FORTUNE'S CALL
A GOLD RUSH ODYSSEY

A NOVEL
FRANK NISSEN

Black Rose Writing | Texas

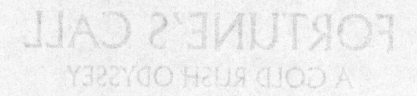

ISBN: 978-1-68513-001-5
PUBLISHED BY BLACK ROSE WRITING
www.blackrosewriting.com

Printed in the United States of America
Suggested Retail Price (SRP) $24.95

Fortune's Call is printed in Baskerville

*As a planet-friendly publisher, Black Rose Writing does its best to eliminate unnecessary waste to
reduce paper usage and energy costs, while never compromising the reading experience. As a result, the
final word count vs. page count may not meet common expectations.

Cover map courtesy of The David Rumsey Map Collection at Stanford University Libraries

For my sister, J.L.
Dear heart and gentle soul.

ACKNOWLEDGMENTS

They say that writing is a solitary pursuit. Perhaps crafting the words themselves can be seen in that light. But the journey of creating a published book is impossible without the participation of valued associates.

Sometimes that participation occurs at the very beginning. It is for that initial spark I want to give special thanks to my friend and colleague, Margot Pipkin. She also gave me crucial early advice and encouragement. She provided key insights that helped shape the bones of the story.

A tale of this sort takes research. I have stacks of reference about the house. But chief among my sources, not to mention my inspirations, was J.S. Holliday's *The World Rushed In*. I depended heavily on the Placer County Archives, in the very heart of the gold country, for all manner of broad strokes, as well as minutiae.

Early readers, especially my friends Richard Lawrence, Erika MacDonald, and Betsy Schwarzentraub, generously shared their invaluable commentary and encouragement. Much further down the road, three obliging beta readers, Kelly Lardner, John Knox, and Corinne Malcolm Ibeling, gave liberally of their time and insights to a full, cohesive manuscript.

My editors, Sheri McGuinn and Rebecca Partridge, took the raw material and shaped and trimmed it into something I'm proud to put my name to. Rebecca further demonstrated her commitment to the project by acting as my Virgil in traversing the *terra incognito* of publishing. Without her advice, encouragement, and unstinting energy, this book would simply not be in your hands.

I belong to an outfit aptly titled Gold Country Writers. These dear, patient folks heard or read disjointed bits of the story—*for years*, it must be said. I am grateful for their comments, encouragement, and perseverance.

I am honored and grateful that Reagan Roche and the good folks at Black Rose Writing found merit in the piece to take on the publishing steps of the journey. Their patience with a first-time writer is admirable, and much appreciated.

I hope you enjoy this novel as you would a good yarn around the campfire.

November 24, 2021Frank Nissen

FORTUNE'S CALL

PROLOGUE

If you'd told me in the autumn of 1849 I would walk across the country, I would have pronounced you crazy where you stood. From Vermont to California is three thousand miles, give or take.

Of course, in 1849, for lots of folks the United States stopped at the Mississippi River. On the far side of the Mississippi lay the Louisiana Purchase. We'd bought it off Napoleon back in '03. We'd won the rest off Mexico in '46, which got us California. But nobody knew very much about that half of the country; even less about California.

My Uncle Rafe was one of the few who did know. He'd been out there. All over it, in fact, trapping and exploring.

I couldn't wait to see it for myself.

This story is how I got my wish.

HOME

CHAPTER 1

I fitted another stone into the rock fence and turned to our beagle, Bugle. "If we were raising rocks, we'd have a bumper crop." Bugle, who took his ease all but underfoot, agreed with a thump of his tail on the bare ground. I picked up another rock and showed it to him. "This should be a potato." It was about the right size and shape, except it was a rock. "Seems like we grow more rocks than anything else on this farm." I found a place for it in the fence.

Bugle was a good audience for such doleful speculations; complaining was not encouraged in our family, and I could count on him to keep my mutterings to himself.

This was my least favorite chore. It would never end. Every year the ground pushed up more rocks, and every year we gathered them up—lest they break the plowshare—and added them to the fences that outlined the fields of our farm.

It wasn't all bad. My dad said doing a simple task gave you time to think something over while still getting something else done. Mostly, I thought of having adventures like my Uncle Rafe. My father's older brother had followed in the footsteps of the Corps of Discovery—Lewis and Clark's trek through the Louisiana Territory. He knew the Rocky Mountains like the back of his hand. He'd trapped with Jedediah Smith, trekked to the Pacific with

Joseph Walker's expedition in '33. He'd seen magnificent places no white man had ever laid eyes on.

My mother had read his letters to me until I could read them for myself. And that I did time and time again now. I dreamed about tramping through all that glorious, untamed country.

The sharp bray of the dinner horn interrupted my thoughts. The sun was at the zenith, right overhead, dinner time. I could picture my mom on the back step, her long apron lifting on the breeze, pointing the horn high and out toward the fields, toward us. Bugle got up and looked at me as if to say, *What are we waiting for?*

I brushed off my hands, and we started back to the house. Bugle made good company. We'd had him since I was a tyke. He was really Dad's dog, in that Dad trained him to be a 'coon hound. But, then, Bugle'd chase anything if he thought he had half a reason to. He was good at letting us know when something needed our attention, like a visitor.

We met my brother Adam on our way to the house—he'd been pulling stumps on newly-cleared land at the north end of the farm. He walked with a brace of oxen Dad had borrowed for the job. Adam was four years older than me, and seldom let me forget it.

He had our dad's height, his light brown hair and blue eyes, and the strapping build that comes from working dawn 'til dark for most of your life. A vitality emanated from him like heat from a stove. This latter quality was not lost on the young women of our neighborhood, one of whom had caught his eye. "See any Indians this morning?" he joshed, falling in step beside me.

I didn't rise to his bait. "No more'n you saw ice on the pond."

"I will see ice soon enough," he smirked. "You, on the other hand, will wait in vain to see one of your beloved heathens."

He was right on both counts. The days were growing steadily colder. Ice would start creeping out from the shore of the pond any day now. Adam had a particular interest in ice. He wanted to start an ice business, like Mr. Schofield, in town. "People'll always need ice," he'd said more than once.

As for my "beloved heathens," they were only phantoms wrested from the descriptions in my uncle's lively letters. Our part of Vermont hadn't seen a wild Indian in more years than anybody could count. Truth be told, my uncle's letters had filled me with a yearning for adventures that seemed far beyond my reach.

Bugle gave a bark. I looked ahead. A trim, gleaming black buggy with red detailing stood out front of the house. A beautiful ebony mare, equally well cared for, with four white socks and a blaze on her forehead, waited patiently in the traces. I needed no more to tell me Mr. Pruitt had come to call.

"Looks like we got company for dinner," I said.

"Mr. Pruitt," Adam confirmed unnecessarily. Adam liked things good and nailed down, no loose ends. "He wants to talk to Pop."

I knew that, too. Mr. Pruitt was one of the few people who got more than a decent living out of the stony ground. He had a thousand acres where most people had forty or fifty. He also owned a sawmill and a gristmill, as well as his farms.

He made a success of just about everything he turned his hand to. My dad said that was because Mr. Pruitt had a shrewd eye and a patient manner. And he was known for giving sound advice. I took special pride, which I never showed to anybody, that when Mr. Pruitt wanted to talk something over, he'd often seek out my dad. They'd sit on the front porch. My mom would bring out two mugs of cider and make sure we kids were otherwise occupied.

"He sure as shootin' doesn't want to talk to me." My brother was not very good at hiding his envy.

I couldn't resist. "Maybe if you'd talk about something besides your darlin' Adriana, or your *beloved* ice company…"

"Well, he sure doesn't want to talk about highin' off to the mountains, chasing after beaver," my brother scoffed.

A guest would normally mean a meal served in the parlor. But Mr. Pruitt almost always insisted on eating in the kitchen, especially at midday, to avoid putting Mom to the extra fuss. For all his wealth and achievements, he never got on his high horse. He was on equally good terms with Tommy, the boot black, as with the honorable S. S. Phelps, the senator we sent down to Washington.

While Adam saw to the oxen, I went into the mud room at the back of the house. After scraping off my shoes, I washed my hands, patted down my hair, and went into the warm kitchen. The salty tang of baked ham filled the room, seconded by the yeasty whiff of fresh-baked biscuits. Amy, my sister, seven years of sass and cheek, was helping Mother put the food on the table. My mother, all four-foot-ten of her, could make a whole dinner and work it all so apple pies had cooled just enough from the oven when we were ready for dessert. Our guest sat to Dad's right, where I usually sat. Mother caught my eye and glanced at the chair I was supposed to take, one more down from Mr. Pruitt.

"Good day to you, Master Pegg," he said, smiling.

Mr. Pruitt had a full-moon face and a bald pate. A stout man, he sported snowy-white side whiskers and shaggy eyebrows nimble as semaphore flags. He was a widower, had been for a long time. My mom's baking was a favorite of his.

"Good day to you, sir," I replied, taking my seat.

My given name is Bartholomew, Bartholomew Pegg. But everybody just called me Pegg. Only the preacher and Mr. Pruitt called me Master Pegg. That's how they addressed boys. My mom called my dad "Jay" because she said he was cheeky, like a blue jay, but his name was James Madison Pegg. My dad called Mom "Darlin'," or "Minerva," as well as "Pru" for Prudence, her given name.

Dad poured cider while Mother and Adam and Amy took their seats. Then he said grace, and we tucked into our dinner. Bowls and platters of hearty victuals were passed around amid cordial talk. We kids practiced our manners. Everybody concentrated on showing my mom how good her cooking was.

When mother was cutting the pie, Mr. Pruitt turned to me and said, "How would you feel about going on an adventure, Son?"

Out of the corner of my eye, I saw Adam nearly drop his fork.

My mom knit up her brow in worry. I caught her reaction on my way to seeing the newspaper article lying by Mr. Pruitt's elbow.

The headline read, *GOLD PLENTIFUL IN FAR WEST!* I'd seen its like before. My dad had been clipping such pieces since the autumn of 1848. It was now the autumn of '49.

Mr. Pruitt held up his clipping. "Here's the latest proclamation to add to your collection, James." He shifted his gaze to Mom. "Now, Prudence, I know you have grave concerns about such an undertaking, but this strikes me as an opportunity to be grasped."

Dad had been saying as much for the past year.

Mr. Pruitt went on. "The reports have been uniformly positive, even allowing for a certain amount of exaggeration. After all, the country is perfectly civilized for almost half the distance."

My mom interrupted him, forsaking her usual decorum. "I realize that, Mr. Pruitt. It's the other half that worries me."

When Dad had showed Mother the first notice about gold out west, she'd laughed out loud. He believed it was the chance of a lifetime. That was rare talk from a farmer. But when he kept showing her clippings, to prove to her it wasn't a fluke, she kicked up a terrible fuss. She said chasing after this gold was a terrible, foolish gamble; it was so far, far away and full of awful dangers, uncharted wilderness and wild beasts being the least of them.

We all fixed on Mother to see if Mr. Pruitt would have any better luck overcoming her objections. He nodded carefully with a patient smile. "It's true that information about the territory west of the Mississippi is scarce, but James and Pegg would be joining an emigrant train in St. Louis and be in the company of a multitude of their fellow citizens. Surely their sheer numbers will be proof against any difficulties they may encounter."

My mom didn't mince words. "James has told me you are willing to loan us the money for this scheme."

"Yes," said Mr. Pruitt. "And since then, several of the neighbors have asked to join in. So, as you can see, many of your friends have the same faith in James that I do."

Even I could tell this was a subtle challenge to my mother to step forward with her support.

She was impervious to the nudge. "You will forgive me, sir, if I have trouble seeing this proposal as anything but placing my family in the most fearful jeopardy."

Dad asked that we move on to less vexatious subjects over dinner, and we did. However my mother felt about the scheme, she sent Mr. Pruitt home with a pot of her blackberry preserves. The discussion between Mother and Dad continued after we children went back to our chores. I could hardly think about piling up rocks. I was about jumping out of my skin!

"James and Pegg" he'd said! My head was full of following the wide Missouri, trapping, exploring the Shining Mountains, prairies covered in buffalo—grizzly bears—Indians!

That night, I practiced my writing by lamp light at the kitchen table, copying out Proverbs 4:1 to 4:13. Mom and Dad debated in the mud room with the door closed. I'm sure they thought they were being quiet enough. But I listened hard.

As she did whenever Dad got wound up to a particular pitch of enthusiasm, Mom came back with mention of the Donner Party of '46.

"We'll be smarter than that. We won't leave it so late," Dad protested.

"And who will run the farm? You aren't just another pair of hands. You make the decisions."

There came a long pause. I could picture him taking both of her hands the way he often did. "Pru, love, if we are to have any hope for a better life, we don't really have a choice."

What he meant was, we didn't have that many acres, and most of what we *did* have was too rocky to expect a decent yield. They'd been trying for sixteen years. Many of the folks around us were in the same fix, breaking their backs to get a living out of reluctant ground and in hock up to their eyes to the bank. So it was easy to see why folks got excited when they heard about gold just lying around for the taking. A lot of people, not just my dad, thought it was worth a try.

And it wasn't like we hadn't ourselves heard stories of success. My aunt, who lived near Irasburg, had told us about her neighbor, Mr. Sinclair. He lit out for California as soon as the news came through, in the fall of '48. He'd come back two months ago with enough money to build a brand-new, two-story house for his wife and eight kids, and a new, bigger barn, *plus* double his acreage! That's when Dad went to see Mr. Pruitt.

"But Pegg's still a boy," said my mother.

I bristled at that, but of course they couldn't see me. I glanced around. Thankfully Amy was in bed and Adam had gone to call on Adriana. It made me feel just a bit better when Dad replied, "He'll turn fourteen when we're on the road. Time he should see something of the world."

"By leaping into the howling jaws of the unknown?" countered my mother.

"We'll take it one step at a time, Darlin'. And Rafe will give us good advice when we see him in St Louis."

Mother's voice became urgent. "We must write them that you're coming."

Dad replied firmly. "I'll see to it."

A pause. I knew they were looking at each other in a way I didn't yet understand.

Then Mother's voice, not far from despair. "How will we get along without you?"

"Adam knows the farm as well as I do, and he can do the heavy work Pegg isn't ready for."

I bristled at that, too, but knew he was right. I almost missed what he said next. "It seems Adriana has already given him notice: if he wants to look for gold, he can look for another fiancée."

"I don't blame her," came my mother's wistful reply.

"He has promised me he will stay on until we get back." There was a pause as I strained to hear more. "And we have good neighbors."

"Because you are a good neighbor," Mother said. So soft I could barely hear.

I bet he was drawing her into his arms. "It's only for a little while, Pru-love. And we'll have a better life for it."

Even though I couldn't see, I had no doubt my mom let herself be hugged.

We were going West!

CHAPTER 2

By the next morning, it had indeed been settled. Adam would run the farm while we were away, so Dad and I were for the gold fields come the spring. Dad assured Mom we'd be gone not much more than a year, though I was pretty sure that was a guess on my dad's part. After all, some of the newspaper articles said it took six months just to get to California; others said it'd take at least seven or eight. And he told her over and over how we would come home rich enough to buy a better place. He wanted to start a dairy farm. As it was, we could only afford four cows, some chickens, and two pigs.

Everybody knew you started in the spring, so you'd be traveling in the summer. So we'd have all winter to plan and prepare. We studied all the newspaper articles and advertisements Dad had saved. Some listed what should make up a "California outfit." Still others offered clever contraptions that guaranteed you'd find gold. None talked about the land we would be passing through. I got that from rereading—for the umpteenth time—all of Uncle Rafe's letters. According to him, there were plenty of mountains and rivers, and plenty of places with no water at all.

When Mother once again dwelt on the hazards we'd face on the trail, Dad pointed out that emigrant trains had been going west for years— so the trail should be well enough established.

"That may well be," she replied. "But promise me you'll join a wagon train with an experienced guide, even if you have to spend some of our money on a fee."

For all the excitement that filled my waking thoughts, there were still chores to do. You'd think, with the crops in and the fodder stacked, there would be plenty of time for planning and preparing. Not so. Every day, no matter the season, our animals had to be fed and watered, the cows milked twice a day—absolutely without fail—and their stalls mucked out. Even if you were sick, you tended to the milking. Eggs had to be gathered, or the hens would stop laying. Newborns, particularly piglets, always needed extra watching. The animals needed people as much as people needed the animals.

Chief among winter chores was mending and sharpening tools, as well as forging new ones. And of course, before the first snowfall, we cut and split enough wood to take us through the cold and for the sugaring when the season started turning warm again.

The days grew steadily colder. Mother got out the winter clothes and coats, mitts and scarves. Ice did, indeed, creep out from the shore of our pond toward the center. The last skeins of Canada geese passed overhead, heading south, honking fretfully as if urging each other on. Blustery winds, often bringing snow squalls, rattled the bare, stark branches.

Mr. Pruitt came over the morning after we had our first real snowfall—six inches. He dug several books out of his saddle bags and brought them into the house. He went straight to the kitchen, where Mother was just putting new loaves in the oven to bake. He said he liked being in the kitchen because it reminded him of his wife, Malora. Mother was quick to brush away stray flour dust before he set the books respectfully on the kitchen table: Mr. Dana's *Two Years Before The Mast*, Mr. Fremont's *Report*, and Mr. Bryant's *What I saw in California*.

"Perhaps they'll be of some help," he said.

Even though they were for our journey, Mother wiped her hands thoroughly on her apron and gazed fondly down at the stack of books. She often said books in the home were as important as the lumber in the walls. Mr. Pruitt offered a brief summation of each volume and answered Mother's questions. She didn't let him leave until he'd had a cup of coffee and a big square of cherry cobbler.

As the days grew shorter and shorter, more chores had to be done by lantern light. Farm kids followed their parents around as soon as they could walk, watching. At a certain age, they were considered old enough to be trusted with carrying the lantern to aid their elders. When that child grew into doing some of those chores themselves, the lantern was passed down to the next in line. That winter of '49-'50 was Amy's second year of carrying the lantern. She peppered me with endless questions about what I was doing while she held up the light.

One day, while Dad inspected our farm wagon to see if it could make the trip, I complained to him about Amy's pestering. He gave me a sad-eyed smile. "Don't you remember? You were just as full of questions when you started carrying the lantern. The chores took twice as long. Adam complained about *you* the same way."

"Was I that bad?"

"It's not bad." He shook his head gently. "It's the best way to learn—asking questions. Like scratching an itch; the itch in this case being curiosity." He rested his hand on my shoulder. "Be patient with her. You are her teacher. And she'll need to do many of your chores while we're gone."

After walking around the wagon a couple of times, appraising, Dad declared, "With some work, it could serve. We can carve some hoops. Mother can sew the covers." He squatted to peer through the wheel spokes. "I'd feel better if we had new bolsters and hounds." Those were parts of the running gear. It would probably mean carving new stakes, too. Stakes held the box on the bolsters.

Once he got started, we ended up pretty much dismantling the whole wagon to check its condition.

While we were rummaging through the tools in the shed for what we needed, I came upon some tins of paint. I was puzzled. Nothing on our farm was yellow or black, which is what the two colors were.

I showed them to my dad. "Can I paint the wagon?"

He smiled. "I thought we were going to the gold rush, not the circus."

"I know…" I scrambled for a good reason. "But we *are* going on a great adventure."

He laughed. "So we are!" Then he got serious. "Don't let it interfere with your chores."

"No, sir! I'll get Will to help." Will was my best friend and lived on the next farm over.

But alerting Will could wait. Dad wanted to instruct me in the finer points of using a draw knife to shape the forward bolster. While we were at it, Mr. Pruitt stopped by. He tapped on the door of the work shed and let himself in, stamping snow off his boots. "Prudence said it would be alright if I interrupted you." He knocked snowflakes off his hat.

Dad smiled. "Oh, she did, did she?" They shook hands.

Mr. Pruitt jigged his eyebrows and chuckled. "Well, you take that up with her when I'm not in the line of fire." He turned to me with his hand out. "Good day to you, Pegg."

We shook. I liked that he didn't call me "Master Pegg" anymore.

Mr. Pruitt regarded the rough-shaped bolster dogged to the saw horse. The newly-carved wood, clean and bright, almost gleamed. "Preparations are well under way, I see."

"Only getting started," corrected my father, "but thanks for the encouragement. And thanks for the books."

"Not at all. Not at all," replied our visitor cheerfully. "I suppose you could call them an enticement of sorts."

Dad eyed Mr. Pruitt. "You are not one to beat around the bush, Sam." Not many people would presume to call Mr. Pruitt by his Christian name, Samuel.

I moved to the other end of the shed and busied myself touching up the blade of the draw knife.

"I'd like to ask a favor," Mr. Pruitt said after a pause.

With the money he was lending us, Mr. Pruitt could have asked for a dozen favors, but he wasn't that kind of man.

"I am happy to hear your least request," my dad replied solemnly. He counted Mr. Pruitt a good friend—someone he could trust—not a foolish man in the least.

Mr. Pruitt sobered, too. "Well I know it, James. Well I know it. And appreciate it... infinitely."

Dad raised his eyebrows as encouragement to the older man.

"I'd ask you to include my stepson, Fred Hoyt, in your party."

Dad took just a bit longer to answer than he could have. "Of course. The more the merrier!"

"I know you don't know him all that well. But I'd be obliged," Mr. Pruitt said. "He's at loose ends right now. His last several business ventures haven't worked out, and this undertaking might be just the thing to give him a sense of purpose—and the means to carry out any plans he might form." He looked down at the ground for a moment, and then said, "The truth is, it's high time he started relying on his *own* resources, not mine—if you take my meaning."

"This sounds like just the thing, then," my dad replied with more enthusiasm.

Mr. Pruitt sighed in relief. "I appreciate your forbearance." He regained some of his good humor. "I think your greatest burden will be his own grand view of himself."

I didn't know much about Fred Hoyt except by reputation. He was about my dad's age, give or take a year or two. He seemed bigger than he was because he carried himself like he expected the world to pay attention, and with his deep voice, rugged features, and full head of dark, wavy hair, the world, for the most part, obliged. Whenever our family went to town, I would seek him out. His stories were the next best thing to Uncle Rafe's letters. Mr. Hoyt could always be found at Gibson's Dry Goods or McCaffey's barbershop in Richford, regaling people with tales of his adventures. In addition to much else, Fred Hoyt had been in the steamboats on the Mississippi, and every kid I knew, including me, wanted to do that!

Their business concluded, my elders fell to discussing the merits of different wagons for our purpose. You could tell they just enjoyed the give and take born of mutual respect.

Dad invited Mr. Pruitt to join us for supper. To my surprise, he declined. "I'd best leave it to you to give Prudence the news. I know she doesn't have the highest regard for Fred."

Dad chuckled, "How considerate of you."

They shared a laugh and, with a wave, Mr. Pruitt stepped out the door.

Since we had a little time after the chores, before supper, Dad let me go tell Will about painting the wagon. By the time I returned, dinner was on the table and apparently Dad had just advised Mother of Mr. Pruitt's request. As we expected, she took a hard line on Fred Hoyt. She declared that his main attribute seemed to be the ability to talk the hind leg off a mule—as if that was an affliction. She pointed out he was a townsman, and, as such, poorly acquainted with honest work.

Dad protested, "At least he'll be an extra pair of hands. I'm sure he'll pitch in when he sees the necessity. And it'll get us home sooner."

Mother allowed, "It would, if he did, but my opinion will remain where it is until shown otherwise."

Then, as she was given to do when it suited her aims, Mom completely changed the subject. "And since Miss Thatcher has abandoned us before a new teacher could be found, I have decided to hold school for Barti and Amy right here." She set her finger tips on the kitchen table. "No child of mine will be lacking an education."

Many of my friends had already started apprenticeships. However, my parents put more value in book learning, and had insisted I remain in school. Unfortunately, Miss Thatcher, who had never been reconciled to Vermont winters, had recently escaped to an offer of matrimony in her native New Jersey. Apparently, Mother was no longer content to wait for a new teacher to take her place. Adam had long since proclaimed he had all the schooling he needed.

"Where will we find the time?" I objected.

Mother knitted her brow. I could hear the strain in her voice. "Come spring, you will be away from any kind of schooling at all for who knows how long. We'll make the time."

I knew that tone brooked no argument. "Yes, ma'am."

We made school an hour each day before the evening milking. Since Amy could read almost as good as me, Mom gave her pages full of handwritten arithmetic exercises. Mother proclaimed my penmanship in need of improvement. When I suggested I copy from Uncle Rafe's letters, she observed, "I am sure you know those by heart. You will learn nothing new that way. Choose something from Fremont's *Report,* or Mr. Dana's novel."

I made a long face.

She gave me a fretful look. "Barti, I know you revere your uncle beyond measure, and he is, truly, a brave and admirable man." She paused for an eye blink. "But his spelling is haphazard, at best, and his punctuation all but nonexistent." She slid the Dana toward me. "There are many new words for you in Mr. Dana's story, correctly spelt, I might add."

As sure as day follows night, the speculation got around to when, exactly, we would leave. Mother didn't want us to go before the

17

sugaring was done. That was collecting sap from the maple trees and rendering it into syrup. Dad didn't argue. Tapping the trees started in March and went through April, when winter was losing its grip, but there was still snow on the ground—poor traveling weather, with almost no grass and lots of mud.

Christmas eve, we had a blizzard. As soon as Dad saw the sky that morning, he instructed Adam and me to rig life lines between the barn, the house, and the chicken coop and the hog house. "It could last an hour; it could last a week. Fill the water barrels in the barns and the mud room."

The snow started before we finished our morning chores. By midday, the flakes were blowing horizontal, and you could hardly see the barn. Dad and Adam, bundled up and gripping the life line out to the barn, did the evening milking. Dad asked me to lay a good fire in the parlor's fireplace. We had a new-fangled Christmas tree in the parlor, which made the room especially festive. In this Mother had defied Reverend Halfpenny, who frowned upon a decorated tree as a pagan custom.

After supper, we gathered there for another Christmas custom which Mother had taken up with enthusiasm: the exchange of presents. This ritual, too, was not that widely followed, for much the same reason. Her gifts to Adam pointed to his new life. She presented him with a quilt she, Mrs. Overby, and Will's mom had been working on for most of the year. But that wasn't all. Nestled in the folds of the quilt was a Bible. Mom never let us miss church, and Adam sang the hymns more ardently than any in our family.

Mother next presented Amy with a new pinafore, probably the last one before Amy started wearing real lady's dresses. Dad gave her a carving of a horse, about seven inches high, painted, with its left foreleg lifted, as if prancing, beautifully carved flaring nostrils, and wildly flowing mane and tail. If I haven't mentioned it before, Dad was a whiz-bang carver.

I was next. Mother placed a large store box in my lap. I opened it slowly, my mind racing to guess. It was a new pair of boots. I was flabbergasted. They weren't little kid shoes, but near knee-high, grown-up boots. When I protested, she said, "You will outgrow them soon enough. They will at least get you off to a good start." She was trying to be stern, but she wasn't pulling it off too good.

"Thank you. They are more than I could've ever hoped for." Smoothing my hands over the shiny leather, I couldn't help but wonder where she had found the money for such fine boots.

Adam got a big grin. "Those'll come in handy out-running your Indians."

Mother turned sharply on him. "That'll be enough of that."

Adam might've been near full-grown, but he was still her child. He ducked his head. "Yes'm." He sat back in his chair and tried to be invisible.

Dad spoke up. "It's Christmas. Let's remember we love each other." He looked around to all of us. "Regardless of missteps." Mother went over to Adam and kissed him on the forehead.

Dad rose from his chair. "If you will excuse me for a moment." He went into the other room and came back with a bundle of old homespun, with a sprig of holly on top. "This is actually from your uncle Rafe." He laid it in my outstretched hands. "But perhaps you could think of it as from all of us."

I gazed down at the parcel, mystified, setting aside the holly sprig.

"Rafe said to give it to you when the time was right. I figure that's now."

Inside was Uncle Rafe's Bowie knife from his trapping days. It was in a beautiful, beaded buckskin sheath, fringes and all. It sure looked Indian. It had seen a lot of hard use, was stained and scuffed, but that just raised it in my esteem. I remembered seeing it when Uncle Rafe came to visit. It was a lot of knife for a kid. It would be like he was at my side.

I looked up at my dad. "Thank you."

Mom said, "Take a piece of paper and thank your Uncle Rafe."

For a second time Dad disappeared and reappeared. This time he cradled a parcel in his arms that was wrapped in store paper. He stepped ceremoniously toward Mother and bowed before her, all the while speaking in a tone a wink away from laughter. "There is no gift worthy of the queen of this house, but perhaps she will accept this humble offering from one who adores her out of all reason." The more he went on, the wider grew my mother's smile.

My sister stared at our father, owl-eyed.

He lowered the parcel onto mother's lap. It had ribbon binding it, which she undid as carefully as if swaddling a newborn. Soon she lifted out a length of cloth. Her eyes went wide too, her lips formed into a silent "O". That cloth was the richest thing I'd ever laid eyes on. It was red, her favorite color, but a deep red: darker than blood, but not as dark as wine. It shimmered in the firelight.

She lifted out more of the cloth. She looked up. "Jay! This is…this is…" She had more to say, but Dad jumped in.

"Beautiful."

That was meant to quell her protests, but it didn't. "Where… how…?"

"None of your business. But I assure you I committed no crimes."

She drew still more of the heavy cloth from the parcel. As it heaped at her feet, the folding reminded me of thick cream.

Dad said, "Enough to make a gown so we can go dancing in New York City."

Mother looked up smiling, with wet eyes, hugging the cloth to her bosom. "When you return loaded down with gold."

Dad smiled back. "We will pour the bounty at your feet."

Gazing intently at him, she got a worried look. "I have nothing nearly so grand for you."

Dad opened his mouth to gush more balderdash, but Amy burst out, "Oh, c'monnnn!"

Everybody had a good laugh at that while Mother lifted the cloth aside, rose from her chair and went into the kitchen. Despite the howl of the wind, we heard the pantry door click, and click again.

She returned with more homespun. Amy and I exchanged puzzled glances. Mother tried the same formality as Dad, but at the last minute she tripped and tumbled into his lap. He encircled her in his arms, and she squirmed for release—not very hard—while he tried to kiss her.

Amy leaned close to me. "He tripped her. I saw."

Mother had knitted him a great, thick wool sweater, colored with acorn, lily of the valley, and marigold. She slipped out of his grasp, stood, and pulled him up to try it on.

"We'll be traveling in summer," he said, as his head reappeared in the neck hole.

"Your brother has told us of a number of mountain passes…" She plucked at the shoulders, smoothed the sleeves, "which you must cross, each higher and more fearsome than the last. This may go some way in warding off the cold."

Dad turned to take her in his arms again, smiling. "Not as much as…" but she broke away and hurried into the kitchen. Dad stood still, his arms suspended in midair.

Amy and I looked at each other. I pointed to the door, indicating a respectful retreat, but Mother returned from the kitchen, her eyes red, smoothing her apron. She walked into my dad's arms and allowed herself to be hugged. Amy and I crept from the room.

• • •

The storm blew itself out in three days, leaving behind three more feet of snow. On the windward sides of the buildings, it drifted up to the eaves. Dad, Adam and I joined the neighbors in clearing the road, and after that we shoveled a way up our own lane. Two days later, about mid-morning, Mr. Pruitt showed up.

"Just came by to see if you'd dug yourselves out yet," he said, hunching in a chair at the kitchen table. He cupped his hands around the mug of steaming coffee my mom set before him. "Would've come sooner, but I had to dig *myself* out."

Dad sat, too. "I wish we'd known. We would've come over. Where's Fred, your stepson?"

Mr. Pruitt let out a sigh. "Down in Philadelphia, looking into some new business opportunity, by his telling."

Mother set another mug in front of Dad and asked, "Does this mean he won't be going?"

"I wish I could say." Mr. Pruitt scowled into his coffee. "Given his recent run, I'd say he'll be back before the thaw."

Mother and Dad exchanged glances. Dad turned back to our visitor. "Well, whatever he decides, we're still committed."

Mr. Pruitt leaned back in his seat. "And I'm still behind you, one hundred percent." He reached inside his coat. "Which reminds me..." He handed me a round object, about the size and shape of a small biscuit, made of yellow metal, intricately engraved. He saw my eyes light up and smiled.

"No. It's only brass."

I opened the lid. It was a compass. Amy stepped closer to see. I tipped the face toward her, watching the fine needle quiver and sway.

Mr. Pruitt said, "It belonged to my father. It's been to China and back several times." His grin grew wider. "It might bring you good luck." Then he chuckled. "At the very least, it'll help you find your way back home!"

Minding my manners, I thanked him, and said maybe I'd visit China after I'd been to California. I didn't know the first thing about China.

Mr. Pruitt laughed. "Well now, you'd be half way there, wouldn't you?"

Mom made a little leather pouch for the compass to hang around my neck.

This adventure of ours may not have been to her liking, but having accepted the fact of it, she would do everything *she* could to make it a success.

CHAPTER 3

Mother threw herself into the planning the way she did everything she put her mind to. She wanted to sell her grandma's brooch and music box, which played "The Magic Flute," but Dad put his foot down. Undaunted, Mother took in mending and made batches of candles to bring in extra money. She said she couldn't be comfortable relying solely on Mr. Pruitt's generosity. My folks spent many hours poring over the lists of provisions suggested in the newspapers. They made list after list, speculating on what we needed to bring.

There were so many decisions to make: Should we take feed for the animals, or count on finding grass along the way? They debated buying what we needed here, or buying it along the way. My mom said here, because, if the stampede was anything like people said, prices would only rise the closer we got to the gold fields. We figured to take some spare parts for the wagon, but which parts? And how many?

One thing that gave my mother no peace was Fred Hoyt. Mr. Pruitt had still received no word from his stepson as to whether he would be joining our adventure. Dad did his best to get her comfortable with the idea just in case. One night in late January, we were in the kitchen, except Adam, who had once again excused himself to visit his lady love. Mother was making soup. Vapors rising from the great pot on the stove moistened the air.

"What do you know about this man?" Mom challenged Dad. "You will be thrown together night and day for who knows how long…"

Amy cautiously cut potatoes into cubes. I tried to do a page of arithmetic Mother had prepared for me. She took the knife gently from Amy and beheaded several parsnips at once.

"Will he be tolerable company?" She handed the knife back to Amy after indicating with the point the lengths she wished the parsnips to be cut.

Lanterns spread yellow light; the windows were painted black with night. Dad shifted in his chair to follow Mother's movements around the room. "It's not like we'll be stranded on a desert island," he said. "We'll be in the company of all and sundry. If friction arises, or a need for variety, we have merely to amble over to another wagon."

Mother wasn't finished. "Is he trustworthy? What will he do in a rough patch?" She peered into the pot. "Can he hitch up a team?" She paused for a breath.

Dad jumped in, but with wobbly conviction. "Everybody knows how to hitch up a team."

She cast a pinch of pepper into the rolling broth. "Can the man even fry bacon?"

Dad furrowed his brow, a rare occurrence. "I don't think Sam would have made the proposal if he thought his stepson would pose us a hazard or be utterly useless."

Mother thrust a big wooden spoon into the boiling pot and stirred with uncommon vigor. "I am entrusting my husband and my son to the company of a man I know only by reputation—a reputation, I might add, that does nothing to inspire confidence."

"Your son and I are not babes in arms, Pru," he said to Mother's back as she disappeared into the pantry. "We can take care of ourselves. We will certainly *not* lay our fate at the feet of Fred Hoyt."

Mom reappeared bearing onions. "I should hope not."

Dad laced his fingers together and suggested in the most offhand way. "Perhaps we should invite him over for supper… and Sam, of course."

"But he's in Philadelphia." She sighed, taking the plate of sliced parsnips Amy offered. "I would just like to know him a little better. Perhaps there is more to him than tall tales."

Dad sounded just as frustrated. "Sam has no idea when he might return."

When we were getting ready for bed, Amy leaned close and whispered, "Was that an argument?"

I thought a minute and realized how rare those were in our house. "Probably as close as we'll ever get to hearing one."

Like a guardian angel answering prayers, Mr. Pruitt appeared the next afternoon. "I've just received a letter from my stepson. He is returning by coach. He expects to be reaching the area on Saturday afternoon. He suggests we meet at the Grape and Swan for supper on that evening."

The Grape and Swan was one of the better inns serving the coach trade on the road between Enosburg and Richford. It was about five miles south of us. My mom was not to be bested by a public inn. "I can certainly prepare a suitable repast…"

Dad held up his hand. "I'm sure you could, my dear. But we have no way to intercept Mr. Hoyt with a message. He is certainly already on his way."

It was Wednesday. The meeting would take place three days hence.

Saturday proved a brilliant, cloudless day, and bitterly cold. The crust on the snow glistened. Amy and I were to be left under the reluctant charge of Adam. We all gathered in the barnyard after dinner, except Adam. He was in the barn, busy with some chore, having not the least interest in the upcoming meeting. Dad already sat King Henry, Mr. Overby's big Morgan.

Mother fussed at our coat collars to make us warmer. "Don't wait up for us. Your brother most likely will sneak off to visit Adriana. Be sure to bank the fire before you go to bed."

"Yes, Mother," said Amy, the obedient one.

Mom stepped back, reluctantly separating from her children. "If it's late enough, we may even stay the night at the inn."

"Or if the weather takes a turn," offered Dad.

Mom mounted Bonnie, our sturdy Quarter horse. Mother seldom rode horses, but when she did, she rode astride, despite the disapproval she endured. "Any fool can see a side saddle is a poor way to hang onto a horse," she always said.

Off they went, crunching through the crust two days of sunshine had made. After supper and evening chores, Adam did, indeed, announce that he was obliged to pay his respects to the Harringtons, who just happened to be the parents of Adriana Harrington.

The next morning at first light, Amy, Adam, and I clambered downstairs. We tracked the smell of coffee and toasted bread, only to find our father busy with the fixings, instead of our mother. He put his finger to his lips for silence as we bustled into the kitchen. "Your mother needs to sleep."

We stopped in our tracks. That was like saying the river needed to stop and rest, or the sun needed to go the other way.

Dad saw our confusion. "We got back only a few hours ago. She insisted on riding through the night." He set out jars of Mother's jellies and preserves. "Luckily, we had a full moon."

Adam took a long swig of his coffee, slathered blackberry preserves on a piece of toasted bread, then took another big swig of coffee. "You're home. That's the important thing," he pronounced. With that he stepped through into the mud room, gripping his toast in his teeth while he shrugged on his coat, and went out to his chores.

Dad watched his eldest depart and turned to us, the coffeepot poised in his grasp. "Well, is it safe to assume you two might be interested in hearing the story?"

Amy and I nodded enthusiastically. My only thought, an envious one, was that Mr. Hoyt kept them there 'til the wee hours with one rousing tale after another.

"Eat up, then, and I'll tell you while we do the milking."

We trudged out to the barn just as pale pink light filled the eastern sky. Icicles hung three feet long, like swords, from the eaves of our buildings, longer on the north sides. Inside, we picked out our milking stools. Then Dad positioned Amy standing between the first two cows, at the back, instructing her to hold the lantern so the light shown on both the cows and, of course, the milkers, Dad and me. We set the pails and warmed our hands against the full udders before we started milking.

But I couldn't wait to hear about the supper at the Grape and Swan. "So how'd it go? Does Mother think any better of him?"

"Who?" piped up Amy.

"Fred Hoyt," I reminded her. "Now let Dad tell it." I was expecting to hear, if only third-hand, more of Mr. Hoyt's fine adventures.

"Sadly, our meeting didn't come to pass." He paused. "Actually, it did, just not in the way we expected."

The admiration in my dad's voice was unmistakable. My interest sharpened. He started squeezing milk into the pail. I figured that was a sign for me to start milking, too.

Dad began the story. "Your mother, Mr. Pruitt and I got to the Grape and Swan in plenty of time. Mr. Pruitt checked with Mr. Swindon, the proprietor, to make sure we hadn't missed the stage, and to let him know we would be wanting supper. We settled ourselves at a table close to the door. Though it was colder, it would be easy to note arrivals. We ordered ales—your mother ordered mulled cider—and passed the time in pleasant conversation."

The barn cat appeared out of the shadows looking for a hand out. Dad turned the teat and squirted a couple of jets of milk at the cat, which the feline missed, then Dad turned it back into the pail.

"The stated arrival time for the coach came and went, but we didn't worry. We knew winter frustrates the best of intentions. Local customers began to arrive for supper. The place filled with a noisy, cheerful crowd. Mrs. Swindon, the hostess, started serving supper."

"My arm's tired," complained Amy.

"Try your other arm," I said.

Dad got up, found a crate, and put it in the place where Amy had stood—beyond a cow's kick. He placed the lantern on it. The light reached much the same area. He bent close to Amy. "You watch the lantern closely, now, and make sure it doesn't tip over." He picked up his stool and went back to milking.

"We waited two hours after the appointed time, during which we ordered our own supper. Poor Mr. Pruitt grew more vexed with each chime of the clock. The mood had soured, and we made what conversation we could. Mr. Pruitt insisted on taking care of the bill for the failure of his stepson.

"We had no sooner gained the yard when, Fred Hoyt appeared out of the night. It was like something out of those adventure novels you like to read, Pegg. There was no mistaking that he had ridden hard; his mount was well-lathered. And in his arms he held an elderly lady, who looked in a terrible state; and who would have swooned right off the horse had he not contained her. That was a puzzle; he said he was coming by coach. Obviously, something had gone amiss."

I left off my milking to listen more keenly.

"The poor horse was near done in and grievously injured—numerous cuts running with blood. Hoyt handed down the woman, who was soaked to the bone. And when Hoyt himself slid from the saddle it was clear he, too, had been the victim of a serious misfortune. He displayed a great gash on his head and his clothes were torn and disheveled. Half fainting, he managed to tell of the fate of the coach he had been riding in."

"What?" I blurted, losing the rhythm of milking after having just restarted.

"The coach left the road and crashed." Dad's voice took on urgency. "You should have seen Sam Pruitt. What a marvel that man is. He lost not a moment in organizing a rescue: He asked for the use of the inn's hay wagon, which he then asked me to drive to the scene, which Hoyt said was two or three miles short of the inn. Your mother would not hear of being left behind, and together we raced off, while Sam rode back to Richford to fetch Doctor Betts.

"We found a scene more terrible than we could imagine. We only found it because one of the other passengers had managed to crawl up to the road. But your mother…"

He stopped. The clatter of milk hitting his pail stopped. I leaned around to see. He had stopped milking, resting his head against the warm bovine belly. "My Lord, Pegg, your mother. She showed the strength of ten men. She shoved and heaved and pulled right next to me. When we got someone loose, she ripped up her own petticoats to bind the wounds we could see, propriety be damned. Together, we hoisted them into the hay wagon when they could not manage for themselves. And she hesitated not a moment to scramble down again to aid another. My love for her multiplied a thousand times."

I had been making pictures in my head as fast as I could, but "Love, a thousand times," came with no pictures.

"The Swindons cleared their common room so we could lay the injured in some comfort while we waited for Sam Pruitt to return with Doctor Betts. By then some of the other patrons lent a hand."

"Did you find out how it happened?"

"I did," he replied. "While your mother and Mrs. Swindon tended the victims, I sought out Fred Hoyt to learn how the tragedy had come about. He said he was riding on top of the coach, among the luggage, with two other gentlemen, the inside being filled right up. The three were in a lively exchange with the driver when the coach came to a sharp bend, and at the same time encountered a large hole concealed by the snow. He said the next thing he knew, the whole rig was crashing down the side of a steep gorge. He and his two companions flew through the air with hurtling luggage.

"By the greatest misfortune, a rocky stream awaited them at the bottom, and there the coach and its passengers came to rest. Hoyt said when he came to his senses, he saw a horrible tangle of horses, harness, and people amidst shattered splinters. He managed to free the elderly lady, but her husband had been trapped in such a way as to drown—that is, if he did not perish outright. Hoyt said he managed to extract one of the team and, with great difficulty, urge the horse back up to the road and on to the inn, where we encountered him." Dad fell silent for a moment. "Your mother and I discovered that, beside the elderly gentleman who'd drowned, the driver had likewise met his end."

We finished the milking in silence. If I was hoping to hear a breathtaking story or two from my parent's outing, I could hardly have asked for better. It was not a story you could cheer, but it showed that Mr. Hoyt was more than a teller of tall tales.

While we were straining and separating the warm milk, I couldn't hold back my question. "Will Mr. Hoyt be all right? Will he still be able to come with us?"

CHAPTER 4

After the passengers who had received care at the Grape and Swan dispersed to their homes, Mother took it upon herself to keep tabs on Mr. Hoyt's recovery. She made sure the nasty cut on his scalp was kept clean and bandaged. Aside from a host of bruises, nothing more serious seemed to have befallen him. A sturdy fellow, indeed. All in all, that incident did not hinder our preparations.

Mother's generosity when it came to Mr. Hoyt included the occasional dish to save Mr. Pruitt the extra work. This was no trifling gesture, it being the dead of winter and the Pruitt farm being situated four miles down the road. The second time she did this, who should she encounter at the Pruitt domicile but Mrs. Chadwick—the town gossip and wife of Deacon Chadwick. She happened to be visiting Mr. Pruitt for her own reasons.

My mom, in recounting the incident, related how the daunting matron was able to express her disapproval with an arched eyebrow, and a comment about "how *unusual* it was for a respectably married woman to call at another gentleman's home, unaccompanied, regardless of the mission."

Dad smirked. "Which is, of course, exactly what *she* was doing."

Mother's eyes popped wide; her hand flew to her mouth to stifle her laugh.

Dad then gave Mother a sidelong look. "Is it safe to say, Dear, by these demonstrations of Christian charity, you have changed your opinion of Mr. Hoyt?"

Mother lifted her chin at him. "My *demonstrations* are small enough in recognition of such courage and self-sacrifice."

Dad dipped his head, smiling. "Hear, hear, and amen."

However, after the encounter with Mrs. Chadwick, my folks decided I should be entrusted with these errands——if not the nursing——from then on. Mr. Hoyt recounted the story of the accident several times over, and I never tired of it. I loved to hear any stories he had, but I could never stay long—— there was always a chore waiting for me at home. Even though Mr. Hoyt was always the king pin of his tales, they still reminded me of my Uncle Rafe.

I couldn't wait to tell Will about Mr. Hoyt's stagecoach crash. I got a chance to do it when he came over to put the finishing touches on our wagon. While I waited for Will, Dad set me to sharpening tools, which was no small chore. There were several kinds of axe, each for its own job, and adzes and shovels, grub hoes, and spuds for debarking, scythes, a multitude of chisels and gouges. And that's not counting the hay knives and reaping hooks.

First, though, I sharpened Uncle Rafe's Bowie knife.

That was a daunting blade, broad and heavy, with its distinctive scoop tapering down to the point. It needed no more than touching up. The first time I became acquainted with that fearsome implement, it was in its sheath at his side. Uncle Rafe was paying his second visit to Mother and Dad's homestead. I was five. He was still in his buckskins, having only recently quit the mountains. I remembered a lean, sharp-featured man with a vigilant gaze. He could move as silently as a shadow. Even at that young age, I knew I wanted to follow in his footsteps.

After I finished with the blade, I left it out where I could glance at it once in a while. I was working on a felling axe when Will stomped into the shed.

33

"Hey, there, Steamboat. What didoes you been cuttin' up?" Will never used a normal name if he had something sassier handy.

I put on a pious air. "Ain't you heard? I'm up for sainthood."

Will was right on my heels. "Saint Pegg. Patron saint of cowpats."

He was the same age as me. We topped out about the same, too, but I was lighter built than him. He sported a soup bowl haircut of corn-silk-pale hair, and bold, blue-green eyes. I had dark hair and eyes: brown, almost black. I was on the quiet side, Will was loud, a little bit of a braggart. He strutted around like he was Paul Bunyan. He liked a good laugh, but never shied away from trouble and already had a broken nose to show for it. All in all, he was a good kid. We were unlikely chums, but chums we were.

Will leaned against the scarred old leg vice at the end of the bench, pushing a shaving around with the toe of his shoe. "Sooo... Pegg-o... you champin' at the bit?"

"Countin' the days."

He spied the Bowie knife. "Say... now here's a toothpick for ya." He lifted it, whistling appreciation at its heft, and turned the blade in the pallid winter light. "This your dad's?"

"No," I said, smug inside. "It's mine."

Will leered at me. "Nooooo. You wore this, it'd drag your britches down into your boots."

"Maybe," I drawled, making brave. "But it'll be good for fightin' off Indians and such."

Then he noticed the beaded, buckskin sheath. He reached for it, warbling envy. "O-ooo-oh. Where'd you get this?" He fingered the long fringes on the trailing edge.

"I've told you about my Uncle Rafe. It's his, from his trapping days. The knife, too. Dad gave it to me at Christmas."

Though I had seen my uncle only a few times in my life, I felt I knew him through his letters. Going to look for gold in California was exciting, sure, but a little dreamlike. Visiting Uncle Rafe in St. Louis was real. I couldn't wait for that.

"We're going to stop and see him on the way west."

Will made a noise in his throat. I finished the felling axe and started work on a mortise axe. We didn't say much for a while. We were usually *doing* something, for good or ill.

Will said, "Gonna be slim around here, with you off runnin' around Lord knows where."

That gave me pause. "Gonna be the same for me, out there. You back here, whackin' at hornets' nests, skinnin' cats an' what all. Won't be anything for us to do when I get back."

"Ha," he scoffed.

He took the felling axe and pretended to examine my work. "'Member when we built that raft?"

I grinned. "Your mom wasn't too happy about having a skull and crossbones painted on one of her sheets."

He said again what he said when we got the dickens for it. "It was for a noble cause."

I thrust the mortise axe into the air like a sword. "Away to the bounding main!" I dropped my sword arm. "'Cept it came apart under us."

Will gave a rueful smile. "Good thing your dad taught us how to swim."

We joked about how Captain Clark and Meriwether Lewis had done all the hard work finding the way, and how Dad and I would just waltz in there, adorned in buffalo robes and feathers, lords of all. It didn't matter that Lewis and Clark had never been to California.

Then we were quiet for a spell. The only sound was the whisk of me scraping the whetstone along the scythe.

Will said, "How long you think this is gonna take? I heard it takes six months just to *get there*."

I started work on a second scythe. "That's what I heard. Then a couple of weeks to stuff our pockets with gold, and six months back. So, I guess a year and some."

Will let out a whistle.

35

"But I did tell Mr. Pruitt I might visit China after California." Right away I knew that wasn't the best thing to say.

Will reared back, wincing in distaste. "You get that far, you might just keep goin'."

It dawned on me what was stuck in his craw. "Good thing the world's round; I'll end up back here, anyway."

Will scoffed, "And I'll be an old man."

We rolled those ideas around in our heads for a minute or two. I rasped the whetstone against the blade, Will had another look at the beaded sheath.

"What're you gonna do?" I asked him. "You got three brothers ahead of you wanting a piece of your dad's farm."

"Pa's been talkin' up curryin' for me. He says Brandt needs an apprentice."

Zebulon Brandt was our local currier. He was widely known for his fine leathers. I scowled at the thought. "Mr. Brandt's gone through three apprentices in the last two years. He must be hard to please."

"Ira Banning said as much," Will replied. "He lasted eight months. I talked to him just before he lit out for New Bedford to go whalin'. Ira said pickin' cotton in Georgia would be a Sunday picnic compared to bendin' all day over a currier's beam, with Brandt breathin' down your neck.'"

"Is Ira from Georgia?"

Will let out a snort. "If Ira Banning is from Georgia, I'm from the moon." He finished with a sneer.

I gave him saucer eyes. "I thought you were."

He nearly toppled over, laughing. I so seldom got one on him. He shifted to stand up straight. I knew he was getting ready to bolt. "Damn, Pegg. This ain't—" he made a fist and struck the bench. He took a minute to look up. "I hope you get at least a coup stick outta this. Or a war bonnet, or somethin'…"

A coup stick was like a long staff the Indians used in battle to count their victories. Will and I soaked up every scrap of Indian lore we came across. "I hope so, too," I said, but he was already out the door trudging off across the farmyard toward the wagon. I called after him. "I'll buy us a couple of Hawkens to go huntin' with."

Then I realized I'd forgotten to tell him Mr. Hoyt's stagecoach story. That was sure to cheer him up. So I ran after him. "You won't believe the story I've got for you!"

While I told him about the accident, Will pulled up a keg to the rear wheel of our wagon and opened the black paint. With the smallest brush we had, he started painting a thin black line down the center of a bright yellow spoke. I jabbered away while he painted a careful stripe on each spoke.

When he was about to start the second wheel, I paused in my retelling and said, "Wait a minute." I got a long timber, stacked some firewood to make a fulcrum, and levered the wheel off the ground just enough so he could turn it after each stripe, and always be painting on the vertical. It went a lot faster after that, and looked better, to boot.

When he finished all four wheels, the stripes looked like rays of the sun coming out from the hub, only in black. They certainly added to the jaunty air of the yellow wagon. Even then he wasn't done. He did a border along the edges of each side of the box, then added fancy curls in each corner.

I'd never seen him be so serious. I said, "You should be an artist."

Will just snorted. He stepped back and said, "Think of this as me ridin' along with you."

• • •

In the weeks leading up to our departure, we must have packed and repacked that wagon ten times, trying to figure out the best way to arrange everything. Mother suggested dividing everything we'd assembled into piles—food, clothing, bedding, cooking gear, tools, spare parts for the wagon, mining gear—that kind of thing.

First, we tried packing everything with an eye toward weight, with the heaviest things on the bottom. We thought that would permit the least shifting, cause the least damage. But that meant the sacks of flour, beans, and rice, which we would use most every day, would be at the bottom, underneath everything else. We'd have to unpack the wagon three times a day to get at our food. Next, we tried packing by shape, so there wasn't a whisker of space left unoccupied, but that had its own drawbacks. Then we tried "frequency of use," which had mining gear on the bottom close to the front.

I never told my dad the times I came upon my mom, standing by herself in the middle of all our kit, helpless tears running down her cheeks. It was at those moments that the size of what we were about to do settled on me.

Mr. Hoyt, restored to health, started coming around while we were loading and unloading the wagon. He pitched in, indeed, with enthusiasm, just as Dad said he would. After moving the sixth sack of flour for the sixth time, he suddenly lurched and grimaced in pain. We eased him onto a nearby keg and gathered around, concerned.

He looked up, contrite. "Just an old wound acting up."

A wound? From the accident? Maybe a battle? Indians? River pirates?

After that, he didn't come around so much. When he did, you could see him grow fidgety at not being able to help. He usually managed to show up just before dinner. If mother didn't invite him to stay to eat with us, he'd make a few jokes, bid us good day, and skitter off.

Sometimes he'd come by with an idea. He thought umbrellas would be good for the rain. They were kind of a new article. He had seen them on a trip to Boston.

"I'll order some up," he offered with a lopsided grin. "They should be here before we leave. How many do you think we'll need?"

My dad said, "Let me think on it, Fred. Our space will be very limited. It seems to me a well-chosen hat'll do much the same job."

Another time Mr. Hoyt announced that he had gone to considerable effort to draw up a list of necessities. After supper that night, Dad and Mother looked over Mr. Hoyt's list, and my mom pointed out that most of the food on the list was better suited to a fancy hotel dining room.

The next time Mr. Hoyt showed up, Mother patiently explained that most of his suggestions were prepared dishes, with sauces and creams that would soon spoil. What was needed were foodstuffs that would keep for weeks and months before use. She offered that if he wanted to bring along a few of the items on his list for the first day or two, that would be fine. He had a look like he'd been accused of growing an extra set of arms. Mother returned his list, and we never heard another word about it.

Toward the end of February, a morning came when we knew the back of winter had broken. The geese hadn't appeared yet, snow was still thick on the ground, but the air felt softer. The sun gave out warmth for the first time in months. At breakfast, Dad said, "Won't be long before we can start tapping the maples."

I about jumped out my chair. We'd get that sap boiled up and be on our way!

Like every year, when sugaring season was close, Dad went out to the barn to inspect last year's spiles, the taps that allowed the rising sap to run out of the tree. Some spiles didn't last from one year to the next. That year Dad said we needed a couple dozen new ones. In two days, I had all the new spiles carved from sumac and bored out with the burning awl. I inspected and stacked all the collecting buckets against the barn wall. Every day I woke up hoping Dad would say today was the day.

That day finally came.

There was still snow on the ground. We loaded up the sled and sleighed out to the maple grove we called "the sugar bush."

Dad and Adam drilled the tap holes with our grandfather's old bitstocks. The angle of the hole had to be just right. This was the third year Dad let me tap the spiles into the holes. This had to be done carefully, gently. We tapped about eighty trees that year, all sugar maples or black maples, which produced the tastiest syrup. Those eighty trees yielded enough sap to boil down to forty gallons of syrup—plenty for our family's use, with extra to sell at market.

For six weeks we made maple syrup. If I wasn't tapping trees, I was hauling buckets to the boiling pans, which Mother and Amy tended. If not that, I was splitting more wood for the fires. And that was in between the regular chores. The whole family was running all the time. We barely had time to notice the return of the blackbirds. They were the first to come back from parts unknown. Nobody had much thought for the gold rush, except me.

I chafed at the uncertainty of when we would be on our way. Our leaving day would be whenever Dad judged the roads dry enough to bear the weight of the loaded wagon. The days got warmer, the snow started to melt, and, little by little, the earth started to breathe again. Lo-and-behold! The very day we found cloudy-looking sap in the buckets, the first of the big Canadas flew over in their vast "V" formations, heading north. Dad stuck a finger in a bucket, screwed up his face at the bitter taste, and said, "Well, that's all we'll be getting this year."

Sugaring season was over. It was difficult to keep from shouting. When we got word that the river ice had broken up, I quietly rejoiced. Then Will spotted the first robin. That was a coveted achievement in our neck of the woods: sighting the first robin of the spring. Now, there'd have to be a good reason NOT to be going. But, though we had settled the stowage of the wagon, our preparations weren't yet complete.

There was considerable discussion about whether to take Bugle, or leave him for the farm. I wanted to take him, and I was pretty sure Dad wanted to take him, too. But he would be good for Mom and Amy to have around, if only to let them know when someone was coming.

"You'll need him more, in that regard, than we will," said Mom. "I dread to think what you will have in the way of visitors out there."

Dad didn't have a good response for that one, so Bugle would join us. That settled, Mother surprised Dad by urging him to take his fiddle. He didn't want to, saying it wasn't essential, but she said, "Nonsense. It weighs almost nothing. You know how it keeps your spirits up."

"You're the one who keeps my spirits up, Sweet." He smiled at her.

She couldn't help but smile back. "Hush. And *I* know how it lifts *other* people's spirits when you play. I'm sure there will be many who will welcome it."

Dad tried another tack. "We don't know how rough it's going to be; I wouldn't want to take a chance…"

My mom was not easily turned aside. "And when you play 'Rose on the Mountain' maybe you'll think of me…" She locked eyes with my dad.

My dad started to say something back, but at that point I left the room, minding my manners.

A number of chores bridged the seasons: chores that prepared for the growing time, yet harked back to the season just gone. One of those chores was picking up the stones in the fields that the freeze had pushed up during the winter. It was a nasty surprise for both man and beast to have their plowing brought up short by a rock lurking in the dirt. Besides, it was cheaper to pick up stones than it was to buy a new plow every year.

I went about that task with a grim sense of triumph: it would be the last time. Our new farm would be someplace that didn't grow rocks.

That night at dinner, Dad announced, "I figure we ought to head out Wednesday."

He concentrated on cutting his potatoes. Adam looked at Dad, Amy looked at Mother. Mother pushed up from the table and went to get the pie. I wanted to stand up on my chair and shout, "Hosanna!" Two days hence, we would be on our way. After dinner, I was dispatched to inform Mr. Pruitt and Mr. Hoyt of the joyous news. When I got back, I saw my mother's eyes and for the briefest instant, I thought, *What are we doing?*

On the evening before our leave-taking, after supper, when nothing much was being said, I went outside for one last look around. I ambled through the barn to check on our sow Rosetta's new litter, and then into the pasture. Bugle followed me, his tongue lolling, hoping we were setting off on an adventure. I looked down at him. "If you only knew."

The sun was a plump, egg yolk ball, almost sitting on the horizon. The shadows stretched long across the fields. Tomorrow was exciting and scary at the same time.

I stopped at one of our stone fences. I looked over my shoulder and said to the sun, "Guess I'll be chasing you for the next little while. I'll catch you, though. You wait and see."

Then I turned back into my shadow and looked at the fence. "One thing I *won't* be doing—ever again—is stacking any more confounded *rocks!*"

Just for good measure, I gave the fence a good kick. It didn't budge but a jolt of pain shot up my foot. I let out a short, sharp cry. Bugle arched his eyebrows, concerned. When I went back into the house, I was limping.

My mom, who had the eyes of a hawk when it came to her children, asked me what was wrong.

"Nothing," I said.

"Beans," she said. "Why are you favoring your foot?"

"I was saying goodbye to the fence."

"Let me see," she said, steering me over to sit in a kitchen chair. She got my shoe and sock off lickety-split. About as quick, she had made her examination of my traitorous foot. Despite biting down on my lower lip, I couldn't keep from yelping when she wiggled the toe next to the big one.

"You've broken your toe," she said.

CHAPTER 5

She looked from my swollen toe to me and I knew what she was going to say, so I headed her off. "It's nothing! Wrap it up good and I'll be good as new. Just like Will!" I blurted, like I was spitting out too-hot porridge. Will had broken his toe a while back, and his mom had wrapped it against the next toe, and it didn't slow him down one bit.

Mom looked up at Dad, who was still sitting at the table.

My dad said, "It ain't like it's his leg, Pru. I'll keep an eye on it."

I knew when my dad called my mom Pru, he was asking her to let things work themselves out, to put her trust in Providence.

And she did. But not before wrapping my toe up good, snug against next toe.

The next morning, the house was even more subdued. Nary a word was spoken. We moved around each other like respectful strangers at a wake. The loaded wagon sat before the barn doors, a brash, bright bird poised for flight. All that remained was to hitch up Achilles and Ajax. Dad and I participated in a last round of morning chores; Mother made a huge breakfast, as if that would keep us many mornings hence. Every bit of me tingled to be on our way. Bugle seemed to be the only other one of like mind; he could not stay out from underfoot.

At last, gathered by the wagon, Mom made us promise to write every day, to stay out of trouble, to mind our own business, and avoid sharp operators. She had even figured out how much gold we would need to bring back in order to buy that new farm and build the new house she wanted. She wrote it down on a piece of paper and put it in my dad's shirt pocket.

She said to me, "You keep up your reading and writing, you hear? It's important."

"Yes, ma'am," I said. "I know. I will." She had drummed that into me more times than I could count.

Dad put in, "We'll find a school as soon as we get to California."

My sister Amy asked me, "Can you bring me back some ribbon?"

I dropped to my knees and gave her a hug. "Squirt, I will bring you back a whole trunk full of new dresses and every one of 'em'll have enough ribbons to choke a horse!"

But my mom wasn't done yet. She leaned close and held both my arms. I knew this would be serious. "I don't care if you don't find one speck of gold out there," she said in a low voice, so only I could hear. "Bring your father home safe to me."

"Yes, ma'am. I will." I was as serious as I had ever been in my whole life. I gave her the biggest hug in the world. I can't tell you how hard it was, walking to the road, my mom and Adam and Amy waving.

I walked beside my dad, who walked beside the mules. With every step, my broken toe sent a stab of pain to remind me of my foolishness. It being squeezed into new boots didn't help any, either. But I didn't say a word. I was off to see the Great West, and I wasn't about to let one toe keep me from it.

We didn't get more than thirty paces when Mom called out and came running up. Dad stopped the mules.

"Barti, you ride until your toe heals!" she said, pushing her hair back in place. Then she grabbed me and hugged me like there was no tomorrow. She turned to my dad. "Jay! You make sure he rides until his toe is healed."

Dad made a stern look. "Yes, ma'am." He turned to me. "You heard your mother. Up you go." After I was up on the seat, she hugged my dad, too, like there was no tomorrow. Finally they pulled apart and Dad and I went on our way.

We were no more'n out of sight of our farm when we heard thundering hooves, someone coming up from behind—hell-bent-for-leather—to overtake us. This was of note. 'Hurry' was not the general pace of things in our neighborhood. Dad stepped closer to Ajax to steady the team and let the person pass. I leaned out to see Will, on their sorrel, Minnie. He couldn't rein her in in time, sailed on past, and had to turn and come back.

He touched his finger to his hat for my dad. "Mornin', Mr. Pegg."

Dad returned the salute. "Mornin', Will."

From my perch on the wagon seat, I grinned at him. "Miss me already?"

Will fairly barked at me. "Try and hang on to your scalp, will ya?" He reined around and took off the way he'd come.

I watched him pound up the road, mud clots flying from Minnie's hooves. I felt terrible.

Our first stop was the Pruitt place to pick up Fred Hoyt. His gear took a while to load. Mr. Pruitt walked back to the main road with us, chatting with my dad and offering encouragement.

"I'll look in on your family now and then, don't you worry," he said to my dad. "Write when you can."

We came into Richford, our town, by way of River Street and turned down Main Street. I had Dad hand up Bugle and I put him in the wagon. Richford was full of dogs, not all of them friendly.

Passing through the village, people pointed at our brilliant golden wagon. We got all kinds of salutes and cheers, and people calling out their good wishes. That's where I first heard we were being called "Californians," before we had even cleared the last store, Mr. Breuer's tannery. This spirit of excitement, like we were being seen off to a great war, was exactly how I felt, so I waved and shouted back.

The trees were still bare and the roads were still muddy from the thaw. Patches of crusty snow hid in the hollows and the shaded north-facing slopes. Dad said the farther south we went, the more advanced the season would be, which meant the roads would be drier. He made me ride on the wagon for the first few days to give my toe a start on mending. That treasonous digit burned like fire, but I kept my mouth shut. I told myself after three days I'd walk. Anything else would be sissy.

Bugle was as excited about the trip as I was. I don't think he cared about the destination; he just liked all the new things on the way. Of course, being a beagle, he wasn't all that big, but he could keep up with the wagon easily enough. In fact, he had plenty of time to dash off and sniff at a fence or chase a rabbit. We spent half our time calling him back from his exploring.

We made about sixteen miles on our first day on the road; a short day, thanks to a late start after loading up Mr. Hoyt's outfit. Tomorrow we would do better. We stopped for the night just shy of Sheldon Junction, by the Missisquoi River, and picked a spot in a meadow with new grass sprouting.

Mr. Hoyt, casting a wary gaze about our prospective campsite, observed, "Why sleep in the dirt when there's a perfectly good inn not a half a mile up ahead?"

Dad didn't stop unloading our cooking gear. "We'd best break ourselves into roughing it while the going's easy."

While I unharnessed the team, Dad pulled the tent canvas and pegs from the wagon. "Could you look after the tent?" he asked, handing Mr. Hoyt the pegs and rope.

"Sure," Mr. Hoyt replied heartily.

Dad went to unload sacks of beans and bacon.

When I got back from hobbling Achilles and Ajax, Dad had a fire going and Mr. Hoyt had found one corner of the tent from the heap at his feet. Dad saved him further embarrassment, saying, "I'll take care of the tent. Why don't you start the coffee?" He handed Mr. Hoyt the coffeepot.

"Now that I can do," replied our partner with a lopsided grin, and he sauntered off to fill the pot.

Darkness closed around us and lights from houses appeared among the trees and across the river. My mom had sent us on our way with loaves of fresh-baked bread, pickled brisket, pots of jam, and a delicious apple strudel, her specialty. Mr. Hoyt helped himself to an extra generous portion of the strudel. But he was also generous with his praise.

As we bedded down for the night, Mr. Hoyt proclaimed for the benefit of anyone within earshot, "Just think, by this time next year, we'll be living in the lap of luxury," along with several other enthusiasms.

For my part, I was glad I was with two adults who could make all the important decisions, while I kept an eye out for Indians and buffalo.

The next morning, Mr. Hoyt offered right away to hunt up firewood, and made another pot of very passable coffee. He begged off making biscuits. "My cooking has been known to lay low the stoutest constitution," he chortled, pleased with his own modesty.

He gobbled down his breakfast and otherwise fidgeted to be under way, worrying aloud about all the people getting to the gold fields ahead of us. Dad said he wanted to break the mules in gradually. Pulling a heavily loaded wagon steadily all day long was a very different proposition from most farm chores, which seldom lasted more than a day, and for a lot of that time the animals stood patiently while we loaded the wagon. Mr. Hoyt, not being a farmer, could offer no argument. That day, and each day afterward, Dad inspected the hooves of the mules and kept an eye out for where the harness chafed. He would put patches of fleece where that occurred.

The frozen ground crunched underfoot in the mornings, but by afternoon the sun turned the roads to mud. At midday our second day, we left the Missisquoi at Swanton and turned south. Swanton was hard by Lake Champlain, which was a little over a mile to the west. I had ardently wanted to clap eyes on that grand body of water ever since I'd heard about it, but it would have meant a detour, so I didn't say anything. We made seventeen miles that day and camped just outside of Saint Albans.

The sun, already below the distant western hills, threw pale orange light up at the clouds. I was carving bacon for supper. I looked around, elated: new hills, new trees. It was all washed in the same pale orange light. The hills were less rugged than those around Richford.

Without warning, the bottom dropped out of my stomach. We weren't going to turn back. This wasn't a day's errand from which we would return home. We would not drive back up the lane with the big elm partly shading the house, with Mother standing at the back door, or smell a stew bubbling on the stove. I wouldn't be able to throw horse apples at Amy. Tomorrow would take us yet farther away, and the day after, farther still.

In that moment, I realized I had made up great adventures for myself from the safety of my bed, but whatever trials lay ahead wouldn't be overcome with a turn of the pillow.

A REAL ADVENTURE

CHAPTER 6

After leaving Saint Albans, the country was still hilly but the roads were good. The towns grew bigger and the country between them was chock full of farms.

As we approached Burlington, we were able to catch glimpses of Lake Champlain, a vast sheet of silver off to the west. I consoled myself that where we were headed, I'd soon see places every bit as grand as that lake.

The morning of our fifth day found us some ten miles south of Burlington in open country. We had passed the town the day before, with Mr. Hoyt making his usual request, to which my dad chided with a smile, "We've barely started and you want to stop?"

Mr. Hoyt reared back with a gruff chuckle. "Well, since you put it that way…"

We had pretty much established our routine. In the morning, Dad packed the tent while I made breakfast. Mr. Hoyt took it upon himself to keep the water barrel filled, as well as make the coffee and find fire wood. For myself, I didn't reckon this a shortcoming. When you lived a life as full of daring and adventures as Mr. Hoyt did, you didn't have time to learn about wrestling canvas or boiling beans. After we ate, Dad hitched the team and inspected the wagon

51

while I cleaned up and packed the cooking gear. Mr. Hoyt paced and fidgeted.

Once under way, I walked beside Ajax, along with Dad, working up some fine blisters to go along with my broken toe. But, often as not, Dad made me ride in the wagon most of the day. At the end of each day he inspected my toe to make sure it was mending properly.

One of my evening chores was taking Ajax and Achilles off to graze while Dad put up the tent and got out the cooking gear. Dad and I shared cooking duties. After supper Dad wrote a letter to Mom while I cleaned up. He always had me read it back to him, and add a little in my own hand, to keep up my reading and writing. He saved them up and mailed them at the next village or town with a post office.

Dad offered Mr. Hoyt paper to write to Mr. Pruitt, but Mr. Hoyt rarely took him up on it. Mr. Hoyt stuck his thumbs in his belt and proclaimed with a grin, "A man of action, as I strive to be, sir, has little tolerance for such maudlin recreations." So Dad took to writing to Mr. Pruitt himself. Not as often as he wrote to Mom, but a lot more than Mr. Hoyt ever did.

The sixth day, Dad woke up first, as he always did. He got me up and we set about our morning chores. Mr. Hoyt woke up while I was cooking and approached the fire with an odd gait. When I asked, he said, "Oh, it's nothing. Just my lumbago acting up."

After we set off, Mr. Hoyt was still limping. My dad told him to get up on the wagon, and he protested he was doing fine, but Dad insisted. I scooted over to make room for Mr. Hoyt. He felt awfully big sitting next to me. He had dark hair, like mine, and he tended it particularly. Mine was cut to fit a soup bowl. He had a watchful look about his eyes. You could tell he'd been places, seen things.

I figured if I came up on the subject of riverboats easy, it wouldn't seem like I was being nosey. "If we weren't going to California, I'd want to be going to the Mississippi to be a steamboat man." I waited a bit. "You ever been on a steamboat, Mr. Hoyt?"

He turned to me with a lopsided grin. "Well now. You've come to the right place, Son. I've been on more steamboats, keel boats, and showboats than is decent to count."

"Are they as grand as people say?"

"Grander!" exclaimed Mr. Hoyt. "There's no sight like it." He stared off, like he was remembering. "They're long and sleek as a greyhound. The gingerbread on the pilot house and the Texas deck dazzling in the sun. Chimneys reaching for the sky." He shook his head. "A marvelous sight!"

"And trailing smoke all the way back to New Orleans!" I added.

"Well, now, as to smoke," said Mr. Hoyt in a fatherly tone, "That's just for show. Most of the time, they don't throw out all that much. When the boat is approaching a landing, the boiler man throws a bunch of pitch pine on the fire, and up out of those chimneys pour great clouds of black smoke—like Old Scratch himself let out a belch—that lets everybody know the steamboat's a-coming!"

"And the whistle," I added. I had to let him know I wasn't completely ignorant.

He grinned. "And the whistle."

I gathered together all my scraps of hearsay and stories. It wasn't enough. "I'd sure like to see one."

His shoulders jigged like he was holding back a belly laugh. "Well, lad, most likely you'll see one or two when we get to Saint Louie—that's how you say Saint Louis if you've been there." And he busted out laughing like he'd made a joke he was proud of.

I sat with a vision in my head of the majestic ship rounding a bend, black smoke billowing, and coming into view. "Which ones have you been on?"

He rubbed his chin thoughtfully. "Well, let's see now. I was on the Natchez a couple of times... you've heard of that one, sure."

"Yessir. I have." Will and I knew the names of the most famous steamboats.

Mr. Hoyt went on. "The Zephyr… the Andrew Jackson… I was on the Mississippi Belle when she blew up." He took off his hat and pulled back his hair. "See that scar?" he tipped his head and pointed to it. A pale welt disappeared back into his greasy hair opposite his newer scar. "A piece of the wheel knocked me into the river. Only reason I'm here to tell it." He put his hat back on. "Burned to the waterline, she did. Lost sixty souls."

"If I could ask, sir, were you the pilot?"

"Oh, now Son!" he chuckled. "Not just anybody can be a pilot. They're a special breed. You've got to learn every snag and sawyer and sandbar for two thousand miles. And they're always changing!"

I wanted to know everything, but I didn't know what to ask next. "What's a sawyer?" I thought it was a man who cut down trees.

"A sawyer is a snag under water that you can't see," replied Mr. Hoyt. "The most dangerous kind."

"And they're big, aren't they—steamboats? Churning up the water like Moses parting the sea?"

"They're big, all right." Mr. Hoyt agreed heartily. "And getting bigger, with every one they build. I was in partnership with Ol' Captain Leathers himself. He's built a whack of steamboats. We were gonna build one two hundred feet long—gonna call her the Olympia—carry four thousand bales of cotton. Twenty-four cabins on the Texas deck! Fancy work all around the pilot house."

"What happened?"

Mr. Hoyt's voice lost some of its enthusiasm. "Captain Leathers and I had a parting of the ways. He didn't have the vision I had. I had plans drawn up for a steamboat three hundred feet long, eight boilers, able to carry five thousand bales of cotton! Forty staterooms!"

I tried to imagine a ship that big. It would take up half the river and have soaring chimneys taller than trees.

"You wait!" he cried, stabbing a finger at the air like a preacher. "They'll build them one day! Mark my word!"

Oh, to be a pilot on that one!

We passed through well-settled country, moving ever southward. We were almost never out of sight of a barn or house or fence, often on both sides. The roads swung in long, gentle curves, often following a stream or creek, and were well trod. The wagons we encountered held local folks on local errands: a load of lumber for a new building or the repair of an old one, seed corn or seed potatoes for the spring planting, forage or hay if they'd run out over the winter.

We got some amused looks for our brightly colored wagon. Some even grinned, "Where's the show?" I will allow we also got a few scowls of disapproval.

Sometimes we passed a wagon full of a family headed into town or coming back, the little kids staring owl-eyed. They'd probably never seen that much bright color in one place. When we came to a bridge and saw somebody approaching, Dad would stop and let them cross first. That courtesy often earned him a friendly greeting and a piece of useful information about the road ahead.

We had to keep a close eye on Bugle, who was busy marking every rock and tree he came to. A lot of these families had dogs, and the canine exchange wasn't always cordial.

If we stopped in a town for any reason—and Mr. Hoyt almost always had a reason—we drew a crowd. Many of the villages weren't any bigger than Richford, and the appearance of a fancy yellow wagon was cause for an indulgence of curiosity. This inspired Mr. Hoyt to hold forth on the grandness of our purpose, the perils that lay ahead, and the triumphs.

We crossed into New York state and soon found the Champlain Canal, a waterway that had been around as long as the Erie Canal. The Champlain canal ran north-south, which suited us fine. In the fields on either side we saw people striding across new-plowed ground, sowing oats. The trees had leafed out here and were filled with birdsong.

Late in our eighth day, at the southern end of the canal, we came to the Hudson River, which, like the canal, teemed with all manner of craft carrying goods and people. The Hudson River Valley was a beautiful, wide-open place often bordered by majestic bluffs that brought forests down to the water's edge.

The country started to gentle out. We crossed the Hudson on a bridge at Schuylerville. While we waited to pay the toll, we met a fellow who said he was going to California, too. He was from Fitchburg, Massachusetts and was a milliner: he made ladies' hats. He traveled light—just his horse, some jerky, and a bed roll. He said he was going to buy his outfit in St Louis. He rode with us for the rest of the afternoon, then wished us Godspeed and pushed ahead.

At least once a day Mr. Hoyt declared what a grand company of adventurers we three were, without mentioning how he was always wanting to sleep in a soft bed. As we came into Albany, he once again wanted to stop for a shave and a "real meal", as he called it. With the patience of Job, my dad sighed and said such luxuries could wait until California, better to keep moving.

As it was, there was plenty to see, just walking through the city. Dad put Bugle up in the wagon so he wouldn't get lost in the bustle. Right off, there were more people than I'd ever hoped to see in one spot. There were tall brick buildings, and businesses and mills and factories galore. There were fancy, polished carriages with fine ladies riding right alongside wagons heaped with barrels or stacked with fresh-sawn lumber. You could smell bread baking, meat roasting, and candy. But we resisted all the temptations Albany had to offer and made our way out of town to the turnpike heading southwest.

Dad said we'd come almost two hundred miles, farther than I'd ever been away from home in my life. I already felt like I'd seen the world.

The weather held fine as we climbed into the Catskills of New York State. These were beautiful, well-wooded mountains, and they had good roads. We trended southwest, making for Pennsylvania. Trees arrayed themselves in bright new leaves; oats sprouted in the fields. The roads teemed with farmers' wagons, coaches, and herds of livestock. My blisters toughened up as my boots broke in and my toe barely ached.

Mr. Hoyt rode as often as he walked, excusing himself with one ailment or another. Every chance I had, I asked him for more stories about his river days, and he would oblige me with tales of rough-and-tumble keelboat men, horrendous boiler explosions, and the exploits of legendary pilots and captains. They were often one and the same, like Joseph La Barge, who started taking steamboats up the Missouri when he was seventeen, who Mr. Hoyt had also known. When the time seemed right, I told Mr. Hoyt about some of my uncle Rafe's adventures in the mountains, just so Mr. Hoyt would know that the Peggs came from the same sturdy stock.

We continued west and south into Pennsylvania, then more southerly to the settled part of the state, which had better roads. Berks, Lancaster, and York counties had some of the best farming country we'd ever seen. The barns and buildings were large and well kept. Fat Dutch cattle grazed on lush, rolling pastures.

"These farms sure look nice," I said to my dad one sunny day.

"Yes! That they do, Son." He gazed out across the fields and got a big smile. "And we'll have a barn as grand as that one, for all our cows." He pointed to a particularly splendid example that towered over the other buildings in its barnyard. "You wait and see."

At day's end, if there was no place to pull off, Dad approached a farmer to ask for the use of a corner of his yard, promising to be away by daybreak. Sometimes the farmer's generosity would extend to hay for our team and supper with his family. Dad would offer some fiddle music in exchange, which was almost always greeted with delight. On even rarer occasions, the farmer would dispatch one of his elder children to make it known to the neighbors that music was in the offing, and the host's house would soon fill not only with Dad's fiddle, but mandolins, banjos, autoharps, spoons, and soaring harmonies.

No matter where we stopped for the night, there were lights scattered in the darkness, dogs barking, or a voice calling.

As we made our way through Ohio, the land grew flatter still. The population thinned out, the towns got smaller, and the farms fewer. We started seeing rougher, log-built houses and barns, and lots of stumps. Those were a sure sign of recent settlement. But it looked like prime land. The plowed fields showed earth glossy black and not a rock in sight!

We met more people on the road who were doing the same thing we were: heading west. One such was a family by the name of Stewart. We came upon them stuck in the mud crossing a stream. Dad used Ajax and Achilles to pull them out. The Stewart party was Oregon-bound. It consisted of Mr. and Mrs. Stewart, Grandma Stewart, Mrs. Stewart's sister, and the nine Stewart children. The younger Mrs. Stewart was obviously going to bring another Stewart into the world any day. They had three big Conestoga wagons. They called those heavy old freight wagons prairie schooners. I loved that name. Mr. Stewart drove one, Mrs. Stewart drove one, and their oldest boy drove the third. They hailed from Virginia. Once a blacksmith, Mr. Stewart was set on planting apple trees. In the wagon driven by his oldest boy, Mr. Stewart had rigged up special shelves to carry three hundred seedlings. That wagon had sunk deepest into the mud. It took every animal available, the teams of their three wagons and ours, to pull it free.

When we were on our way again, Mr. Hoyt beckoned me close. "Now there's a man of vision," he said, casting a quick glance back at the Stewart wagons. "There are a lot of fools in this world, Peggson—timid men afraid of dreaming big—like old Captain Leathers

I was telling you about. If you have the gumption to dream big, go after it. That's the way people will look up to you. Stewart, there, is such a man, mark my word."

We soon pulled ahead of the Stewarts. Those three Conestogas of theirs were just plain more work. We had only two mules to hitch up each morning. They had eighteen animals: three yoke for each wagon.

Indiana was about as flat as you could want. And it rained: a deluge that lasted for days. The roads became a mess of foot-deep mud. We were never dry.

When weather permitted, Dad liked to end the day with a little fiddle music. If we happened to camp near other travelers, those folks often wandered over to listen. You could see everybody felt better hearing the music, just as Mother said they would. One evening Dad had just finished playing "Rose on the Mountain" when a tall, gangly man with sandy-colored hair under his hat walked into the firelight, following the sound of a violin, he said. Dad put down his fiddle and stood to greet him. The man, who carried a banjo on his back, shook hands with great enthusiasm and introduced himself as Linnaeus Peabody from Connecticut. After exchanging a few pleasantries, Dad made bold to ask the man what was his calling.

Mr. Peabody smiled and looked down at Bugle, who was sniffing at his trouser cuffs. He reached down his hand. Bugle sniffed at it and wagged his tail. This Mr. Peabody was okay in his book. Our visitor looked up, smiling even wider. "I was a teacher— a distinguished professor, if you believed the pamphlet advertising the institution. I held a position at Miss Crawford's Academy for Young Ladies in Hartford, Connecticut."

Dad popped his eyebrows high. Mr. Hoyt sneered. I wondered, *a whole school, just for girls?*

Mr. Peabody went on. "It was pleasant enough, teaching young ladies drawing and Latin, but what I received for my services kept me poor as a church mouse. The news of instant wealth on the western shores seemed a handsome remedy, indeed. So here I am, headed west."

He unslung his banjo and played a few lively tunes, then he and Dad played a few songs together.

Mr. Peabody seemed to be as interested in finding out about us as we were in learning about him. He had been to the Continent—Europe—where, he said, cities were far grander and older than anything in America. He spoke of museums and tumbled ruins and vast, gilded palaces. Mr. Hoyt expressed his doubts that anything could be grander than Philadelphia or Baltimore or New York City.

"Ah. If I may say, sir," replied our visitor, "seeing is believing."

Mr. Hoyt jigged his shoulders and chuckled like he knew better, but said no more. Linnaeus Peabody stayed to talk long after we should have turned in.

The best part was, for the next few days Mr. Peabody slowed his pace to ours. He rode a sleek bay gelding and trailed a string of pack mules. He soon revealed himself to be one of those people who would ask questions that most people wouldn't think were questions at all. Or they'd scold that it was God's business. Questions like, how do trees stand up? Or how does water reflect things? A lot of Linnaeus' questions couldn't be answered, but that didn't keep him from asking them. And we had many a good time trying. Mr. Hoyt observed it was unseemly for a grown man to occupy his mind with such useless speculations, but it made the rainy days pass easier.

And at the end of the day Dad and Linnaeus—he soon insisted on that address—would fill the camp with music: Dad on his violin, Linnaeus on his banjo. When the rain didn't quit for the night, they'd play inside the wagon.

Linnaeus heaped praises on Dad's playing. He asked if he might try the violin himself. He tucked it gently under his chin and played some of the most beautiful music I had ever heard.

My dad was thunderstruck. "You have brought more beauty from that violin than I would have thought possible."

"Well, sir, I can only take half the credit," Linnaeus replied. "Rarely have I played on a finer instrument than this." He inspected the violin closely. "If I'm not mistaken, this is a Dalla Costa."

"So I'm told. It was my Grandfather's."

Sometimes they swapped instruments. That's how I learned my dad could play the banjo as well as the fiddle. As ever, if there were others camped close by they would gather to listen.

Seven soggy days later we crossed into Illinois and the rain finally stopped.

CHAPTER 7

Illinois gave me the willies.

It couldn't be any flatter than Indiana had been, but it sure felt like it. When you grow up in hills or mountains, you get kind of spooked when you're out on the flat. The roads got rougher, and more and more of the travelers we met were heading west. A few of those folks had scraps of knowledge we found welcome. One such was that all of us travelers would be using the same road until it forked somewhere in the middle of the Great American Desert. The north fork took you to Oregon Territory, and the south fork to California.

I'd long since taken to walking every day, usually along side my dad. One day, I turned to him and said, "I can smell the West."

Of course that was silly. What I *could* smell was earth and grass.

But he humored me with a noisy inhale. "So can I, Pegg-son, so surely can I."

Mr. Hoyt jumped in the fun. "What I can smell is gold! And if we're not careful, all these other jokers will get there ahead of us!"

Each evening I told the setting sun, "I'm gettin' closer."

. . .

Ten days later we came to the mighty Mississippi River. We pulled up to the outer edge of a great, sprawling camp, all waiting to cross; too far back to even see the river. Uncle Rafe told us in his letter the Choctaw Indians called it the Father of Waters. St. Louis lay on the west bank, in the last real state: Missouri. West of Missouri, everything was called a territory.

I couldn't wait to see my uncle, but that's just what I had to do—wait.

Wagons were jammed together as if everyone wanted to get as close to the river as they could. Mr. Hoyt could find no firewood. All the driftwood and deadfall had been used up long ago. Most of the trees had been cut down, as well. About then a man came through with a wagon, selling firewood. Both my father and Mr. Hoyt grumbled at the price we had to pay for a few sticks.

"Highway robbery!" Mr. Hoyt shouted at the man's back as he drove away.

Without turning, the wood seller hoisted a rude gesture as he faded into the haze of cook fire smoke.

After the dishes were done, I could wait no longer. I had to go look at this legend of a river. I tied a lead on Bugle's collar and Dad smiled. "Make note of what you pass so you can find your way back." With Bugle straining at the lead, off we went.

A fat full moon rose behind me, blushing orange and near bright as day. Threading my way among the encampments, I spotted people we had met on the road. I recognized the Stewart's three big Conestoga wagons looming over the humbler sorts of rig. How had they gotten ahead of us? I heard banjo music and wondered if it might be Linnaeus Peabody. We hadn't seen him for several days.

I wasn't the only one curious to behold the mighty stream. Other emigrants stood quietly on the bank, looking. Little groups, couples, the men puffing thoughtfully on their squat clay pipes, the women with shawls and their arms crossed like they do when they're skeptical. Maybe these were folks who, like myself, came from places that didn't feature big waters. Maybe they were thinking what I was thinking.

Up to now, each river we crossed seemed more majestic than the one before: the Hudson, the Susquehanna, the Monongahela. But the Mississippi was stupendously grand—maybe because I was seeing it with my uncle Rafe's eyes, maybe because across this river waited the wild unknown. It looked so quiet and peaceful, until I saw a whole tree race by; then I knew the power of this river.

I spotted a boy standing by himself, off to my left, watching the tree float by. He looked about eight or nine, a little sprig of a kid. Tufts of red hair stuck out from under a black, flat-brimmed hat that was too big for him. He wasn't wearing long pants yet, maybe in a year or two. I thought he might need company as much as I did.

I went over to him with a grin. "Ever seen that much water in one place?"

He turned to watch me step up to him. "No," he said. "I'm from Virginia."

I introduced myself and let him know I had come farther than him.

"Bobby Bequette," he said. He and his family hailed from a wide spot in the road called Merriman's Shop, which he said lay east of Lynchburg. It didn't matter, I didn't know where Lynchburg was, either. His dad had been a barber in Merriman's Shop. They had a cousin in Oregon already. Bobby glanced down at Bugle. "Can I pet your dog?"

"Sure. He doesn't bite." I bent down to address my canine. "This here's Bobby Bequette. Say hello."

Bugle gave the kid a grin and put up his right forepaw.

Young Bobby broke into a bigger grin and dropped to his knees, petting Bugle like he was his own.

Then we went back to studying the Father of Waters.

"I sure wouldn't want to try to swim against that current," I ventured.

Bobby swung around. "You can swim?"

When I told him I could, he asked me a slew of questions about it. He all but begged me to teach him how. I persuaded him the mighty Mississippi would not be the best place to hope to survive the lessons.

Bobby Bequette sank back.

"If we find some swimmin' hole out there," I swept my arm out to the west, "someplace that won't carry us away, I'll sure-as-shootin' teach you how to swim." *If I ever see you again.* Looking at all the folks waiting to cross the river, that didn't seem likely.

Like clusters of fireflies hugging the other shore, the lights of the city peeked out between the black shapes of boats pulled up. Their reflections scribbled bright lines on the ink-dark waters.

On this side of the river were mostly ferries, in the business of getting people across the river. Working by torch light, ferrymen were taking advantage of the moonlight, working as fast as they could, loading wagons for the crossing.

The next morning we learned many had been waiting days to cross. One man said there were probably two hundred wagons for every ferry. His neighbor chimed in, "More like four hundred!"

Like a lot of folks, we used the waiting time to repack our wagon. But there was time for visiting, too. Mr. Hoyt took himself off to seek out useful information. Dad and I talked to people from all over the country. There was a lot of horsing around, and guns going off. Kids were running everywhere. I bumped into Bobby Bequette now and then. He seemed like a good sort, if on the timid side.

One kid, a few years older than me, wanted to buy Uncle Rafe's Bowie knife and sheath. He looked like he had already had a run-in with one—a sizable scar ran from his left ear to his chin. I had a dickens of a time convincing him it wasn't for sale.

About supper time on our second day of waiting, Mr. Hoyt reappeared to announce that he had happened upon an extraordinary piece of luck. A large party, under the able leadership of a Colonel Horatio Hamilton Baines, was intent on

California. They were calling themselves The Baines Company. Mr. Hoyt said they would be willing to accept us into their organization. They had splendid uniforms, wagons all painted the same color, and were well-armed.

"Everybody around here is well-armed," said my father.

A gunshot cracked a few wagons over. I couldn't help but smile. Dad just turned the bacon in the pan.

Mr. Hoyt was unfazed. "These fellows are highly organized. They've drawn up rules. They have uniforms."

"And would we be obliged to purchase uniforms and repaint our wagon in their colors, were we to sign up with this outfit?"

"I expect so," replied Mr. Hoyt. He was quickly frustrated at Dad's lack of enthusiasm, but still blustered, "That's nothing! Why take a chance on our safety?"

"Until somebody made a bad decision," my dad said, handing Mr. Hoyt a plate of beans and bacon.

They continued to debate the merits of this idea over supper. Simple arithmetic ended the discussion. It turned out that the total cost of entry into the Baines Company—fees, paint, uniforms, and all—would use up half the money we'd set aside for expenses in California. This, my father said, was not agreeable to him. It sounded down right foolish to me, but I said nothing.

When it came time to do the dishes, Mr. Hoyt excused himself to go make his apologies to Colonel Baines.

Dad regarded our partner, perplexed. "What need is there for apologies?"

Mr. Hoyt glowered at the ground, loath to speak "I just assumed…"

Dad struck an uncommonly gentle note. "Perhaps in your enthusiasm you promised too much?"

"In a word, yes," came the gruff reply, and he stalked off to his disagreeable errand.

A little later we heard the drone of a fiddle tuning up, followed quickly by the twang of a banjo. People drifted toward the music.

I looked at my dad, "Could that be Mr. Peabody?"

Smiling, Dad dug in the wagon for his violin case. "Let's go find out."

Sure enough, when we got to the dance ground, we spied Linnaeus Peabody among the musicians. He gave us a hearty wave. Dad went up and joined in.

About noon on our third day of waiting we finally loaded onto a ferry. I put Bugle in the wagon so he wouldn't be underfoot.

The loading area was a great din of noise and dust: ferrymen shouting, men yelling at their teams and each other, animals bawling and braying. I'd never been on any kind of boat before, unless you wanted to count the raft Will and I built. This ferry was kind of a raft, except much bigger. It was made of rough timber and had a flimsy wooden railing running around the edge, except where you got on. It looked like it could hold two to three wagons and their teams. One outfit had loaded before us. The deck of the ferry still bobbed and swayed from those folks.

Dad was going ahead, backing up, holding the lead rope, coaxing the team forward. We got up the wide ramp from the shore, but the mules were stepping cautiously. Achilles and Ajax had never been on a boat either, it seems, because they put one hoof on that shifting, unsteady deck and reared right back. Dad almost got pulled into the muddy water.

Perched on the wagon seat, I flapped the reins on the team's backs. "Giddap! Giddap!" Bugle poked his head out next to me, eager to see what was going on. Mr. Hoyt already stood on the ferry.

The mules gave me as good back, honking and braying and throwing their heads. Dad tried to settle our animals. People started calling out, protesting the hold up. The ferryman came over and slapped Ajax on his rump. "Get on, there!" he bellowed.

Dad tugged on the lead rope, firmly but not too sudden.

I whistled and flapped the reins. "Come on, Ajax! Come on, Achilles!" I looped the reins around the brake and climbed into the wagon. Then I called out, "Hey, Dad!"

He looked up. I showed him an apple. Then I tossed it to him. He caught it one-handed and held it up so Ajax and Achilles could see it. He weaved it back and forth between them like he was asking, *Which one of you wants this?* Then he started backing up, pulling gently on the lead rope. The mules stepped forward to get the apple. Dad kept backing up. By then the deck wasn't moving too much. The front wheels of our wagon clunked onto the deck. Dad held the apple a little closer to the mules and kept backing up. The rear wheels clunked onto the deck. The ferry dipped a little, but the mules seemed not to notice. The ferryman told Dad where he wanted him to park. As soon as we were set, I jumped off the wagon with another apple. Dad and I fed the mules their treats.

As we crossed the river, Dad stayed with the team to quiet them. I went to stand at the railing, but I didn't put my weight on it. St. Louis spread along the far side of the river as far as the eye could see. The shore itself was hidden by countless boats of every kind. Even from this far away, you could smell the coal smoke.

Mr. Hoyt wandered over to join me. Gazing out, he remarked, "It's hard to believe the whole waterfront burned down last year."

We had heard nothing of it in Vermont. I worried how Uncle Rafe and his family had fared in that calamity. It made me all the more anxious to see him.

Mr. Hoyt pointed to a magnificent side-wheeler. The name painted on the paddle box was hidden by a smaller craft, but he said, "That's the Anita B." He pointed to another. "There's the Sultan." He turned to me. "How many steamboats you reckon are tied up over there?"

I laughed as I scanned the far shore. It seemed like a forest of tall, black chimneys.

He grinned. "Go on. Take a guess."

"Just steamboats?"

"The rest are scows!" he mocked. "Not worthy!" He gave me an encouraging grin. "How many?"

I stared across the river. I tried, but they moved. At last, I said, "I don't know. Lots!"

He leaned his elbow on the railing. "Twenty dollars says there's a hundred and fifty, at the very least."

I blinked. This was a world I wasn't used to. Sure, Will and I bet each other all the time. But the wager was always for ten frogs or a mountain of taffy. My enthusiasm faded. "I don't have twenty dollars."

"Not a sporting man. I see."

"My dad doesn't hold much with games of chance."

"Well, maybe that's to the good."

We went back to watching the scene.

Countless wagons and drays were loading and unloading bales of cotton, barrels of sugar, flour, or bacon, great coils of hemp. There had to be more people here even than in Albany. The shouting and the noise grew to an exuberant clamor as the ferry approached, and finally nudged the western shore.

Dreams of finding fistfuls of gold faded before the prospect of seeing Uncle Rafe again. Dad followed the map he'd put in his letter and found their house right off. Bugle jumped all over my uncle like he'd recovered a long-lost friend, and was rewarded with a good scratch. Uncle Rafe sized up our bright yellow wagon and asked, "You fixin' on joinin' the circus?"

My dad and I just laughed.

I confess I struggled to square the lean woods runner in fringed buckskins who resided in my imagination with the robust figure who stood before me. To be sure, the eyes were the same, the long, straight nose, the broad brow. But now the sharp chin was hidden behind a great spade of whiskers. His frame was heavier, the limbs powerful from his work as a builder. His girth proclaimed him well-fed and comfortable. Whatever the outward differences, when he spoke, I knew he was my beloved uncle.

Our welcome was warm and unsparing. I'd always been puzzled, even a little disappointed, that Uncle Rafe could give up such an exciting life, roaming the wild mountains, for settling in one spot to build other people's houses. But the way Uncle Rafe told it, he'd come under the gaze of one Ramona Santiago Rivera, a rancher's daughter. She had rescued him, half frozen, from a late blizzard and nursed him back to health. He said after he met Ramona, being alone in the mountains didn't seem like such a good idea anymore. Now he was making a real success in St. Louis as a builder. This wasn't a big surprise. He and my dad had helped their father build the family home and barn, and then he had helped Dad build our house and our first barn.

"After last year's fire, I'm busier than ever," he said. "And people are pouring in, wanting houses, stores." He gave Dad a wry smile. "I don't suppose I could persuade you…"

Dad held up his hands in defense. "And what should I tell Pru?" He shook his head, smiling. "No, for better or worse, our fate is bound up in California."

Uncle Rafe's wife, Ramona, reached about to his shoulder, which was tall for her people. She had a great mane of raven black hair which she kept trapped in a bun during the day, but let down after supper, when her laughter seemed to emerge, as well. Her strong cheek bones set off her bright ebony eyes. Child-bearing had softened her figure, but not her spirit. She ruled her home with the decisiveness of a military commander. It was easy to see that Uncle Rafe was no less besotted than the day she'd pulled him from the snow.

When Mr. Hoyt saw Uncle Rafe's children scampering and squealing around their father's legs, he begged off the hospitality he was offered, saying he had old friends he was obliged to seek out in the city. Bugle, for his part, fairly wallowed in all the attention those same kids gave him.

The first night, after a supper of food I'd never tasted before, I thanked Uncle Rafe for the Bowie knife, which hung at my right hip.

He nodded toward it. "I hope it serves you as well as it served me." He gave me a small whetstone to keep it sharp.

Throughout our stay, lively talk always followed supper. Ramona would sit with us until it was the kids' bedtime. Dad and Uncle Rafe held forth. I was happy to hug my knees and listen. When the talk wasn't about the wild times of their youth, it was about the trip ahead of us. Uncle Rafe had been out there before there was an Oregon Trail, or pretty much any trail. He talked about how much some of the rivers changed with the seasons. Unlike back East, where they flowed pretty steady the whole year, he said many rivers out west were impassable for weeks and weeks in the spring, and then all but disappeared in high summer.

"Have you caulked your wagon?" he asked.

I piped up. "You mean like on a ship?" Despite my mom's chiding, sometimes I forgot myself and interrupted.

Uncle Rafe didn't seem to take offense. He nodded and smiled. "The same."

"No, we haven't," my dad said. "River crossings?"

Uncle Rafe lifted one of his sleeping children off his lap and handed her to Ramona. Then he answered. "Rivers far outnumber ferries between here and California."

The next day we went to the outfitters, bought a tub of caulking, and filled every crack, split, and gap in our wagon box. When I mewled about the caulking wrecking our beautiful paint work, Dad said, "That may be, but who would you rather enjoy your paint work—us or the fish?"

My uncle's advice did not end with caulking. He recommended trading our mules for oxen. We didn't have a very big wagon, so we would only need two.

"First off," he said, "they'll eat almost any kind of grass or weed you come across. Not like mules or horses, who are more fussy eaters. They're slower, true, but they can pull more, and they'll outlast mules and horses ten to one. And the best part is, the Indians have no use for 'em, as mounts anyway, while they'll sure have their eye on mules and horses."

So that's what we did. I was sure sorry to lose Ajax and Achilles. I gave 'em hugs before they were led away.

Then my dad said to me, "We have some fine new beasts to help us get to California. But they'll need names, just like the mules did." And he smiled. "Why don't you see what you can come up with?"

Good names would take some time. We ended up staying there a few days, I think mostly because we were so enjoying sleeping in real beds. The other good thing about staying was I got to hear more stories about Uncle Rafe's days in the wilderness. One night, after everyone else had turned in, it was just him and me by the dying fire.

"How're you holding up, Pegg?" he asked me after a silence.

"Fine, sir. Fine."

"Your dad says you're good with the animals."

"Thank you, sir. But I just do what he taught me."

Uncle Rafe smiled. "I suspect there's a little more to it than that, but I doubt you could find a better teacher."

"Yessir."

He smiled even more. "And your momma's seen to your sociable aspects."

I grinned like a fool and nodded. "Probably more than is healthy, Will says. Will is my best friend back home."

We were quiet for a minute. Then he said, "You've come a fair piece..."

"We've walked more miles than I thought I ever would walk, but, even so, not near as many as you."

"Well," he laughed. "That's more than a body should decently walk in one lifetime." He laced his fingers over his belly. "What you've walked so far is a good shakeout for what's up ahead."

"I figure I'm ready to see some of the places you've seen."

"Some of the most interesting parts are yet to come, that's for certain."

"I'm ready for 'em," I said, patting his Bowie knife in my belt.

CHAPTER 8

I had my fourteenth birthday while we were in St. Louis. Ramona made a chocolate cake and a piñata. I had never had that much chocolate at one sitting in my life! I think the piñata, which I had never heard of before, was more for her kids' sake than mine. They shrieked with glee, bashing it to pieces, and scrambling after the candy that spilled out.

My dad, for his part, relished time with his brother. The days were full of visiting. Uncle Rafe took us around to meet all his neighbors and friends, or they came over. Ramona and her lady relatives cooked up feast after feast, and I tasted many new things.

As much as we were enjoying the visit, we knew other emigrants were rushing through the city, among them many gold seekers. With no little regret, we fixed the day of our departure. We expected to have to chase down Mr. Hoyt, but while Dad and I were repacking, finding places for the dried peppers, tortillas, cornmeal, and dried beans Ramona had given us, he appeared in the canvas opening at the rear of the wagon. "I have great news," he said as a hearty greeting.

Dad paused and regarded him, then said dryly, "Colonel Baines has offered us a reduced rate to join his company."

Mr. Hoyt's grin only widened. "You jest, sir. But the truth is quite above anything you might anticipate."

Dad moved to climb out of the wagon. He made no effort to hide his skepticism. "I am eager to hear it."

I thought it best to hang back.

When my dad stood before him, Mr. Hoyt pronounced, "I have been approached by a group of gentlemen representing the renowned Captain Leathers. Those of us with river experience know that when Captain Leathers speaks, we listen."

As I remembered, Mr. Hoyt didn't have a very high opinion of Captain Leathers. I crept close to the end of the wagon, the better to hear, but kept out of sight, sitting on a bag of beans.

Mr. Hoyt continued in the same lofty tone. "I have been asked to lend my expertise to the Captain's new enterprise, in return for a portion of the proceeds."

My dad said nothing.

Smug laughter bubbled out of Mr. Hoyt. "It is unexpected, I grant you. It was as much a surprise to me as I'm sure it is to you."

My dad's voice was flat and hard. He was really mad. "You have already committed yourself to a partnership from which you will receive a portion of the proceeds. Will you not honor that?"

"I don't remember signing any papers," snapped Mr. Hoyt.

"Nor did I," came my father's reply, just as quick. "But I gave my word, and I mean to keep it."

When Mr. Hoyt spoke again he wasn't exactly pleading, but he was close. "But it must be apparent to a man of your intelligence that this gold-hunting business was always a terrible gamble. We've all heard the stories."

"There are as many good stories as bad."

Mr. Hoyt made a more friendly voice, like my dad was his best buddy. "But why take a chance? I have, right here, at my fingertips, an opportunity that guarantees a king's ransom without risking life and limb."

Dad didn't say anything.

Mr. Hoyt said, "I would be the worst of fools to turn my back on it."

Silence. What could my dad say to change Mr. Hoyt's mind?

I thought I heard defeat in my father's voice. "I do not deny that there are many hardships ahead. From what I hear, conditions that test a man to his limits." Surely he was thinking of Uncle Rafe's stories. He paused again. "Perhaps it's for the best that you show your colors before other lives depend on you."

My jaw dropped. My dad almost never spoke so baldly. Most men would take those as fightin' words. I wished desperately I could see Mr. Hoyt's face. Would they come to blows?

Mr. Hoyt let out a low chuckle, but it had no humor. "Well, sir. You have cut me to the quick, and it prompts me to confess that I have joined Captain Leather's new venture not for personal gain but to legitimize my suit to my life's love, a lady who I had thought lost to me, but who has, through the kindest stroke of fortune, been restored to me in this very city."

Whoa! What? I was glad I was sitting down. You couldn't ask for a bigger surprise.

Dad took it in stride. "Would that be Miss Rochester? I thought she was in New Hampshire."

Mr. Hoyt barked in surprise. "No, it is not Miss Rochester." He took a moment to regain his composure. "The fine lady who awaits my return goes by the name of Mirabelle Devereux. She comes from one of the finest French families in New Orleans."

A longer silence. Then Dad spoke again. "So this is your choice, then? You will not be swayed?"

No doubt Mr. Hoyt wore his lopsided grin. "I am merely accepting what destiny has placed before me."

Dad assumed his formal, town-hall-meeting voice. "Far be it from me to stand in the way of true love. I wish you every success and happiness."

"That's very generous of you, sir, and gratefully received." Mr. Hoyt's tone was syrupy with triumph.

"Well, don't let us detain you." My father's hand grasped the top of the tail gate, preparing to climb back into the wagon.

Mr. Hoyt cleared his throat importantly. "But I will have to trouble you for my portion of our resources, so that I can conduct myself in a manner befitting my situation."

"By rights, that is Mr. Pruitt's money, since he bankrolled your participation."

"I'll settle up with Pruitt. You don't have to worry about that."

Dad stuck his head in the opening and found me in the shadows. Even in the gloom I could see his anger, but his voice was calm. "Pegg, get the money box, will you?"

We had built a compartment under the floorboards to hold valuables. It was under several heavy barrels. I dug it out and handed it to him. Once revealed, I stayed in the opening to watch what went on.

Dad rummaged in the box and handed Mr. Hoyt a sheaf of bills. *Vermont money. Will it be accepted here?*

"Good day to you, sir," declared Mr. Hoyt, as if Dad was a perfect stranger. He turned on his heel and strode away. No "thank you", no "safe travels", no "good luck."

I watched him go with mixed feelings. I would miss his colorful stories, but that was nothing compared to losing the extra pair of hands. How could he cast off his obligations as one would flick ash from his shoulder?

My dad watched him, too. "That's probably the last we'll see of him." He turned to climb back into the wagon. "I'm afraid I've let Mr. Pruitt down. I'll have to write him about this."

"What'll we do now?" I scooted out of the way to make room for him.

Dad smiled. "We'll go to California to dig for gold, just like we've set out to do."

I managed a smile in return, but it was tainted with worry.

He put the money box back in its cubby hole. "We still have four sturdy hands to do the work. It'll just take a little longer."

Inwardly, I was proud he considered my labor equal to his, but I was still worried. "Do we have enough money?"

"We have less. We will have to be careful. A great desire to win is as important as a pocket full of silver."

In all, we stayed five days in St. Louis. The fourth day Mr. Hoyt left us, and the next day Dad said we should be on our way. I had names for our team.

Dad, Bugle, Uncle Rafe, and his two oldest kids were my audience. I stood where we would walk with them, as we had with the mules. I grasped a horn of the darker, caramel-colored one. "This is Boreas," I said. "He'll be the leader." Then I pointed over the yoke to the offside ox. "And that is Yellowstone."

"You never do anything slipshod, Pegg," my dad said. "Enlighten us."

I looked at Boreas. He had white patches on his legs and along his spine. "Boreas is one of the four winds of the Greeks. He will carry us swiftly on our way."

My dad's eyebrows shot up. "I only hope so."

"And Yellowstone is named for a river out West Uncle Rafe talked about. It stands for all the wonders we'll see."

"Hear, hear!" called Uncle Rafe, clapping.

Dad smiled. "Boreas and Yellowstone it shall be then, and good omens, too." He patted my shoulder. "Well done, well done."

After hugs, goodbyes, and lots of waving, we hit the road, without Mr. Hoyt.

CHAPTER 9

It was early May. The grass was tall, the roads were dry. We joined a river of wagons threading its way west out of St. Louis, all rattling and clanking and thumping. If you weren't at the very front, you travelled in a cloud of dust. Children squealed, running ahead; dogs barked. People looked forward with eager faces. *The great journey begins!* The townspeople ignored us. They saw this procession every day.

Once clear of the last buildings, wagons spread out so as to avoid each other's dust. It was easy to pick out the Baines Company Mr. Hoyt wanted us to join. They looked very smart in their light blue coats and plumed caps. I counted thirty men riding two abreast, not counting the good colonel and his flag bearer, or their teamsters. They had four sturdy wagons painted in the same light blue color, with the name in fancy letters on the sides. Each wagon was pulled by a six-mule team. Apparently, they had not heard of the advice about oxen, or chose to ignore it.

Let 'em have their blue wagons. I was proud of our cheerful, sunny, yellow wagon with Will's smart black striping. And we had Boreas and Yellowstone, two fine, steadfast, willing animals.

The Baines Company aside, not many had yet seen the wisdom of forming into groups with leaders. We were nothing more than a great, wooly mob, each wagon making its way as best it could.

It turned out the Bequette wagon always seemed to be close by, so I got to know Bobby a little more. He'd point out the tiniest spit of a puddle as a possible swimming hole, until I had to give him some practical dimensions. Another kid started coming by, too, a skinny, long-legged kid about my age but taller, with dirty blonde hair that hung in his eyes. Ben Parker didn't walk; he ambled like he was made with loose hinges, arms swinging. He was the oldest of seven kids, all boys. The Parker family was bound for Oregon. Ben had already apprenticed as a farrier back in Massachusetts, but was happy to leave it. He found he had little interest in the care of horses. He wanted to run a mill or a store; he wanted to be the boss.

"How about bein' a captain on a stern wheeler, or a Baltimore clipper?" I crowed.

"Too wet by half," he scoffed with a flap of his arm.

Ben told jokes, endlessly. But, to be fair, he was good at it.

Indeed, there were kids of all ages on the emigrant trail. Lots of women tended newborns. Others were large with child.

My dad, watching one lady straighten awkwardly with her swollen belly, observed quietly, "A hard time to be traveling into the wilderness."

I was surprised to see farms on this side of the river—nothing like New York or Pennsylvania, to be sure, but people getting a foothold. I thought once we crossed the Mississippi, we would plunge into howling wilderness.

Almost immediately there were mishaps: poorly maintained harnesses broke, badly packed wagons spilled baggage at the least bump. Mismatched, untrained teams stumbled into each other, bellowing their frustration. Add to that the shouting and cursing and cracking of whips, and we made a raucous bunch.

But most folks were just glad to be on the way. Minor calamities were put to rights with good humor. A sense of purpose spread among the host. However casually they had progressed so far, people took the bit. More walked than rode; a bumpy ride on a wagon was a lot rougher on the backside than picking your way on foot.

Soon we met with realities that would beset us for much of the journey: the teams struggled to pull overloaded wagons. Discarded possessions lined our route almost from the outset: grandma's bedstead, the hallway mirror. Fuel for our cook fires proved scarce. Trees hugged the streams we crossed, but those folks who had gone before us had used up much of the deadfall and felled many of the smaller trees.

Dad and I walked with the team, me to the left of Boreas, keeping a loose hold on his lead rope in case he needed guiding. Dad walked to the right of Yellowstone. Sometimes Dad and I swapped places. We nattered at them and sang songs to them. It helped pass the time. They seemed content. The pace was such that I could take Bugle off for a run and still catch up to our wagon.

Linnaeus reappeared on a new mount, a fine, roan Kentucky Saddler. He kept pace with us for a few days, talking with Dad and me during the days and playing music with Dad at night. Then his eagerness got the better of him and he surged ahead, his banjo twanging as it bounced against his back.

The Baines Company displayed military precision, waking up everybody within earshot with a shrill blast of their trumpet, and were usually the first to be under way. They soon outpaced our plodding oxen. By the third day they left us behind entirely.

Each day our great motley parade changed order. Some folks stopped early; many pushed on until the sun was half sunk in the horizon. People moved about their chores soberly. Children, tired after a day of walking, sat close by the camp kettle, waiting for supper. As darkness fell, campfires flickered like fireflies, seemingly to the horizon.

The land spread wide on either hand. The grass was already drying out under the bright sun. The horizon seemed to pull farther and farther away, taunting us to catch it. We began to see multitudes of birds: great flocks of ducks of every variety, wild geese, and hawks soaring; more turkeys than I'd ever seen. This abundance was not lost on the boys who had rifles. They raced into the surrounding meadows, blasting away, laughing and shouting. Luckily, they didn't hit each other. Mostly they wasted a lot of ammunition.

At the end of one day, I saw one kid had actually bagged a prairie chicken, but he didn't have a gun. Seeing the wrung neck of the bird, I asked, "How'd you do that without a gun?"

But I already had a good hunch.

He confirmed it. "A rock."

He was ten, I guessed. A little shorter than me, sturdily made.

"Show me," I challenged, which meant *prove it,* without being a toad about it, as Will would say.

Without a word, he got a bucket and an egg and stepped off about thirty paces. Then he set the bucket upside down and put the egg on top. Then he came back to us—a few of the other boys were as skeptical as I was. Digging a small rock out of his trouser pocket, he turned, held still for a heartbeat, then hurled the stone side-arm, the way you do when you skip a stone on water. The egg exploded, shell pieces twirling away, innards flying out in loopy strands. He turned to his audience. Those who weren't staring at the remains of the feat were staring at the kid.

I was pretty good with a rock myself, but not that good. "Good shot."

One of the other boys dared him to do it again. He did it again, but with an apple the second time. His mother chased him away when he went for another egg.

Most of the others drifted off to their suppers. I stuck out my hand. "Bartholomew Pegg, proud to meet you."

"Mattie Shilo."

I liked this kid. He kept still but his eyes were watchful. We exchanged particulars. He was from Ohio. His dad was a wainwright, a man who made wagons. Oregon bound, too, his folks and him. He was a rare one; he didn't have any brothers or sisters.

Two days after Mattie Shilo's demonstration, I bagged a turkey with Dad's rifle. I was not above pride, and carefully explained my technique to every awestruck youngster who came to view my trophy. Roast turkey was a welcome change from bacon and beans. I kept a tail feather for my hat.

After almost a month and a half on the road, we came to the fabled Missouri River, much of which Captain Clark and Mr. Lewis had navigated on their great trek to the Pacific. The ferry that was supposed to take us across looked so flimsy I was sure it would fall to pieces and sink as soon as we set foot on it.

Here, too, a great, impatient mob waited to cross. The river itself was almost as crowded, with ferrymen and steamboats jostling for right-of-way, and smaller craft of every sort darting between. The steamboats, towering above all else, seemed likely to sink under their own weight, crammed as they were with wagons, wood, people, freight and gear. Cursing and name-calling, the like of which I had never heard before, peppered the dusty air.

Our own crossing very nearly came to grief. The ferry we rode, along with three other outfits, found itself in the path of a great palace of a side-wheeler chugging relentlessly upriver. The steamboat's whistle screamed a warning, the ferryman had only his fist to shake, and oaths to hurl. Neither craft could be called nimble.

Only a few yards separated us from disaster. I was convinced we were going to be crushed to splinters.

At the last possible moment, the steamboat blew off steam, lost way with the help of the river, and the passengers of each crowded their respective railings to watch the two vessels graze by each other, with the larger sheering off a few out-riding timbers from stern of the lesser.

The steamboat's whistle ripped the air with a long, punishing blast, and the two captains exchanged blasphemies and rude gestures until they were lost to each other's sight.

Most of the steamboats were sternwheelers, called by Uncle Rafe mountain boats, I guess because they followed the Missouri all the way to the mountains. Most of the steamboats on the Mississippi had been side-wheelers.

When I had questioned the difference with my uncle, he'd said, "The Missouri is called Old Misery for a reason. It's a meaner river. For one thing, it's worse full of snags. When the wheel's at the back, you've got less chance of wrecking your paddles on a snag. The boat'll take the blow before the wheel. With a side-wheeler, both wheels are out there, waiting to get struck."

We reached the western shore and saw a steamboat pulled up to the bank. Men were carrying shrouded forms off the boat and up to a group of other men digging graves. "Cholera," people whispered to each other in terror. Cholera inspired such fear because it struck anyone and everyone, and no one, not even doctors, knew where it came from or how it spread. Just like smallpox or the bloody flux.

Despite my fear for his safety, Dad insisted on going to help with the digging. I went and got shovels out of the wagon, but Dad said, "You wait here with Bugle, Pegg-son. No sense in taking more chances than we have to."

"What if you get sick by helping them?"

"We can't let that keep us from doing what we can," Dad answered in a somber voice. "We'd appreciate the help if we were in their place."

"Yessir, I suppose so."

He rested his hand on my shoulder. "Pray the good Lord watches over us, Pegg-son." And off he went.

Those were the first graves we'd seen, but they wouldn't be the last, not by a long shot.

The cholera laid waste to the emigrants in the weeks that followed, taking people with terrifying swiftness. Dad kept helping with the burials. I was sick with fear that he would catch it himself, but I couldn't share that with anyone.

Because of how it bends, we had to cross the Missouri twice. The second time was at a little trading post known as Rocheport. This place looked more primitive than anything we had seen so far. We caught up to Linnaeus there, and he pointed out that the name was left over from when the French had the run of this part of the country.

"Would that be true of St. Louis, and St. Joseph, too?" I asked him.

"I would say so," he replied. "Often you can tell something of the history of a place by the names people leave behind."

Two days after we left Rocheport, Mr. Hoyt reappeared.

CHAPTER 10

We had stopped for the night, and were in the middle of supper when Mr. Hoyt rode up on a broken-down old nag. I stared in disbelief. My dad set his plate aside and stood. Mr. Hoyt dismounted and strode into camp like he'd only been away the day.

Dad moved to meet him and spoke first. "This is an unexpected surprise."

"Am I unwelcome?" replied Mr. Hoyt. But he kept coming, leading the horse. The nag plodded sluggishly, her head hung low; the poor beast was near done in.

"To what do we owe this singular honor?"

"Fortune struck a cruel blow." Mr. Hoyt frowned. "Two cruel blows, in fact."

Dad still stood between Mr. Hoyt and the fire. "That is unfortunate, most unfortunate." Good manners prevented Dad from prying.

Mr. Hoyt stopped at a respectful distance. He pulled off his hat and held it in his hands. "I was robbed." He lifted his chin defiantly. "Without funds to bring to the endeavor, Dr. Leather's people had no further truck with me."

I watched Mr. Hoyt shift uncomfortably. *What about your expertise? Isn't that still needed?*

Dad said, "I'm sorry to hear that." He gave the man a chance to continue. When Hoyt remained silent, Dad prompted, "You said two."

Mr. Hoyt puffed up his chest defensively. "Miss Devereux suggested we resume our association when I was better able to provide for her."

I could see Dad relax a little. "That cannot have been easy to hear. But the ladies do like to be taken care of."

Mr. Hoyt brought forth a small leather sack about the size of my fist. The lumps suggested coins inside. "In a desperate effort to improve my condition, I reluctantly took to the gaming tables. Lady luck smiled upon me and I came away with a modest bounty." He held the sack out to Dad. "Minus the cost of the horse, of course."

Dad wasn't going to just roll over. "What's this for?"

Mr. Hoyt drew his brows together and thrust the little sack forward. "I know it's not near what I took out of the pot, but if you need it spelt out, it's my way of askin' back in." He jigged the bag again. Dad still didn't take it. Mr. Hoyt's scowl deepened. "I'll top it up as the opportunity arises." His voice got rough with unease. "It's the best I can do."

Dad took the sack and moved to let Mr. Hoyt step closer to the fire. He looked at me. "Pegg, would you please see to Mr. Hoyt's horse?"

"Yessir." I put down my plate and went to unsaddle the horse. The saddle looked as desperate as the animal. I took the nag out to where Boreas and Yellowstone were grazing. After hobbling her, I stroked her muzzle and scratched her cheeks. "We'll have you good as new in no time." I walked around her slowly, smoothing my hand along her withers and flanks, muttering friendly nonsense. No injuries; nothing a steady diet of good grass and easy handling wouldn't fix.

When I got back, Dad had served up a plate of beans and bacon to Mr. Hoyt, who wolfed it down like a starving man.

Mr. Hoyt asked my dad, "Have you written to Pruitt yet?"

Dad forked another piece of bacon onto the other man's plate. "This'll be just between us. We all make mistakes."

I wondered how being robbed was a mistake. Maybe this was a grown-up code. Will and I had our own code.

Mr. Hoyt took a swig of coffee. "I'd be much obliged." He made an arc with the cup, taking in our bright yellow wagon and our fire. "I'll do my part. I won't let you down."

To his credit, he was as good as his word. Despite his several infirmities, he resumed his old chores, and did them with dispatch and good cheer. It certainly made a difference when he pitched in, but Will's voice sniggered in the back of my thoughts, *Wouldn't you hustle if you were trying to scramble back into the lifeboat?*

It took seven more days to reach Independence, Missouri. Uncle Rafe had said Independence was the true gateway to the West. Beyond would be buffalo, Blackfoot, Sioux, and Pawnee. Out there were lofty mountains and boundless plains, he said, where you could wander for weeks without seeing another soul.

When we rolled into town, we discovered hordes and hordes of emigrants filling the streets, just like in St. Louis. The feeling of impatience, of anticipation, buzzed in the town like a swarm of insects. There was so much merchandise it was displayed on the street itself. Sacks of flour and beans were snapped up as they came off the freight wagons. Wainwrights, wheelwrights, and blacksmiths worked night and day making wagons to satisfy the demand. People outbid each other for them before they were even finished. Insults, threats, and even fights broke out over the buying of animals to make up teams.

Amid the throng I spied a few individuals to make my heart race: trappers and mountain men--what my Uncle Rafe had been. They sauntered about as if they were kings of the realm, cradling their beautiful, old-fashioned Pennsylvania long rifles. I had never seen an Indian, but it seemed to me these shaggy, sunburnt men in their buckskins, furs, and feathers would be barely distinguishable from wild Indians. I wondered if wearing buckskins would be any cooler than the scratchy woolens or homespun we emigrants wore.

This was the last place to mail letters for a good while. Dad had saved up the ones he had been writing since St. Louis, and now wrote a long one, saying letters might not be as regular from now on, but reassuring my mom we were in the best of health and spirits, and well-equipped for the journey ahead. He gave me a page of my own.

"What should I write about?" I asked.

"Why don't you tell her about your mountain men?"

I filled the page without any trouble at all.

As at other river crossings, we had to wait our turn. We still feared the cholera, which seemed to strike most when there were great mobs of us together, but we didn't talk about it. Dad gave Mr. Hoyt some of the partnership money to go buy supplies. Dad, himself, watched men training their ox teams to see what he could learn.

Mr. Hoyt came back with a bulky-looking contraption he called a "Road-o-meter." He proudly explained that it would keep track of how far we got each day.

"Where's the salt and flour?" My dad asked, casting a skeptical eye on the homely collection of wooden cogs.

Mr. Hoyt lifted his chin, a smug twist to his mouth. "We can buy food anywhere. This is a much better investment. I'm sure my stepfather would agree."

"Well," said Dad, "since Mr. Pruitt isn't here to speak for himself, and since he entrusted his money to me, I find myself obliged to disagree. Other things will be more important to our success. Like feed for the oxen, if need be, or a new wagon wheel, or food for our own bellies."

"But…" Mr. Hoyt sputtered, then stopped.

Dad waited, but Mr. Hoyt offered no further argument. Finally, Dad spoke. "Well, the milk is spilt. Nobody's going to trade a good sack of beans for that." He squatted down for a closer look. It wasn't easy to figure. "It looks like it might even slow the wagon down."

Mr. Hoyt took that as an insult. "We won't know until we try it, will we?"

Dad stood up, still eyeing the lumpish machine. "If it slows us down, it's out."

Mr. Hoyt had neglected to get any instructions with the device, claiming learning such a simple machine would be child's play. We three each made a try, attempting it on all four wheels— since that was the one bit of the operation everyone agreed on— to no avail. Still, he refused to have it thrown out.

As well, he continued to pester Dad about joining a company. Dad finally went around and talked to people and, indeed, it looked like everybody had joined one kind of group or another. Nobody wanted to challenge those vast distances, not to mention the Indians, on their own. Even more, this was confirmed by the people we talked to who were heading east, on their way back home. They all said not to chance it alone.

Mr. Hoyt remained eager for us to join Colonel Baines's company. He brought news that they had tarried in Independence, looking to replace members they had lost.

Dad asked around and discovered that two of those members had been booted out for fighting and another three had quit in disgust at what they called "mule-headed leadership." Dad learned all this from another Baines man who, of a like opinion, had joined a different company. Mr. Hoyt protested that a few bad apples— that old saw—but my dad responded that the man had also revealed that neither Colonel Baines, nor any of his company, had been farther west than Philadelphia.

Abandoning the Baines people, Mr. Hoyt continued his search. The very next evening he returned from his ramblings flush with excitement. He poured himself a cup of coffee, bursting to reveal all. "I have solved our problem."

"I didn't know we had one," Dad replied mildly.

I bent down and scrubbed Bugle's ears to hide my laugh.

Though confounded, Mr. Hoyt tried to retain his dignity. "I have found us a company. Something more to your liking, I think."

Dad broke into a smile. "If it'll solve our problem and I'll like it, what more could one ask?"

I snuck a look at Mr. Hoyt, who was clearly abashed by my dad's ripostes. He closed his eyes and made a scowl, as if to reaffirm the importance of his news. "I have located an outfit quite the contrary in all regards to the Baines Company."

"Indeed." Dad finally put down his own coffee cup. "That would be an improvement. You spoke with them?"

Now that he had our interest, our partner took on a grave manner. "I spoke at length with the man in charge, one Abraham Chalmers. It seems he's done the trip before."

Mr. Hoyt went on to explain that the Chalmers' Company had no rule book, brandished no flag, nor did they sport fancy uniforms. "Perhaps best of all, they charge no fees, and ask only good behavior of the members, as well as willing participation toward the common good or the common defense." He sat back to assess the impact of his news.

Dad glanced at me. I could offer nothing but a smile.

Mr. Hoyt spoke earnestly. "I would not hesitate to inquire. Given the accomplishments of Chalmers and his guide, many are eager to join them. I pressed our case most ardently. I spoke of your reputation for generosity and fair dealing in our community back home."

Now it was Dad's turn to be abashed. "You are most generous. I hope I can live up to it." He stood up. "We'd best look into it, then."

I stood up, too. He nodded to me and gestured to Mr. Hoyt to set us on our way.

"You go on," Mr. Hoyt demurred. "I've done what good I can. I have other obligations." He told us where to find the Chalmers people and Dad, Bugle, and I set out.

Abraham Chalmers proved to be a towering bull of a man with a leonine mane and a fine, flaring, ginger-colored beard. You just knew he was a leader as soon as you laid eyes on him. Not only because he could pound you flat with a fist the size of a maul, but by the way he carried himself; the quiet way he spoke.

As impressive as Mr. Chalmers might've been, my attention was drawn to his guide—a pilot, to use a river term—who he presented as his second-in-command. Gideon MacIver, a crusty stick of a man, was every inch a mountain man—fringed buckskin shirt, moccasins, the whole rig. His fur hat, fashioned from a skunk pelt, sported several feathers. He looked almost Indian, and that was fine by me. Gideon MacIver claimed to have trapped every river and stream that ran to the Pacific. Mr. MacIver also claimed that he, himself, had laid eyes on the Yosemite Valley, which many held to be a mythical place of Indian lore.

Mr. Chalmers had been democratically elected by the assembled company, which didn't have an official name, much less his.

"I've got forty-eight wagons so far," he said. "I'll take on no more than another half dozen. Your partner spoke very highly of you. You're welcome, if you've a mind to join us."

I was immensely pleased that Dad glanced at me before accepting Mr. Chalmers' invitation.

When Mr. Chalmers inquired after Dad's trade, and Dad told him, he said, "We have a goodly number of farmers among our people." We soon learned that, in addition to the farmers, the company hosted a collection of men from the mechanical trades, a handful of coal miners, three storekeepers, a tailor, two coopers, a glazier, a blacksmith, three lawyers, and a doctor. Almost all were family men, which meant a selection of wives and children in tow.

When Mr. Hoyt belatedly worried that Mr. Chalmers was taking his people to Oregon, my dad pointed out that several wagons in the company were in fact bound for California. He said that he was sure that, up ahead, when the trail forked for California, we would find plenty of people going our way that we could join. Until then, he would put his trust in Mr. Chalmers' and Mr. MacIver's experience with the country.

"And," he reminded Mr. Hoyt, "they have a real doctor."

I considered the choice a good one for the same reasons as my dad, and for the kids I spotted amongst the families of the company. Even better, before the first day's travel was out, I discovered that the Bequette family, the Parkers, and the Shilos all thought Mr. Chalmers the best choice, too, and had joined his company. So whatever else came about, I would have ever-hopeful Bobby, joke-spinning Ben, and deadly marksman Mattie for company, and I was glad of that.

THE CHALMERS COMPANY

CHAPTER 11

Leaving Independence, we weren't just a river of wagons—we were a sea! At least a dozen companies, some made up of only four or five wagons, many with twenty or more. The Chalmers Company was comprised of fifty-five wagons, mostly one family to a wagon, a bit over two hundred souls in all.

I imagined perching on the tallest building back in town and looking westward: I would see regiments of little white humps of canvas spread over the grassy plain, shivering and flapping when the wagons lurched and bumped. Once again, the proud Baines Company forged ahead of the lumbering multitude.

At the end of the day, Mr. Chalmers and Mr. MacIver insisted we start getting into the habit of drawing our wagons into a circle.

"We'll start with two circles of twenty wagons," Mr. Chalmers addressed the assembled drivers. "But farther on, the size will be determined by the availability of grass and fuel."

Mr. MacIver waited for the hubbub to die down. "We may not need it today or tomorrow," he said, regarding his audience with a flinty gaze. "But there'll be a time when we will."

Despite their tutelage, when we tried this circling operation, it produced a great tangle of beast and wagon.

A few days in it rained, and the mud only added to the misery of those folks unaccustomed to living rough. With hundreds upon hundreds of wagons and thousands of animals moving through, the trail was chewed up good. And everybody was carrying too much, so the wagons sank to their hubs in the muck.

We grew accustomed to the clatter and thump of things being thrown out to lighten loads. The choices of what to abandon were odd: An essential sack of flour would be discarded alongside an ornately carved table, a perfectly good pair of shoes with a butter churn.

Dad and I helped folks dig out when they needed it, and they returned the favor. One time a family named Forsyth got stuck. When we got there, we found the daughter, Hally, right next to her dad, up to her knees in muck, shoveling for all she was worth. Mud spattered, hair flying, she scooped out mud like there was no tomorrow. I thought, *Now, there's a girl cut from different cloth.*

None of the pamphlets or advertisements that talked up going west mentioned meeting your Maker on the way. Though any fool knew it could happen, I doubt anyone expected it to be so common. When the first few poor souls were lost, everybody stopped out of sympathy and the burials were well attended. After a time, people were left to their burying chores, to catch up as best they could.

And we weren't losing people just to cholera. Fevers, accidents, broken spirits took their toll, too. Six-year-old Ottie, Ben Parker's next to youngest brother, had a run-in with a rattlesnake. He put up a good fight, but the poison finally took him. Ben didn't tell many jokes for a good while after that.

Another kid, A. J., jumped off his wagon. Didn't judge it right, fell under the left rear wheel. Doctor Yarborough, the doctor in our company, gave him all the laudanum he could swallow. A. J. hung on for two days before he gave up the ghost. His mother near went mad with grief.

Our company wasn't alone in these calamities. Sometimes there were so many graves at the places we stopped, it was hard to find a place for the tents.

We were no strangers to death. Dad had put his folks in the ground when their time came, and he helped Mom do the same for hers. I'd been old enough to understand when it came to my mom's folks. I'd seen Granny Hester laid out in the front hall, in the box Dad made for her, so people could pay their respects. Death had its place, its season, as the Good Book says, but it had never seemed overwhelming.

But on that rutted emigrant trail, tragedy and tribulation, great and small, seemed a ceaseless parade. People grew quiet.

Dad didn't play his fiddle as often. Mr. Hoyt took on the manner of a hunted man, throwing wary glances over his shoulders as if expecting an attack from any quarter. At night, in the darkness of the tent, he would mutter, "Are we going to just wait for death to strike us down?"

But as the days wore on, people toughened up. Those who couldn't, turned for home. Mr. Chalmers and his wife strove to keep everyone trained on the positive. Mrs. Chalmers corralled Dad and Linnaeus Peabody to play for dancing of an evening. Much to my delight, Mr. Peabody had decided to travel with Chalmers and made a habit of swinging by every few days, when he could have easily outpaced us.

Even crusty old Mr. MacIver pitched in to raise spirits by telling us kids stories when we pestered him.

One evening, when I asked him why we hadn't seen any wild Indians yet, he explained that the local tribes had been decimated by diseases from us and warfare amongst themselves. Then he slapped his knee and said, "But don't worry, sonny. If you don't lose your hair to the Pawnee, you'll see some fine Lakota, Cheyenne, or Blackfoot up ahead, sure as shootin'." He would not guarantee sighting buffalo, though. "They have minds of their own. Which is to say, the matriarch of each herd has a mind of her own. They could be anywhere from the Mexican border to the Canadian prairies."

"Do the buffalo stop at the Mexican border?" I asked.

He tilted his head and gave me a hard look. "Don't much appreciate smart alecks." And he got up and left.

One of the other kids, the Forsyth girl, said, "You shouldn't be such a smart mouth like that. He won't talk to us anymore." Hally was a very serious person for somebody who was only eleven. She was the only person who asked Mr. MacIver as many questions as I did. Unlike myself, she always asked serious questions. Before I could defend my pride, she spun on her heel, her long dark braids swinging like scythes in the field, and walked away.

Mr. MacIver wasn't the only person we got our learning from. Mrs. Chalmers held lessons after supper for the kids. Hally Fortsyth, Bobby Bequette and Mattie Shilo were among her ten students. When I protested to my dad that she was teaching stuff I already knew, he spoke to Mrs. Chalmers about giving me something challenging, which she did. When I complained to Mr. Peabody that I should have kept my mouth shut, he told me I was lucky to be continuing my education. I'd forgotten he'd been a teacher.

Hally was just as serious about learning arithmetic as she was about Indian tribes. When she overheard what Mrs. Chalmers was teaching me, she lugged her seat over and horned in. Hally did double duty in Mrs. Chalmers' school by looking after Mrs. Chalmers' three-year-old, Lilly. I paid it no mind until Lilly decided I merited closer inspection. She would stand at my knee and regard me with eyes as big and blue as my sister's. Hally would drag her away, and after a few minutes the tyke would be back, studying me. Mrs. Chalmers soon recruited me and Mattie to set up kegs and boxes before class, which only gave little Lilly more chance to tail me. She stayed quiet and out of the way, so I didn't mind. She reminded me of my sister Amy and I found that to my liking.

Dad had me put what I was learning in our letters home.

"To help convince your mother we aren't descending into utter savagery." He smiled. If it helped keep her from worrying, I was happy to do it.

Every morning, as soon as we were on our way, I checked my compass to make sure we were heading west, mostly. And every evening I made my promise to the setting sun, *I'll catch you one day*.

To break the monotony of the miles, there were always critters around: rabbits, prairie dogs, plovers, doves, and prairie chickens. Far off, deer gave us a wide berth, as did tawny, white-rumped antelopes Mr. MacIver called pronghorns. I was sure we would see buffalo soon enough. I taught some of the other boys to shoot better so they could add to their family cook pots.

The heat out on this prairie was more fierce than anything I'd ever felt back in Vermont. We did have a constant companion—the wind. It tugged at aprons and bonnets and hats. And the wind pushed not only the heat around, but dust, as well. That dust, whether kicked up by the wagons and animals or brought on the unrelenting wind, covered everything. It got in your eyes, your mouth, your nose.

One morning I went out to gather in the stock: Boreas and Yellowstone, and Mr. Hoyt's mount. The horse was missing.

When I told Mr. Hoyt, he said, "I sold her, and the saddle. She was nothin' but a bag of bones, anyway. And the saddle was about ready to fall apart."

Dad and I looked puzzled.

He snorted smugly. "To Whitton, a harness maker from New Jersey. I met him the other day. He paid twice what she was worth. I threw in the saddle."

We waited to see if there was more to his story.

Mr. Hoyt shrugged restlessly. "Besides, it didn't feel right, riding, with you two walking." He fished a small bag out of his vest pocket and handed it to my dad. "I said I'd pay back what I borrowed of our funds." He lifted his chin pridefully. "I'll not have it said Fred Hoyt doesn't honor his commitments." Dad handed him a cup of coffee. "I'm sure everybody'd appreciate that."

I took a long look at Mr. Hoyt as he sat himself down by the fire. Will sneered in a corner of my mind, *How long was he going to keep the money? Did he hope you wouldn't notice the horse was missing?* I did not want to be so quick to condemn. He might be unpredictable, but he'd come good in the end.

We traveled steadily northwestward for several weeks before arriving at Fort Kearney. This outpost consisted of just a few rough buildings perched on a rise above the Platte River. No imposing palisade, no stout block houses on the corners. As we got closer, I said to Mr. MacIver, "It doesn't look much like a fort."

"Well, give it time, Sonny. It's only been here a couple of years. Besides that, in case you hadn't noticed, there ain't much in the way of timber in these parts."

I didn't want to be taken for stupid, so I told him I had surely noticed that hundreds of emigrants were camped below the fort. Tents and wagons were all higgledy-piggledy. Discarded articles, both practical and impractical, were heaped and scattered all about. People were still reluctantly throwing stuff out of their wagons in an effort to spare their teams. Mr. Chalmers led us over to one side where we could stay together.

We put all the stock out to graze and set to soaking our wagon wheels and filling our water barrels. Mr. Chalmers went up to the fort to collect what information he could.

He came back and gathered everyone around his wagon. Standing on the wagon seat, he held up his arms for quiet.

His voice boomed out. "The lieutenant tells me thousands of wagons are passing through every day, so we best not dally. The last train through near cleaned him and his sutler out of their stores, and we won't have another chance to resupply until Fort Laramie. That's over three hundred miles from here. So be thrifty with your provisions."

The army and the trader had no supplies to spare?

He let people chew on that for a minute. Then he said, "They've started a mail service between Independence and Salt Lake City. There's a coach at the fort right now, heading east. If you've got letters saved up for mailing, or you want to write one, get them to Mr. MacIver. We'll stay three hours, no more." People scattered to their wagons. Hardly anybody heard him repeat, "Three hours!"

My dad gave me all the letters we had written to take to Mr. MacIver while he went to check on the wheels that had been soaking. We barely got our wheels back on before Mr. Chalmers started clanging that old cowbell of his, his signal to hitch up and move out. The sun was in our eyes. We could make maybe another ten or twelve miles before we stopped for supper.

We kept close to the south bank of the Platte River. Mr. MacIver advised everyone to keep their weapons close to hand and keep together. "We're heading into Cheyenne country, and the Sioux and the Cheyenne are havin' disagreements and both find it convenient to take out their ire on a lone wagon."

I thought I might get to see my war party at last.

But most people fretted. He told them, "Long as we keep together, folks, we shouldn't have any trouble. They like going after lone wagons, so don't get behind. Besides, we got somethin' they don't want any part of, and that's the cholera and smallpox. Like as not, they'll keep their distance. Just keep a sharp lookout and we'll be fine."

As everybody was breaking up, Mr. MacIver touched my shoulder and I knew I should wait a little. When it was just him and me, he said in a quiet voice, "Now, Sonny, you want to see the plains warrior at his finest, you'll see that in the Sioux and the Cheyenne, as proud and handsome a people as ever strode this earth." He leaned a little closer, almost whispering, "One of them chiefs, in his war bonnet and paint, on his pony—well, it's a sight to set your heart a-racin'—an' not just because he might want your hair!" He busted out laughing.

I heard a frightened gasp behind me and turned to see Hally, and a couple of other kids who were hanging on his every word. They scattered when Mr. MacIver swung around.

"Nothin' like a little bit o' scared to keep you on your toes," he chuckled, and sauntered off.

One day I was walking with Mattie Shilo. He was always looking for rocks and pebbles of a certain quality. I was telling him how any day now we should be seeing buffalo. Just then Mr. MacIver went riding by, and I waved to him.

He came over and slowed his horse to a walk. "You boys been keepin' a sharp eye out for hostiles?"

"Yessir. But they seem to be as scarce as the buffalo." I knew from listening to Dad and Mr. Chalmers talk that Mr. MacIver scouted ahead for us, looking for grass and water. So I asked, "Have you seen any buffalo, yet, Mr. MacIver?"

He made a show of looking over the broad plain. "This is prime buffalo country. If we're gonna see 'em, this is where we'll see 'em." He shifted his cap. "It's why we're not seein' many Injuns, either. They follow the buffalo, just like the buffs follow the grass."

Well, the very next day I got my wish. The shout, "Buffalo! Buffalo!" was passed down from wagon to wagon. Everybody grabbed up their rifles. It seemed the animals were crossing our path at the front of our train and moving down the valley to our left, running full out. I climbed onto our wagon seat and stood to get a better view.

By the time the buffalo hove into sight, several of our fellows, already on horseback, were giving chase; one or two had only side arms. Even I could guess a hand gun would be nigh on useless. Foolishly, some people even dashed out on foot. The ground trembled. Men had to calm their teams.

Suddenly, Linnaeus Peabody rode up to our wagon. His horse was greatly agitated. He shouted to me, "C'mon! Let's go have a look!"

I looked down at my dad. He had hold of Boreas' lead rope. He smiled and nodded. I was off the wagon in a flash and Mr. Peabody hauled me up to sit behind him, and off we went. Bugle started out after us, but I shouted back at him, "Stay!" and he stopped. My dad whistled to him and he went back. I was glad I didn't have to worry about him getting trampled by buffalo.

It took me only a minute to realize that neither of us had a weapon of any kind, but by then we were well away. We quickly passed those on foot and gained on the horsemen. The buffalo ran in a dense, shifting bunch. Much of their fur was dark, so it was difficult to separate the mob into individuals. As well, they were kicking up a furious cloud of dust! It was impossible to count them all. There were surely above fifty; there might have been a hundred! Their pursuers fired off their weapons wildly or not, depending on their skill.

Mr. Peabody shouted back to me. "MacIver told me this was a Buffalo Pony when he sold it to me! He was acting up even before we saw the beasts! Highly prized by the Indians for this very purpose! Now I see what he means!"

And, indeed, the horse was flying across the plain, even with my extra weight, making a straight line for the stampeding buffalo. We were very soon passing the other riders, who were whooping and hollering and firing carelessly, but still behind the buffalo.

All but a dozen of the animals veered suddenly and charged over a ridge. The other riders were caught off guard. Not so, Linnaeus Peabody's mount, who veered smoothly with the majority's path, as if one of them.

Our compatriots chose to pursue the splintered dozen, which left the remainder to Linnaeus and me. Unbelievably, the horse was gaining on the buffalo! We were soon enveloped in a choking world of dust. Since we had no weapons, we did not know what was in store for us. In no time at all we were among the beasts. The very earth shook. The thundering of hooves pounded in my ears. I could hear them breathing, huffing, their nostrils flared. Mounted, we were taller than the buffalo, who, up close, revealed themselves to be compact, muscular creatures. I looked down on the great, shaggy humps, the massive heads with their even shaggier crowns, the glinting, curved horns. Strings of spit flew from their mouths. Had I wished to throw my life away, I could have easily leapt onto the back of one of them, they were so close!

These buffalo seemed great chunks of the very earth! Heaved up! And running! We had no choice but to run with them. We ate dust and hung on for dear life. I marveled at the horse, who showed no sign of flagging. Linnaeus shouted something but I couldn't hear it. I was looking into the dark faces of the beasts that veered close enough.

A large bull suddenly swung toward us, tilting his horns to gore the horse, but the horse seemed to know and swerved away.

We were running flat out in a roiling mass of buffalo. The horse must have been avoiding prairie dog holes by sheer instinct! I was sure I was going to lose my grip and get pitched off any second.

Suddenly, the beasts split into two groups and headed off in opposite directions, as if they had come to a fork in an invisible road. I guessed they thought we wouldn't be able to decide which half to follow. With some difficulty, Linnaeus persuaded his horse to give up the chase. We followed the sound of gunfire back toward our wagons.

CHAPTER 12

When we came to Chimney Rock, one of the landmarks on the trail, Mr. Chalmers said we'd lay up for a day or so, to give the animals a rest. A bunch of us kids—Ben, Mattie, Bobby Bequette, even Hally, lit out to add our names to the hundreds of others that people had carved or painted on the rock. Sarah Prichard went along not to be left out, but she didn't climb any. Too unladylike, no doubt. If you climb high enough on Chimney Rock you might find where I scratched my name and the date, "Bartholomew Pegg—July 3, 1850".

Sarah Prichard was a friend of Hally's. At thirteen, she was very proud of the fact that she could wear a woman's dress, no longer a little girl's pinafore—an attainment which seemed to bestow upon her a sure knowledge of everything.

We were all chums. There'd always be one or two of us at one of the other's wagon, walking along, horsing around. Ben kept us in jokes; Bobby laughed so hard he doubled over. Sarah pronounced on all and sundry with great authority. When pestered, Mattie would throw a rock or two and amaze us. Hally brought Lilly, the Chalmers' little girl, over to the Pegg wagon a lot, claiming it was Lilly's request. Hally and I had fierce debates, full of foolishness, but she'd be back for more the next day. We had laughter, too. She almost always showed up with a treat for Bugle—no wonder he liked her.

One of the things that bound us kids together was the collecting of buffalo chips each day for the cook fires. A job of no small significance on the treeless plain.

This was kind of the kids' job, along with picking up rocks out of the road and fetching water. We used old blankets or sacking, whatever would hold the most chips. And you needed a lot of 'em, because they burned fast, being little more than grass.

Back home in Vermont we called them cow pies, or cowpats. Even if you've never been around a cow, you can guess what they were. Buffalo, being a heftier animal, could be relied on to leave a good-sized pie. But like I said, they were called chips. The city kids among us had to learn not to pick up the ones that were still wet.

Sarah was the kind of girl who wanted to collect buffalo chips without touching 'em. She had Ben sharpen her a long, stout stick. She would stab the chip with her stick and then scrap it off into her sack with the toe of her shoe.

One afternoon, we were out collecting chips when Bobby B. complained, "Sure wish there was a way to get a jump on everybody. I never get enough." We all looked at him, then everybody ended up looking at me.

Mattie Shilo said, "You always seem to find the most. What do you think?"

I wasn't used to being on the spot like that. I hatched a plan on the fly. "Maybe that's what we ought to do. Start sooner." *Think, think!* My companions stared, mystified. "In the late afternoon, as soon as I see MacIver standing at the spot where he wants the wagons to circle, I'll climb onto the wagon seat and look out to see where the most chips are."

Mattie was right on my tail. "How you gonna let us know?"

I reached for a chip, thinking like mad. "I'll give a whistle." I demonstrated with a sharp, loud whistle my mom used to call in her wandering children. It carried a mile, easy.

Bobby jumped; Sarah winced.

"One whistle means go left, two whistles means go right." There seemed to be a piece missing. "Hang your chip-carryin' bags or blankets off the back end of your wagons so you can just grab 'em and go."

To my surprise, our success was marked. Bobby B. happily bowed under the weight of his haul. I fixed up a piece of rope to keep Bugle at the wagon while we went off. It would be too easy for him to find trouble.

After about the fifth day, we agreed the idea was working. I suggested we call ourselves "The Buffalo Chip Gang."

The other kids said I should be leader, at which Ben pouted.

I told him, "You can be leader. I don't care."

Ben flustered. "I can't whistle like that. You go ahead."

When we came back with stories of coyotes and rattlesnakes, my dad gave me his Colt Walker, and a shoulder satchel supplied with fixing's—caps, balls, patches, powder. The satchel wasn't like the big hunting bag Mom had made him, but it would fill the need. I wasn't new to any of it. Hunting was part of our life.

A few days later, as the afternoon wore on, I spotted a goodly number of chips off to our left, to the south. As soon as I saw Mr. MacIver standing where he wanted the wagons to circle, I let out one whistle; we grabbed our blankets and gunny sacks and ran.

The easy pickings petered out sooner than I expected. We kept following the ones we found. The other kids were scattering quite a bit, so I called out, "Keep each other in sight!"

I topped a rise and found myself looking down into a wide, shallow stream bed, running roughly east-west. It looked like it had dried out a long time ago. It was generously peppered with buffalo chips. "Over here!" I yelled. Everybody came running, and we scrambled pell-mell down into the gully.

Well, that turned out to be a bonanza of buffalo chips. Our sacks and blankets would be bulging. Ben was making jokes and Bobby was laughing to beat the band. Even Sarah was stabbing and scraping with some enthusiasm. The gully did a slow, lazy curve toward the south, and the buffalo chips kept leading us on. When everybody was loaded with all their sacks could carry, we turned for home. I figured we would just retrace our steps back to where we'd gone down into the gully and then strike north for the wagons.

Finding the place where we had entered the gully was harder than I thought. There were several spots on the north slope that looked disturbed, as if a bunch of kids might have tumbled down the side. I came to a place where the disturbance looked fresher than the rest, and latched onto that. "Here we are," I pronounced confidently, and proceeded to climb the slope to the top.

I didn't recognize anything. There was a rise of ground to the north. I let down my sack and turned to make sure everyone was following. Hally was last, struggling to find her footing, hanging onto her sack, and helping Lilly. I scrambled back down, passing Mattie and Bobby, and scooped up Lilly. "Come on, Lilly-girl. Almost home."

We all stood on the gully's rim, looking around. The shadows were already stretching out. The wind was slacking off. Something was wrong. I looked all around again, hoping like crazy for one familiar-looking twig or lump of dirt. A cold fist closed around my heart. We were lost.

I felt everybody looking at me.

The only thing that felt right was which side of the gully we were on, which was the side we'd gone in. I could tell that by the sun lowering toward the horizon.

I was sure there had been a rise of ground right before we went into the gully. "I'm gonna go up on that rise and see if I can see the wagons. Everybody stay right here. Don't go wandering off."

Standing on the rise was no help. The same grass, brush, and dirt spread out in every direction. No sign of our wagons, not even the thin threads of smoke from the cook fires. *Is this the same rise I stood on just before entering the gully?* I knew we had come at the gully from the north, and we'd never gone out the other side, to the south. Which left only three directions to look: west, north, and east. I dutifully searched in those directions. I didn't need my compass. The sun was well in the west. The rest I could figure out. How far had we gone along the gully? Had we retraced our steps back far enough? I had seen no tracks in the gully, but I could have easily missed them. I was no Gideon MacIver, after all.

Finally I went back to them and said, "I think we better go to that high ground and wait there for our folks to come get us. It's no good wandering around and getting even more lost." The cat was out of the bag.

"Are we lost?" Bobby asked.

I didn't want to feed the fear. "Not as much as we could be." And set off to return to the mound.

Behind me, Ben groused, "What the hell does that mean?"

Having no better idea what to do, everybody followed me to the rise. At its modest peak, they searched in every direction, shading their eyes from the lowering sun, sure deliverance would appear in the next moment. At a distance, a hawk lifted out of the brush, dangling its struggling supper, and flew away. Silence yawned wide to every horizon. The wind tugged impishly at the girls' bonnet strings.

Ben said, "I ain't waitin'. I'm heading back." He gave me a brittle look of triumph. "You can do what you want."

I had to keep the other kids from catching his fear. "Which way you gonna go?" I asked.

Ben looked around. He even looked across the gully, and I knew we hadn't come from that direction. He jabbed his finger out past the rise, away from the gully. North. "That way." He hefted his sack on his back. The irony was, he was right—*if* we were in the right place.

Sarah, her mouth slack with dread, picked up her blanket.

I tried to keep my voice calm. "We should all stick together. And being up here will make it easier to spot us."

"You do what you want," Ben grumped, and set off.

Sarah waited a minute, looking at us, and then toward Ben. She swung her sack onto her back and took out after him. She forgot her poking stick on the ground.

"Sarah, it's a better idea to stay together," I called after her. Fear crept over me, too. And doubt. If Ben was right about the direction, so much to the good. But if he wasn't, they'd just be getting farther away, harder to find. I wrestled with going after them and trying to talk 'em back, but I had responsibilities standing all around me. It was scary enough now. Wait 'til it got dark.

Bobby Bequette said, "How will our folks find us?"

"They have horses," I said, trying to sound confident. "They can cover a lot more ground quicker. We're probably not that far away." *All we have to hope is that some grown-up noticed which way we headed.*

We watched Ben and Sarah get smaller and smaller until the ragged clumps of sagebrush cut off our view. Everybody found a spot to sit down. The top of the rise—it wasn't really a hill—was about the size of a barnyard, pretty flat, and about as bare. We sat smack-dab in the center.

After a minute, Hally said, "Shouldn't we make a fire?"

Then Bobby Bequette piped up, excited. "Why don't we make smoke signals, like the Indians do. Our folks'll see 'em."

Mattie twisted to look at Bobby. "They'll think our smoke signals are Indians and won't come near us."

Hally pondered the other side of the coin. "What if other Indians think it's an enemy and come looking?"

I looked around and raised my hand. "Who's for trying smoke signals?"

Everybody raised their hands. Lilly looked at all of us and raised her hand, too. Then a worry thumped me in the back of the head. I didn't have flint or steel on me. Will snickered in my head, *Can't make a fire by wishing.* I lowered my arm. "Who has fire-making gear with 'em?"

I knew from all the long faces that nobody did. I feared Bobbie's idea would meet a quick death. Then one of MacIver's many stories popped into my head. I reached into the satchel and took out the powder flask. By its heft it was over half full. A good thing. "I have an idea. Everybody gather up dry grass and twigs, little stuff, for kindling." I called out to them as they scattered. "And we need lots of smoke, so look for damp and green stuff, too." Which was silly: anybody could see it hadn't rained around there in weeks, most likely months.

Mattie called back, "Everything around here is dry as tinder."

I busied myself laying the main fire. When they got back, nobody had anything green or damp. We were going to be short on smoke. I looked at the only one of us with extra clothes. "Hally. Would you mind donating your petticoat?"

She stared at me like I'd asked her to strip buck naked.

Perhaps a little explaining would help. "I figure if we tore it up into little strips they wouldn't smother the fire, and, hopefully, they would make some smoke before catching."

Hally found her voice. She was not quite cross. "My mother would skin me alive if I came home without my petticoat."

I was getting desperate. If this idea was going to work, we needed smoke, besides which, the daylight wasn't going to wait around while we argued. "You'd add quite a bit to your chances of seeing your mother again if you let us use your petticoat."

She gave me a look that would turn Medusa to stone. "Everybody turn around."

Everybody just stared at her.

"You heard her," I barked, giving her my back. "Turn around."

A moment later, I felt a nudge on my arm. I turned and Hally handed me her bunched-up petticoat.

Everybody gathered 'round to watch while I cut the cloth into strips about two inches wide. I was still worried about how much smoke these strips of cloth would produce. If they couldn't be green, at least they could be damp. "It'll work better if they were damp. Who——"

We must have been having like thoughts, because Hally snatched the strips from me and said, "Everybody has to look the other way." And she walked away from us.

We all did what she asked. While she was off, I arranged a little mound of grass and twigs on the edge of the main fire fuel. I checked the Colt. All the chambers in the cylinder were loaded.

Some minutes later, Hally came back and handed me the wet strips of petticoat. She leaned close. "If you tell anybody about this, I'll skin you alive."

On my knees, I answered her soberly, "Yes, ma'am," and set the strips down next to the little mound. Hally crouched next to me. One thing about her, she wasn't afraid to get her knees dirty.

"What are you going to do?" she whispered.

I got out the powder flask again and pulled out the stopper. "Use gun powder to start the tinder. MacIver told me about it while you were off playin' with your dolls." I knew that'd get her dander up, which I liked doing. "Now, if you insist on getting a face full of powder burns, be quiet and watch."

She kept quiet for a minute. I sprinkled black powder from the flask, tapping the narrow neck lightly with my finger, making sure the grains were evenly distributed on the kindling. The faint stink of rotten eggs drifted up to my nostrils.

"You're mean," she murmured next to me.

I could hear real hurt. I spoke quiet back. "I'm sorry. I was just joshin'." I capped the flask and put it away. Then I said, quiet, like it was just the two of us, "The trick is to fire the gun close enough to the tinder so the muzzle flash ignites the sprinkled powder, which will, with luck, fire up the grass and twigs." I glanced at her to see if she was following. "Be ready with some of those bigger twigs."

I pulled the Colt out of my belt. I turned to the others. "Everybody stand behind me." I held the muzzle of the Colt right next to the little mound. Praying, I pulled back the hammer and fired. The report in the quiet afternoon hit us like a clap of thunder. The muzzle spit fire. The ball slammed into the dirt.

Nothing. The powder clung cold and dry on the little mound. I sat back on my heels with a sinking feeling. Had I not remembered MacIver's story right? Had I left out a step? How many tries would it take? The petticoat strips were drying out.

A touch at my sleeve. I turned. Hally held forward a wispy clump of shredded grass "What if you put this all around the muzzle. It might have a better chance."

I looked from her offering to her face.

"With more gunpowder, of course," she added earnestly.

I was ready for anything that might better my chances. I dug out the flask again as Hally nested her collection next to the old one. I was a little more generous with powder, but not so much as to cause an explosion. *Set aside the flask. Pull back the hammer and worm the muzzle carefully into the center of the fibers... don't disturb the loose powder. Pray, squeeze the trigger...*

Another thunder clap. Hally flinched. Burning gunpowder flared out of the muzzle and a spit of dust kicked up as the ball plowed into the ground. Hally's grass caught. Tiny flames licked up. Then the twigs caught. I put on some more greasewood twigs and when the flames were strong enough, I held out my hand. Hally handed me some bigger twigs. When those caught, watching the flames grow, I held out my hand again. "Now a chip." I broke it in two and laid the pieces carefully on the fire, making sure plenty of air got in to feed the flames. When the first chip was burning good, I added a couple more. Soon we had a good fire. I had everybody empty their blankets and bags of chips into one pile. That was going to be our fuel supply.

We compared our blankets and gunny sacks. I had the biggest blanket, so we used mine. With Ben and Sarah gone, we had only four kids tall enough, Hally, Mattie, Bobby and me, to hold a corner of the blanket above the flames.

I lay some strips of damp petticoat on the fire and we took up our corners. An unmistakable tang rose into the air, but nobody said a word. As I had hoped, the strips smoked. *This might work, after all.* We waited for the smoke to collect under the blanket. But it leaked out all sides! We were holding the blanket too tight. I told the others to ease up on the blanket a little and reached under it with Sarah's poking stick, pushing up the center to create a kind of tent. When there was a bunch of smoke, I yelled to take away the blanket. In the confusion, Bobby didn't let go soon enough, and a wobbly ball of smoke escaped his way, sending him coughing. He dropped the blanket. While we watched the shreds of smoke drift away in the wind, the blanket caught fire. I reached for it, but too late. Several spots were already aflame. I jerked the blanket off the fire and threw it to the side. Mattie stomped on it until it was out.

We gathered around the sorry remains of the blanket. I bent down and found two corners. I handed one toward Mattie; he understood. We lifted the blanket up and let it hang. Three char-fringed holes I could put my fist through, and three smaller ones ended the blanket's usefulness for smoke signals. Hally's blanket was too small to hold enough smoke; the gunny sacks wouldn't hold the smoke much at all. The smoke signal idea was done. Besides, the petticoat strips were all but dry by now. I stamped out the fire to save any unburned fuel.

I dug the two balls out of the ground. They were too misshapen to be used again. I dropped them in the satchel, figuring I'd Melt them down later to make new ones. *Two shots spent on the smoke signal idea. Four left in the cylinder. How many shots will it take to start another fire? We'll need a fire, come darkness, to keep critters at bay. How many more shots in the satchel?*

Hally's voice broke into my thoughts. "We need the fire, anyway, don't we?"

"We'll need it even more after it gets dark. And we've only got so much fuel." I didn't say anything about animals. Everybody was scared enough already.

"Will we still be here when it's dark?" Bobby's voice trembled.

"I don't know," I said, softening my voice. Then I spoke louder for everyone to hear. "But let's collect everything we can that will burn, just in case."

In the fading light, we fanned out to gather up every last scrap of anything that would burn. Even the meager patches of withered grass. "Stay in sight of each other!" I called, like always. This time there was no horsing around.

I used my knife to cut some of the bigger brush, thanking Uncle Rafe for the hefty blade. Every few minutes I looked up and counted souls. I kept Lilly with me. She collected the tiniest, little bitty twigs, but I kept it all.

When we were back together, I asked Hally and Mattie to sort the fuel by size; buffalo chips separate. Better than standing around. Bobby Bequette joined them. Lilly hovered close at my elbow while I dug everything out of the satchel: the metal powder flask, a dozen patches, half a dozen caps, and eighteen good balls plus the two spent ones. Several lengths of rawhide thong lay in the bottom. I let those be.

The flask and bullet-makings I spread out on Hally's blanket—and was struck with dismay. The caps ignited the gunpowder. Without them, everything else might as well have been mud and river pebbles. The caps decided it. I could make six shots from what was in the bag, if all the caps were good. Caps were store-bought. In a handful, you might find a dud or two. When those six caps were gone, I'd be out of ammunition.

Lilly bent and picked up a patch; a little round piece of grey felt you could rest on the tip of your finger.

"You want that?" I asked her. I had more than I needed.

She looked at me very seriously, pinching the little disc between her thumb and finger. Then she put it back carefully.

"Thank you, ma'am." I patted her back and turned to regard the fixings. I scowled that I hadn't checked the satchel before we left, but I was expecting nothing more than a rattlesnake, not getting lost.

I reloaded the two empty chambers in the cylinder. My arsenal consisted of ten shots; six in the Colt, and potentially four more in the satchel.

I gave Mattie and Bobby the job of picking up any stones that were the right size for throwing and making little piles spaced in a ring around our spot. Mattie knew what they were for, but Bobby asked, so I told him, "We'll probably have visitors during the night. Rocks won't be nearly as persuasive as bullets, but I'm going to run out of bullets a lot sooner than we'll run out of rocks."

They made twenty or so piles in a circle about twenty-five feet across. That was our outermost defenses. We sat inside that, with the fire and extra fuel at the center. Then there was nothing more to do but wait, hopefully for our folks.

I held off as late as possible into the twilight to rekindle the fire. My luck wasn't any better the second time. It took two shots to ignite the powder.

While the light from the fire was still strong, I reloaded the two empty chambers again. That left two caps in the satchel. I looked up to see Mattie watching me with a somber gaze. I tried a grin. "We've got a lot more rocks than we've got bullets."

CHAPTER 13

Darkness was complete when Ben rushed into the firelight with Sarah close behind, lookin' like they'd seen ghosts. They were both scratched up good, and out of breath. Sarah's hem was shredded. Ben had lost his hat. I was relieved to see them, but dismayed. Somewhere out there, in their tramping, they had abandoned their loads of precious fuel.

Before I could speak, Ben scooped up an armful of chips from our reserve and threw them on the fire. "We've got to make it big!" he shouted. Sparks showered up. He almost smothered the blaze.

I reached in and pulled the chips out. "No! No! It's only gotta be big enough to keep us warm and keep the critters at bay." I knocked off the burning bits and put the chips aside.

I dared not put them back on the reserve pile. I found Bobby among the shadowed figures and pointed at the smoldering chips. "Keep an eye on those. Make sure they're out."

Sarah blurted, "We could hardly see the fire. How do you expect our folks to see it unless it's bigger?"

I was angry. "Indians can see a fire just as good as our folks."

She stared at me, her eyes full of uncertainty and terror, but she made no answer.

I looked around at everyone. "I vote for keeping the critters at bay, and takin' our chances on who sees the fire. If the good Lord is with us, it'll be our folks." Mattie and Hally and Bobby nodded mutely.

I remembered how MacIver had talked to us about the dangers of quicksand on river banks and flash floods. I took on his no-nonsense tone. "Now, there may or may not be Indians out there, but it's a good bet there's critters out there who'd like nothing better than to gnaw on our bones." I let that sink in. "We've got to make the fuel we've got last as long as we can, at least 'til daylight." I looked hard at Ben and Sarah: I couldn't help takin' a jab. "'Course, we'd have a better chance of that if you'd a brought back your loads."

Looking miserable, Ben and Sarah sank to their haunches, curled up and tried their best to disappear. Nobody had anything more to say. One of the critters did, though, so far away as to be little more than a ripple of the night breeze—a long, lonely howl. Still, it sent a shiver through me.

I took on the role of fire tender. I fought a battle between Sarah's instinct for the fire to be seen, and my certainty that we needed to keep it going all night as our best defense against the animals. "Get some sleep, if you can," I said to nobody in particular and everybody. The kids quieted. I stood watch to make sure no one rolled into the fire as they dropped into slumber. Weariness overtook me so I sat cross-legged where I could replenish the fire.

Lilly came over and stood regarding me as she did so often. Her eyes seemed to say, *I understand,* but I knew that was foolish, she was only three. I held out my hand, and she stepped closer. I gathered her into my lap and drew my singed blanket around both of us. She was like a little warming brick my mother put at the foot of the bed in winter. The sting in my hands told me I had gotten a little too friendly with the burning chips.

"I'm thirsty," she said in a drowsy voice.

"I am, too, Lilly-girl. We all are. But we're gonna have to wait a while. Can you do that?"

She rubbed her head *Yes* against my shirt. "And then we'll jump in that ol' North Platte River and drink our fill."

You can't believe how black the night can be when you are out in the middle of nowhere with no lights and no moon. Our little circle of firelight didn't reach much farther out than where we sat.

Then we heard the sound I didn't want to hear. A yip, almost like a dog, but high, sharp. One here, one there. Coyotes. And if that wasn't bad enough, a heartbeat later another howl, long and mournful, far off, but not as far as that earlier one. From a different direction, another howl. The yap of coyotes was one thing, the howl of wolves was another. I drew the Colt and checked the chambers. Six shots.

I eased Lilly off my lap. "Hally, would you mind keeping Lilly with you? I've got to move around a bit."

I bent close to Lilly, trying to say it how my dad would say it to Amy. "Darlin', I'll be right close by. But I gotta have you sit with Hally for a while. Can you do that for me?" She nodded. I kissed the top of her head. "Good girl. When we get home, I'm gonna tell your momma and your poppa what a brave girl you are." I lifted her over to Hally and stood up.

"Pegg!" Sarah called out.

I looked across the fire and saw what she was pointing at. Yellow eyes glowed in the dark, close to the ground, moving, coming closer. One pair, then two, then three! The coyotes. And those were just the ones close enough to catch the firelight in their eyes. I looked all around the perimeter.

"Shoot 'em!" Ben shouted.

"We've only got eight shots. We're gonna have to make 'em count." I said, still looking out into the dark, trying to count. Another pair.

"Shoot 'em!" Ben shouted again, his voice rising.

I could hear the fear in him. The little ones were all sitting up now. I held the Colt against my leg so no one would see my hand trembling. I wondered if they could hear my heart thudding like a frantic drum. I wished Ben had a little more sand in him.

"There's ten of 'em out there!" I called to him. "Probably more. Which one you want me to shoot first?" I didn't want to do any shooting until I had no other choice.

Ben went quiet. I moved out past the circle of kids to the piles of stones Bobby and Mattie had set out. I picked up a rock and aimed for a pair of eyes. And missed. *What good are you going to be if you can't hit anything?* Gun or rock, I needed to be able to hit what I was aiming at. And I couldn't afford to run out of rocks improving my aim. *But I know somebody who already has a good aim—a deadly aim.* I went over to Mattie Shilo and handed him a stone. "Wanna help me patrol?"

Without a word, he took the stone, found a pair of those yellow eyes and let fly. The eyes jumped as the coyote yelped and disappeared. *At least stunned, not likely dead.* I pointed to the other side of our circle. "You take that side. We'll circle." Mattie nodded and went off. I liked his way.

By now, everyone was alert, watching out in different directions, backs to the fire. I added chips sparingly, but a buffalo chip isn't anything like a piece of oak, or even pine. We were burning through them a lot faster than I wanted to.

The coyotes got bolder, some coming close enough we could see their grey-yellow bodies at the edge of the light. I tried counting again. Close to a dozen pairs of eyes out there. Mattie lobbed a rock now and then, to be rewarded with a yelp. Then, almost as one, the coyotes fell back, fading into the ink black of the night. A few moments later, the reason for their retreat appeared. A set of larger eyes, wider apart, higher off the ground; the coyote's cousin, the wolf, had come to call. There were two, right off, but wolves hunted in packs, too.

Mattie and I kept walking the circle. He threw a stone when a pair of eyes ventured close. I heard one of the kids crying and somebody else trying to comfort them, but I didn't stop to see. Whoever it was didn't need me calling attention to their fear.

I shouted and threw rocks. I sang crazy songs at the top of my lungs. I ran out, lunging at them, screaming and waving my arms.

Hally yelled, "Pegg!"

I came to my senses and scuttled back to the safety of the fire.

The wolves were not impressed. They separated, circling like Mattie and I were. Maybe a gunshot would give 'em second thoughts. They must have learned to be wary when people pointed things at them, because whenever I tried to get a bead on one, it would slip back into the dark. I decided I would use two shots, and if I didn't get any I would go back to rocks and save my last six rounds for the direst need. I had to act quick, not give away what I was up to. I shot—and missed. In my desperation I yanked back the hammer and fired again. That one missed, too.

I kicked myself for the miss, which shouldn't have been a miss. Somebody behind me screamed. I whipped around to see a wolf pulling on Mattie Shilo's leg.

Somebody else wailed in terror—*Lilly?*

Mattie was on the ground, screaming his head off, scrabbling to keep from being dragged off. A second wolf was moving in to help its mate.

I don't remember getting over there, but in the next instant I was leaning over Mattie, lookin' the wolf in the eyes. The wolf was working too hard at hauling off his protesting supper to pay me much mind. I didn't give him time to think it over. I put the Colt to the critter's forehead and fired. Most of his brains left out the back of his head. I brought the pistol up and found the second wolf, closer now. I couldn't miss this close. The wolf and I were frozen in place for less than a heartbeat, then I dropped the mate.

The night swallowed up those two gunshots and the commotion as if they had never been. The kids stared for a minute, then broke into cheers. Except Hally. She knelt beside Mattie and tore at his pant leg to inspect his wounds. Mattie, for his part, settled as soon as Hally had him in hand. His shank was chewed on pretty good, but he'd survive. Hally asked Sarah to sacrifice a piece of her petticoat to bind Mattie's leg.

"What? Never! Use your own petticoat," came the horrified reply.

"I already have," said Hally in a hard voice.

Sarah stared at her, goggle-eyed, no doubt imagining the most shocking things, but she relented.

Hally asked for my knife and I soon heard tearing sounds. I occupied myself dragging the carcasses of the wolves outside our circle, beyond the firelight.

Ben came over to help. "People aren't going to believe us."

If we get to tell anybody about it. But I kept that to myself. "We'll just show 'em Mattie's leg."

I hoped the deaths of the wolves would discourage the rest of the pack, which was more'n likely still out there. The coyotes, for their part, did not let the opportunity go to waste. Then, too, maybe it only whetted their appetites.

I kept tending the fire, fretting about every chip I put on. I had only two shots left in the Colt. If the coyotes or the rest of the wolf pack decided to come for us in earnest there would be no time to load my last two shots from the satchel.

My legs felt wobbly. I sat down where I could still feed the fire. I must have dozed, because I woke up to find Lilly climbing into my lap again. I jerked my head up and peered out into the dark all around. Hally crouched close by. "I'm sorry, Pegg," she whispered. "She wouldn't take no…."

"It's okay," I whispered back.

Hally settled down close. "There's eyes out there, but they're staying back."

"Thanks." *How long did I sleep?* "How's Mattie?"

She glanced over in his direction. "Asleep, thank goodness."

I wrapped the blanket closer around Lilly and she curled herself up like a chipmunk in a nest. I put an arm around her, but kept the Colt in my other hand. I looked around as much as I could. "You mind keeping watch the other way?" I whispered to Hally, pointing behind me. "In case they make another try."

She scooted around and took up her vigil. After a few minutes, she whispered, "Our folks are sure to see the fire."

I pushed down my own doubts. "They shouldn't have any trouble. It's the only one out here."

When I put the last three chips on the fire, I was gentle, but sparks showered up into the black sky anyway. When those three were burned up, we couldn't do much but watch the fire fade and grow cold. It was still the deepest night; we had hours yet before first light. I didn't want to think about what might happen when daylight came. Would we still be here two days from now, half of us dragged off into the bushes, the other half waiting to die?

I didn't tell anybody I peed my pants that night. If they smelled it, they didn't say anything. Besides, I could tell I wasn't the only one.

The next time I woke up, the fire was just a pile of powdery gray ash, giving itself up, little by little, to the breeze. There was plenty of light in the sky; the sun would be coming up soon. The world looked bigger and more lonesome than it ever had. The coyotes were taking their ease about a hundred yards off to the east.

A pop sound, way off, short and flat. Too far to tell where it came from. But we all knew it was a gunshot. Friend or foe? A lone hunter, not expecting a reply? I handed Lilly to Hally, snatched up the Colt, and scrambled to my feet, pulling back the hammer. My burned hands protested the abuse. The other kids looked at me. I held the old gun high, pointing at the sky just off the zenith, and pulled the trigger. After all the quiet, the gun roared like a cannon. Everybody flinched. One more shot and I would have to reload my last two rounds. We had given ourselves away—to a rescue party or a war party?

Ben shouted, "Let's go meet 'em!" He was ready to run.

I yelled, "No, Ben! Which way you gonna go?"

"Toward the gunshot, stupid!"

"Which way is that?" I yelled back, trying to shout him down.

Ben was desperate to do *something*! Sarah looked like she would do anything Ben was going to do.

I said as hard as I could, "You take off runnin' and those coyotes will be on you in a heartbeat. Besides, this is the only way they'll find us! Stayin' put!" And I prayed like the dickens they would.

A second shot rang out, closer, to the north.

"There! God almighty!" Ben screamed, pointing. "There!"

The kids were looking from Ben to me. Little Lilly pressed her face against my leg.

I thumbed back the hammer for the last shot and raised the Colt until it pointed at the sky. I fired. Lilly flinched and clung tighter. I dropped to one knee and swung the satchel off my shoulder to reload. If they were hostile, two more rounds wasn't much of a defense. And that only if I could get them reloaded in time. If they were friendly, it was up to them. I didn't want to spend my last two shots drawing friends closer. If they couldn't find us now, the coyotes had nothing to stop 'em but a few rocks.

A third shot cracked the air. This one was closer yet. From the north, no mistake.

Kids were smiling, crying, looking from one to the other. Then, as if we were one, we started yelling and screaming our heads off. That spooked the coyotes. They stood up, watching us. A minute later we heard barking and right after that Bugle came racing into view. As soon as he saw us he stopped and bayed loud and clear, then ran toward us. The coyotes melted into the brush like smoke. In Bugle's wake, a half a dozen riders came pounding up over a far rise. Pretty quick we could see it was my dad, Mr. Chalmers, Mr. MacIver, and Linnaeus Peabody, with Mr. Forsyth and Mr. Bequette right behind.

That's when we ran.

I hugged Bugle almost hard enough to break his bones. Tears flowed and I didn't care. "You are the best dog in the whole world!"

They had water, which we were mighty grateful for, and biscuits. Linnaeus made it his business to go around and make sure every kid had a good swallow or two, and two or three biscuits. Everybody else was too busy hugging and laughing and crying.

When he got to me he said, "Drink up. There's plenty." While I drank, he added in a low voice, "Well done, sir."

Questions flew and all the kids tried to tell the story at once. Hally and her dad hugged each other for a long time without saying anything.

I saw my dad and Mr. MacIver wandering around over near the fire, looking at the dead critters. My dad bent and picked up a rock from one of Bobby and Mattie's little piles. He looked around the circle and then pitched the rock side-armed into the brush. When they came back, I handed Dad his Colt. He shook his head and said, "No, you keep it. I think you've earned it."

After we got back, Mrs. Chalmers brought Dr. Yarborough over to look at my hands. I protested, but she made me sit still. He gave me some liniment with instructions to apply it twice a day. With Dad's encouragement, I climbed into the wagon and slept half the day away.

That night, my dad and I were sitting at the fire after cleaning up. Mr. Hoyt was, as usual, off visiting. I was scratching Bugle.

"I don't think we'll want to tell your mother about this little incident," my dad said. "She's worried enough as it is."

I smiled at him. "She'd make us go home right now."

Dad smiled, too. "Boreas and Yellowstone wouldn't be able to turn the wagon fast enough."

"How did you know where to look for us?"

Dad smiled even wider and chuckled. "We just followed Bugle."

"Whoa!" I leaned down and scratched Bugle even better. "Good boy! Good boy!" Bugle rolled onto his back for more. "Boy! You're our savior! How will I ever repay you?"

After a minute, my dad said, "I am proud of you, Son. You cannot know how proud."

I shrugged. "I couldn't miss those wolves. But Mattie's the sure shot."

My dad shook his head. "Not for that. For things of much greater importance. For keeping your head. You didn't panic. For staying in one place, keeping everyone together. That was the right thing to do." He paused. "And I have a good idea you kept everyone else from losing heart."

He didn't know how fragile a thing it was. Then he asked me to tell him the story of the stones and wolves. I told him the whole thing. Mr. MacIver came by and I told it again. He gave me a spare piece of flint, and a couple days later, I found a little piece of steel in an abandoned tool box, maybe from a broken chisel. From now on, as long as I could find fuel, I would never again be without fire. Soon after, at another stop, I found among the castoffs a little leather pouch. With that I hung my fire-making kit around my neck next to my compass.

CHAPTER 14

Approaching Fort Laramie from the east, you had a good look at the whole spread. It was a whole other kettle of fish from Fort Kearney. It was a much bigger place, for a start, surrounded by a high wall, with block houses on the corners and a big gate, everything I thought a fort should have. Even better, Indian tipis, maybe a dozen, clustered nearby, the first sign of Indian life we'd seen. My head filled with questions for Mr. MacIver: *What tribe? Are they friendly? Are they waiting to attack?* Not likely, since the tipis were scattered within spitting distance of the fort.

We got there in the early afternoon. When I came back after putting the team out to graze, Dad said, "I'm going to write some letters and look over our provisions." He swung his hand wide, offering me the world, or at least the immediate vicinity. "Be back in time to help with supper."

I knew what I wanted to do, but the best chances of doing it advised against seeking approval. I would have taken Will, but he was back in Vermont. I went off to find Mattie Shilo, and where I found Mattie, I'd likely find Bobby Bequette. They were playing mumbly-peg in the dirt beside Mattie's wagon. I sauntered up to them like I had nothing particular in mind. "You fellas see the Indian tipis while we were comin' in?"

Mattie flipped the knife off his elbow.

"Yeah," they said together.

But Mattie knew me better than I thought he did. "You thinkin' about payin' 'em a visit?"

The way he said it told me he didn't think it was a good idea. Bobby went bug-eyed, and forgot to pick up the knife.

I shrugged. "They don't look like they're on the warpath right now. Can't hurt to have look-see, can it?"

Mattie handed Bobby the knife and scolded me. "Ain't you heard the stories? They 'specially like stealin' kids, to make 'em into new Indians."

Bobby found his voice. "My folks would tan my hide if I was to do that."

Mattie scowled at him. "They would if they ever got you back."

I could see I was losing ground in the convincing department. "We could always run to the fort if they made to grab us."

Mattie was getting his dander up. "I'd rather not give 'em the chance, by just not goin' in the first place."

"C'mon, you guys. Don't you want to see some real Indians?"

"What you want me to tell your dad?" He tilted his head up and looked innocent. "Oh, Gee, Sir, he's over there, palaverin' with the Injuns. Don't expect him back any time soon. Six, eight years, if you're lucky."

I'd never seen Mattie so riled. Well, in the end they talked me out of it. We went scavenging instead.

Wagons weren't drawn up in neat circles the way they would be out on the trail. The Chalmers company simply found a spot at the edge of the formless mass of the wagons that had arrived before us.

"Last time we stopped," Mattie enthused as we set out, "I found a general's epaulets, and a battle flag from an infantry regiment."

"What's an epaulet?" asked Bobby.

"Those gold braid thingamajigs they wear on their shoulders. Makes 'em look bigger."

We picked our way through the confusion. Everywhere were disorderly heaps of possessions and provisions, the castoffs of those who had passed through. We weren't the only ones scavenging: soldiers from the fort were collecting sacks of beans, rice, and barrels of hard biscuit—flour, too—that had been foolishly discarded. Furniture and cooking utensils of every kind, weapons, whole trunkfuls of clothing, mining tools, shoes—all thrown away! I found a pair of new shoes that fit. My Christmas boots were getting snug, and the soles would be worn through before we reached California, where a new pair would no doubt cost a king's ransom. I tied my find up in a handy scrap of cloth for future use.

Of course, we weren't really looking for such sensible stuff. We each wanted to find things that told the other two what a sharp eye for the unusual we had.

Pretty quick, Bobby spied a brand-new Sharp's carbine, not a scratch on it. I came upon a brass statue of an elephant, its trunk raised up, long, curving tusks. It gleamed so in the sun I fancied it was made of gold, though I knew better. The figure must have been solid through and through. With the base, it weighed thirty pounds, if it weighed an ounce. You had to wonder how such a thing made it into the wagon in the first place, let alone this far. I had just set it back down when Mattie called out. "Hey! Over here."

Bobby and I trotted over to him. He was standing next to a stack of large, flat, wooden boxes. A very unusual shape for a box, only a few inches deep. Finely crafted, like cabinetry. *What could they be used for?* Somebody had stacked them neatly, not just tossed them out willy-nilly. Mattie was standing smug next to his trophy and pointed us to a closer look. They were specimen cases. From a professor or somebody who studied bugs. Beneath the glass lids, bugs and butterflies of all shapes and sizes were arranged in neat rows, with tiny writing next to each one. Some critters were so small, you had to peer down close to make them out at all. I recognized a few, like the Monarch and Swallowtail butterflies, and the cicada and the bottle fly. But as we lifted off each case to see the next one below, the critters became stranger and stranger.

"Look at that one!" Mattie exclaimed. "It's almost as big as my hand." It was, indeed, bigger than any bug I'd ever seen, a real monster, with bold black and white markings, and a shell that looked like a knight's armor. Mattie screwed up his face in distaste. "I don't think I'd want to live where that lives."

There were eighteen cases in all and we looked over every one, exclaiming over the ever more bizarre critters. When we were crouched over the bottommost case, Bobby said, "I guess he didn't like spiders."

Mattie and I looked at each other, saucer-eyed. As we restacked the pile, we checked. No spiders. We congratulated Bobby and chewed on that a while. *Why no spiders?*

Farther on, I found something that maybe wasn't all that odd, but it was something I knew my mom would treasure—an eight-book set of the works of William Shakespeare. It was quite an armful. Bobby and Mattie helped me carry them back to our wagon. My dad looked up from addressing an envelope as we approached.

"Look what I found for Mom!" I crowed.

Mattie and Bobby added the books they carried to my stack and took their leave. "Good luck," Mattie whispered.

Dad looked over the collection. "Well, now. That's very thoughtful of you, Son. I'm sure she would be delighted."

"It's more Shakespeare than we have at home, by a long shot." We had *Romeo and Juliet,* and *Midsummer Night's Dream*, to be exact.

"And you propose to take these to California, and hence back to Vermont?"

I could hear a "No" coming and resorted to pleading. "Shakespeare's her favorite."

"After Keats," corrected my father. "I'm sorry, Son. I can't very well criticize Fred Hoyt's mileage contraption, and then take on more weight with a commodity we can easily purchase once we get back home."

"But these are books. We can't just leave them."

Dad regarded my long face and then sighed. "I tell you what. Choose one, for your schooling. Mother would be pleased to hear that. The others may likewise find a home."

I made no attempt to hide my disappointment. "Yessir."

He smiled. "You may be sure Boreas and Yellowstone will appreciate it." He collected up his envelopes. "And when the time comes, we'll buy your mother every word Mr. Shakespeare ever wrote."

He let me keep the shoes. I picked out "The Tempest" and tied the rest of the books in the cloth that had held the shoes. "I can see to the books," he said, proffering me the letters. "Would you mind taking these up to the fort?"

"That's all right. I can do both."

"And if you see Mr. Hoyt, ask him not to be late for supper."

As I wound my way through the camps toward the fort, an idea hatched from my father's comment. The smoke of cook fires began to thread into the great bowl of the sky. People were adding to the piles of discards, having learned that the country ahead was rougher and steeper than any they had so far crossed. Now they were desperate. I spied Mr. MacIver trudging ahead of me with a considerable load of mail. I caught up with him.

He nodded at the high walls ahead. "This fort more to you likin'?"

"Yessir, it is." I smiled at him and shifted my gaze. He would catch that. "Are those Indian tipis off to the side, there?"

"Well, they sure ain't your Uncle Henry's corncribs."

I had long since toughened to his jibes. "What tribe are they?"

"Most likely Pawnee. Maybe Arapaho, maybe Cheyenne."

"Is there a way to tell?"

"Not so easy from here. They all use what's called three-pole lodges—even though there's more than three poles. See how the poles are bunched tight together where they cross? That's what tells you. Other tribes use what's called a four-pole lodge, and the sticks look looser."

I watched the tipis as we walked closer by them. Mattie's cautions kept me at MacIver's side. A stout woman tended a fire while a naked toddler clung unsteadily to her skirt. A man sat cross-legged before his tipi, bent to some task that required close attention. Two other braves stood by a horse, talking quietly. One of the men stroked the muzzle of the animal, while the other sported a single feather in his hair. A listless dog ambled along, sniffed at the child, and, after a few more paces, flopped down on his belly. None of this squared well with the Indians I expected to meet—wild, painted warriors bedecked in feathered war bonnets, tearing across the prairie on equally decorated ponies, waving their coup sticks and screaming death and destruction.

"Why are they camped so close to the fort?" I asked.

"Trading, most likely. And seein' what they can sucker out of the emigrants." MacIver snorted a laugh.

"Why aren't they out huntin' buffalo?"

"You seen any buffalo the last three, four days?"

"No, sir, I haven't."

"Maybe they haven't, either."

Lots of times Mr. MacIver made me look at a thing from a different side than I was used to. "This fort looks pretty new, too."

"It used to be built of logs, back when it was only a tradin' post, but they rebuilt it in adobe 'bout nine, ten year back. They heard you were comin', and knowed you'd want to be impressed."

I laughed in surprise.

Mr. MacIver went on with a perfectly sober face. "Even when I was through here back in '36, the trade in beaver pelts was givin' over to buffalo robes. Now it's nothin' but robes."

Sure enough, inside the sutler's trading post, one whole end of the room was stacked almost to the ceiling in shaggy buffalo hides. I lost track of Mr. MacIver right away. The room was crowded with people—a few soldiers, to be sure, but many from the wagon trains, including our own: Mrs. Chalmers, Dr. Yarborough, Mrs. Forsyth and Hally, and Mr. Shilo, Mattie's dad. The sutler, the trader, presided over the hubbub from behind a high, rough wooden counter, dispensing prices and directions, refusing to haggle, while two scrawny underlings fetched the articles requested.

I marched up to the sutler and untied the cloth on his counter. He regarded the books as if I'd presented him with fresh manure. "What's this, then?" His dark brows drew together.

"Something very valuable," I replied, trying to sound as if we were in it together.

He snorted. "I don't buy, I sell." He turned to answer a customer's question.

I tried to sound even more cunning. "That's exactly the point. You put these on that shelf there..." I pointed to an empty shelf behind him, "... and the right person will pay good money for them." *Think fast. Who?* "The commanding officer. Or his wife. A lawyer coming through."

"I reckon you found these in the trash outside and—" grumped the sutler.

Nothing to lose, I cut him off. "And I knew right off how valuable they are."

The sutler was intrigued. "If they're so valuable, whyn't you take 'em for yourself?"

I played the sated glutton. "I've already taken what I wanted."

His eyes popped wide. "There were more?" Avarice had him.

Another customer drew his attention and I slipped away, hoping for the best.

After depositing my dad's letters, I wandered over to have a closer look at the buffalo hides. Somehow, they had a majesty about them. They gave off a warm, musky, earth smell. I ran my hand through the wiry black hair that crowned their heads, thinking of the puffing, pounding, lunging beasts Linnaeus and I had ridden among.

A familiar voice spoke behind me. "They smell like cows."

Hally Forsyth, no doubt looking for a spar.

I turned to her as she stepped up. "Do you know what a cow smells like?"

If I haven't already mentioned it, Hally and her family came from Baltimore, Maryland. I decided not to lecture her on cows. She'd only ask more questions. I still had my hands buried in buffalo fur. "I bet these'd keep you plenty warm, come winter."

She wasn't impressed, and looked up and down the wall of hides. "If you took all the meat that was inside all these hides you could feed an army—a city." She sounded downright cross.

I had a choice bit to parlay. "Mr. MacIver says the Indians don't have much that isn't made from some part of the buffalo."

Our duel was brought up short by Hally's mother calling her away.

"See you." She actually smiled before she rushed off.

She didn't think like other girls. I watched her go—right past three grave-looking fellows who stood apart, by the door. Their long black hair streamed over their shoulders, longer than any man I knew would ever wear his. They stood close together, very still, while the shoppers bustled around them. *An island*, I thought. Only their eyes moved in their bronzed, chiseled faces. Wrapped in trade blankets, even though it was summer, they reminded me of hawks on a high branch, aloof and watchful. My first up close Indians!

When I stepped past them to leave the sutler's store, I remembered Dad's request about Mr. Hoyt. Our partner hadn't been inside. Could he be somewhere else in the fort? I didn't relish searching through the whole sprawling emigrant camp for him. He was an adult. If he wanted his supper, he should know to be back in time. I did.

Fortunately, the man himself saved me the trouble. My attention was drawn to a group of soldiers at the edge of the parade ground, gathered in a rough circle, laughing heartily. Then a finger stabbed the air above their heads in best preacher fashion, a favorite gesticulation of Mr. Hoyt when he was on a tear. Indeed, wedging my way through the gaggle to the front, I discovered him holding forth in high form. He was in the middle of a story.

"Where upon, she had the gall to demand that I preserve her honor by escorting her to the nearest shrine of matrimony, wherein we would be united in holy wedlock." A dramatic sweep of his arm. "To which I replied in righteous indignation, 'Madam! Do not prattle to me of honor. For I have it on the best authority that you have entertained…'" Here he paused, casting a baleful eye around the circle while laughter erupted. "The entirety of…" Mr. Hoyt's gaze fell on me and he clammed up tight.

All eyes turned to me, some in confusion, some in vexation. A grumble of discontent replaced the laughter. A soldier called out, "Of what?"

I was the plug in the jug. I figured I'd better deliver my message and skedaddle so Mr. Hoyt could carry on. "Dad says if you want supper, be home in time."

I didn't wait for an answer. I wormed my way back out of the crowd, surrounded by raucous laughter, heartier than before, and darted away. Mr. Hoyt did not appear for supper.

CHAPTER 15

The next morning we departed Fort Laramie and made for the Laramie Mountains. Here we found trees and grass and water aplenty, things we had not seen in some time! Buffalo populated the big meadows. Here, too, were horses sporting great, flowing manes and tails. Proud, graceful creatures, they glided across the fields as if they, themselves, were made of wind. I asked Mr. MacIver who they belonged to.

"Anyone who can catch 'em and break 'em," he said.

We were blessed in this part of the trip with having enough grass and fresh water. We didn't have to look for buffalo chips anymore; there was plenty of wood around. Everybody's spirits lifted. But no doubt about it, it was rougher country.

To our great relief the cholera seemed to have lost its grip. As the days rolled by, fewer people got sick, and then it was gone. That in itself put a spring in people's step. Dr. Yarborough put it down to the mountain air, but confessed he wasn't sure. And it didn't mean we were free of sickness. Right before we got to the Upper Ferry it struck right close to home.

My dad got a fever.

One evening, I noticed he wasn't talking much over supper, but I just thought he was tired from the day. The next morning, I

135

noticed Dad wasn't stepping along with Boreas and Yellowstone, chatting encouragement to them like he usually did. He shuffled along silently, his head drooping.

When I asked if anything was wrong, he said, "No. Just feeling a little poorly this morning."

But he didn't look at me, which was mighty odd. He seemed like he was using all his energy for putting one foot in front of the other. And I could see his face was red.

Right away, I thought it might be cholera. I wasn't going to take any chances. Mr. Hoyt was off talking to people, so I ran and got Mrs. Chalmers, who went and got Dr. Yarborough. When we got back, Mr. Hoyt was helping my dad to his feet, brushing dust off Dad's clothes.

"Where you been, boy?" Mr. Hoyt said crossly. "Can't you see your dad is ailing?"

"Easy, Hoyt. He came to get us," Dr. Yarborough said in a stern voice.

He made Mr. Hoyt help my dad up onto the wagon seat. Then Dr. Yarborough climbed up himself to look my dad over and ask him some questions. Mr. Hoyt went up by the team where Dad usually walked.

I went to the other side and urged the team to keep moving. I didn't want to lose our place in line until there was no other choice, but I kept an eye on my dad and the doctor. Then Dr. Yarborough called to me. "Pegg, Son, would you hand up some water?"

"Yessir," I almost shouted, glad for something to do for my dad.

Dr. Yarborough made him drink the whole dipper. Then he helped him over the back of the seat and made him sit among our provisions, resting against the back of the seat box. When Dr. Yarborough got down off the wagon, he told me, "Make sure he rests and gets plenty of water."

I leaned close, all but tugging at his sleeve. "What is it?"

He looked from me to Mrs. Chalmers. Mr. Hoyt was just ahead, shouting unnecessarily at the oxen.

"Well, it doesn't appear to be cholera," the doctor said. "For that we can be thankful."

"But what is it?" I blurted out.

"From the symptoms I can see, I'd say it's fever. I'm afraid that's all I *can* say until, or if, other symptoms show themselves," he said. "Do you know if he's had measles or smallpox or malaria?"

I wracked my brain. I remembered Mom saying Dad had had measles. Smallpox, if you survived it at all, left you badly marked. "I think he's had measles, sir. I don't know about smallpox." I knew almost nothing of malaria.

The doctor nodded. "Let's keep an eye on him. With luck and care—and our prayers—he'll beat it." He lowered his eyebrows and raised a finger. "Remember, no matter what he says, plenty of rest and water."

I stepped in his way. "Is it like Mr. Clifton's fever? You pulled *him* out of it fine."

Dr. Yarborough chuckled with his chin tucked in. "Every fever is different, Son, the origin, the character. Your father's in his prime. That is our best hope." He turned to Mrs. Chalmers. "Can you make him some soup?"

"I can make soup!" I bleated. My voice broke right in the middle of my utterance. Soup hadn't been in Mom's cooking lessons, but I'd seen her make soup plenty of times.

Mrs. Chalmers smiled at me. "I would be happy to make some, Pegg. You already have enough to do."

Dr. Yarborough put his hand on my shoulder. "Try to keep him cool. A damp cloth on his forehead will help." He looked up at our wagon. "I'll check on him this evening."

At our nooning, I gave Dad some bacon and a biscuit. He ate listlessly. Between bites, he said, "I'm sorry, Pegg. I just need a little rest." His voice drifted off some. "Just a little tired."

"Doc Yarborough says you can beat the fever with rest and water. So that's what you gotta do." I brought a bucket of water and wedged it between a couple of sacks next to my dad where it wouldn't fall over. I set the dipper in the water. "The doc says you've got to drink a lot of water." I put my hand to his forehead just like my mom did when I was sick. He was burning up. I found a piece of cloth and wet it and wiped his face down.

When I left him, he mumbled, "Be right as rain... just a little rest..."

I rolled the canvas up on the sides of the wagon, to let the air move through. I couldn't do anything about how hot it was. He would get some relief once the sun went down.

When we were under way again, Mr. Hoyt walked beside me and the oxen instead of rushing off to do his visiting. He seemed genuinely concerned when he asked, "How is he?"

"Burning up," I replied. "I'll see to the team. Could you make sure he drinks lots of water?"

"Surely," said Mr. Hoyt, no trace of bravado in his voice.

It would mean more weight for the oxen to pull, but I was better with the animals. I walked beside the team for the rest of the day, worrying and praying, praying and worrying, glancing up at the wagon. Mr. Hoyt was as good as his word, clambering up into the moving wagon again and again, helping my dad drink water.

That night, when we stopped, I asked Mr. Hoyt to look for firewood while I got out our cooking gear. Dad didn't look any better. He was sweating up a storm. I wiped his face down with the wet cloth. He felt hotter than he had in the morning.

He swallowed with effort. "I'm sorry for putting the extra load on Boreas and Yellowstone, not being able to help with chores..."

I said, over and over, "You just have to get better, is all. Okay? That's all you have to do."

"I'm trying, Son. I'm trying."

When I heard wood rattling outside, I said to my dad, "I'll get some supper going. You've got to keep your strength up."

Dad smiled and nodded. "Mother would be pleased with your cooking."

I climbed out of the wagon to find Ben Parker dumping out some of his wood by our cooking utensils. He was adding it to another pile—Mr. Hoyt's. Ben shrugged with a sheepish grin. "Heard a good joke. I'll tell you tomorrow." And he scuttled away.

Mr. Hoyt came around the corner of our wagon with a pot full of water. "For the beans, or rice." He'd no sooner put the pot down than he cast around, perplexed, until he spied the empty coffeepot. He snatched it up to go fill it.

I didn't have the heart to tell him that you don't just boil up beans lickety split. I would be heating up beans I had boiled at our nooning, which had soaked in water through last night. Biscuits could be made fresh, but not beans.

I laid a fire and started on the biscuits. Mrs. Chalmers brought over a steaming kettle of beef-barley soup.

"Thank you," I told her. "We are beholdin' to you."

She smiled. "This from the young man who brought our little girl back."

It smelled delicious. Dad managed a little of it when I held the bowl under his nose.

Back outside, I found Mr. Hoyt had helped himself to a generous portion. "This *is* mighty fine soup, indeed, Ma'am," he proclaimed. A frown of displeasure flashed across Mrs. Chalmers' face. Her lips parted to speak, but she checked it and turned back to me, smiling. "You must let me know the very minute you need anything else."

"Yes, ma'am. I will."

Mrs. Chalmers turned to leave just as Linnaeus Peabody rode up and slid off his horse. He tipped his hat. "A good evening to you, Mrs. Chalmers."

The lady nodded. "And to you, Mr. Peabody." But she kept moving away toward her wagon.

Mr. Peabody came up to the fire. "I heard your dad was ailing. How is he? Can I do anything?"

I tried to sound lighthearted. "Tell me what's wrong with him?"

Linnaeus Peabody stepped closer. "I would want to more than anything, Pegg, but I'm no doctor." He glanced around our camp. He nodded. "Mr. Hoyt."

Mr. Hoyt barely managed a grunt between mouthfuls.

I said, "Dad's in the wagon. I know he'd be happy to see you if you're not afraid of catching whatever he's got."

"I'll take my chances," he replied soberly. "However brief our friendship, he already feels like a brother." He stepped toward the wagon. "If you'll excuse me."

He didn't have to excuse himself to a kid, but he did. That's one of the reasons I liked him. As he climbed up I asked, "Have you had your supper?"

"No, but don't trouble yourself."

"I've made fresh biscuits to go with the beans."

While Mr. Peabody was in talking with Dad, Dr. Yarborough came by. "Any change?"

I stood up from putting another stick on the fire. "At supper, he felt a little hotter than he did this morning. But he ate some."

"That's good. And water?"

"Yessir. Mr. Hoyt said he drank lots of water. All day."

The doctor adjusted his hat. "Good."

"Our friend Linnaeus Peabody is visiting with him. Should I call him away?"

But Mr. Peabody must have heard us, for he came down from the wagon. He exchanged greetings with Dr. Yarborough. The doctor could see the worry in his face, and said, "He's strong. We can hope for the best."

Dr. Yarborough climbed up into the wagon and had a look at Dad. After a while he looked out through the opening in the canvas and called to me. "Let's rearrange some of your gear so he can lie down. I'd rather have him sleeping in here than on the ground."

I climbed in and we handed things down to Mr. Hoyt and Mr. Peabody. We made a kind of trough in all our gear and lined it with anything soft: extra clothes, extra blankets, sacks of flour and beans. Then we got my dad comfortable. He complained about not wanting to be a bother. Dr. Yarborough scolded him gently as he put the dampened cloth on his forehead. We ended up leaving some gear by the trail, tools mostly, so the wagon wouldn't be too much heavier with my dad riding in it.

CHAPTER 16

The next morning Dad insisted he was feeling better and wanted to walk. His forehead still felt pretty warm to me, but he wouldn't listen to my arguments. Dr. Yarborough came by and convinced him to at least ride in the seat if he insisted on seeing what was going on.

I walked with the team, but kept looking up to check on Dad. He was holding onto the seat, but he'd give me a weak smile. Mr. Hoyt hung close by the wagon, too, walking beside the off-side ox, Yellowstone. That was not like him. Usually, he'd find a reason to be off visiting or say he was checking with Mr. Chalmers.

Midmorning I looked up and Dad wasn't there. *Holy Dinah! He's fallen under the wheels! Why didn't I hear him? How long ago? Why didn't Mr. Hoyt call out—or anybody else in the following wagons?* But Mr. Hoyt wasn't by Yellowstone. I rushed to the back of the wagon, expecting the worst. Dad wasn't lying in the road, no matter how far back I looked. I turned back to see movement in the opening of the canvas of our wagon. That had to be Mr. Hoyt or Dad. My heart stopped thudding in my chest. I trotted back and looked in. Dad lay in his new bed. Mr. Hoyt, hovering over him, saw me and put his finger to his lips. I climbed in.

Dad appeared to be sleeping. He felt as hot as ever. He opened his eyes when he felt my touch. A sheen of sweat covered his face. Mr. Hoyt left us. To calm myself, I gave Dad a dipper of water. I tried to smile. "You gave me a good fright. I thought I'd find you squashed like a bug under the wheels."

"I'm sorry, Barti…should have said something." He sipped a little water. "Just had to lay down for a while. Don't say anything to your mother, will you?" He handed me the half-empty dipper.

Why would he talk about Mom like she was with us? "No, I won't." I gave him back the dipper. "You have to finish it."

Dad stayed in the wagon the rest of the day. Mr. Hoyt climbed up and made sure he drank plenty of water and took care of the resulting necessities.

By the third day, it was clear my dad's ailment was no passing vexation. He stayed in the wagon. He ate less said less.

Mr. Hoyt maintained his water duty—especially making sure the water barrel on the side of the wagon stayed full—and tried to make himself useful around camp, sticking to chores where he could do the least damage. His moods were no less predictable. Often he was short-tempered for no apparent reason. But still, this was a very different Mr. Hoyt. I picked carefully what I said to him. His one consistency was his attention to my dad. He added taking up meals to his water duties.

After supper and dishes were done, I sat in the wagon with Dad, giving him water, replacing the damp cloth. Though asleep, he gave me a new fright—he broke into a spell of shivering. As soon as I piled blankets on him it slackened and he shrugged the blankets off.

I poked my head out to look for Mr. Hoyt. He was nowhere to be seen. I jumped out to go for Doctor Yarborough. He was approaching our wagon. I walked with him, describing what had just occurred.

"How long are fevers supposed to last?" I asked.

Doctor Yarborough rested one hand on the tailgate before he went up. "In an otherwise healthy person, fever will usually run its course in a few days, three or four." And he hoisted himself up.

"Dad was healthy as a horse before this," I blurted out, following him into the wagon.

"Indeed," replied the doctor, laying his hand on Dad's brow.

Dad slept right through the doctor's visit. When we were outside the wagon again, Doctor Yarborough spoke as if finishing his thought. "So we should look forward to a change for the better very soon." A few steps away, he stopped and turned. "But a few prayers on his behalf certainly wouldn't do any harm."

Hope guttered in me like a candle in a harsh wind. That night I slept in the wagon.

The following morning was a Sunday.

Mr. Chalmers and Mr. MacIver put the word around that, since rougher country lay ahead, we would stay put a day and rest the animals while there was good graze and water, and look after ourselves. Do laundry, soak the wagon wheels, mend whatever needed mending. Mr. Chalmers offered to read from the Good Book for those who wished to hear it. To my surprise, Mr. Hoyt took up the washboard and soap and offered to do our laundry in the stream. While he was away, Mr. MacIver came by. By now everybody knew about my dad. Most people stayed away. He glanced at the wagon. "How's your pa gettin' along?"

I left off daubing tar on the rear wheel. "Doctor Yarborough says he should come out of it any day now."

The old scout could see I was bothered. I dreaded closer questions. I told him about how Mr. Hoyt had been acting. Helpful, but cranky.

He said, "He's scared, Sonny, is all. He's scared. He knows your dad is the brains of this outfit. He knows without your dad he's sunk."

"My dad isn't going to die!" I swallowed what felt like a rock. "Is he?"

Mr. MacIver was quiet for a minute. I looked up at him, trying to read his weathered face. If anybody had ready answers, he did.

At last he spoke, looking me square in the eye. "Mrs. Chalmers would have my hide if she were here, and Dr. Yarborough would be none too happy, either. But I'll have my say and hope you have as much sand as I think you have." Mr. MacIver never beat around the bush like that. My gut knotted up. He settled his hand on my shoulder. "I'm sure enough pullin' for your pa to lick this fever, Son, but... you might put some thought into who you'd want to hook up with if it don't work out that way."

I didn't want to think about that. My dad was going to pull through. People had fevers all the time and came out of them fine. Besides, he had a real doctor taking care of him. We had only lost four people in our whole company to cholera, none to fever. He was going to be fine.

. . .

Dad was no better nor any worse after our day of rest.

We left the forest, the easy grass, and plentiful water for a high, broken country that was dry, barren, and poisonous. The pools were surrounded by dead oxen, horses, and mules. Mr. MacIver warned us about this water, saying it was alkaline. Most people heeded his advice; those that didn't soon found themselves without a team.

The men cut grass wherever we found it and piled it into the wagons, to tide us over in the many places where there was none. Mr. MacIver led us to the few good places to drink. I tethered Bugle to the wagon so he wouldn't run off drinking water that would kill him. Once again, we scrounged for fuel for our fires, relying on greasewood and sage or abandoned wagons and furniture, which still lined the trail. I became heartless about chopping up other people's possessions they'd left behind.

Dad was no better on the sixth day.

Mrs. Chalmers brought over more soup, but he could only eat a few spoonfuls. The mysterious shivers came and went. Mr. Hoyt, Bugle and I subsisted on less water for Dad's sake. The fever showed no sign of releasing its grip. Dr. Yarborough didn't say it in so many words, but he was mystified by why Dad hadn't gotten better or been carried off. On several visits, he gave Dad something to help him sleep. All we could do was make sure my dad had plenty to drink and get him to eat as much as he could. Each evening, I put up the tent for Mr. Hoyt, but I slept in the wagon. I didn't care whether I caught his fever or not.

At supper, Mr. Hoyt tried to cheer me up. "Now don't you fret, Pegg, lad. Your papa's gonna be just fine, just fine. We've got this thing almost licked. You got to keep a bright outlook. It helps us all keep our spirits up." He looked up from his plate. "He asked after you today." I looked up sharply. Dad hadn't uttered a word since yesterday.

But Mr. Hoyt nattered on. "I don't want to have to tell him you're draggin' around with a long face. That wouldn't do him any good at all, now, would it?"

That made me feel worse than ever. I answered, "No, sir, it wouldn't."

And he went back to shoveling down his supper.

Walking with Boreas and Yellowstone, nattering nonsense and encouragement to them, kept my spirits from sinking too low. Sometimes I let Bugle loose and we'd play fetch with a stick.

The seventh day of our vigil, Hally brought Lilly over. They fell in step beside me.

"Well, good mornin', ladies," I said, letting a smile come to play.

Hally smiled and blushed. "Lilly insisted on coming over." She reached down and scratched Bugle. "Mrs. Chalmers said we could only stay a minute. She doesn't want us bothering you at your chores."

"She's not worried about Lilly catchin' Dad's fever?"

Hally used her don't-be-stupid voice. "I'm sure if she was, we wouldn't be here."

I didn't want to get into one of our arguments. I picked Lilly up. "Well, Lilly girl, aren't you the best friend in the whole wide world?" And, without even thinking about it, I kissed her cheek. She lay against me and put her arms around my neck. I looked over at Hally. "How do I deserve this?"

"Maybe she's thanking you for keeping her from being some coyote's supper," Hally said, giving me her serious look. "I know I do." She looked down quick.

That got me flustered. I tucked in my chin and said quiet to Lilly, "You want to ride on Boreas for a minute?"

Lilly looked up and nodded her head, yes.

After I made sure the little girl was firmly seated, I turned back to Hally. "This is a treat. Thanks for comin' by." I kept my right hand resting on Boreas, close to Lilly.

Hally tossed her head in Lilly's direction. "Oh! Don't forget, it was her idea." Then Hally got her serious look back. "I'm sorry about your dad. How's he doing?"

I said what I wanted to be true. "He's doing fine, as well as can be expected. Dr. Yarborough says that with fever you just have to let it run its course."

When it was time for them to go, I lifted Lilly off Boreas and set her on the ground. "Thanks for the visit. I appreciate it."

"You're welcome." Hally blushed again. A little smile snuck out. She took Lilly's hand and looked down at her. "Can you say thank you for the ride, Mr. Pegg?"

"*Mister* Pegg?" I protested.

"Well…" now Hally was flustered.

But Lilly busted in. "Thank you for the ride," she chirped.

I did a silly bow. "You're very welcome, Princess. And thank your momma for letting you come by." Then I looked up at Hally. "Thanks."

"You're welcome, too," she said.

I kept smiling long after they went away.

•　•　•

That evening, after Dr. Yarborough had been to see my dad, he came over to the fire and told me Dad wanted to see me. Mr. Hoyt jumped to his feet. Dr. Yarborough put out his hand. "Please stay where you are, Mr. Hoyt. Mr. Pegg would like to speak with his son privately." And he kept his hand out until Mr. Hoyt sat back down.

I ran over and scrambled up into the wagon. My heart sank. He was so thin and tired-looking. I settled next to him. His eyes were closed. I didn't know if he was asleep. "Dad?" I said, real soft.

He opened his eyes. He looked like he had to come back from someplace far away.

"There's my boy," he said in a weary voice. I'd never heard that voice in him before, so weak and scratchy, like a scrap of cloth sinking at the bottom of a well.

"I'm here." I leaned close. I could feel the heat coming from his fever.

He took hold of my hand. "How you holding up?"

"I'm doing okay."

He kept his eyes on me.

"It's a rough part of the trail," I said.

"I can tell." A little smile came to his parched lips. Of course, he meant the bumpy wagon ride. "You think we ought to give up? Go home?"

That took me by surprise. "No. No, I mean the wagon is holding up fine. Our provisions are good, if we're careful, like you said... as long as we take care of the team..." I worked up a smile. "We got a dairy farm to buy, remember?"

He blinked at me slowly a couple of times, making me wonder if he had heard anything I said. He licked his lips and I gave him some water. He went on. "The toughest part of the trip is yet to come… Your uncle Rafe said… said… You've never seen…mountains like the Sierra Nevada. They're like teeth…covered in snow and ice…"

I grasped his arm. "That's why you've got to get better before we tackle them."

"How would you feel about tackling them with Mr. Hoyt?"

"What do you mean?" I said.

"You'll need a… grown-up to help you with other grown-ups."

"I've got you." My voice rattled with fear.

"I don't think you'll be able to count on me."

"What? No. You'll get better."

"Pegg," he interrupted, which he almost never did. "Son, if you want to keep going, you'll need someone to stand up for you, when need be." He closed his eyes, gathering strength. "And I don't think it'll be me…"

"Stop saying that! It has to be you! Who else could it be?" I was close to losing control.

He put his hand over mine. "Mr. Hoyt has assured me… that he will see out his commitment to the partnership, and…to you… make sure you get home safe." He patted my hand. His hand was too warm. "You must…work together to make sure…you both get home." He held my gaze like he wanted my assurance. I could only nod my head. He patted my hand again. "I've entrusted the purse to Mr. Hoyt, and extracted his promise…that he will use it only to provide for your most pressing needs."

"You'll get better! We'll have a big new farm…"

"You shouldn't need to spend much…between here and California. And once you're there, our obligations to Mr. Pruitt should inspire him to spend…what money is left wisely…"

Mr. Hoyt might be wise about money, but he couldn't cook, and he wasn't very good with the team. "Do I have to do everything he says?"

"I think he will be counting on you as much as you will have to count on him," Dad said. "Partners watch out for each other. Be a good partner."

"I will."

We sat in silence for a minute. Then my dad said, "Wait a minute..." and he tapped his shirt pocket with a feeble hand. "You'll need this..."

I reached into his pocket and drew out the folded-up paper with my mom's calculations on it: how much we'd need to buy a new farm and build a house.

"And when you get back home..." He gave my hand a little jig. He hadn't let go of it this whole time. "I want you to look after your sister..."

I jumped in. I was desperate. "You can't! I promised Mom! I promised her I'd bring you home safe!"

I heard Bugle whine. He was under the wagon.

Dad gave my hand a feebler squeeze. "Tell your mother that I love her...very much... and I am sorry that I couldn't come home to her..."

Well, that's where I crumbled. I blubbered right where I sat. I knew I was too old to be crying. My dad let me carry on for a few minutes and then he squeezed my hand again.

"If you want to turn around and go home, I'll understand," he said. "And I'm sure Mr. Pruitt will look kindly on your... decision and make provisions for the debt."

Now he was saying things that I didn't understand. He closed his eyes again for a minute. Then he said, "It's up to you...and I won't think any different of you one way or the other ..." He rested for a minute.

I tried to calm down. I put the slip of paper in my pocket. Dad licked his lips again, and I gave him more water.

"Get some sleep," he said. "You need yours as much as I need mine."

I laid my head on his chest and hugged him, just like I used to do when I was a little kid. Sometime later, a change in his breathing woke me. I sat up and looked at my dad in the faint moon light. He held my gaze. His mouth was moving like he was trying to say something. I leaned down closer.

His voice was barely more than a shredded whisper. "Know…Pegg-son, that…I am proud…proud of who you are…and only regret…that…that I will not be able to see you grow…" He rested. "Into your…your maturity."

I was confused but I nodded, yes.

He had his left hand resting over his heart. He patted his chest weakly. "Trust… in… here," he said.

That, I thought I understood. I nodded again. It was all I could do. My eyes were getting all blurry.

"Give…love to…your… mother…"

Then he wasn't looking at me anymore. He wasn't looking at anything. I just sat there, staring down at him, desperately wanting him to blink or swallow, but he didn't. He couldn't. I sat there trying to accept it. I don't know how long it was before Mr. Hoyt climbed back up and closed my father's eyes and put his other hand up on his chest. Then he went and got Mr. Chalmers and Doctor Yarborough.

All of a sudden, the world became immensely big, starkly empty, heartless. And I knew with a powerful force that I was very, very far away from anything or anyone I could cling to.

Mrs. Chalmers came back with her husband. Mr. MacIver wasn't far behind.

"We won't get a hole dug by dark, but we can make a start," Mr. Chalmers said. "If you don't mind, Son, we'll tend to the buryin' in the morning." Then Mr. Chalmers went off to put together a digging party.

Word spread quick.

Mattie and his father appeared out of the darkness. Mattie's dad offered to make a box for Dad. "It's the least I can do," he said. He stayed up half the night making a box out of discarded wagon pieces. My dad was lucky in that regard. Many people were buried in such haste they were only wrapped in a sheet or a blanket. While Mr. Shilo worked, I washed Dad, trimmed his hair, and dressed him in clean clothes. It was the proper way of things. Last, I dug out the sweater Mom had given him for Christmas and wrestled it on him, telling myself he might need it for the winter.

Mr. Hoyt paced and fidgeted, approached and retreated, clearly at a loss. I put him to spiffing up Dad's shoes out by the fire.

I was probably harsher than I should've been.

At first light the next morning, Mr. Chalmers, Mr. MacIver, and Mr. Bequette finished digging the grave. Mr. Chalmers had chosen some high ground, a ways off the trail, for the spot. You could see a long way, all around. No trees, barely any grass—a lonely spot. He set me to collecting rocks. Ben and Hally and Mattie helped. This wasn't easy, because it wasn't very rocky country. But it was necessary if I wished the grave undisturbed by animals. Lilly came over, offering me a pebble in her little fist. I stopped and gave her a long hug.

When it was time to close up the box, I wanted to leave Dad's violin with him, but all my elders expressed such dismay at this idea that I gave it up. While he was laid to rest and words were said and the dirt was mounded over him, the rest of the company was hitching up their teams. I used my rock fence building skills to pack the rocks tight, and since everybody was pitching in, I found myself advising more than anything else, which felt odd, since they were my elders.

Mr. Hoyt surprised me by appearing with a marker: a cross with "J. M. Pegg" carved in the cross piece.

When they all left, I knelt beside the cairn of rocks we'd laid over my dad. Bugle sat on his haunches next to me. Little uncertain whines escaped his throat. I heard the wagon train set out. The rattle, creak, and clank, what before had been a herald of life and movement now seemed brittle and grating, so sunk was I in mourning. Anger, fear, disbelief, bottomless grief, coursed through me like a buffeting wind, each vying to kick me over. When the last teamster's shout faded, pinched out by the boundless silence, I glanced over my shoulder.

Our wagon stood alone. It was only sixty yards away, but it felt tiny, naked, helpless. Somebody had hitched up the team. Not Mr. Hoyt. He wouldn't know a nose band from a heel chain. A great patch of trampled ground and smoldering fire circles were the only signs the Chalmers Company had tarried here. Mr. Hoyt stood by the wagon in a formal way, feet apart, hands clasped in front holding his hat, the way men did outside a church. He was giving me my time to grieve.

I turned back to the long mound before me. I tried to accept that my dad was under that pile of dirt and rocks, that he wasn't going anywhere but there. I'd probably never see this place again, or even be able to find it. My mom would never get to see it, to say her own goodbyes to him.

Footsteps approached behind me, stopping a few paces back. Bugle turned to look. I didn't.

Mr. Hoyt didn't speak for a time. When he did, his tone was modest, respectful. "I know you're hurtin', lad, but they ain't gonna wait on us. If we don't get a move on, we'll never catch up."

I made no response. Mr. Hoyt waited a moment more and then retreated to the wagon. The needs of everyday life seemed a cruel joke, pointless. I had to figure out how to fill this huge, gaping hole that used to be me…no, used to be filled with my dad. He wasn't going to be with me anymore. I would have to learn to get along without him, try to remember the things he told me.

Mr. Hoyt came forward again, not as close as before. I kept my back to him. He raised his voice a little to carry. "It ain't a good idea to be out here on our own. Who knows but there's heathens just over the hill."

I heard him but I didn't listen. My thoughts clung to one image. Dad was like a tree, a straight, strong, well-formed tree. Quiet, steady, firmly rooted, there day and night, rain or shine, ready to give you shelter if you sought it. *What would Dad do in this situation?* He'd go forward. I'd have to remember the way he was, how he worked, how he treated people, how he was with my mom and my little sister.

Mr. Hoyt waited a few minutes, then retreated again. I could hear him pacing by the wagon. Soon he returned, staying well back, raising his voice more urgently. "You may not care about dyin' out here, but I do." He waited to see if that would uproot me. It didn't. "We've got commitments. We can't be thinkin' only of ourselves."

I crouched lower and covered my ears. My mind thrashed and flailed. How could I go on without my dad? How was I going to tell my mom that he was gone, that I wouldn't be able to keep my promise to bring him home safe to her, after all? I couldn't separate how lost she was going to feel from how lost I felt.

Mr. Hoyt didn't go away. His voice was strained, almost shrill. "Pegg. He's in the ground. There's nothing more you can do."

"Go to hell!" My voice broke, rasping. *Did that come out of me?*

He was quiet. Maybe he was just as surprised. He made a noise of frustration in his throat. When he spoke again, he was chiding. "I made a solemn promise to your poppa I'd see to your safety. You don't want to make a liar out of me, do you?"

Who is thinking only of himself? Still I didn't turn. "Shut your mouth." Now I was scaring myself.

Mr. Hoyt tried again. "We have to go on. We owe it to Mr. Pruitt and your father. It's what he wanted us to do!"

How can this man presume to know my father? "You don't know what he'd want."

"I do Pegg, lad. I do! We had good talks, your pop and I, while I was tendin' to his needs."

I was suspicious of that. Dad had all but stopped talking by the fifth day of the fever. He was sleeping or out of his head for most of the rest of the time. But I had no way of knowing what they had talked about, what had been promised. I sat back on my heels, feeling blindfolded.

Mr. Hoyt smelled victory. "He made me promise to press on, to make sure you didn't lose heart. To get to California and get rich so we could take care of our families."

Dad had said different things to me. Mr. Hoyt didn't have a family that I knew of, other than Mr. Pruitt, and that gentleman was well able to take care of himself.

I would have no peace while Mr. Hoyt fretted. He had ruined my vigil. I didn't want to provoke him into more brazen proclamations. I stood up. Bugle was more loyal than I was. *How many times have you been hunting with Dad?* "Come on, Bugle..."

He turned his head to me and whined.

I patted the side of my leg. "Come on, Boy. People're waitin'."

Mr. Hoyt broke into his lopsided grin, but he wasn't happy. "Well now. At last, we see some sense in the boy." He thumped me on the shoulder as I trudged past him. "You've more than paid your respects, Pegg, lad. Time to get on with livin'."

I kept heading toward the wagon. I didn't trust myself to speak. Based on recent evidence, I couldn't be sure what might come out of my mouth.

He hustled to catch up. "We'll have to shake a leg to catch the train at the nooning."

I gave Boreas and Yellowstone a drink of water out of my hat before we started out. It's what Dad always did.

Now that things were going his way, Mr. Hoyt could afford a little cheer. "We don't want to give those hostiles more opportunity than we need to."

I dearly wished to shut him up. "We ain't seen a single Indian since we left Fort Laramie." I jigged Boreas' lead rope and clucked to him. He and Yellowstone leaned into the yoke. The wagon creaked and rolled forward.

I didn't look back at the grave, then or after. I'd want to go back. Maybe Dad'd be sitting there, one leg stretched out straight, the other hitched up, the way he did. Like it had all been a big mistake.

I nattered at the oxen to divert my mind, watched the dust puff up as their hooves clomped along. Mr. Hoyt strode briskly ahead, no ailments hindering him this time. I took it as his eagerness to rejoin the train, or maybe he wanted to get away from the war party that was surely on our heels.

I didn't care. I was in no mind to listen to his blather and preachments.

CHAPTER 17

We caught up to the Company at their nooning, on the west bank of a lively stream. The smell of bacon and biscuits came to us on the breeze. We were lucky—crossing the stream had slowed them down. Mr. MacIver rode out to meet us. He could've probably seen us comin' for a mile or more. I wondered why he wasn't scouting ahead of the train, looking for the night's stop.

He passed Mr. Hoyt and rode up to me. "Still got your hair, I see."

MacIver raised my spirits just by his gruffness, but I could muster no sass. "Ain't seen a hostile since Fort Laramie. Have you?"

He came around and walked his horse beside me. "I seen sign, but it was old. No sense in scarin' folks without cause."

I pulled the wagon up next to Mr. Chalmers and ran off to collect firewood. People were well along fixing their dinners. I had had no breakfast; I didn't want to miss another meal.

When I got back to our wagon, Mr. MacIver and Mr. Hoyt were talking and Mr. Chalmers was with them, listening. When I got closer, they stopped and watched me approach.

"Glad you're back, Pegg," Mr. Chalmers said. "We were just discussing your situation."

I dropped my load of twigs and branches and waited. Adults always had serious things to say when they called it a situation.

Mr. MacIver said, "Hoyt, here, says the trip's over. You're turning for home."

Mr. Hoyt blustered, "I'll not have you putting words in my mouth, sir."

"Well, that's what it amounts to, don't it?" Mr. MacIver glared at Mr. Hoyt.

Mr. Chalmers said, "Gentlemen, please…"

I stared at them, my mouth hanging open. Did my dad die for nothing? Were we just going to throw it all away? My mom was back home, waiting for a better farm, waiting for him!

Mr. MacIver went on. "He says with your pa gone, you've shown yourself to be unmanageable. Says it came as a shock to him."

I stared at Mr. Hoyt. "What do you mean? I don't understand!"

He looked anywhere but at me.

The scout spoke for him. "He says he can't assume responsibility for you or your mission under such circumstances."

When people used a word like that, they were usually hiding something ugly they didn't want to name. I looked at each man in turn. "What circumstances?"

Mr. Chalmers entered the fray with a calm voice. "Now, Son. Mr. Hoyt's concern is that you have no clear idea of the dangers and hardships that lie ahead, that you will, in some foolish manner, put his life and your own in mortal peril."

Mr. Hoyt burst out, "I said no such thing!"

MacIver shot back, "'He doesn't realize he's the greatest danger to the entire enterprise.' Your very words."

I couldn't go home without even trying. I would be going home with *less*. Without a father. Or a husband for my mother. I yelped, "I won't be a burden! I won't talk back! I promise! I'll walk with the team. I'll cook and wash up and hitch up the team, just like always!" I tried to get Mr. Hoyt's attention, but he was looking at the ground. I fairly barked at him. "We have to keep going!"

Everybody looked at each other, except Mr. Hoyt. He kept his gaze fixed on the ground.

"What say you, Mr. Hoyt?" inquired the wagon master.

Mr. Hoyt looked up at Mr. Chalmers and squared his shoulders. "To honor the father, I'll agree. It's against my better judgment, but. . .we'll see."

Mr. MacIver said to me, "What Hoyt, here, is gettin' at is, with your pa gone, he wants to be sure there's no question about who's in charge in your outfit."

I'd turned fourteen in St. Louis. I knew how to do my chores, but I knew I had a while yet before I reached my majority, "Dad said Mr. Hoyt was the grown-up, that he'd take care of things. He said that as partners we should support each other." I looked from one to the other.

I had a strong sense that they were expecting more. I nodded in Mr. Hoyt's direction. "But he's the boss."

Everybody was quiet for a minute. Then Mr. Chalmers said, with clear relief, "Well, gentlemen, I think we understand each other." He looked at me. "You are welcome to continue with us, with Mr. Hoyt in charge." He looked at the other two. "Now, if there is no more to discuss, let's finish up dinner and see if we can't make a few more miles today."

They went about their business. Mr. Hoyt went off, too, and I was glad for that. Boreas and Yellowstone stood with their heads down, like they knew something bad had happened. I laid a fire, made coffee and fried some bacon; no time for anything more. The wagon seemed like it was from a different time, a different place. The bright, confident colors and graceful detailing were fading, spattered with mud and dust.

Nothing would be the same without my dad. Some part of me had been hacked off. I could walk beside Boreas and Yellowstone. I could climb in the wagon. But it wouldn't be the same.

Mr. Hoyt kept his distance the rest of the day. I minded Boreas and Yellowstone extra special and kept Bugle close. I couldn't think of anything but leaving my dad farther and farther behind. Where we'd left him tugged at me something fierce. I kept wanting to turn back. I was sure we'd find him sitting there, waiting for us. He'd smile and wave as we came up, and everything would be all right.

While I was cooking supper, Mr. Hoyt came back. He cast about, like he didn't know where to settle. At last, he said, "You do understand don't you, Pegg-boy? A ship's got to have a captain. Someone being in charge is what keeps the whole thing running smoothly. Just like Mr. Chalmers keeps our whole wagon train running smooth, I'll keep our little company—you and me— running smooth. I owe it to your father. It's what he wanted."

I put my head down and concentrated on frying griddle cakes.

Mr. Hoyt poked at the fire with a stick. "It'll be tough without him; I know that as well as anyone. But if we each remember our part, why, then, everything will be fine." Stirred-up cinders settled on the griddle cakes.

I felt he wanted an answer. "Yessir," I said, but I kept looking at the griddle cakes.

After supper, he went off like always to gather his information. Mr. Hoyt seldom shared whatever he had gathered. And, of course, it was impolite to inquire too insistently. He could have been off playing cards, gambling, for all we knew, or perhaps just visiting. At least he never asked Dad for money. Dad had remarked that he was glad our partner was not given to drink.

It was as well Mr. Hoyt was away; I had to figure out what I would say in the letter I knew I had to write. I took an extra-long time cleaning up, trying out different ways to tell her. When it came to putting the words down on paper, the awful reality, the weight of it, crushed me. All I wanted to do was crawl into my mom's lap and have her hold me, tell me it wasn't my fault. I sat there, pen in hand, but the only thing marking the paper were my tears.

Without my dad, who was I? I didn't hold his hand anymore; I was too old for that. But it was always there; on my shoulder, or on my back, if I needed it. No more. How could I tell my mom I couldn't keep my promise to bring my father home? They still held hands; people smiled at them.

Bugle didn't help. He watched me blubbering over the paper and let out a howl of despair—several, in fact. I wished I could do the same. But I didn't have that luxury. I pushed the tears away with my fist and made a start.

Dear Mother,

We made South Pass yesterday—

What I had to say next ripped a fresh hole in me. I bowed my head and squeezed my eyes shut. How was I going to write this letter?

．．．

When Mr. Hoyt got back from his visiting, I was bowed over the paper, on my third try. I had already wrecked two sheets of paper with words that were horrible, and hard, and wrong. Mother would frown in dismay at the waste, but I had to get it right.

Mr. Hoyt looked at me and the crumpled balls of paper. "Don't fret yourself, lad. I'll take care of that. I know just what needs saying."

"It's all right, sir. It's for me to do."

"You're grieving, Son." Mr. Hoyt touched my shoulder. "You can't be expected to put words together at such a terrible time. I'll see to it. Don't fret yourself."

"Well," I hated to admit it, but I was relieved. "Thank you, sir."

Mr. Hoyt peered into the coffeepot. "Consider it done, lad. Consider it done."

"I'll make some more coffee."

"Much obliged, Pegg-son. Much obliged." He handed me the pot.

The next day I was walking beside Boreas, complimenting him on his best qualities, when Mrs. Chalmers came up with Lilly in tow.

"Lilly insisted on a visit." Mrs. Chalmers smiled. "I hope you don't mind." Whenever that lady smiled it seemed like the sun coming out.

"That's fine, ma'am. Couldn't ask for better company." I lifted Lilly onto Boreas's broad back.

"Oh, Pegg. You've inherited your father's way with…" Her face got serious and she looked away.

I didn't want her to feel bad. "That's all right, ma'am. Dad and Mother used to say stuff like that to each other all the time. It was all in fun."

Mrs. Chalmers looked at me surprised for a minute, then she smiled again, nicer than ever. "If you'd like, Pegg, I'll help you write a letter to your family. To let them know."

"Thank you kindly, ma'am, but Mr. Hoyt said he'd write the letter."

Mrs. Chalmers got a serious look. "Are you sure? It would be no trouble at all."

"It's all right, ma'am. Mr. Hoyt said he'd do it. Thanks all the same, though."

She hesitated. I could tell there was something else, but she only said, "Of course, Pegg. Of course."

She made to go, but then she asked, "Are you sure Lilly won't be a bother right now?"

"No, ma'am. Not at all. She's my own little ray of sunshine." My dad used to say that about my sister Amy.

Mrs. Chalmers smiled again. "I'll fetch her for dinner, then." She turned to go. After a couple of steps she turned back. "If you change your mind about the letter, please let me know. I assure you, it would be no trouble."

"Thank you, ma'am. I will."

The daily routine helped me keep on going. I missed Dad powerfully, like an ache deep in my chest, but at least I wasn't holding back tears so much anymore.

Eventually we came to a place where the trail split. One part, called the Mormon Trail, continued southwestward, toward the Great Salt Lake where the Mormons settled. I figured they must be pretty important if they had a trail named after them, or else a lot of 'em took that way. I didn't know anything about them, so the next chance I had, I asked Linnaeus Peabody. He knew everything.

"They're a religious group. They have some ideas that other people don't agree with and they've suffered for it. Often badly," he explained.

"But Dad says everyone is free to worship as they see fit."

"And we are. But not everybody abides by that. The Mormons have moved west so that they can worship their way." Mr. Peabody smiled. "They picked a spot they thought nobody else would want."

"A big, salty lake." Not good for livestock, not good for people.

"Exactly," he agreed. "But they're a hardworking, sober bunch. I'm sure they'll make a success of it."

The fork we took, Sublette's Cuttoff, headed more directly west. According to Mr. MacIver, this Sublette fellow had done more, seen more, trapped more streams, than even he, Mr. MacIver, had. If Mr. MacIver held Mr. Sublette in such high regard, he must be a truly remarkable fellow.

He pointed off to our right, to the northwest, to distant blue peaks. "Over there's the Wind River Range. Used to be good beaver country."

Almost as soon as we got onto Sublette's Cutoff, we came to a desert. We saw more and more dead animals, along with the castoffs, by the side of the trail. The smell and the flies were something awful. The animals hadn't died from bad water—the only water was what the wagons carried. No, these animals were just plain worn out, driven too hard by people who didn't know any better, worn out pulling a wagon that was *still* loaded with too much! I promised myself that Boreas and Yellowstone would *not* end up that way. My dad cared about all our animals, even the chickens, for which I had no great love.

One night, Mr. Hoyt remarked that the water barrels were lower than he thought they would be. "But they don't look like they're leaking," he said.

"They're not," I said, putting away the dishes. "I'm just making sure Boreas and Yellowstone are getting enough to drink. Without them we're sunk."

Mr. Hoyt regarded me for a minute. "You've got a good head on your shoulders, lad. We make a good team. Your pa can rest easy."

The sun beat down on us in that desert like nothing I'd ever seen before. You liked to choke on the dust everybody was kicking up. Mrs. Chalmers came by. She walked with me for a ways. Her shoes were the same color as the dirt, same as mine.

"Mr. Chalmers says this desert is only about forty miles wide. That shouldn't be too bad," she said.

"Yes, ma'am. And after that is the Green River, Mr. MacIver says, and then more mountains." I laughed to accompany my brilliant wit.

Mrs. Chalmers only smiled. We walked in silence for a few minutes.

"How are you getting along, Pegg, dear?" she asked.

I probably took longer to answer than was polite. "Fine, ma'am. Fine."

Next she spoke softer and more hesitantly, so I knew I was supposed to listen extra careful. "I know it's important for you to get to California. It was your father's hope for a better life. And goodness knows, you've come so far—we've *all* come so far." She turned to look at me. "But it's a huge job to take on that dream by yourself. From what we've all heard, California is a wild, lawless place. You should not have to face that on your own."

"Thank you, ma'am, but I'm not by myself exactly." I was surprised she'd forgotten. "I've got Mr. Hoyt."

She looked away and then back with more resolve. "I just want you to know that Mr. Chalmers and I have discussed it, and we would be *very* happy to have you travel with us." She gave a quick, small smile. "And I know one little girl who would think that was the best idea in the world."

Then she turned to look down at where she was walking. "We're going to Oregon, I know, but it would give you some time to sort yourself out, and then, if you wanted, to figure out a way to get back home."

Well, Mrs. Chalmers's speech was the next best thing to a hug. And then she gave me one, and I realized how much I missed my mom.

Then she favored me with a warm smile. "Please think about it."

"I will, ma'am." I said, filled up to the brim with a good feeling for her. "I surely will."

. . .

On we tramped through the powdery white dust. The sun lowered in the sky to stare me in the face, teasing, *You'll never catch me.* Mr. Hoyt showed up for supper.

I could see he was in a dark mood. After a minute he said, "The Chalmers talked to me about you going off with them. That was hurtful news, lad, hurtful news." He waited for me to say something.

I sensed I was on tricky ground. I was still formulating what to say when he went on. "I do dearly hope that wasn't your idea."

"No, sir. It wasn't."

"Well, now," he sighed. "I'm glad to hear that."

I had an impulse to say more about it, but I had an equal impulse to keep quiet. I kept quiet.

"Your poppa asked me to look after you," Mr. Hoyt said, "and to make sure you got back home to your family safe and sound."

My mind was churned up worse than a creek in spring. My dad stood on one bank, the Chalmers family stood on the other.

Mr. Hoyt said, "I gave him my solemn word I would do just that."

I felt like I had less and less choice the more Mr. Hoyt talked. And he kept on talking.

"I figure we can do better than that, Pegg, lad. We can go home rich as kings and do everything your poppa wanted to do. But we've got to stick together. What do you say?"

"Yessir."

"Good," he said. "Good lad."

He said no more. Just ate his beans and bacon and went into the tent. I guess at least in *his* mind the matter was settled. I was left wondering what an odd duck Mr. Hoyt was. *When Dad died, he pronounced me a mortal danger to his well-being. Now he's moaning about me abandoning him.* Then I remembered what Mr. MacIver said about him when Dad first took sick: "He's scared. He knows your dad is the brains of the outfit." And, later, my dad said to me: "Mr. Hoyt's going to count on you as much as you're going to count on him." Each was saying Mr. Hoyt wouldn't last a day out here on his own. He couldn't hitch a team or pitch a tent to save his soul. No wonder he didn't want me highin' off with the Chalmers.

The next morning, he offered to do the dishes. I'd have sooner expected toads to fall from the sky. Most times, he'd be off to do his visiting as soon as he put his plate down.

"Okay," I said. "I'll get the water." And I reached for the bucket.

"No need, lad," Mr. Hoyt said, staying my hand. "I'll see to it. You take care of the animals."

I wasn't about to look a gift horse in the mouth. He couldn't do much damage to tin dishes and iron cook pots. I went off to collect Boreas and Yellowstone to hitch them up. When I got back, the dishes were done.

Well, this was a new Mr. Hoyt. That night he helped put up the tent, sort of. I figured he'd get the hang of it if he kept at it, but I didn't say anything. And he did the dishes again! *And* the next morning! I scolded myself to accept the help and not worry about the why. I concentrated on the animals and the cooking. Those needed two things that were in short supply in that part of the country—fuel and forage. I took to darting off any time I saw a likely clump of grass, cutting it and stowing it in the wagon in case Mr. MacIver couldn't find us any grass at the end of the day. His main interest was water. You could eat a cold supper and sleep just about anywhere, but you and your animals couldn't do without water.

It was a relief to get to the Green River.

After the river, we came to what Mr. MacIver declared were the Wasatch Mountains. This was one of several ranges, mostly running north to south. Uncle Rafe had spoken of the Wasatch Mountains, among many others in this part of the country. Though we made steady progress, I could see Boreas and Yellowstone were struggling.

At supper I told Mr. Hoyt we had to lighten the load, for the sake of the animals. He rubbed his chin. "Are you sure, lad? We've done that four or five times already. We're down to the bare bones."

I'd already thought about it. "I'd say it wouldn't hurt to toss the Roadometer. We never could get it to work properly."

Mr. Hoyt knitted up his brow. "But that's only ten pounds, maybe fifteen."

"Every pound feels like two going uphill."

"I still maintain it was a good investment," he said.

I had never had much truck with cash money. My world was chores and animals, knowing that only our own sweat and toil put food on the table. Dad and Mother used money to buy things they couldn't make, like thread and salt. I knew Mr. Hoyt should've spent the money Dad gave him for real supplies, not the Roadometer. That was partnership money. But I suppose you could say Mr. Hoyt, being a partner, took it upon himself to decide the Roadometer would help us.

All that was water under the bridge. I just wanted to keep the new Mr. Hoyt happy. If we didn't find any gold in California, the Roadometer would just be part of the baggage we left behind. If we found gold, a few nuggets in the jubilation of the moment would settle the matter. "Well, we can set aside some nuggets from our first strike to pay you back for the loss of the Roadometer."

"Done!" Mr. Hoyt said with a grin, slapping his knee.

The Roadometer was out. I kept going. I didn't want to throw out what little we had in the way of mining equipment; from all the talk I'd heard it would probably be twice or three times as expensive if we were to buy it when we got to the gold fields. Only one other portion of the load could be discarded without harm to ourselves. I took a gulp. "And the extra guns. They can go."

Mr. Hoyt had been collecting rifles and sidearms and ammunition from the castoffs along the trail. He gave me a pleading look. "But Pegg-boy! Those are valuable! We can sell them and get ourselves the best outfit money can buy."

I pointed out they were the heaviest things in the wagon.

He made to agree with my logic. "That may be true, lad, that may be true. But it'd take three or four rifles and a dozen pistols to equal a sack of flour."

I was not used to contradicting my elders. "I don't think we should be throwing out food." I could see Mr. Hoyt was not convinced. "I can make pancakes and biscuits out of flour. I can't make breakfast out of a rifle."

Mr. Hoyt busted out laughing. "You got me there, lad!" He laughed some more. "We sure can't eat rifles, now can we?"

He was still chuckling to himself. He waved his hand in the air. "Do your worst, lad. Do your worst."

Maybe this partnership will work out after all.

CHAPTER 18

There wasn't much to do during the day but walk. There wasn't so much worrying to do following the river, water and grass were close at hand. But I didn't take the grass for granted. I kept up my habit of darting off after a particularly good bunch for the oxen. Bugle stuck close and whined a lot. I knew he was still missing Dad. I gave him extra attention. And I kept up a patter with Boreas and Yellowstone, remembering the encouragement Dad would give them, and the scratching. I'd rest my hand on their side as we walked along. Just the touching seemed to help, maybe because it's what Dad put such great store by. He was always putting his arm around Mom, or holding her hand while he talked to her, when she wasn't busy with a chore. Or he'd hug Amy out of the blue. Anything I did that was like him tore my heart apart all over again.

Still, walking all day gave me time to worry about my mom and sister back in Vermont and the wild, lawless place I was headed for. I didn't worry about my brother Adam too much. He was grown and almost on his own. He'd get married and get his ice business started. He'd be okay.

Mr. MacIver would ride by and ask me how the animals were doing or if I'd seen any hostiles. It was an old joke with us. I knew he was just being neighborly, but I appreciated it all the same.

Sometimes he'd catch me at a good moment, and I'd give him some sass back, and he'd snort and grin, and say, "Attaboy!"

Hally came by, too, and she'd just walk beside me. A lot of the times, she'd have Lilly with her. Lilly would walk a while and then want to ride Boreas. We made up stories for Lilly. Hally always had her bonnet hanging down her back, her glossy, dark hair pulled into two long braids. When I tried to make a joke, she'd fix me with her serious, dark eyes. I took comfort in their visits, but I couldn't tell you why.

One afternoon, after we'd stopped for the day, I went with the other kids to gather firewood. Ben always reminded me of a grasshopper standing up on its hind legs. His ears stuck out like mine did, which gave me consolation that I wasn't the only one so afflicted.

Ben said, "So why don't you come to Oregon with us? What do you want to muck around in the mud for? My pop says it's just wild stories."

On the other side of me, Hally said, "I think it would be nice to travel with the Chalmers. They're really nice people."

Somehow, Hally must have heard about Mrs. Chalmers' idea. I know I didn't tell her about it. I said, "The Chalmers *are* nice people. But look, you've got your families with you. You can go anywhere you want." I picked up another twig. "My family's back in Vermont, and they're counting on us, on me, to bring back enough gold to buy a new farm, a better farm."

"Well, I sure can't argue with that," Ben said.

After a minute Hally said, "Will there be other kids in California?"

Of the California-bound wagons in our company, I was the only one. "I can't say. Maybe." Then I smiled at Hally. "When I'm loaded down with gold, I'll come up to Oregon in my shiny new landau and matching pair, to visit you. How's that?"

Hally blushed and bent to pick up a stick.

They didn't bother me about going to Oregon after that, but they unsettled what had been settled in my mind.

Mr. Hoyt was a puzzle. Before Dad died, about all he did was collect firewood—when he was around. Now he was doing the dishes regular, and helping with the tent, *and* getting the hang of it. And he went after water and wood, most of the time without being asked. He left the animals to me, and I was fine with that.

If he seemed to linger after the supper dishes were done, and I judged him to be in an amiable mood, I would ask him for a story from one of his adventures. I made sure the coffeepot was full so the telling wouldn't be interrupted.

So many of his stories about steamboats included disasters that I quietly put aside my ambition for being a riverboat man. But then Will snickered from a corner of my mind. *So who would want to listen to a story that had no ruckus, and everybody came out of it smiling?*

One of those stories, though, struck me as having the same qualities Mr. Hoyt had shown after the stagecoach wreck back home, before we knew him well.

He said *this* story happened on a sternwheeler named the *Mandan,* on the Missouri, back in '44. Before he went on, Mr. Hoyt took a swig of coffee. "We had stopped at a wood-yard on the south bank, upriver from Fort James. Every able-bodied man lent a hand loading wood. Word was out the Sioux were making trouble. Well, they showed up, whoopin' and hollerin'. The wood crew barely got back on board before the captain pulled up the gangplank and cast off. The side of the boat looked like a porcupine by the time the captain put some water between us and the hostiles. But the pilot, in his haste, hit a snag." Mr. Hoyt gave a snort. "Like a spear through a soft belly. Everyone climbed up onto the Texas deck, trusting in the stories of the shallow river. That just made 'em better targets." He took another drink of his coffee. My own coffee grew cold.

"But fate had a crueler trick in store. Impaled on the snag, the *Mandan* twisted and shuddered like a beast in torment. The boilers

171

exploded, hurling passengers and cargo alike into the sky. What was left of the mutilated hulk sank like a stone. Only the canted chimneys marked her grave. Those who survived were flung into the muddy stream. Lots couldn't swim and were quickly lost." He was quiet for a moment.

The pictures that must be going through his mind.

He finished his coffee. "I only escaped by clinging to a large scrap of the wreckage. It was every man for himself."

"But you made it," I offered cheerfully. "Why didn't you swim?"

"Never learned," he replied gruffly, pouring himself more from the pot. "While I rejoiced at cheating death, I spied a young passenger who was not going to be so fortunate. Worse, she clasped to her bosom a babe in arms. Without a thought, I maneuvered the plank in her way and helped her grab hold.

"But we weren't out of danger. The savages ran along the shore picking off, one by one, those who were, by whatever means, still afloat. Any fool who made the south bank met a gruesome end at the hands of the savages.

"The young mother and I avoided slaughter by concealing ourselves in a vast tangle of driftwood. I urged her to feed the infant, lest its cries betray us. There we hid into the next day, when we clambered out and walked fifty miles to another wood-yard. The poor creature, having lost her shoes, nearly gave out, but I took up the infant myself, dragged the mother to her feet and pushed her on, if only for the sake of the child."

Mr. Hoyt finished the last of his coffee with a loud smack. "She lives in Trenton now. She still writes."

I sat, goggle-eyed.

Some evenings, Mrs. Chalmers would invite me over. I looked forward to that. She talked to me like I was older than I was. Other times, once Mr. Hoyt was off for the evening, I'd sit by my fire with Bugle, giving him a good scratch. He was a good listener.

"So what do you think about this idea?" I said.

Bugle licked his chops and went back to panting, eager to hear what else I had to say.

"Hally's right. I like the Chalmers and they *are* good people. If I were with them, I could stop worrying about all that's coming, stop worrying about all that I don't know."

Bugle knew there was more to it than that, but he let me figure the rest of it out.

"That's a good part of what parents do for you. They do a lot of worrying so you can be a kid." I scratched his head. Bugle didn't take his eyes off me.

"If I can't have my dad, I don't see anybody around who would do better than Mr. Chalmers. And when Mrs. Chalmers talks to me and smiles at me, well, that makes me feel like the best person in the whole world."

I smiled down at Bugle. He smiled back in his canine way.

"And Lilly is almost like having Amy around—except there *is* Amy, and Mom. Waiting, counting on me. And Mr. Hoyt's getting better." I sighed.

The time to choose was drawing closer every day. But if I chose Oregon, what would Mr. Hoyt do?

* * *

At a big bend in the Bear River, the trail forked again. This was *another* cutoff, called Hudspeth's Cutoff. Mr. MacIver said it was brand new, made for people in a hurry to get to California.

He pointed up the trail we were on. "Going by way of Fort Hall is a little longer. But there's more grass and water." He nodded at the new trail. "Hudspeth's Cutoff is some shorter, but it's rougher country, without much water."

He let people chew on that a minute. He glanced at Mr. Chalmers, who gave him a short nod. Mr. MacIver finished his speech. "For the sake of your animals, it's best to stay together to Fort Hall."

Despite this recommendation, two parties of gold seekers headed off on Hudspeth's Cutoff. People shook their heads and wondered what fate awaited those impatient men.

The trail we chose was rough enough. We were still losing animals, and the wagons seemed to be falling apart from under us. The wood was so dry, the iron tires slipped off the wheels and rolled away into the brush. Hospitality was sorely tested. Tempers were short.

Everybody heaved a sigh of relief when Fort Hall came in sight at last.

It was no Fort Laramie, not by a long shot, but it was still an important stop for emigrants. Both places had started out as trading posts. Fort Hall was the last chance to top up supplies. The fort sat hard by the south bank of the Snake River, which we would follow until we got to the place where the Oregon Trail split off. At that fork we would have to say goodbye once and for all. You could feel that day coming in the whole company.

Mrs. Chalmers let me know in the gentlest, nicest way that their offer was still open, though they knew I felt responsible to follow through with my dad's plans.

After dinner Mr. Hoyt said, "I'm going up to the fort. Do we need anything? Salt? Beans? Coffee?"

"No. I don't think so."

He grinned his off-kilter grin. "There's nothing between here and California. Are you sure?"

I climbed into the wagon and looked through our stores. I hadn't gotten very far when I realized we would probably have enough because we had one less mouth to feed. That stopped me in my tracks. My eyes smarted, but I scolded myself to keep going. I climbed back out of the wagon.

"If we're sensible, we should have enough," I said.

"Good lad." Mr. Hoyt tossed out the last of his coffee and stood up.

"Do you have my mother's letter to mail?" I asked.

His eyes popped wide, as if surprised. He scuttled over to our wagon and climbed in. A minute later he came back out. He patted his coat pocket.

"Thanks for reminding me." And off he went.

"Thanks," I said to his back.

I found a good patch of grass for Boreas and Yellowstone and checked the grease on our wheels.

Mr. Hoyt was gone most of the afternoon. As I was laying a fire for supper, Bugle barked. I saw Mr. Hoyt approaching with a short, skinny man dressed in dark clothes.

"Pegg, lad! You'll never guess who I bumped into! A fellow scalawag from my river days!"

All of our clothes were patched and dusty. This new fellow's clothes were so travel-worn they were almost rags.

Mr. Hoyt grinned down at his friend. "Allow me to introduce Mister Vernon Tucker, Esquire, a magician of truly extraordinary powers."

I stuck out my hand. "Bartholomew Pegg. Pleased to meet you, Mr. Tucker."

"Likewise, young fellow, likewise." He grinned at Mr. Hoyt. "This your boy, then, Fred?"

Mr. Hoyt barked a nervous laugh. "No! Goodness, no!" Then he caught himself. "What I mean is, I'm not so lucky. Pegg, here, is a neighbor boy. No! Better yet, he's my partner. We're on our way to California to make our fortunes!"

I'd seen Mr. Hoyt lay it on thick with other people, so I didn't pay this much mind.

He turned to me, keeping up his jovial air. "Pegg, lad. I've invited Vern to supper. Is it too late to add more beans to the pot?"

Now wasn't the time to embarrass Mr. Hoyt about his persistent lack of knowledge about the preparation of beans. Thankfully, I always soaked enough beans to last us through several meals. *I'll just dish out some of that extra to our guest.* "No, not at all." I carved off some more bacon.

They settled themselves to visit.

Mr. Tucker seemed anxious to please. "I've told you about what I've been up to, Fred. How about you? How have you been? What's it been? Five years since we were in New Orleans?"

Mr. Hoyt grinned back at Mr. Tucker. "I've been keeping myself busy. You know me."

"I thought sure you'd have your mansion on the hill by now."

Mr. Hoyt reared back, grinning even wider. "When we get back from California, I'll have that mansion, *and* the hill, and the valley all around!"

Mr. Tucker nodded approvingly. "I don't doubt it for a minute!" He stared off, maybe imagining the splendid mansion. Then he said, "Say, whatever became of Miss Mirabelle? We thought sure you'd settle down with her."

I glanced over my shoulder, but kept minding the bacon. Back in St. Louis, Mr. Hoyt had talked about meeting a Miss Mirabelle.

When he responded I could hear his high spirits dim a little. "I'm a man for tomorrow, Vern. You know that. Nothing to be gained by dwelling on yesterday."

Mr. Tucker noticed me listening. "Miss Mirabelle was an angel. Sweetest little lady ever walked a wire." He saw that I didn't understand. "Has Fred never told you about his showboating days?" He gave a quick look to Mr. Hoyt. "That's how we know each other. He was known up and down the river, Mr. Mississippi! We played every village and settlement with a stump to tie up to."

Mr. Hoyt shifted in his seat and pulled at his hat. "Now don't get carried away, Vernon."

"I couldn't do better than the truth, Fred!" Mr. Tucker turned to me with his eyes dancing. "Fred had three showboats, all at the same time."

Again, he turned to Mr. Hoyt. "I was always amazed at how you kept it all going." He swung back to me. "Most showboats just put on plays and such. Fred did a whole heck of a lot more! He had acrobats! Strongmen! Minstrels! Strange beasts and opera singers!"

"And magicians." Mr. Hoyt grinned.

Mr. Tucker reached up and pulled a playing card from out of Mr. Hoyt's ear. Mr. Hoyt reared back. Mr. Tucker made the card disappear just as quickly. He beamed at me. "His showboats were bigger, with more banners and fancy work than anybody else's."

"You can do a lot when you don't have to have an engine." Mr. Hoyt offered.

I turned to be a better audience. "How did you get around?"

"A steam tug pushed us around," replied Mr. Tucker. "And he had the Great Santorini and the Divine Miss Mirabelle!"

Mr. Hoyt grew quiet.

Mr. Tucker didn't notice. He was just getting warmed up. "The Great Santorini and Miss Mirabelle were the best high wire act you ever saw! She did triple backflips, she stood on his shoulders! It was something to see, I tell ya!"

"Not as amazing as your fire-in-the-hat trick," Mr. Hoyt said.

Mr. Tucker scoffed and turned to me. "We all thought the world of Miss Mirabelle, but it was Fred, here, who had the gall to woo her right from under the Great Santorini's nose!" He slapped his knee while he chuckled. Then the magician got a serious look. "Then, one night, we were pulled up, putting on a show; don't even remember the name of the town…"

"La Grange," Mr. Hoyt offered quietly.

Vernon charged on. "And…bad luck…a tree floating down the river hit the showboat. It wasn't more'n a nudge, but Miss Mirabelle lost her balance and crashed to the deck! We couldn't believe it."

Mr. Hoyt was scowling at the ground.

Mr. Tucker had a pleading look. "They took her into town." He turned to Mr. Hoyt. "You made us finish the show. That was hard. But you were right, of course."

Mr. Hoyt still looked at the ground. He spoke in a grave voice. "You know my motto, Vernon. Honor your commitments, no matter what."

Vernon told the rest of the story to Mr. Hoyt, who already knew it. I listened hard just the same. "The doctor said she couldn't be moved. You said we couldn't wait. She could catch up with us when she got better. Santorini threw a fit."

Mr. Hoyt snorted in contempt. "Santorini was always throwing fits."

"He accused you of all kinds of terrible things! We thought sure you were going to sling him in the river right then and there!" Mr. Tucker then turned back to me with a grin. "Nobody threw mud on Fred Hoyt's name and got away with it!"

Mr. Hoyt shook himself like a fly was pestering him.

"What happened in New Orleans?" Mr. Tucker tried to look into Mr. Hoyt's face. "You went into town, like you always did, and the next thing we knew, the sheriff came out to the boat and told us to clear out. When we asked him what was going on, he told us it was none of our concern. Just clear out."

Mr. Hoyt was scraping at the dirt with his boot. He spoke and his voice was full of muffled thunder. "Like I said, Vernon, it does no good to dwell on the past."

Mr. Tucker gulped. "That's the truth, Fred. It surely is." He shot me a quick glance. He had something close to fear in his eyes. He stood up abruptly. "Well, I'd better be getting back now. It was nice to see you, Fred." He started backing away. "Best of luck in California, hear?"

I straightened up from my stirring. "Supper's almost ready."

"Much obliged, Son, but it's best I be heading back. I'm sorry for your trouble." He turned and hurried off into the lengthening shadows.

After Mr. Tucker took his leave, Mr. Hoyt heaved himself up and stomped off in the opposite direction.

"Supper's just about ready," I called after him.

"Ain't hungry," he grumbled, and kept moving.

In the end, I had more food prepared than I could eat. I gave Bugle the extra bacon and ate my fill of beans, all the while wondering why Mr. Hoyt had not told Mr. Tucker about seeing Miss Mirabelle in St. Louis. And why would Miss Mirabelle have a kind word for him in St. Louis if he abandoned her in that small town, La Grange? I thought I knew what she must have felt like, being left alone in a strange place, facing an uncertain future.

Was she even in St. Louis when Mr. Hoyt said she was? And if she wasn't, why would he use her as his excuse for getting out of the partnership? If she wasn't in St. Louis, where was she? Still in La Grange, after all these years? Somewhere along the river, lost in one of the countless landings and villages? And why did Mr. Hoyt get angry with Mr. Tucker for telling the story? As my friend Will was fond of saying about people, Mr. Hoyt was certainly an odd duck.

He would bear watching.

Maybe Dad would want me to go with the Chalmers, after all.

Mr. Chalmers and Mr. MacIver were eager to get us moving again. The summer was well advanced, and we still had hundreds of miles yet to go. Those headed to California had more to worry about. According to Mr. MacIver, winter could come to the Sierras any time now. All he had to say was "Donner Party" and people hustled.

On the third day out of Fort Hall we came to the fork in the trail where the Oregon people would leave us. They probably thought of it as us leaving them. We made our dinner in a big meadow on the west bank of the Raft River. I went over to the Chalmers' wagon.

"Well, hello, Pegg," Mrs. Chalmers said with a smile, "Will you eat with us?"

"Thank you, ma'am. I've already eaten. Thank you just the same."

Lilly came over and took my hand and led me to a seat. Then she settled herself beside me. Bugle came up to Lilly and gave her his sad eyes until she petted the top of his head.

Mrs. Chalmers came over and sat down near me. "Have you thought over what you'd like to do, Pegg?"

It would be so easy to hook up with them, but my dad and I had set out with such big dreams. Now Dad was gone. I wouldn't be bringing him home. The only thing left was to honor his dream. Make it come true.

"I have, ma'am. I have to go to California. My family is counting on it."

Mrs. Chalmers looked at me steady for a couple of minutes. But it was a kind look. "I understand." She clasped her hands together. "I am disappointed, truly, but I understand. I will keep you in my prayers. And I wish you all the success in the world."

Just then, Mr. Chalmers and Mr. MacIver came up.

Both Mrs. Chalmers and I stood.

"Pegg has decided to push on to California. To our loss," Mrs. Chalmers announced.

Mr. Chalmers regarded me for a minute. He stuck out his hand. "I salute such courage, young man. I wish you great success. May the good Lord bless and keep you." We shook hands.

"Thank you, sir."

Mr. MacIver's eyes crinkled up in a smile. "Well, I'll make sure he stays out of trouble for the next six hundred miles, anyway. After that, it really will be up to the Good Lord."

That's how I learned Gideon MacIver would be guiding us to California, while Mr. Chalmers was taking the others to Oregon.

I knelt down in front of Lilly. "Well, Princess." I choked up, surprised at myself, then cleared my throat. "We have to go different ways. Will you think of me once in a while? I'll think of you."

She stepped closer and put her arms around my neck. She was so much like my sister Amy. I hugged her tight.

After a long minute, I leaned back. "Our paths may cross again someday. I would like that." I put my finger under her chin to get her to look at me. "Until then, you grow up strong and brave and true for me. Okay?" And I kissed her cheek.

I had to leave before I changed my mind.

Mrs. Chalmers stepped over and gave me a hug. "Now we will miss you more than ever." Her eyes were welling up.

"Good luck to you all. God Bless," I said, and skedaddled before I started blubbering.

I found Mattie and Bobby and Ben and said goodbye to them.

Ben said, "Send me some gold. I want to buy a steamboat."

I found Hally's wagon, but her mom said she was down at the river getting water with Sarah.

I went toward the river. I prayed my voice wouldn't crack, saying what I had to say. Pretty quick I saw two figures sitting close together on a little shelf under a big, old cottonwood tree. There were a few other people by the river, but these two were off by themselves. I was pretty sure they were who I wanted. Bugle *was* sure. He ran ahead and pestered Hally.

I was still approaching when Sarah Prichard jumped up and came toward me. I slowed to talk to her, but she kept up her head of steam. "Have fun in Californi-o!" she sang as she passed.

"Thanks. You, too, in Oregoni-o," I called after her. *How did she know?*

Feeling very foolish, I made my way on to the remaining figure on the riverbank.

I came to a stop and looked down at the top of Hally's head. "Am I interrupting anything?"

"No," she said. It wasn't the warmest welcome in the world.

Bugle gave her a sad look. She stroked the top of his head.

"May I sit down?" I was good until "sit." At "down," my voice pitched up several notches. I wanted to crawl under a rock, but there were none handy.

"If you want to," she said.

I looked at the unfilled water buckets on the muddy shore below her feet. I sat down beside her. Bugle went off in search of something interesting at the water's edge.

I wrestled with what to say. I'd already said goodbye to half a dozen people. Why was it so hard to say it to Hally? She turned her dark, serious eyes on me and I realized why. She could look right through me, but somehow I knew that was okay. A dozen pictures flashed through my mind: Hally asking Mr. MacIver about Indians; her coming up with Lilly on her hip, smiling, and walking along; us arguing about some silly thing; her laughing at something I said; her handing me her wet petticoat strips when we were lost and needed them to make the fire smoke.

Hally said, "So I suppose you're going to California."

"News travels fast."

I thought that was a pretty good comeback, especially since I'd only just told the Chalmers my decision.

Hally didn't laugh. She kept looking out at the river. "From what I hear, you've got the hardest part of the trip ahead of you."

"So I hear." I watched the river a minute, too. "But Mr. MacIver will be leading us. I figure we're in good hands."

I got the impression Hally didn't care who was leading who.

I looked up where little ragged clouds scattered in rows across the sky.

"How long will you stay?" she asked.

"'Til I get enough gold to buy a farm. Oh! And a steamboat. Ben wants a steamboat." Then I remembered. "And some ribbon. My sister Amy wants some ribbon."

I turned to her, to see if her spirits had lifted any. "How about you? Can I bring you anything?"

"Would you bring it to Oregon?"

"Sure I would."

She concentrated on the river. "Did you ever think..." She stopped.

"I try not to do it too often." I smiled. I really wanted to lighten things up.

"Don't be stupid." She said it like she hurt, somehow.

Whatever it was, I didn't want that. "Sorry."

She didn't look at me. "Do you really have to go to California?"

"It's the only place I've heard of with gold lying around."

That didn't go over very well, either. She swatted me. I suppose I deserved it.

I tried again. "Hally, look. With my dad gone, I'm the only one who can do what we set out to do. I owe it to him..."

She cut me off. "But it's such a dangerous place. I've heard..."

I cut *her* off. I had to beat back my own fear. "Can you think of a better way to grow up?"

Her eyes flashed anger. "Oh! You're impossible!" And she sprang to her feet.

I don't know why, but I grabbed her hand. "What? Wait a minute!" I stammered.

She didn't pull away, which I thought sure she would. I got to my feet, still holding onto her hand. "Hally, I don't really have a choice."

Her dark eyes bored into me. "Couldn't you make a new farm in Oregon?"

"It isn't as simple as that. I have to think about Mr. Pruitt and the neighbors. They backed this trip."

"And you don't have room to think about anybody else?"

"I think about my family all the time," I said. *Why are we still holding hands?*

We were standing so close together I could tell she was watching my mouth, not my eyes.

She dropped her gaze to the ground. "Well, they're lucky then."

I reached and took her other hand. It seemed as natural as pie. "We had a good time. I'll always remember you." I jigged her hands a little. "Will you remember me?"

She nodded. Then she looked up at me and I realized I had upset her even more. "H—have a good time in California," she said in a broken voice. She leaned in quick and pecked me on the cheek. As quick, she pulled her hands away and ran off toward the camp, her braids slapping at her back.

"Hally! Wait!" I watched her for a long minute, but she didn't stop.

I was surprised by my hand feeling empty. I swore I could still feel the warmth of her fingers. I tried to fathom what had just passed, but it kept slipping out of reach, no matter how I came at it. I looked around for Bugle. He was marking a big piece of driftwood. Then I saw Hally had forgotten her water buckets. I filled them and started after her.

"Bugle! Come on, boy!"

By the time I got back to her wagon, Hally was nowhere to be seen. Her mother said, "Hello, Pegg," in a kindly way, like she knew what had happened. I set the buckets down. She thanked me for the water and then tipped her head toward their wagon. I nodded a *thank you* to her and went over to the tailgate.

"Hally, I'm sorry if I said something wrong." I called loud enough for anyone in the wagon to hear.

"Go look for your stupid gold! See if I care!" the wagon shouted back.

Hally's mom gave me an expression that I knew meant *Don't worry. She'll come around*. I smiled and nodded to thank her again and went back to my own wagon.

Girls were unknown, not to mention unpredictable and mysterious territory. Little sisters were fine, if sometimes vexing. Mothers were necessary and mostly a comfort. But girls?

As I crawled under my blankets that night, I realized I'd never felt before what I felt when I had to say goodbye to Hally.

CHAPTER 19

THE CALIFORNIA TRAIL

CHAPTER 19

Seventeen wagons set off down the California trail. Those wagons carried forty-nine souls. Seven more men, who had lost their wagons, were on foot. The whole was as varied as the original Chalmers company had been—except there were no women, and no other kids besides me. That felt strange. People who I might have seen only once in a while earlier on the trail were now constant companions.

Linnaeus Peabody was with us, and of that I was glad. He'd climb down from his horse and walk along with me, telling me about ancient Rome, or Marco Polo, or the Vikings. If the time was right, I'd ask him to stay for dinner or supper so I could hear more stories, ask him more questions.

In the wagon ahead of us was Big Joe Porter. He was a longshoreman from Louisiana. He boasted he could load cotton faster than any man alive. He had formed a company, with merely a hand shake, with Quentin Miller, a cooper from Massachusetts, and Thomas Averill an engraver from Philadelphia. They'd met at Council Bluffs.

The wagon behind us held two gentlemen who fascinated me. Bill Marburger was a boiler man from Baltimore, Maryland. He claimed to have shoveled coal on the first steamship to cross the

Atlantic Ocean, the *SS Great Western*. He liked to joke that he had broken his back shoveling coal for seven paying passengers. Mr. Quincey, his partner, had blue arms and hands. He had worked in a tannery and dye works in Kentucky.

I could keep going, but those were the people I talked to the most.

Our first night away from the Oregon-bound folks, Mr. MacIver asked me to go around to everyone and tell them that he wanted to say a few words after folks had finished their suppers. When we had gathered, Mr. MacIver climbed up to stand on the seat of the Pegg wagon and held his hands up for quiet.

After we all settled down, he began. "Gentlemen. You have made it this far on grit and determination. And for that you are to be commended. You have escaped the cholera and every other misfortune this trail has been burdened with. Well, gents, that was just the warm-up. That was just to shake out the wrinkles. The country ahead will test your limits. In fact, it'll do its best to kill you. You think you've been thirsty? You think you've been dusty? Hungry? Exhausted? At your wit's end? What's up ahead will teach you what those words really mean."

He let everybody digest that for a minute. Then he said, "I know many of you have lost friends, even loved ones. You've abandoned treasured keepsakes, lost your wagons. I only speak to impress upon you the need for caution and good sense in the days and weeks ahead. We'll need every ounce of charity toward each other that we can muster to make it through." He looked around at the upturned faces. "Think on it."

The next day we came to a place that proved what Mr. MacIver had said. It was a high, steep drop off—a thousand feet, maybe more—and we had to get to the bottom of it. The wheels had to be chained so they wouldn't turn. Men at the top of the slope held the wagons back with long ropes so they wouldn't overrun the teams. Even so, the incline was steep enough the teams had trouble keeping their feet under them. The few men not needed for immediate tasks spaced themselves along the slope, like spectators along a race track, ready to jump to assistance.

Three wagons went down without a hitch.

Then it was Mr. Marburger's turn. They had gotten a good start, maybe seventy or eighty yards, when Daisy, his lead ox, slipped and went down. People shouted in alarm.

Because of the yoke, Daisy took Oscar, the offside leader, down with her. The two following oxen, Beau and Beamer, stumbled into the first two, and in a flash all four were down, a tangled, bawling mess, swerving and sliding down the hill. The wagon skewed one way, then the other, and then came back and tipped over onto its side. You could hear their gear clattering and crashing and thumping inside. More men at the top of the hill grabbed on to the ropes to try to slow it down. Falling on its side sprung some of the hoops that arched over the wagon, sending them flying like arrows and taking most of the canvas cover with them. With the canvas gone, their outfit spilled out in the wake. Mr. Marburger and Mr. Quincey gave up and ran clear.

Mr. MacIver shouted to the men at the top, "Let go those ropes! Let 'em go!" — lest they be pulled down the hill with the runaway rig. The oxen were still sliding, bawling, still dragging the wagon. A rear wheel had already sheared off. Then the wagon hit a rock, which caught it for a second. It flipped clean into the air, flinging clothes, blankets, cook pots, and sacks of food like so many fireworks. The wagon came down on its back with a terrible crash and exploded into thousands of pieces of dry wood. The men along the side ducked the flying splinters.

A front wheel rolled, wobbling, to the bottom of the slope. It all seemed over in a couple of heartbeats. Mr. Marburger and Mr. Quincey stared, thunderstruck, at their scattered wreckage.

I watched all this from the top of the hill. Growing alarm made a knot in the pit of my stomach. We were next. Mr. Hoyt helped the men put chains through the wheels. But then he stepped out of the way. That was probably for the best. I wished mightily that my dad was here.

I stood in front with Boreas and Yellowstone, holding Boreas' lead rope. Mr. MacIver picked up Bugle and nodded to let me know he'd keep him safe.

But we had to wait while men cleared the wreckage out of the way. Daisy and the rest of the team were cut loose and led away. Miraculously, they escaped their ordeal with only scratches.

I talked to Boreas and Yellowstone, scratching their foreheads. I tried to imagine what my dad would say to them.

"It's gonna be okay. We just have to take it slow and careful, hear? Slow and careful. It'll be okay." I sang them a song. I was reassuring myself as much as them.

Finally, one of the men down the slope yelled, "All clear!"

Mr. MacIver was standing off to one side, watching the men on the ropes and me. He called out, "Ready on the ropes?"

"Ready!" came a jumbled chorus.

Then Mr. MacIver turned to me. "All right, Son. Easy does it," he said in a calm voice, like he knew I could do it. Bugle let out a whine, then kept still.

I clucked to Boreas. That was his signal to start. I did it the way my dad did it. I watched their feet. They stepped onto the steep slope. They faltered, their eyes rolling, looking for a more secure footing. I leaned close to Boreas' big head.

"It's okay, boys. One foot at a time. It's okay. Take your time."

They stepped forward, stiff-legged, onto the steep slope. They dipped their heads awkwardly.

"Slow, boys. Slow. Eeee-zeeee…" I said in a low voice. "That's good. Slow, now."

Someone farther down the hill shouted, "Better stand clear, boy, in case she goes!"

I ignored him. The wagon rolled slowly over the lip and tilted down.

"Man the ropes there!" Mr. MacIver shouted.

Fifteen men on each rope pulled them tight.

The wagon was now fully on the slope. The locked iron tires screeched and threw sparks as they scraped across rocks. So far, so good.

I took a quick look farther down the hill, in front of the wagon. The way seemed clear, nothing I couldn't toss to the side.

I soothed Boreas and Yellowstone, "You're doing swell, boys, swell. Easy, easy, easy does it."

They snorted, they tossed their heads, their big, gentle eyes staring. They were as nervous as I was. Behind me, I heard Mr. Hoyt say, "Easy does it, boy." *He must be walking down the slope along the side lines.*

The wagon creaked and groaned. The wheels screeched. I could hear other men already at the bottom calling out encouragement, those above calling out caution.

I looked around again. Ahead, I saw a rock I hadn't noticed before, and pieces from the wrecked wagon. Boreas or Yellowstone could slip on even the smallest piece. The rock was worse. I had a little time, though.

"You're doing swell," I said to them. "I'll be right back."

I ran out ahead, pointing, and shouted, "Somebody please get that rock!" I snatched up pieces of wood and tossed them clear. A couple of men wrestled with the rock. It wasn't all that big, but it was big enough to throw Boreas if he stepped on it; it was on his side of the path. It wouldn't budge.

I ran back to the team. I grabbed Boreas' lead rope and gently pulled on it. I kept my voice calm and reassuring.

"Gee, Boreas, Boy. Gee, now." That meant turn right. Haw was turn left. That's what my dad used.

I kept a steady pressure on the lead rope. Boreas and Yellowstone turned slowly to the right. I darted in to grab bits of wood out of their path. It was only a few feet, but it was enough. They, and the wagon, cleared the rock. I relaxed the lead rope.

"Good boys! Good boys!" I said, patting Boreas on the shoulder. "Good. Good." But I quickly saw that if we kept this angle the wagon could easily tip over. I tightened the lead rope again, back to the left.

"Haw, Boreas, Boy. Haw. Back. Haw, Boy."

Boreas brought the wagon back to going straight down the slope.

There was more wreckage now, bits other people thought wouldn't be dangerous. I scurried around, throwing pieces out of the way, even the smallest.

People at the bottom called out, "You're gonna get run over, boy!" and "Get outta the way, kid!"

"You're courting sudden death, Sonny!" shouted another.

I guess they thought they were looking out for my safety. I was looking out for my team and my wagon. Out of the corner of my eye I saw Mr. Peabody dart into our path and help me. A man named Riley, from one of the wagons already at the bottom, did the same. I was tossing stuff as fast as I found it. I didn't care where it landed, as long as it was away from my team.

Somebody shouted, "Hey! Watch where you're throwing that!"

At last, the steep slope started to gentle out. Boreas and Yellowstone found firmer footing and stepped more confidently. At the bottom, I eased Boreas to a stop.

"Whoa, boys. Whoa." I made sure to pat Yellowstone, too. "Good job. Good job."

A few onlookers were clapping and cheering. Men scrambled to untie the ropes from my wagon. The men at the top of the hill dragged them back up to attach to the next wagon. Mr. Hoyt came over to help take the chains off the wheels.

After I led Boreas and Yellowstone and our wagon out of the way, I gave them a drink of water and a good scratching, heaping praise on them. "You boys are the best team in the whole world, you hear? The whole world! Dad would be proud of you! *I'm* proud of you!" I gave special attention behind their ears. "Yessiree! The best! The very best!"

I thanked Mr. Riley for helping to throw debris out of the team's way, and I looked around to thank Mr. Peabody, too, but he was helping Mr. Marburger and Mr. Quincey collect their gear. I went over to lend a hand.

"Thank you for your help, Mr. Peabody."

"My goodness!" He gave me a mocking-injured look. "I thought we'd gotten over the 'Mister Peabody' business."

"Yessir." I wasn't sure my mom would approve of me calling a grown-up by his Christian name, but I reckoned we had enough miles together to warrant it. "Thank you, Linnaeus."

"That's better," he replied, still smiling. "Don't mention it, Pegg. I'm sure your father is very pleased."

Linnaeus was not sloppy in his choice of words and what he said gave me a shiver. I could only hope my dad was watching over me. "You didn't have to help," I said, "but you did. I really appreciate it."

He got a serious look. "Seldom are we privileged to witness bravery and compassion in one display."

Sometimes he said stuff like that, too. All my mom's lessons in manners hadn't prepared me for something like that. So I just said, "Thank you, sir."

He grinned again. "You're very welcome, sir."

While the other wagons were being lowered down the slope, Mr. Marburger and Mr. Quincey had the difficult and unhappy task of deciding what they could carry on their own backs. They sold their oxen and became backpackers.

At the fording of Goose Creek we came upon a sad encampment. I counted a dozen souls, all that remained of Colonel Baines' Company. Their uniforms were faded and dusty. Worn-out jackets and trousers had been replaced with what they could find along the way. The proud band of adventurers had been reduced to an exhausted, unhappy rabble, ready to quarrel at the slightest excuse. The great flag that had once heralded their arrival was now attempting to cover their one remaining wagon. The noble colonel was nowhere to be seen. I glanced at Mr. Hoyt, but his face revealed nothing.

"We lost Colonel Baines to cholera at Ash Hollow, rest his soul," said the young fellow who presented himself as their new leader. He asked Mr. MacIver if they might join our group for the remainder of the journey.

Mr. MacIver fixed him with a stern eye. "I'll tolerate no fighting, no slackers, and no stealin'." He gazed around at the haggard newcomers. "The land ahead will beat you up bad enough; no sense in you bringin' even more misery on each other. The best way you're gonna get through this is tending to your own business, and helping your neighbor, if you're so inclined." He passed his gaze over them again, hard as flint. "Is that understood?" He received a ragged volley of nods.

Just as Mr. MacIver said, the land got worse. There wasn't a lot of water, and often it was alkaline, which was fatal to man and beast. We had to be very careful where we let the animals drink. Grass was scarce and withered. We had to stop to fill our barrels and cut hay, as we were pleased to call the dry grass, whenever we came upon it. We had to halt to let the teams rest more often. And still they gave out, crumpling over in their traces. Buzzards, flies, and the stench of rot were our constant companions.

The only things that were in any abundance were the wagons abandoned by the trail. We never lacked for fuel. You could tell how long a wagon had been sitting there by how much of it was missing. The possessions within went untouched.

We passed through miles where it seemed the infernal regions were breaking through and torturing the land with boiling waters, foul gases, and spouting geysers. We took to traveling at dusk and at night to spare the teams, and ourselves, from the merciless heat of the day. Many ran out of water and relied on charity. I made sure Boreas, Yellowstone, and Bugle had water before we did.

Mr. Hoyt sank into gloom. He ate in silence. He still went off to do his usual visiting, but more often he came back smelling of liquor. He trudged beside the wagon, staring at the ground.

Those who still had wagons slept under them during the day. Others rigged shade with blankets as best they could. The heat was unbearable, suffocating. Any movement kicked up powdery dust that got in your mouth and nose. There was little relief for the poor animals. They stood in the blazing sun, lowing and groaning in their misery while we rested. There was little for them to eat, and we dared not let them wander to find it. The job of guarding our animals fell to those who still had weapons.

Linnaeus often camped near our wagon. He played his banjo and told stories about the Moors in Spain.

One afternoon as we prepared to head out, Linnaeus went out to collect his horse. When I brought in Boreas and Yellowstone and hitched them up, Linnaeus still had not returned. Unease shifted in my stomach. We would be heading out soon.

When Linnaeus did come back in, he was on foot. That was odd. His face was bleak. That was odder still. Unease gave way to dread. "Where's your horse?"

He shook his head slowly. "The alkali got him." He ran his hand through his hair and let his hand drop to his side. "He wandered off from the rest of the stock. Joe Porter and Tom Averill were on guard. They said they didn't see a thing."

I handed him a cup of coffee. "Are you sure it was the water?"

"I found him about half a mile farther out, beyond a knoll. I followed the buzzards."

Mr. MacIver came up. "No time for socializing, Gents. We'll be moving out in short order."

"Mr. Peabody's lost his horse."

Mr. MacIver, set to move on, paused and lifted an eyebrow.

"Alkali water," Linnaeus offered.

Mr. MacIver drew his brows together, dark as storm clouds. "I told them…"

"He wandered off." Linnaeus interjected. "The guards didn't even see it."

Mr. MacIver grunted, "Well, I'm sorry to hear it." He turned to me. "You willin' to carry his kit 'til our noonin'? He can make up a pack then."

Linnaeus made to protest. "Oh, no. I wouldn't…"

MacIver cut him off. "We could, on the other hand, leave you here with your kit to make do as you can. At noon you can get some help makin' up a pack." And he left us.

Linnaeus and I were loading his outfit into the wagon when Mr. Hoyt reappeared. "What's this?" he huffed.

"It's just 'til noon." I knew Mr. Hoyt had little regard for Linnaeus. "He lost his horse."

Mr. Hoyt gave Linnaeus a rakish leer. "He slip out from under you when you were ridin' side saddle?"

That was mean. Uncalled for, my mom would say. I was sad that my partner chose to be so unsparing.

If Linnaeus was insulted, he didn't let it show. He regarded Mr. Hoyt with a level gaze for only a second before he bent to pick up his saddle.

Mr. Hoyt nodded at the saddle. "That's going to put an awful strain on our animals. You sure you need it? You got no nag to put it on."

"It's only 'til noon," I said again. Then I asked myself, *What will he do with it then?*

At our nooning, Mr. Marburger and I helped Linnaeus make up a pack, with other backpackers offering advice on lashings. When he was all but done up, I cast a quick glance around. I didn't see Mr. Hoyt. I picked up Linnaeus's banjo, and leaned close with a low voice. "I know what to do with this."

Linnaeus gave me a questioning look. I put my finger to my lips. "Sshhhhhhh," and made off with it toward my wagon. I stowed the banjo in the same blanket I kept my dad's fiddle wrapped in. I didn't think I had to worry about objections from Mr. Hoyt. The last time he had been in the wagon was when Dad was sick.

It did not surprise me that Linnaeus took to backpacking with nary a grumble, and fell in with the other backpackers, spreading good cheer. I *was* surprised that he sold the saddle for eight dollars to Big Joe Porter, who felt bad about losing track of the horse.

Linnaeus' misfortune was one of many. Every day the desert beat on us, taunting, taking an animal one day, a wagon the next, testing our resolve, sapping our spirits.

MacIver said, "Buck up. This is pussycat stuff. Up ahead the tiger's waitin'—the Sierra Nevada Mountains."

After some ninety miles of that dismal terrain, we came to the headwaters of the Humboldt River. It was the first decent water and grass we had seen in seven days.

Mr. MacIver gathered us together for another meeting.

"We'll be some three weeks following this here 'Humbug' River. It ain't much to look at, and it tastes worse in places, but it has two things we need: water and grass. It's our lifeline through some of the most miserable acreage ever conceived." He looked around at the exhausted, sunburnt faces. "We'll continue to travel at night. We'll need to be extra vigilant. The few wretched hostiles that scratch a living out of this wasteland find our livestock easy pickings."

But we lost more of our animals to exhaustion than to hostiles. And those who lost their animals were forced to abandon their wagons and become backpackers. Their numbers increased as the days wore on. Some fashioned rough frames from discarded wood to carry their kit. One fellow rigged up a ladder back chair to serve the same purpose. Many rolled the barest essentials up in a blanket and lashed that across their backs.

The backpackers trudged out wide to either side of the trail, like scattered, shambling scarecrows, to avoid the swirling dust of the teams and wagons. They would rejoin us when we rested. They had, after all, been our companions for many hundreds of miles. And, inevitably, as they began to run out of provisions, they began to beg for food. Mr. Hoyt took a hard line when it came to backpackers. After he had turned several of them away from our supper, he stated his position.

"Their condition is no fault of mine," he said in a stern voice. "Men who would launch themselves on such an enterprise with only meager preparations must suffer the consequences of their poor judgment."

It was more than he had said in days. I handed him his plate of beans. He wolfed down several mouthfuls before continuing his speech. "What has befallen them is the product of their own foolishness. If they become desperate enough, who knows what villainy they will resort to?"

I thought that a harsh outlook. No one can be blamed when a poor beast who has faithfully pulled a wagon for hundreds and hundreds of miles finally expires for want of water or grass. Who is at fault when a dried-out wagon wheel, after months of torture on a rough and rutted trail, finally shatters on a rock? But I had been raised to listen respectfully when my elders were speaking.

And Mr. Hoyt wasn't done. "How can we be expected to jeopardize our own well-being—indeed, our very survival—to benefit fools who have made such poor choices?"

Finally, he seemed to have exhausted his ire and went back to his supper. I regarded him over my own plate. Never before had I heard him speak so severely.

Perhaps Mr. Hoyt saw some aspect of the situation that I could not. Perhaps he was just exhausted, or alarmed at the misery that was so evident among our company. The dust choked us no matter when we traveled. At night the light was poor even when the moon was out. And trying to sleep during the day was like trying to sleep on a hot stove.

I found I could not adopt the grim judgement Mr. Hoyt meted out to the unlucky men who became backpackers. And while I did not surrender a drop of water, I was not against handing out the odd cup of beans or rice. The only price I asked was sealed lips about where it came from. After all, our wagon carried provisions for three, with only two consuming them. Linnaeus was now among those who were afoot, and though he never asked, he never left one of our visits without a chunk of bacon or a couple of biscuits in his pocket.

We came to a spot where a new trail split off and headed more directly west. The main trail tended strongly toward the south. It was time to make another decision.

"This trail you see goin' off to your right is a new cutoff," said Mr. MacIver. "It's called Lawson's Cutoff, or Lassen's Cutoff, depending on who you ask. Some folks swear by it. They say it's the easier way over the mountains. I say, hogwash. There *is* no easy way over the Sierras. It's about twice as long as the Carson route. The country it passes through makes what you've just been through seem like a stroll in the park."

He pointed at the new cutoff again. "It's a hundred and fifty miles of pure misery. And smack dab in the middle of it is a choice piece of property called the Black Rock Desert. You'd be more comfortable crawlin' through a steamboat boiler."

Mr. MacIver's audience murmured approval of his speech.

"Now, the way we're goin' ain't much better, but at least it's shorter."

"How can it be any worse than it's already been?" came a voice from the back of the crowd.

"It can and it will," said Mr. MacIver.

Groans and protests rippled through the weary mob.

Mr. MacIver let them settle. "We'll be getting to the Humboldt Sink in two days, maybe a little less. That's where this fine waterway finally gives up the fight. There'll be water and grass. We'll cut hay and fill up our water barrels and anything else that will hold water." He paused. "It's also where the trail forks again."

"Again?" called Jess Riley, who still had his sense of humor. A few of us laughed, but feebly.

"Thank you, Mr. Riley," Mr. MacIver intoned without regarding the speaker. Then he resumed his address. "We'll be on the Carson Trail. The Truckee Trail forks off it. They both follow rivers through the mountains. But to get to those rivers, whichever one we decide to take, we have to cross forty miles of the meanest, flattest, hottest, most unforgiving desert in all creation."

It was pretty clear which route Mr. MacIver favored, so we took his advice.

When we got to the Humboldt Sink, we stayed three days. The river spread out in a wide, flat valley, making a vast marsh of shallow lakes and pools, with islands of lush grass. The water never left the valley, but sank at last, unseen, into the ground.

We rested ourselves and our stock, and cut grass with assorted knives. Nobody had thought to bring a scythe. We threw out even more from the wagons to make room for the fodder. We had at last come to realize that for those of us who still had wagons, nothing— *nothing*—was more important than grass and water. We soaked our water barrels and wheels so the wood would swell up. We filled up every thimble and bucket we could lay our hands on. In all, we gathered our strength, preparing ourselves for the final push over the mountains.

Humboldt Sink is also where Mr. Hoyt and I became backpackers.

CHAPTER 20

On the third afternoon of our stay at the Humboldt Sink, Mr. MacIver announced we would be moving on that night. "Make an early supper of it," he said. "I want to be on the move by sunset, so we can make at least halfway before we stop."

When the sun was lowering in the west, Mr. MacIver, Linnaeus Peabody, and Silas Lidmer went to bring in the stock, which we let graze in the willow thickets along the river. The animals really spread out in their search for food, so I was not surprised when the men took a long time getting back.

I'm sure it took longer than Mr. MacIver wanted it to take. He came over to me before I could go collect Boreas and Yellowstone.

"Pegg, lad, I've got bad news. They kilt Yellowstone, and the other one's run off, or they took him with 'em."

I stared at him, stunned. He could not have said a worse thing. "Are you sure?" By "they" I knew he meant Indians.

"We found Yellowstone lying on his side with three arrows in 'im."

I still stared. I couldn't believe it. They had come so far... *we* had come so far.

Mr. MacIver said, "We looked for your other one as long as we could before we had to come back."

"Boreas." I felt like my whole body had turned to lead.

"With them scalawags makin' bold, we'd best be on the move. I'll find Hoyt and tell him," Mr. MacIver said. "Be as quick as you can so you can catch up."

What he was saying was: become a backpacker. Go through your wagon, pick out *only* what you can carry on your own back. It was almost a death sentence, unless we were really lucky.

But I didn't do what he said at all. I ran to the river, looking for Yellowstone, hoping desperately that Boreas would magically step into view. I stumbled a lot; my eyes were all blurry. I had to keep calling Bugle back to me. The danger of hostiles lurking in any thicket didn't get past the anguish tearing at my breast.

I finally found Yellowstone. He was just like Mr. MacIver said. I knelt beside him and put my hand on his great, curly forehead, and sobbed without shame. Bugle knew something was very wrong. He whined in his worried way and cast about, trying to make sense of it. Then I pulled the arrows out of Yellowstone, saying, "I'm sorry" over and over, and broke the shafts over my knee. I suddenly got crazy angry. I dragged the Colt out of my belt and fired off two or three wild shots back upstream, where I thought the thieves might have gone. Again, I was heedless of the unwelcome attention this might gain me. I ran through thicket after thicket, searching for Boreas, calling his name, not caring if I scared up some Indians or not, hoping Boreas was in the next stand of willows. While I scrambled along, I thought about all the miles we'd walked together, all the songs I'd sung to them, all the times they'd drunk water out of my hat.

Linnaeus found me a good mile and a half upstream. He was riding Mr. MacIver's horse.

"There's nothing to be done, Son. We must move on," he said gently, without dismounting.

"If we get some more people, we can fan out," I blubbered.

"Pegg, there are many lives depending on Mr. MacIver's wisdom. He knows you have lost your beloved team, but he must think of *everyone*," Linnaeus said.

I looked upstream, hoping one last hope.

Linnaeus' voice was now a little more firm. "Let's go back now. You have much to do." He held out his hand and took his foot out of the stirrup for me to climb up.

I whistled for Bugle to keep up. He knew. He stayed close, on our left.

Back in our camp, I found Mr. Hoyt throwing a fit.

"This is an outrage! I demand retribution!" he shouted at Mr. MacIver. A few others had gathered round. Mr. Hoyt's face was red with anger. "This transgression cannot go unpunished!"

Mr. MacIver replied in a calm voice. "It's a tough break, Mr. Hoyt. It could have been anybody's team. This time it was yours."

Mr. Hoyt tipped forward threateningly. "Others may sit meekly by while their property is plundered, but I will not, sir. I will not!"

Mr. MacIver stood his ground. "And how do you propose visitin' your punishment upon the scoundrels?"

"I will not be mocked, sir!" Mr. Hoyt fumed. "It couldn't be more obvious! Pursue them without delay! Run them to ground, as one does any vermin!"

My own anger, though strongly mixed with desolation, was not far short of my partner's.

"Mr. Hoyt." Mr. MacIver stayed calm. "May I remind you that, however much we might find it lacking, this country is their home. They know every pebble and stick the way you know the back of your hand. They can melt into it the way rain soaks into sand."

"But we have horses!" Mr. Hoyt blurted.

Now Mr. MacIver's voice took on a sterner tone. "What we *don't* have, sir, is time. The longer we take to get to the mountains, and get over 'em, the greater our chances of getting buried in snow. It's already late in the season. I've seen it snow in those mountains as early as August. We're halfway through September, sittin' right here."

"But how are we to carry on without our team?" Mr. Hoyt was almost pleading.

Mr. MacIver said, even more quietly, "I suggest you turn your considerable energies to choosing what you want to carry on your back. If you don't dither, you should be able to catch up." And he walked away.

"You can't leave us here!" Mr. Hoyt yelped.

"I don't want to, but that's up to you," Mr. MacIver called out over his shoulder.

I chased after him and asked, "How many days should we provide for?"

He swung around, giving me a hard look. "I thought you was smarter'n that."

I was startled and confused. "I don't know how long it will…"

Mr. MacIver broke in, very cross. "Goin' after your critters when it would do no good. Puttin' yourself out there for target practice with nothin' to lose but your hide."

That shut me up. I felt five years old. But he was right. "Yessir. I understand. It won't happen again."

"See to it." He settled back. "Fifteen days, give or take."

I gawped at him like a fresh-caught fish.

He explained. "It ain't much as the crow flies. It's climbin' up the ridges and down the canyons after we leave the river that adds the time." He turned and strode off.

I was shaking in my boots. I didn't want to get left behind. *What if we couldn't catch up? What if…* I stopped thinking right away. I let down the tailgate of our wagon. We would have to be much more ruthless in our decisions than ever before. I figured if we spread everything out on the ground we could make our decisions quicker. When I said this to Mr. Hoyt, he just growled and waved his hand dismissively.

I started by throwing aside all the grass we had just cut. My heart wrenched, but at least I didn't start crying again.

Quentin Miller came over. "My team could sure make use of your grass, Pegg."

I said, "Sure. Help yourself."

Mr. Hoyt spoke up. "Not so fast. What's it worth to you, Miller?"

Mr. Miller spread his hands in appeal. "I've got no money left. I just thought…"

"We have nothing for freeloaders. Be off with you," came the sharp reply.

I stared at Mr. Hoyt. What had gotten into him? There was no cause for that.

Mr. Miller shot me a glance and turned away.

Then Linnaeus came and got his banjo, which set off Mr. Hoyt as if I'd hidden a hod of bricks on him. "And you kept carping at me to lighten the load! This bodes ill, boy." He looked around at the stuff already out of the wagon. "It bodes ill."

I kept emptying the wagon while he sputtered and fumed, demanding to know what other trickery I had pulled on him. Finally, he threw up his hands and stomped off.

Bugle inspected everything as I set it out on the ground. He didn't seem worried. I scolded myself that I should be able to keep my wits about me, too. But the truth was, my mind was choked with panic. Our chances of making it to California were now in grave jeopardy. Our only provisions would be what we could carry. Food and clothing, nothing more. If we misjudged and ran out of anything, we would be at the mercy of our companions, or the land itself.

I looked at everything that had been in the wagon. It was but a fraction of what we had packed back home, but it seemed now a king's ransom. Now we would have to pick a few essentials of what was left and hoist it on our backs. I called to Mr. Hoyt to come look, but he just growled and kicked at the dust where he was.

Mr. MacIver came by when I was looking over my clothes, trying to decide.

"If takin' care of your animals was important to keeping your wagon going, then takin' care of your feet is important to keeping *you* going," he said.

"Socks," I said.

Mr. MacIver nodded and went on his way. I set aside every pair of socks I had. I set out fifteen days worth of bacon. Then I doubled that for Bugle's portion. Bugle, for his part, had seen this frenzied activity before, seven months ago in Vermont, and he had the good sense to watch from the sidelines.

To my surprise, Mr. Hoyt had his pack made up in no time at all. I was afraid he might leave me. He stood up with the pack on his back and staggered backward, arms windmillling. He almost fell over. Even worse, the pack came apart and spilled to the ground. He cursed and kicked his gear and waved his fists around. Then he dropped to his knees and tried again. The same thing happened when he stood up the second time. This time, he only stared down at the wreckage. I offered to help.

Mr. Hoyt scowled, "Tend to yourself, Pegg-boy. I've got this licked."

The first pack I made was too heavy to even lift. I was sure I had been ruthless in my choices. I would have to be more ruthless yet. I had just laid out my choices again when Mr. MacIver called for everyone to start. Panic gripped me anew.

He came over to us. "Trail's clear enough. If you don't catch up to us tonight, you'll catch us sleeping in the morning."

Mr. Hoyt all but whined. "It ain't right, leaving us like this. What difference will a couple of hours make, if you wait for us."

Mr. MacIver gave him a level look. "It could make all the difference." He turned back to me. "It's awful dusty out there. Careful with your water."

"Yessir. Thank you, sir," I said.

Mr. Hoyt waited until Mr. MacIver was gone before he spoke. "MacIver's right, Son. We ought to think about saving water where we can."

"We don't have the oxen to worry about anymore," I said. "We should be all right. We just have to be thrifty."

Mr. Hoyt rubbed his chin. "Well, Son. I don't know if you've noticed, but the mutt there is awful thirsty for his size."

Anger struck me out of nowhere like a hammer. "You don't worry about Bugle, you hear? You worry about yourself. He can have part of my portion, if that's what's worrying you!"

Mr. Hoyt held up his hands in defense, turning his head. "Whoa, now! Whoa! Whatever you say. It was just a thought. No need to get your back up."

I realized I had made fists. I relaxed them. "What were you thinking? Leaving him behind?"

"We don't know what lies ahead, lad," Mr. Hoyt replied calmly. "It could be the most humane thing."

"I'll go without if I have to. We're not leaving him."

Mr. Hoyt got some of his bluster back. "Just trying to think about surviving this misery, is all. Forget I said anything." He bent to rummage through his gear.

The sight of the rest of our party leaving put a great fear in me, but it also spurred me on. Once I got it to where I could lift it, I stood up with my pack on—and it fell apart, just like Mr. Hoyt's first time. I fought down my fear and tried a different arrangement. After the third try, I had one that worked.

I ended up with a pack that weighed about eighty pounds and stood almost as tall as me. Aside from my socks, it was mostly food: beans, rice, bacon, and some hard biscuits. I figured there wouldn't be much time for making biscuits or griddle cakes, so I didn't take flour. I packed the makings for around a hundred rounds of ammunition for the Colt. I had my bedroll and a change of clothes, and a pair of long johns. I included the cook pot and a cup and spoon. I figured the cup could do double duty for drinking and eating.

In the end, I had to choose between "The Tempest" and my dad's violin. *I can always buy another copy of the book, but I'll never be able to replace my dad's violin.* I found Will lurking in a corner of my mind. *Your ma doesn't know about the book, but she'd never abide you leaving your dad's violin behind.*

I wrapped it in a heavy coat I had for the coldest parts of the mountains and tied it onto everything else. By now it was all but dark, so I built a fire for us to work by.

Mr. Hoyt was so frustrated trying to get a good pack made he was almost in tears, although he would never admit to it. He was slamming things around, yanking on ropes, cursing a blue streak. I began to wonder if we'd ever get on our way. I went over to him.

"Can I try?"

He threw down a pair of bright blue suspenders and got out of the way, muttering, "Ain't right at all…"

It went against the grain of everything I was used to, but I didn't ask his opinion on anything. I packed the same things for Mr. Hoyt I had packed for myself. I used what I had learned from making up my own pack, so we had him ready to go pretty quick. We wrapped some extra cloth around the ropes so they wouldn't bite so badly into his shoulders.

I took a last look at our once-cheerful wagon. It seemed to shift and wobble in the wavering firelight. The relentless desert sun had bleached the color away. It was now only a box, shrunken, splintering, useless without a team to pull it. And it would sit there, surrounded by all that we couldn't take, crumbling under countless suns and countless moons. Maybe chewed at by people who needed firewood, maybe just left to rot, like so many others. I promised myself, no matter how merciless the sun, no matter how thirsty I got, or how rugged the mountains, I would not end that way.

We stepped away from the flickering light into darkness. The ground still gave back heat from the day. The parched clay appeared ghostly pale under our feet. Thankfully, a quarter moon rose to give us a little light. It took some doing to get used to the packs on our backs, but Mr. Hoyt's spirits lifted considerably now that we were underway.

"That scurvy mountain man thinks he can get the better of us! We'll show him, won't we, Pegg-boy! Thinks he can just traipse off and leave us to the wolves."

Mr. Hoyt may have had more such thoughts but recited them to himself, which suited me just fine. We had gone only a couple of hundred yards, and he was already breathing hard.

Thousands of wagon wheels, and even more feet, had ground the clay to a fine powder, with countless cowpats pulverized into the mix. This awful concoction billowed up into the air at the slightest disturbance. It got in your nose and stung your eyes. My teeth and the inside of my mouth felt coated with chalk. Even so, I wanted to see how long I could go without a drink of water. I put a small round pebble in my mouth and sucked on it. It was a trick Mr. MacIver had showed me. It held thirst at bay.

Having no such exercise in mind, Mr. Hoyt drank liberally from his canteen. I couldn't criticize him for refreshing himself so often, but I wanted to hold out as long as I could.

I couldn't expect Bugle to suck on a pebble, so I gave him a drink once in a while.

There was little chance of getting lost. Indeed, on each side of the trail lay heaps of wagon castoffs and dead animals. The buzzing, squawking scavengers scattered at our approach and returned after we passed. The sickly, sour stench of decay all but overwhelmed us.

We tramped steadily for three hours or more, walking wide apart, each lost in our own thoughts.

Then Mr. Hoyt said, "Pegg-lad, I'm completely parched. Do you think you could spare me a sip from your canteen?"

I jumped. The only sound for the longest while had been the creak of our packs. I fought an instinct to refuse, but then I thought of him refusing Mr. Miller the discarded grass. I wouldn't be that way. I handed him my canteen, and he took a good swig and rinsed out his mouth with noisy sloshing sounds and spat it out. I stared at him, disbelieving. Then he took another swig, swallowed that, and handed back my canteen.

"Ahhhh, thank you, lad, thank you. Much obliged. That was sorely needed." He gave me a hearty grin. "I'll pay you back when we get to the Carson River." And then he laughed.

I set myself to thinking of ways I could refuse the next time.

Mr. Hoyt and I walked all night. He never asked for another drink, and took only small sips from his own canteen. The angle he held it while he drank told me it was over half full. Why did he ask me for water when he had his own? He had a devilish streak I'd better be careful of.

An hour after sunrise we could just make out a tiny lump of dark on the bleached horizon. It didn't move, so we figured—we hoped—it was Mr. MacIver and the others. It was already boiling hot. I tied a kerchief around my head and jammed my hat back on. Even so, sweat ran in my eyes. Between Bugle and myself, my canteens were nearly empty. The distant lump grew slowly, steadily bigger and we could make out a few threads of smoke.

Somehow, Mr. Hoyt found a last scrap of energy to pick up his lurching pace. When we were still a hundred yards from them, Mr. MacIver came out to greet us. "Good to see you. Make yourselves your supper and get some sleep. We're about half a day's march from the Carson River."

Everyone else in our party was already bedded down for the day, trying their best to sleep in the broiling heat.

I asked around and managed to get at least one canteen refilled, a little here, a little there. I would have to make that last for Bugle and me to the Carson River. When we started off that night, I walked with Linnaeus instead of Mr. Hoyt. Let him waste somebody else's water.

We came to the Carson Sink before we came to the Carson River. The river ended its travels out of the mountains the same way the Humboldt River did, losing itself in a vast marshland. We stopped only long enough to top up our water supplies. I noticed Mr. Hoyt empty his canteens and refill them with fresh water. I wondered once again why he'd asked me for water when he still had some.

We reached the Carson River at midnight and forded it to follow the south bank. The waxing moon gave us even more light to travel by. We stopped at sunrise and camped. Mr. MacIver gathered us together again for one of his talks.

"We'll stay put here until tomorrow morning, no need to be stumbling around these mountains in the dark." Mr. MacIver held up his hand. He had more to say. "We'll be back to traveling by day from here on out. We're going to follow the Carson River up into the mountains to its headwaters. We'll take the west fork when we get to it, then go over the crest at Carson's Pass and down into the Sacramento Valley to Sutter's trading post."

Those who still had some spare energy managed a feeble cheer.

"Sounds easy, don't it?" Mr. MacIver challenged, eyebrows arching high. "Well, these mountains give meanin' to the word mean. Up ahead there's places where the trail ain't a trail at all, just a space with littler rocks set between bigger rocks! Those of you who still have wagons will be wishing you didn't. You will be praying for just one square inch of level ground."

"I thought we've just been through the meanest part of the country?" Quentin Miller called out.

"That was flat and hot mean. This country comin' up is steep and cold mean. Steep as a barn wall and every bit as keen to lick you."

"It ain't licked us, yet," Jess Riley called out.

"That's the spirit!" Mr. MacIver grinned. "May the Great Mystery smile upon you, my son."

"I plan on it," replied Mr. Riley.

I had to chuckle at that, and hope I possessed the same grit.

Mr. MacIver went on. "And if there ain't already enough to love about this country, nature has seen fit to provide us a welcoming committee, in the form of the mountain lion and the grizzly bear."

No mischief danced in his eye. That sobered me up right quick. A glance around told me everyone was equally intent.

"And that's if we don't meet any wolves first," Mr. MacIver said.

He was more serious than I'd ever seen him. A shiver went down my spine.

Mr. MacIver had a hard set to his jaw. "I cannot say this enough ways or enough times, gentlemen. Keep your eyes peeled. The mountain lion will drop on you from a branch overhead silent as a snowflake. The grizz' is as big as a house, has bad eyesight, and a worse temper when it comes to havin' his peace disturbed."

My dad had sharp eyes, if only he were here. I wished I could grow eyes in the back of my head. I looked down at Bugle. He could be my extra pair of eyes.

Our guide looked around the crowd. "Mr. Averill!"

Mr. Averill called out. "Yo."

"How much you weigh?"

"One hundred and seventy pounds, give or take," Mr. Averill replied cheerfully. "Why?"

"Most of the time, the grizz' lives on gophers and squirrels, berries, and fish. Think on what a feast a hunnert and seventy pounds of Thomas Averill would make, should he happen to stumble in the critter's way."

Here Mr. MacIver reached into his buckskin shirt and pulled out a long piece of curved, discolored ivory suspended from a leather thong. It had a knob where the thong went through. The other end came to a sharp point. "This here's a grizzly bear's claw," he said, holding it up. It was easily five inches long. "This animal comes equipped with twenty of 'em, five on each foot, and he knows how to use 'em."

As was my habit, I stood close to the guide, so I got a good look at the ferocious claw.

MacIver held the claw higher. "Both these critters are capable of shredding you like soft cheese. It's not a pleasant way to go." He put the claw away. "The western face of the Sierra Nevada has plenty of dense forest, broken country, and steep canyons, all favorite haunts of the cat and the bear." He looked around. "So, I say again, gentlemen, keep your eyes open."

Men drifted away.

MacIver turned to me. "You keep your hound close, hear? No explorin' for him."

"Yessir." I called Bugle in close.

We kept to the bottomland by the river as much as we could, but the farther we went, the higher the land rose, and the channel the river had cut grew deeper and narrower. Eventually, the trail climbed up away from the river and over the shoulders of the dull yellow hills. Even so, we were roughly following the river.

The higher we climbed, the cooler the air became. For that we were all grateful. We could see pine trees spreading down from the tops of the hills ahead. The trail and the river veered sharply south. I checked my compass and thought to ask Mr. MacIver about it. But I saw him helping a man who had stumbled, and figured he didn't need any guff from me. *He knows the way. Shut up and walk.*

Each ridge we topped brought another into view, higher yet, all covered in ancient forest. The air carried the scent of pine and cedar, not heat and decay. In plenty of places our path met one of Mr. MacIver's barn walls of sheer bare rock. Those places we helped unload the wagons and knock them down into their separate parts. Then *it all* had to be hoisted up the cliff face with the ropes, reassembled and reloaded before we could move on. We'd done that once or twice in the Rocky Mountains. In the Sierra Nevada we did it two, maybe three times *a day.*

The forests of those mountains held none of the trees I was used to back home. In Vermont we had our great beech trees and spreading maples, mighty oaks and elms, but few of those could match the girth, much less the solemn majesty of the trees through which our company moved. The groves were filled with pines that reached the sky, rising on trunks more massive than I could ever have imagined.

I stepped out of line for a moment. Linnaeus came to stand beside me, gazing around in awe, as I was.

"It looks like this place has been here since the beginning of time. Pristine." Linnaeus pointed to a trunk that had to be ten feet across where it met the ground. "Even the Black Forest," he said in a hushed voice, "which is a wondrous place, has nothing to compare to this."

I rested my hand on the slabs of thick, crusty bark. It seemed like ancient, cracked hide. What's more, the trees were free of limbs to many feet above the ground. Good lumber trees. In the still, shaded groves the air was moist and cool, spiced with resin. The forest floor was free of undergrowth. Young trees grew beside old, standing placidly cheek by jowl.

MacIver approached us, heading back to urge on stragglers. "They're called sugar pines." As he drew abreast he spoke in a quiet voice. "Like bein' in church, ain't it?" And went on his way.

I looked up again at the lofty branches. He was right. I wished my dad could see these trees. I knew he would marvel. *Will is never going to believe me when I pace off the breadth of one of these trunks for him.*

The trees cloaked the ridges and crowded the canyons. At the bottom of the gorges, we clambered across rambunctious streams that surged around boulders and under logs fallen like jackstraws. We were constantly climbing or sliding, often separated from the wagons.

They were forced to seek out paths that would allow the passage of their wheels. I had pity for the teams, who had already plodded limitless miles, and were now asked to struggle over country that, as Mr. MacIver promised, held not one square inch of level ground!

We lost over half the remaining wagons in the mountains, tipping and tumbling down mountainsides, taking their doomed teams with them. If the men could reach their wreckage, Mr. MacIver rushed them into a quick assembly of the most essential provisions. Our company of gold seekers quickly became a ragtag army of backpackers.

Charity was, indeed, in short supply. But my friend Linnaeus, even though he had lost his horse and most of his gear, never lost his good will. Many evenings he would regale us with lively tunes: "A Ripping Trip," "Joe Bowers," or "Jim along Josey." The weary travelers, gathered around fires fueled with wrecked wagon parts, sang or tapped time, smiling, forgetting the trials of the day.

On one such evening, Linnaeus was dealt another blow, I think more grievous than the loss of his mount. He had just begun to play a request for "Old Virginia Shore" when out of the shadows stumbled Mr. Hoyt. His lurch showed all too clearly that he had got hold of too much liquor. This wasn't the first time, but it soon proved to be the worst yet.

"Who's makin' that infernal racket?" he bawled as he advanced. He stopped, weaving, in front of Linnaeus. He made an exaggerated expression of surprise.

Is he drawing on his days on the showboats? He clearly expects appreciation for his antics. Only a few of the audience laughed, some uncomfortably.

"Why, if it ain't the exalted perfesser, hisself." He leered around at the others, his arms flailing. "When he ain't lookin' down from his high horse." Mr. Hoyt's eyes popped wide and his hand flew to cover the "o" he made with his mouth. "Oh, I forgot." He hunched over, leering. "He ain't got his horse no more!" He swung to take in the laughter he expected. When none came, he caught his balance and bawled at the circle of men. "And when he ain't feedin' us a bunch of hornswoggle about places ain't nobody seen but *himmm*," he flung an accusing finger at Linnaeus, "he's bangin' out what he's pleased to call music on that gut box of his." He snatched the banjo from Linnaeus's hands.

Everybody froze.

Almost halfway round the circle, I leapt to my feet.

Linnaeus lunged up at Mr. Hoyt to take his banjo back. Mr. Hoyt yanked out of his reach and staggered in my direction. I watched aghast while my drunken partner thrashed at the banjo in a horrible parody of playing, bellowing and slurring the lyrics to "Sweet Betsy from Pike."

At the right moment I stepped out to grab him. He shied, his eyes rolling wildly, and jerked the banjo away from my reach. He weaved and turned, dancing his way around the onlookers, pulling and scraping at the strings. I trailed him, inching closer for another chance to grab the instrument.

One of the Baines men, his pale blue jacket threadbare, stepped out of the circle to intercept Mr. Hoyt. A slightly-built fellow, he could not hope to match Mr Hoyt's strength. The drunk swung the banjo at him like an axe. The Baines man threw up his arms in defense and fell back. Mr. Hoyt stumbled on his way, waving the banjo over his head.

When he came around again, Linnaeus stood in his way and grabbed for the banjo. Mr. Hoyt reared back, eluding his grasp, lost his balance, and tumbled into the fire.

Linnaeus twisted to follow Mr. Hoyt's fall, not to rescue his banjo, but Mr. Hoyt. Only a step behind, I reached in to help drag him clear. Mr. Marbuger and Joe Porter reached in, too, braving the flames to save the drunk.

We pounded on him with hats and hands to put out his burning clothes and smoldering hair. The drunk, heedless of his plight, thought he was under attack and fought back accordingly. Someone brought a blanket, and we rolled him in it despite his protests. At last, he quieted. Everyone heaved a sigh of relief when it became clear that Mr. Hoyt had, miraculously, suffered no more than singed hair and scorched clothes.

Linnaeus's banjo had not fared as well. I looked over to see my friend sitting on the same keg, cradling the charred remains of the instrument in his lap, staring at them in disbelief. I stepped closer. The neck had broken clean off and was still in the fire, and the pot he held was in sad shape. I could smell the burnt skin of the head on the night air. Somewhere in the embers the bridge and the tailpiece, which anchored the strings, were being consumed. The strings had burned away as fast as the head.

Linnaeus looked up at me, his eyes wide and wet and staring. I'd seen people who'd lost children look like that. I'm not even sure he saw me.

"I'm sorry, Linnaeus. Almighty sorry." I wanted to apologize for Mr. Hoyt. But what good would that do? It wouldn't restore the banjo. "I wish…"

Linnaeus rose to his feet; I stepped back. He went to the fire and dropped the remains of his banjo into the flames. Then he paced off into the darkness.

Mr. Hoyt began to snore.

In the morning, even with a roaring headache to remind him, Mr. Hoyt claimed no recollection of the calamity. After my rendition of the events, I pointed to his burnt clothes. "If you don't want to believe *me*, ask Mr. MacIver or Mr. Marburger."

Mr. Hoyt picked at his charred coat sleeve. "Who pulled me out of the fire?"

"Linnaeus. Mr. Marburger and Joe Porter helped him."

A strange kind of shame kept me from including myself among his rescuers. Wasn't it enough that I had to be his partner?

Mr. Hoyt jerked his head with a smirk. "For once his majesty made himself useful."

I knew he meant Linnaeus. Anger swelled in my throat. "Yes. He chose to save you instead of his banjo." Will leered at me in my mind. *Not sure he made the best choice.*

Mr. Hoyt rolled onto one hip, as if preparing to get to his feet. "Well, now he'll have less weight to carry. He ought to be grateful." Mr. Hoyt held out his hand like he wanted help up.

I stayed where I was.

He clambered to his feet by his own unsteady effort and tottered off to relieve himself.

Linnaeus didn't come around for some days. I let him be, taking some of the blame on myself. It was little enough I could do.

It grew steadily colder the higher we went. I quickly forgot the scorching heat of the desert.

Mr. MacIver urged us on with fearsome tales of early blizzards and snowdrifts five times the height of a man. I think everyone was thankful for the plentiful fuel and water. I was. We built hearty fires in the evenings to ward off the cold. Some wore every last scrap of clothing they possessed. I looked around at the circle of huddled men, some clasping steaming cups of coffee, others holding out their hands for warmth. Gaunt, hollow-eyed faces stared into the flames. Only the eerie howling of the wolves rose above the crackling and snapping of the fires.

CHAPTER 21

Having gained the rockiest heights, we awoke one morning to a low ceiling of grey clouds. Mr. MacIver moved through the camp, jabbing the muzzle of his rifle at the clouds. "This is snow, gentlemen, any time now. Get your fannies moving. We can't outrun it, but every thousand feet farther down we can get, the less she'll dump on us."

He instructed the back packers to follow the ravine until we met an intersecting stream, and to wait there for him to bring the wagons down. Linnaeus and Bill Marburger went to help with the wagons.

Large, soft snowflakes began drifting down. The ground was soon white and slippery. With no wind, wet snow piled up where it landed, and the world fell into a hush. Some backpackers were cautious, others less so. Many skidded and fell, their heavy packs pulling them down.

In two hours, the snow became too deep for Bugle. I scooped him up and carried him under my arm.

As we entered the trees, I thought they might shelter us a little from the snow, but we were not so fortunate, fighting our way through knee-deep drifts. Our line of march spread out along the narrow trail. The figures ahead of me took on a ghostly appearance.

Mr. Hoyt was behind me. I glanced back every few minutes to make sure he was coming along. There were others behind him, but I could not see them.

I came upon one of the Baines men trying to repack his gear. To my dismay, it was the same fellow who had tried to help save Linnaeus' banjo. It was pretty clear the man's pack had come apart on him. Tears streamed down his face. From frustration? Fear? Another Baines man, a companion, knelt beside him, but merely held a pair of socks. I'm not proud to admit my own fear kept me from stopping to help.

I passed under the low branch of a tree that leaned out over the trail. A moment later, I heard a cry of alarm behind me and turned to see the last of Mr. Hoyt tumbling over the edge of the trail and out of sight.

I dropped Bugle and ran back to the spot where he'd disappeared.

Mr. Hoyt lay still about ten feet down in a narrow gully.

I shrugged off my pack and clambered down to him.

Mr. Hoyt was crumpled under his pack, his teeth gritted, eyes squeezed tight. At least he was alive. He started to move, but that ended quick enough in a howl of pain. He froze and blinked his eyes open.

I crouched down so he could see my face. "Where are you hurt?"

"My leg." He groaned.

I glanced at his baggy trousers and dusty boots. Nothing odd. "What happened?"

"Blasted rock moved," Mr. Hoyt replied through his grimace.

Can't gainsay that. Rocks have moved on me, too. "Can you get up?" I rose to my feet, ready to help.

He only began, but yelped in pain, slumping back to the ground with clenched teeth.

Panic swelled in my chest. I looked around. I looked up. A lone figure, indistinct in the flurries, trudged by on the trail above.

They can't just leave us! "Wait!" I yelled. "Wait!"

The man paused in his struggles, peering down at us. "I'll send MacIver back when I get to the bottom," he said, and moved on.

The people coming after gave us a glance as they passed, but no one stopped. How could I expect compassion when I, given the chance, had offered none?

Still, I called out. "Please! Could you help us?" They barely slowed down. "Tell Mr. MacIver that Mr. Hoyt's hurt!"

What if they don't? What if they're too concerned with their own safety? What if Mr. MacIver decides it isn't worth risking the safety of the party to come back for two of us?

Snow kept falling. It was beginning to collect on Mr. Hoyt. I brushed it off him. I felt completely helpless. I watched the trail and called for help whenever anybody stumbled past.

Mr. Hoyt tried to help my appeals. "Stop!" he bawled, his voice rattling with frustration. He didn't say anything else. Perhaps he thought better of abusing any would-be rescuers.

The last of the stragglers hurried by. I hoped for one more, but we were alone.

I was sick with fear. I gave Mr. Hoyt a drink of water. "Would it help to take off your pack?"

He made a noise that sounded like he meant "Yes."

Mr. Hoyt winced and yelped at every turn, but we got it off him. I unpacked his bed roll and spread the blanket over him. Then I wedged the pack behind him for a rough pillow.

He settled his head back. "Obliged, lad," he croaked.

I turned to climb out of the gully. He grumbled behind me. "So you're abandoning me, too?"

Will sneered in a dark corner of my mind. *What a wretch. A pure wretch.* I could manage only, "No. I'll be back." I regained the trail, gathered up Bugle, got my bedroll from my pack, and climbed down to rejoin Mr. Hoyt.

After gathering the blanket around my shoulders as a cloak, I looked at his trousers again. It was hard to tell anything was amiss. At least there was no blood. "Which leg is it?"

He tapped gingerly at his left limb.

"Do you think it's broken?"

Mr. Hoyt clenched his teeth. "Don't be daft, Boy! Of course it is."

I had no wish to question his judgment.

We were in a real fix. Dr. Yarborough was on his way to Oregon. I couldn't just sit and wait. "I'll go and get Mr. MacIver."

Mr. Hoyt grabbed my sleeve. "They'll send someone back. Just sit tight."

"But Mr. MacIver will know what to do."

"Don't leave me, lad," Mr. Hoyt all but begged. "There's wolves."

He had the same fear I did. *Who will reach us first, Mr. MacIver or the predators?*

"If I go now, I can bring him back sooner."

"No, boy, no." Mr. Hoyt grasped my sleeve all the harder. "You've got to stay. It's our only hope."

Now he wasn't even making sense. I sat quiet. I imagined MacIver coming into the rendezvous and hearing about us. I scratched Bugle. I checked the Colt. Then I had an idea, and rose to my feet.

He grabbed my pant leg. "Where are you going?"

"I'm going to look for wood to make splints." I didn't know much about setting broken bones, but I knew there were splints to keep everything in place.

"Don't go far. Stay where I can see you." Desperation colored his speech.

I knelt beside Bugle and scrubbed his ears. "You are the best dog in the whole world. I'm going to give you a medal for patience when we get out of this."

Bugle thumped his tail and whined. I could tell he was worried. "Can you wait a little longer? Just a little. Mr. MacIver will be here soon. Okay? Wait just a little longer." I gave him a hug. "I have to look for some wood. Stay here and keep Mr. Hoyt company."

I climbed back up to my pack to get my axe.

"Stay where I can see you, Pegg-boy, hear?" Mr. Hoyt called again.

The snowflakes made it difficult to see him clearly. "Yessir," I said.

I looked around, trying to spot saplings, or low branches, that were straight and just the right thickness. I had to explore a bit, but I kept my pack in view. I wasn't going to make the mistake I'd made back on the prairie.

Mr. Hoyt kept calling out, "Pegg?" or, "You there?"

"Yessir. Almost done."

Pretty soon, I collected five pieces. Two sticks from deadfall, already on the ground. Two were saplings and one was a branch off a tree. I trimmed the branches off the saplings and cut everything to the same length, grateful for taking on my Dad's habit of keeping tools sharp. I whittled one side of each splint flat to fit against his leg, then propped them against my pack so we could find them.

I dug my extra trousers out of my pack and cut lengths for tying on the splints. I figured it was sturdier cloth than my shirt.

Finally, I could think of no more to do—except wait, hope and worry. Big flakes drifted down in deathly silence. Anything that didn't move wore a tall crown of snow.

I brushed snow off Mr. Hoyt, who appeared to be sleeping.

It grew colder and the weak light dimmed. There was no telling how long it would take Mr. MacIver to get the wagons down to the rendezvous. I shrugged off my blanket and laid it over Mr. Hoyt. He was shivering.

He managed only a groggy mumble. "Good lad, good lad. Much obliged. Much…"

"Mr. MacIver should be here soon," I said.

"If they don't just leave us."

My partner's despair scared me so, I could make no reply. I just hoped like crazy he was wrong. I looked up at the snow coming down through the tangled branches. Would it ever let up? Making a fire was impossible; I couldn't find anything dry enough. There was nothing else to do but hunker down and wait. I gathered Bugle close for warmth, fighting off grim thoughts of what darkness would bring.

The trees were ink-black silhouettes and the sky a deepening grey when a sharp whistle split the air. Bugle stood up and barked in reply. Was it a bird call? I got to my feet. Another whistle. Relief swept through me. It was a ways off, down the trail. The whistle sounded again. Mr. Hoyt stirred.

I yelled, "Here!" and scrambled back up to the trail.

Bugle sent up a frantic bark. I yelled again. "Here!"

Soon Mr. MacIver came into view. He had Linnaeus Peabody and Bill Marburger with him.

I waved my arms and yelled, "Here!"

"Settle down, Sonny," Mr. MacIver shouted with a smile. "We got you in our sights, sure enough." He walked up, jerking his thumb at his two companions. "I would have brought the President and the Congress, but they were busy."

I couldn't stop grinning. "Thank you, sir." I turned to the other two. "Thank you, thank you."

Mr. MacIver gazed down at Mr. Hoyt. "So your partner's got himself in a fix, has he?" And he began to climb down to him.

"He slipped on a rock." I scuttled down after him. "He's broken his leg."

Mr. MacIver made no reply. He squatted next to Mr. Hoyt and flipped the bedding aside.

Mr. Hoyt touched his left leg without being asked.

Mr. MacIver sliced through the trouser and long johns and carefully pulled off the boot. Probing very gently, he found the break in the lower leg; a large lump on the outside of Mr. Hoyt's calf that shouldn't have been there.

"Broke, all right," Mr. MacIver observed. He glanced up at Mr. Hoyt's ashen face. "You're lucky." Without explaining why, he turned to me. "Them sticks and bandages up there your handiwork?"

"Yessir, I thought…"

He interrupted me in a low voice, "Worthy, worthy." He tapped his temple with his finger. He turned to look up to Linnaeus and Mr. Marburger.

"You boys mind bringin' those splints and bandages down here? We'll get this here argonaut put right and be on our way."

"You'll take us with you, won't you?" I asked.

If he heard the fear in my voice, he let it pass. "With all that gold waiting for you?" he answered with a grin. "Now, how could we not?"

With Mr. Marburger and Linnaeus holding Mr. Hoyt down— practically sitting on him—and him yelling and screaming and cussing, Mr. MacIver pulled on the leg and set it. He placed the splints and held them while I tied them up.

Mr. MacIver sat back on his heels, regarding Mr. Hoyt. He spoke with genuine sympathy, "I sure do hope you have better luck on the creeks than you're havin' in these mountains."

It was even more of a chore hauling Mr. Hoyt and his trussed-up leg back up onto the trail. Bill Marburger offered to carry Mr. Hoyt's pack down to the camp. With Mr. MacIver on one side of Mr. Hoyt and Linnaeus on the other, they set off down the trail. Watching them push through the drifts, I marveled that Linnaeus would even offer his aid, after Mr. Hoyt had so wantonly destroyed his beloved banjo. That speculation only raised my esteem for the teacher all the more.

I rolled up the blankets, tied them on my pack, and hurried after with Bugle under my arm. There was four feet of snow now, and still more sifted down. I was lucky they were breaking trail for me.

Because of the delay, we camped at the rendezvous point, and Mr. MacIver made Mr. Hoyt a proper crutch.

Brushing aside Mr. Hoyt's thanks, MacIver grinned. "You can buy me a steak dinner if we see each other in San Francisco." Then he scowled. "But you got to get there first."

Mr. Hoyt could no longer support a full pack, so, once again we set to the unwelcome task of reducing his kit to what he could manage. Mr. MacIver stopped by and regarded my glum partner and then his belongings. "Save his vittles and chuck the rest. We're not more'n a few days from someplace he can buy clothes."

Mr. Hoyt jerked his head but said nothing.

I said, "Thank you again, for everything." But Mr. MacIver was already turning to go about other business.

We settled on twenty pounds of food and socks and an extra shirt. At the last I added Mr. Hoyt's canteen. I wanted him making use of his own water.

The next day, even with the lighter load, Mr. Hoyt had to learn to walk with a crutch, a process he accompanied with many an oath. Linnaeus offered to lend a hand however he could and, though rebuffed by the cranky invalid, stayed with us. We quickly fell behind the others. Following the trampled snow kept us from getting lost. And it finally stopped snowing.

I was happy Linnaeus continued to walk with Mr. Hoyt and me, because my partner wasn't in a very talkative mood. Besides, Linnaeus had so many wonderful things to tell. I didn't realize at the time that I was getting an education in the bargain. He was careful to point out which was legend and which was fact, but it was all a great feast to me.

Two days later, in the afternoon, we topped a ridge. Looking west, every ridge ahead of us was lower than we were. When the light began to fade, Mr. MacIver stopped in a clearing and announced it would be our camp. I found a gap among the towering trees where I could see the setting sun: *Almost got you, now.*

After our supper, Mr. MacIver called us together for another talk. "If you ain't smelled the gold by now, you got a dull sniffer," he started with a grin. "In a day or so we'll be in the gold country. Now, I'm supposed to take you as far as Sutter's Fort, and I'll do that for those who desire it. But I'm here to tell you you'd be wastin' your time. The hills below are peppered with towns that are well stocked with what you'll need. It'll be perhaps more expensive than Sutter's, but it'll save you trudgin' halfway across the Sacramento Valley and back again when you can buy your outfit right in the middle of the diggings." Then he grinned again. "And I expect you're right sick of trudgin'."

After getting Mr. Hoyt comfortable for the night, I went to find Linnaeus. He was by another fire with Joe Porter, Mr. Marburger, and Mr. Quincey. When there was a quiet moment, I asked Linnaeus if I might speak with him. "Will you stay with us when we dig for gold?" I asked. "We could be neighbors."

"Ah, Pegg." He held out his palms. "Look at these hands."

I could see they had never done farm work, or any kind of rough work, for that matter.

"I'm not cut out for such work." He smiled like he was apologizing.

"But you came all this way?"

He stretched his arms wide. "I came all this way for a new start, for the opportunities that are everywhere you turn."

"But what will you do?" It was scary to me, how he was talking—no set plan, no goal.

"I'll get work in one of those towns Gideon was talking about, perhaps provide entertainment. Certainly go see what San Francisco has to offer."

"Tell stories?" I said, remembering how he'd entertained me with stories.

Linnaeus laughed gently. "Ah, wouldn't that be wonderful? But I think a jolly tune to dance to, to restore the weary spirit, will be much more in demand."

"But you have no instrument. Your banjo…" I couldn't say the terrible words, *burned up in the fire.*

"I'm sure there will be pianos in some of the establishments, or I can borrow someone's banjo."

"Wait!" I cried and ran off.

I dug through my pack and ran back to him.

"Use this," I said, handing him Dad's fiddle and bow.

Linnaeus reared back in surprise. "Your father's violin?" He took it carefully from my hands. "You've carried it all this way?"

"Yes."

He gazed fondly at the violin, then he looked up and started to hand it back. "That is very kind of you, but I couldn't take it. It was your father's… now yours."

"I never learned to play," I said. "I'll bet he'd be glad it was being used, especially by you." I pressed it gently back toward him.

He ran his palm slowly over the polished wood. "Then I thank you both, with all my heart." His voice trembled. "This is a truly precious gift." He tucked the fiddle under his chin. "It will be a challenge to live up to your father's playing." And he drew the bow across the strings, the same tuning up Dad always did. Like he couldn't stop himself, like it was as natural as drawing breath, Linnaeus played "Rose on the Mountain," my mother's special song, right there and then.

As he drew out the last note and lifted away the bow, he opened his eyes and beamed a smile at me. "Here's an idea. Why don't you come with me? You could sing and I could play the violin." He sat up straighter. "What a team we would be."

It was a wonderful idea. I smiled back for a brief second, then looked at the ground. "I have promises to keep."

He put the violin back in its case. "I understand." And I knew he did. He smiled again. "But if you change your mind, just follow the fiddle music."

In the middle of the night, I almost went and asked for it back. I'm not proud of that moment, but it was the last piece of my dad I had. Without it, I would have nothing. I was too young to put much stock in memories, even though I sure had plenty of them. Whether it was Saturday sociables or on our back porch after a long summer day, my dad's fiddle playing made the time far sweeter than it had any right to be. He always said music was to the soul what well-chosen words were to the mind. Maybe the best way to keep him was to know Linnaeus was giving people what my dad had given them with his violin.

. . .

Finally, the hills began to gentle out. Oak trees started to appear among the pine and cedar—same leaves as oaks back home, but scrawny things. And there were other trees that were new to me. One, with a slender trunk, displayed a smooth, orange bark which seemed to peel easily.

"That's a madrone," Mr. MacIver said, when I asked him.

"Mah-drone." I experimented with it. "Mah-drone."

"That's right. Madrone. It's Spanish. You're gonna find a lot of Spanish names out here. San Francisco, Sacramento, Sierra Nevada, even California itself—they're all Spanish names. The Spanish've been here a long time. We're latecomers. But it's ours now."

The rivers still cut deep canyons. Mr. MacIver informed us that what we easterners called a "gorge," the westerners called a "canyon". That was Spanish, too.

I was pleased to see they had a kind of blue jay here too, as noisy and cheeky as ours back East.

We began to meet miners long before we came to any town. Some were in groups; some alone. Wherever they were, the streams were muddy and the ground all around was torn up, piled and pitted. Above the streams, the hillsides were stripped bare of all but the biggest trees. Every last twig had gone into cooking fires or the construction of crude shelters and cabins. The miners looked as weary and threadbare as we who had just tramped thousands of miles.

I had expected to stumble over nuggets underfoot, to see miners dancing in the streets and celebrating each other's triumphs, to hear joyous shouts filling the air. To the contrary, what I saw before me was a world of relentless drudgery, populated with work-worn men who had no expression but grim determination.

"Don't be fooled," Mr. MacIver smirked. "Like as not, they've got a stash in the express company's safe. With no ladies around to impress, they let the finer points slide. Usually they clean up pretty good."

We were making our way south, following a stream as it tumbled down the hillside.

"This here, what we're followin', is called Simpson's Creek," MacIver said. "It empties into the south fork of the American River."

He had us take a rest and went over and talked to a group of miners. I found a large rock off by itself and helped Mr. Hoyt sit down with his back against it. I handed him his canteen. "Well, it sure is good to be in California, isn't it, Mr. Hoyt?"

He didn't look happy. Hobbling up and down steep terrain on one leg and a crutch had exhausted him, so I wasn't surprised when he said back, "And the sooner we get what we've come for and get home, the happier I'll be."

"Yessir. We'll do that," I said, wanting to lift his spirits. "To be sure. We'll do just that."

He didn't seem interested in conversation, just nodded, closed his eyes, and leaned back. When Mr. MacIver returned, I joined our group to hear what he had to say.

"There's a new town where Simpson's Creek empties into the south fork. About a mile downstream from here. It's called Grizzly Bar, at least for now. They say it's been there most of a year and has everything you need. If you don't like the look of that, you can come on to Sutter's trading post with me."

The sun had dipped behind the western ridge of the canyon we were in, but there was still plenty of light in the sky. Linnaeus and I walked slower than the rest because of Mr. Hoyt. All we really had to do was follow the miners making their way to the town. We came upon a short, burly man with a great scrub of wiry, dark whiskers hiding his chin. He ambled along, his shapeless hat pushed back on his broad round forehead, in no particular hurry, whistling a tune. He, at least, looked content.

He glanced over at our little group: Mr. Hoyt, Linnaeus, Bugle, and me, and broke into a grin. "You folks just arrived?"

Linnaeus answered with good cheer. "That we have, sir, and glad to finally be here."

"Radley's has the best prices," the man offered, adjusting his hat. "Radley's General Merchandise. Tell 'em Caleb Johnson sent you."

"Well, thank you, sir," Linnaeus said, "Thank you kindly. That's much appreciated." Linnaeus turned to me. "Got that? Radley's General Merchandise."

I nodded. "Is this a good spot?" I asked Caleb Johnson.

Mr. Johnson knitted up his brow and repeated my question thoughtfully. "Is this a good spot?" He figured out what I was asking and let out a big belly laugh. "Sonny, far as I know, the whole blamed state is a good spot. I've been on the Feather River, the Yuba, and all three forks of the American. I've got fifty thousand dollars in a bank in San Francisco."

We stared at him, goggle-eyed. It was hard to believe. Fifty thousand dollars was a king's fortune. "You've been at it awhile, then," Linnaeus said.

"Jumped ship in May of '48. The *Enid Claire*, out of Baltimore. The whole crew did," Caleb Johnson declared. "Barney Noble, he was our second mate, Barney was in San Francisco last month and said she was still sittin' there in the bay. She'd been turned into a hotel. He said the whole bay was filled with abandoned ships."

Linnaeus grinned. "Do you suppose there's any gold left for us?"

"There's lots more. You just can't scoop it up with your hand anymore, is all. I'd sell you my claim, but I promised it to Barney when I'm done with it."

"When will you be finished with it?" I asked Mr. Johnson.

Caleb moved closer and dug into his bulging trouser pocket. He brought out a misshapen lump of yellow rock that had a dull gleam. It was about half the size of his thumb. "When it stops producing these." He winked at me. "Here you go, Sonny. Get you off to a good start." He tossed the nugget to me.

I was so surprised, I barely caught it. No sooner had I grasped it than someone called out, "Hey, Mister, you got one of those for me?"

We turned to see, shambling close by, the Baines man I had seen kneeling in the snow, weeping over his ruined pack. He now wore a foolish grin, his spirits apparently revived. His silent friend was again at his side.

Caleb Johnson returned the man's unfettered grin, gave him a rude gesture and no more. He turned back to us in time to see Mr. Hoyt pluck the nugget from my fingers. I started. Mr. Hoyt had not been that lively in days.

"Excuse me, mister," Caleb said with a scowl. "That was meant for the boy."

I caught Linnaeus's frown. I felt bad that storm clouds were gathering again.

Mr. Hoyt studied the nugget without looking at Caleb Johnson. "It's one and the same. We're partners. I'm in charge, if you need to know."

The prospector threw me a glance, one eyebrow cocked up.

"It's okay, Mr. Johnson." I tried to smile. "We're partners, like he said."

Mr. Johnson didn't sound exactly convinced. "If you say so, lad."

I was just glad Mr. Hoyt was coming out of his gloom. He brought the nugget up to his mouth and bit carefully into it with his side teeth. I thought his teeth would shatter. They sank into it!

"Oh, it's the genuine article, all right." Caleb Johnson grinned, his good cheer restored.

Mr. Hoyt put the nugget in his pocket.

Someone called out to Mr. Johnson. He looked off toward a man waving farther down the trail. "Ah! There's Barney." He turned back to us. "Well, good luck to you, gents. Don't forget, Radley's." He gave us a little salute and went off to join his friend.

Linnaeus said to me, "Can you believe it? He gave you a *whole* nugget! Just *gave* it to you!"

Mr. Hoyt grinned at Linnaeus. "Ain't you forgetting something, professor?"

Linnaeus looked at Mr. Hoyt, perplexed. Then he grinned. "Of course! How foolish of me! I meant both of you!"

"Can I see it again?" I asked.

Mr. Hoyt dug the nugget out of his pocket. I cupped it in the palm of my hand, turning it with my finger. It had a nice weight to it. There were Mr. Hoyt's tooth marks. After a minute he took it back and smiled his lopsided smile. "The first of our fortune, eh, Pegg-lad? I'll be banker, just like your Pa wanted. What do you say? This'll be a breeze compared to running a steamboat."

"I should think that the boy could—" Linnaeus began.

But Mr. Hoyt cut him off sharp. "Hold your peace, Professor. This is between the boy and me."

I didn't want bad blood between the two men I counted on. "It's okay, Mr. Peabody. Dad said he should look after the money." I headed down the trail. "Let's go see Grizzly Bar."

We came to the place where Simpson's Creek emptied into the north shore of the river. The south fork of the American River was no Mississippi by any stretch, and it didn't look all that deep. It curved gently off to the southwest. Grizzly Bar was not in sight, but we could hear its noise, off to the right—the sound of music and laughter and loud voices, plus the occasional gunshot. Indeed, it sounded like a big party. We came around a bend and saw a riot of buildings, a riot of people. Most of the buildings were tents of various shapes and sizes. Others were partly tents and partly wood. A few were entirely of wood—logs mostly, very little sawn lumber. They all looked like they had been thrown up in a great hurry.

Signs were attached to every available surface, announcing every kind of business. Haircuts! Beds! Meals! Signs! Dry goods! Some of these signs were fancier than the structures they were stuck to. The dusty street was as crowded with merchandise and supplies as it was with people. We threaded our way through crates of smoked oysters and tinned cheese, piles of mining equipment, barrels of black powder and sacks of rice. I heard a bell coming from one of the buildings and watched a crowd of men rush into it.

Many of the buildings seemed to be hosting their own celebrations. Garish light, tinkling piano music and loud voices spilled from the windows and doorways. Men streamed in and out of these places. Others looked to be asleep on the plank sidewalks. A few sat staring at nothing, as if puzzled at finding themselves here. The air had a sharp tang. I asked Linnaeus, but Mr. Hoyt spoke up first. "Whiskey and piss, Pegg, lad. Whiskey and piss. The stink of foolish men."

I was suddenly struck with the fear of losing Bugle in this crowd. I looked down to see him right at my heel. "Stay close, Boy." Even as I said it, I knew it wasn't all up to him. I asked Linnaeus to get the bit of line I kept for a lead out of my pack.

"That's a very good idea," he said.

With Bugle on his rope, I could concentrate on weaving through the people. Then we had to find Mr. Hoyt, who had kept going.

As we picked our way along the street, full dark settled over us. The scene became a shifting landscape of orange light and ink-black shadow. We came abreast of one place just as a fight tumbled out of the entrance and into the street. We had to jump out of the way. Amidst the rough gaiety, I saw one man consoling another quietly. The second man was hunched over, sobbing wretchedly. I nearly tripped over a man who was sitting in the middle of the street, his legs splayed out in front of him. His battered hat sat primly on his lap. He was singing, no, bellowing, at the top of his voice, heedless of the traffic swirling around him.

If Mom could see what I'm walking through, she'd faint. Then she'd drag me home by my ear.

GRIZZLY BAR

CHAPTER 22

Grizzly Bar had sprung up like a rank weed on the banks of the south fork. And like a weed it was unruly and willy-nilly.

Navigating it at night was even trickier than during the day. Linnaeus stumbled over one of the webs of ropes that anchored this tent city. Farther on, he bumped his head on a piece of lumber sticking out from a construction project. Mr. Hoyt, still learning how to use his crutch, fared little better. He was often jostled by the careless, milling crowd, or had his crutch kicked. At one point, he plunged his crutch into a hole in the road and nearly toppled over. A hand reached out to steady him. This helping hand belonged to a lady. She appeared to be part of the festivities, for she had plumes in her hair and a brightly colored dress. She smiled at us and melted into the crowd as magically as she had appeared.

That solitary lady made me realize Grizzly Bar was a town composed almost entirely of men. If there were more ladies in this town, they must be inside the buildings. And I had seen no children.

In all this bustle, there was a confusion of different languages, too. True, you heard foreign tongues on the emigrant trail, speech that Linnaeus said was Swedish or German, but they were few. Here in Grizzly Bar it seemed like every other mouth spouted a colorful gibberish. *How do they all talk to each other?*

Sure enough, we came upon Radley's General Merchandise, on our left. It was a grand tent, as big as a barn, with American flags on tall poles flying from each corner. Arrayed along the front, shovels and picks, pry bars and pans, not to mention hats, pants, shirts, boots, and kettles, all announced what the customer could expect within. Radley's was lit up with enough lanterns for a Saturday night dance. Just a glimpse through the opening revealed that it was packed with men buying their outfits.

As we came abreast of a large, plain, wooden building, the smell of roast beef filled the air. The smell made my mouth water. Fancy lettering stretched across the entire front of the building proclaiming, "*American House. Fine Food*". I looked up at Mr. Hoyt. He was standing with his eyes closed, swaying slightly on his crutch. Perhaps he was smelling the delicious aroma, too.

"Can we use a little of our money to buy supper?" I asked.

Mr. Hoyt blinked his eyes open. He cleared his throat, as if composing himself. "Well, I suppose it would be a good investment to fortify ourselves for our coming labors," he pronounced solemnly.

I smiled up at Linnaeus and in we went.

We entered a room crammed with men furiously eating. They hunched over their plates, shoveling their food, or grabbed for another helping from large bowls and platters on the tables. Calls for more food, along with the scrape of platters and plates, filled the smoky air. After the riot of noise outside in the street, this chewing, muttering mob seemed sedate as a Sunday meeting.

A burly man in a filthy apron came up to us, barring our way. "You gents'll have to wait outside. Next sitting's in fifteen minutes." He scowled at us with his arms crossed. "And no animals."

We went back outside.

"Shall we look for someplace else?" Linnaeus asked.

Mr. Hoyt pointed to a tent across the street. "They're all going to be the same."

The sign outside that tent, crudely painted in simple black letters, said, *Meals—$2.* The tent had no front, so it was easy to see it was just as crowded. I looked up and down the rambunctious, muddy street. Mr. Hoyt could well be right. Setting down my pack in a little space away from the doors of American House, I tied Bugle to it and scrubbed his ears. "Stay, okay? We won't be long."

Linnaeus set his pack next to mine, and helped Mr. Hoyt with his. Then we went back to the front doors so we could be first in line.

A crowd began to gather around us. *They must know the restaurant's schedule.* Soon the press of the crowd pushed us against the rough wooden planks. The smell of roast beef lost out to the reek of tobacco, unwashed bodies, and dirty clothes.

Finally, the door opened. All the men who had been inside pushed their way out into the street. We fell back as best we could to let them pass, trying to keep our place at the front of the crowd. When the building was empty, we heard a bell ring and our mob surged into the room. I had a quick glimpse of the setup as miners scrambled for seats. American House, Fine Food may have been one of the very few wooden buildings, but it had a dirt floor. The only furniture consisted of two long plank tables with benches on either side. Men in grubby aprons came through a door in the back wall, bearing steaming bowls and platters of food. These they set in a row down the middle of the tables. Another man set out small bottles among the bowls. Tin plates and simple metal knives and forks completed the settings.

In the general commotion, I lost sight of Mr. Hoyt and Linnaeus. Then I heard Mr. Hoyt shout, "C'mon!" I wormed my way through to them and we managed to grab three seats at the end of the farther table. Linnaeus helped Mr. Hoyt sit down at the very end, so he could stretch out his splinted leg. Then he leaned Mr. Hoyt's crutch against the bare wood wall.

I waited for everyone to quiet down so someone could say grace, but that was folly. As soon as a man took his seat, he lunged for a bowl of food and scooped a helping onto his plate. Most of the diners, no matter what they had chosen, then doused their food with a generous slathering of molasses from one of those little bottles. I never heard the words I had grown up with, words that had been drummed into me—please and thank you. The scene was a frenzy of elbows and reaching, chewing and shoveling. It was every man for himself. Mr. Hoyt understood the situation perfectly, and, in a flash, heaped his plate with watery stew, boiled potatoes, and a great slab of roast meat. He tucked into it as if he hadn't eaten in weeks. My plate was still empty. Linnaeus looked stunned.

I grabbed a bowl that sat for an instant unclaimed, regardless of its contents. The bowl was already half empty. The concoction looked like thick gravy and smelled funny. I scooped some onto my plate, hoping it would be agreeable. Linnaeus regained his wits and leaned close to look at my choice.

"Ah! Curry!" He exclaimed with pleasure.

"What's that?" I asked.

"From India. Delicious!" He gestured toward the bowl. "May I?"

I had never heard the word curry before, nor smelled such an unusual aroma coming from food. I handed him the bowl and he emptied it onto his plate. It was mostly a thick, yellow-colored sauce with chunks in it. The mystery chunks were completely covered with the gravy.

I looked for what else might be within reach. Nearby, a server reached over the bent heads of the diners and set down a heaping platter of sliced, roasted meat. Juices ran off the platter onto the table. Almost as one, like lightning, a dozen forks stabbed at the heap. I speared in underneath all the outstretched arms and forked three slices across the table to my plate, then transferred one slice to Linnaeus' plate. Another slice went into my pocket for Bugle.

Linnaeus paused in serving himself some rice. "Why, thank you, kind sir. Allow me to return the favor." He spooned some rice onto my plate. "Goes very well with the curry," he said.

I cautiously tasted a bit of the yellow gravy from this curry and found it to my liking right off. Linnaeus was right. It was delicious—spicy, but delicious. The mystery chunks turned out to be chicken, potatoes and onions. The first onion I'd tasted in months! I hesitated no more and gobbled up my supper. Having cleaned my plate, I reached for another bowl. It proved empty. I tried three other bowls before accepting that not a scrap remained.

Most of ten minutes had passed. One or two slowpokes were still chewing. Men took out their pipes and plugs, and a hubbub of conversation began. Suddenly, across the room, a big, thunderous voice bellowed, "A child?"

Immediately, all eyes turned to me. A ripple of voices swept through the room like a tide, demanding to see. Without warning, or asking, a pair of arms lifted me off the bench and stood me on the table among the empty bowls and platters. I looked around at a sea of sun-browned, hairy faces wreathed in smoke. Standing on the table at home would have gotten me in serious trouble, but here I was, standing on this table, with no one objecting at all.

Another voice called out, "Ain't seen one of them in a year or more!"

This remark inspired others. I could make out only a few in the growing noise. "Last one I saw was in San Francisco," and "Hey, Sonny, why didn't you bring your sister?" and "What's your name, boy?" and "Where you from?"

I didn't know if I was supposed to try and answer all these questions. I kept turning to try.

Shouts came from every part of the crowded room. "Sing us a song, young'un!" and "Can you dance, lad? Give us a dance!" and "Do you know 'Little Topsy's Song?'"

I knew the songs my mom had taught me, but I didn't know anything about dancing. The thought of trying to sing in front of all these strangers turned my knees to water. More requests rang out amid the general din. People were trying to outshout each other. Something struck me in the chest, like a small fist. I looked down. A small leather pouch landed with a thump on the table. Something similar hit me in the back, but I didn't turn to see. I was getting a little scared. *Are these people angry at me? Did I take too much food?* Linnaeus stood up at that moment, but whatever he was going to do or say was cut short by the burly, scowling man.

From his station by the kitchen door, he boomed over all the voices. "If it's singin' and dancin' you want, get your…" the rest of what he said was drowned out by the noise of the crowd getting up, almost as one, to converge on the scowling man. From my vantage point I could see they were paying for their suppers. I was relieved that the diners gave up their interest in me as quickly as they had discovered it.

Linnaeus helped me climb down from the table. "I dare say that wasn't very pleasant. Are you all right?"

I wasn't sure which was more unnerving: standing on the table or being challenged to sing. "Why did they do that?"

Linnaeus handed me my hat. "I would guess that children are even more rarely seen in this benighted place than women."

Mr. Hoyt was weighing with his hand the little sack someone had thrown at me. The second one had probably fallen under the table.

Linnaeus offered to pay for our meals. He approached the burly man and spoke to him. The burly man took a large, flat book down from a shelf, and Linnaeus wrote in it.

When he returned to us, he explained. "We owe the gentleman six dollars. Two dollars each for supper. To be paid when we have found some gold."

"Highway robbery," grumbled Mr. Hoyt.

"They trust us?" I asked. We were strangers. We could be in the next county before sunrise.

"I said we had money," replied Linnaeus, "but the gentleman said he preferred gold. I suppose because no one argues about its value."

The burly man and his helpers were already rushing to gather up the bowls and plates. We were the last to leave, keeping pace with Mr. Hoyt.

Outside again, I was relieved to see our packs had not been disturbed in any way. I gave Bugle his supper, wondering when I would get a chance to wash my trousers. They smelled of roast beef for days after that. We considered our next move, where to spend the night. Linnaeus spotted a sign across the street, *The Gold Mountain Hotel*. It was a crude wooden building two stories high with one door and no windows.

"You go ahead. I'll wait here and look after Bugle," Linnaeus said with a smile.

When Mr. Hoyt and I got inside we found ourselves in one large, bare, poorly-lit room. A ladder set against a side wall led to the second floor. On the first floor, there were two levels of shelves all along the four walls, each wide enough for a man to lie down. This is where men were sleeping. Cots filled the center of the room, too. People were even sleeping on the floor.

A man sat at a simple wooden table near the door. "Three dollars a night. Provide your own bedding," he said without looking up. "Another two dollars for bedding. And you leave your guns with me."

Mr. Hoyt protested. "Isn't that a bit steep? We've just paid two dollars for dinner, which, in itself—"

The man looked up at us. "You new here?"

"What difference does that make?" said Mr. Hoyt, sticking out his chin.

The hotelman was not impressed. "There's The Palace down the street. They're four dollars a night. Monte Carlo is six dollars a night."

I tugged at Mr. Hoyt's sleeve. He seemed not to notice. I tugged again. Finally he turned to me.

"You need a good rest, sir," I said. "This seems to be the cheapest place. Linnaeus and I can find a hayloft or something."

"These prices are outrageous. I'll not be taken for a fool," Mr. Hoyt hissed through gritted teeth.

"Yessir. I understand that. But the sooner you get better, the better it'll be for us," I said.

So, Mr. Hoyt signed his promise in the hotelman's ledger just as Linnaeus had done in the restaurant's book.

I unpacked Mr. Hoyt's bedroll and helped him get settled on one of the lower shelves. We stored his pack on the floor beneath him.

"Wait for us here," I said, trying to sound cheerful. "We'll be back in the morning. Then we can go hunting for gold."

But I was worried. I remembered all the miners we had seen as we made our way down the canyons with Mr. MacIver. Only a small portion of those had joined us in making our way toward the town at sunset. If *all* these people were hunting for gold in the nearby countryside, it would be difficult to find a spot that wasn't already occupied.

I found Linnaeus perched on a barrel, chatting quietly with another man. He turned to me as I came up to him. "Ah." He smiled. "All settled, then?"

"Yessir. I got Mr. Hoyt all settled."

"What about you?" Linnaeus asked, concerned.

"We have to watch our pennies. I'll figure something out. Mr. Hoyt needs a good rest."

Linnaeus nodded and gestured to the man he had been talking with. "Allow me to introduce Mr. Felix Fourier, late of Marseilles, France, by way of New Orleans and Panama."

Felix Fourier was a man of medium height and a swarthy complexion. Like so many here, he sported a red flannel shirt and a shaggy beard.

Linnaeus turned back to Mr. Fourier. "May I present, Monsieur, Master Bartholomew Pegg, better known as Pegg. As fine a traveling companion as one could hope for."

Mr. Fourier and I had barely time to shake hands before Linnaeus continued, for my benefit. "Mr. Fourier and I were just comparing notes on our favorite city, *La Paree*. That's 'Paris' to us Yankees." He turned back to Mr. Fourier. *"Oui? N'est-ce pas?"*

Whatever Linnaeus was saying, it made Mr. Fourier smile and nod. Linnaeus turned back to me and said, "It turns out Mr. Fourier's aunt was my landlady back on Rue Huchette while I was at the Sorbonne. What a small world."

He returned to his conversation with Mr. Fourier from Marseilles, France, speaking a language I didn't understand, but assumed was French. I set my pack down next to the barrel and sat with my back against it. Bugle settled next to me. I gave him a scratch.

The next thing I knew, Linnaeus was gently shaking my shoulder. "Wake up, weary Argonaut, wake up." Mr. Fourier had departed. Linnaeus had his own pack slung over his shoulder.

"Time to find you a place to sleep," he said, straightening up and waiting for me to get to my feet.

"Mr. Hoyt has our money," I said to Linnaeus as we trudged up the street. There were fewer people than before, but it was still busy.

"I'm about out, myself," Linnaeus said, looking all around as he walked. "We'll just have to find a nice pile of straw, or maybe a cave." Then he stopped.

I stopped, too. Linnaeus darted off to the side, between two piles of merchandise. "This way," he whispered over his shoulder.

Away from the street, we were swallowed up in shadow. But Linnaeus soon stopped and turned to me with a flourish. "I give you *le Hôtel Baril*. He swept his hand to indicate a large, empty barrel lying on its side. It was the largest among a whole collection of empty barrels and crates. Linnaeus settled his hand on the side like a doting uncle.

"Very reasonably priced. Spacious. Plenty of fresh air. Privacy almost guaranteed."

"Does *baril* mean barrel in French?" I asked him.

Linnaeus grinned. "Indeed, Pegg-o. Indeed. Why, we'll make a linguist of you, yet."

"What's a linguist?"

"I'll tell you tomorrow," he said crisply. "Well, what do you think?"

"It'll never fit both of us," I said, bending down to peer into the shadowed space.

"Oh, no. This is for you," Linnaeus protested. "The night is young. I have adventures yet to pursue. I want to see if I can, with the help of your father's fiddle, earn what I owe American House for my supper."

It was not my place to argue he needed his rest, too. "See you in the morning, then."

"Sleep well." Linnaeus said it like a genuine wish.

"Good luck," I said.

After he left us I unpacked my bed roll and crawled into the barrel. It wobbled. I turned to Bugle. "What if it rolls away with us?"

I found several scraps of crating and wedged them on either side of it, and pushed at the barrel. Rock steady. "Wouldn't want to be rolling into San Francisco Bay, would we?" Bugle stood up and sat down again.

The inside of the barrel smelled of salt and vinegar. What had been in it before me? I beckoned to Bugle to come into the barrel. There was enough room. "C'mon, boy. We can keep each other warm."

Bugle curled up against me and I was soon asleep.

I must have slept well, for it seemed like moments later I was awakened by Bugle's barking. The sun was not above the ridge, but there was plenty of light, though it was muted by fog shrouding the town. The fog seemed to muffle sounds, too. I climbed out and stood up. Another dog stood several paces from the opening of the barrel, but when he saw me he trotted off.

My head crowded with questions. How did Mr. Hoyt get on at the hotel? Where did Linnaeus spend the night? How do we start looking for gold? I rolled up my bedding and put on my pack.

I asked Bugle, "You ready for our new adventure?"

CHAPTER 23

The first person I hunted up was Mr. MacIver. I knew he would be on the move early. I found him at the edge of town on the road west. He was hustling the people who wanted to push on to Sutter's post. A half-dozen of our party were staying in Grizzly Bar—most of them from the former Baines Company. I told Mr. MacIver Mr. Hoyt and I would be, too.

"As good a place as any, I suppose," he replied.

"Thank you for getting us safely to California, sir."

He looked off in the distance for a minute. Then he turned his gaze back to me. "It was as much your grit and good sense as it was me, but thankee just the same."

"And thanks for telling us so much about the Indians and all."

"You and that Forsyth girl had more questions than a dog has fleas." He bent down and scratched Bugle's head. "No offense meant, dog." Bugle thumped his tail on the ground, gazing up at Mr. MacIver with loving eyes. Mr. MacIver straightened and hollered at a slow poke. He turned to me. "I was happy to oblige." Then he sighed. "Country's changin' though. Injuns an' buffs, alike, don't stand a chance against the white man's push."

"How can that be?" I exclaimed. "Seems to me there's plenty room enough out there for everybody *and* the buffalo."

Mr. MacIver merely grunted. Then he fixed me with a squint. "I know it's none of my business, but I got one thing to say." He made sure I was paying attention. "Your pa was a fine man. I reckon he left you some good things." He tapped his temple. "You grow into his like, wherever you end up will be the better for it." He stuck out his hand. "Keep an eye out for wolves. They come in all shapes and sizes."

We shook hands.

He looked around again. "I've got everybody tallied but your friend, Mr. Peabody. He said he's comin' with us. If you see either of 'em, tell 'em we're pullin' out in an hour." Mr. MacIver started to turn away, and waved his hand to include the town, the river. "Good luck with all this."

"Thank you, sir." I knew he wanted no part of it.

He went off, urging on his people. To him, I was one of an endless parade. But I wouldn't forget him. He was a real mountain man, and I had gotten to walk with him a ways. He was rough as a cob, but his heart was generous and true. He didn't take nonsense from anyone. He had told us kids a tiny fraction of what he knew. If I could be half of what he was, I figured I could look the world square in the eye, the way he did.

I headed back to find Linnaeus and Mr. Hoyt. There was a different man sitting at the little table in The Gold Mountain Hotel.

"I'm here looking for a friend," I said to him.

"Have a look," he said.

The spot on the bench where I had left Mr. Hoyt was now occupied by someone else. Mr. Hoyt's pack was not there, either. I went back to the man at the desk.

"Did you see a man with a crutch leave? He stayed here last night."

"Seems he's a popular fellow," said the hotelman, with no pleasure in his voice.

I didn't know what that could mean so I stuck to my immediate concern. "He's not here now."

"Threw him out hours ago," he said without looking up.

"What? Why?" I blurted out, completely forgetting my manners. Panic surged into my mind.

"Creating a ruckus. Threw 'em both out," said the hotelman.

"But where did he go?" I had no care for who the other person might be. My worry was Mr. Hoyt.

"Once they're out that door, Sonny, I've got no truck with 'em. Now, you want a bed or not?" He sounded weary and bored.

"No, sir. I don't need a bed."

"Then kindly step aside for the paying customer behind you."

I whirled around. Indeed, a rumpled man was standing behind me, looking as if he was already half asleep.

"Thank you, sir," I said to the hotelman, like I'd been taught to.

"Glad to be of service," he replied, just as woodenly.

I went back outside. Mr. Hoyt could be anywhere. *Where to start looking?* I looked up and down the street. The fog was already starting to burn off. I counted three people, besides myself. None of them were Mr. Hoyt. I looked in the space between the hotel and the next building. It was filled with rubbish. I went to check the alleyway on the other side. There I found Linnaeus, kneeling with his back to me. I also saw Mr. Hoyt's pack leaning up against the building.

Bugle barked at Linnaeus. He turned to me.

"Linnaeus?" I said.

"Ah. Good morning, Pegg," he said cheerfully. "I was just asking Mr. Hoyt if he knew where you might be."

I stepped into the narrow space. "I was looking for Mr. Hoyt."

"As was I." He smiled. "When I found your barrel empty, I thought you might already be with him."

Mr. Hoyt was awake, but in a very cross mood.

Linnaeus went on. "No doubt you asked at the hotel, got the same information, and came in search of our man, here."

Mr. Hoyt muttered some not very nice things about the hotel man. Linnaeus helped him to his feet.

"That may be so, my dear fellow," Linnaeus said, "but it's water under the bridge, no?"

It was clear that Mr. Hoyt had not had a restful night.

"I'm for some breakfast. What do you say?" Linnaeus said brightly, taking up Mr. Hoyt's pack and canteen.

"Mr. MacIver says they're leaving in an hour."

Linnaeus helped Mr. Hoyt get his crutch under his arm. "I think we can still get some breakfast."

We followed the smell of frying griddle cakes. We came to a shed made of sticks and canvas, with one side open to the street. There was no sign at all. The man making the griddle cakes called them flapjacks. It seemed everything out here had a different name. His griddle was a large, flat sheet of iron held up over the fire by four stacks of rocks. To the cook's left was a pile of firewood which reached almost to the roof of the tent. To his right several crates grouped together held his pitcher of batter, assorted implements, and a bowl of eggs.

Four homemade tables had lengths of stout logs set on end to serve as chairs. We got the last empty table. The whole place wasn't much bigger than my mother's kitchen. The cook addressed us without interrupting his tending the flapjacks.

"Short stack's a dollar. A stack of four is a dollar and a half." He flipped a flapjack. "Eggs, any way you like 'em, three dollars each."

Mr. Hoyt growled his disgust at the prices. But he ordered a stack of four and three eggs, over easy.

I wanted to ask Linnaeus if he had made any money playing Dad's violin, but it was not proper to be so forward, especially about money. Instead, I asked if he'd had a good rest.

"I wish I could say I did, Pegg. But people kept asking for one more tune, and I was only too happy to oblige." Linnaeus smiled, patting his trouser pocket slyly.

I smiled back. "I'm glad my father's fiddle has been so helpful to you, then."

"What are you two talking about?" Mr. Hoyt said, squirming on his seat, which meant he felt left out. We talked about the weather after that.

In that crude, slapdash place, the cook made perfectly round, perfectly golden-brown griddle cakes, or flapjacks, every bit as good as my mom's. I saved one for Bugle. Various containers held molasses, jams, and preserves.

While we were eating, Linnaeus coaxed the story of the hotel from Mr. Hoyt. It seemed that, in his sleep, Mr. Hoyt had rolled off his bed onto the floor. But there was somebody sleeping on the floor right where he landed. This was an unpleasant surprise for both parties. Neither man had been at all happy at having his sleep interrupted and insults were soon flying. This woke up even more people, which only added to the commotion. The hotelman had restored order by throwing out both Mr. Hoyt and the man he had landed on. Linnaeus offered his sympathy that Mr. Hoyt hadn't had a better night's rest.

"That rat trap will not have my business again, you have my word on that," Mr. Hoyt pronounced. When it came time to pay for our breakfast, Linnaeus drew a pouch from his coat and handed it to the cook. "For the three breakfasts," he said.

Mr. Hoyt put out his hand and said, "Your charity's not needed, professor. We can look after ourselves." He pulled a small pouch from his pocket. It looked familiar. Then I remembered, it was one of the little pouches that had been thrown at me the night before, when I was standing on the table.

Mr. Hoyt nodded in Linnaeus' direction and said, "Take his out of his pouch and the boy's and mine out of this one. Nobody's gonna owe anybody anything." He tossed his pouch to the cook.

The cook reached to the back of his counter and produced a small set of brass scales. Into one dish he placed a few weights. Into the other he gently poured out some of the contents of Linnaeus' pouch. The dust glittered, and the nuggets clanked as they landed in the metal scale dish. When the two dishes on either side of the scale were exactly even, the cook closed the little sack and handed it back to Linnaeus. The cook emptied the dish holding Linnaeus' gold into his own, larger sack. Then, after adding another weight, he went through the same steps with the pouch Mr. Hoyt had given him.

Linnaeus nodded in the cooks' direction with a smile, but then turned to me. "You'd probably have ten times those two little bags if you'd actually sung them a song last night."

Those people would give me gold to sing for them?

When we were back on the street, Linnaeus turned to us, rubbing his belly contentedly. "Well, gentlemen, I thank you for the delightful company, but if you'll excuse me now, I must go find Mr. MacIver. I don't want him leaving for Sutter's trading post without me."

"You're sure you have to go to San Francisco?" I asked, though my real purpose was to delay Linnaeus' leaving.

"That's *my* bonanza," he grinned. "It's bursting with possibilities." Linnaeus looked troubled. He put both hands on my shoulders.

"But I can leave you with something Mr. Fourier mentioned last night. Something that you might want to consider. He said lots of good news is coming down from the north fork of the American River."

We looked at each other for a minute. I had the impulse to try once more, but I knew he was as set on his course as I was on mine.

"It was an honor. You take care, hear?" he said softly. He dropped his hands. "Mr. Hoyt," he said more formally. He held out his hand. "Good luck to you, sir." Mr. Hoyt shook his hand briefly. Linnaeus added, "Look after Pegg. See him home safe."

Mr. Hoyt's spirits seemed to have improved with breakfast. He gave Linnaeus his lopsided grin. "You don't have to worry about us, professor. We'll take care of our business; you take care of yours."

Linnaeus got a few steps into his journey before he turned with a smile and called to me, "Come see me in San Francisco. Just follow the fiddle music."

Watching Linnaeus walk away into the busy street, I felt more alone than I'd felt in a long time. It was like I was losing my dad for the second time. I was supposed to be at the beginning of a great adventure, and I didn't have the least idea how to start, or if I would even be able to handle it once I got it started.

CHAPTER 24

Linnaeus was soon lost to sight in the busy street. I wondered if I would ever see him again. Would I ever get to San Francisco? But I scolded myself this was no time for sad thoughts. I looked around to see Mr. Hoyt settling himself, with difficulty, onto a handy crate by the side of the street. I wondered if the fall he had suffered during the night had done any harm to his broken leg. He didn't look like he was ready to go tramping through canyons.

I approached him with caution. "How are you feeling, Mr. Hoyt?"

"Ohhh…" He laughed shakily. "I've been better, Pegg-boy, I've been better." He hung onto his crutch like he still needed the support, even though he was sitting.

We were interrupted by a salutation. Two of the Baines men approached. I recognized them as the two I'd passed on the mountain; the two who had wanted their own nugget from Caleb Johnson. *Are they tailing us to some purpose?*

They both looked like they'd been dragged through a war. They'd surely gotten less sleep than Mr. Hoyt. The stink of their liquor reached us before they did. They shuffled to a stop and the sturdier one spoke first. "How be you this fine morning, Mr. H… Holt?"

Mr. Hoyt, without looking, waved them away. "Go on. Be off with you."

The Baines men stayed put. One had a Colt thrust through his belt, just like me. He brought his hand to rest on the butt. "We were wondering if you could loan us your nugget. We're just a little short."

Mr. Hoyt burst into a harsh laugh. "A little short of brains, I'd say."

I thought to lure them on their way. "Mr. MacIver said he's leaving in a few minutes."

Mr. Hoyt put his hand up to quiet me. "Leave it to me, Boy."

The Baines man ignored me. Nor did he appear to take offense at Mr. Hoyt's gibe. He took a step forward. "We'd pay you back right away. We just need a break."

Mr. Hoyt regarded him for a moment, then let out a snort. "Do I look like I was born yesterday? You think I don't know you'll drink it up like you've done the rest of your money?" His voice grew rougher with emotion. "No, this nugget has much worthier uses, I can assure you."

The slight one swept his lank hair out of his eyes. "Please, Mister. You can find another one." He raised a wavering finger in my direction. "Maybe the boy'll get lucky again."

The other Baines man shuffled around Mr. Hoyt. *Was he leaving the convincing to his skinny friend?*

Mr. Hoyt snarled, "Leave the boy out of this."

I barely caught a flick of a glance between the Baines men before the skinny one lunged clumsily at Mr. Hoyt. They tumbled together off the crate.

At the same time Mr. Hoyt struck out with his crutch. But his stroke was aimed at the man behind him. Lurching back to avoid the blow, the man took me down with him. Bugle started barking up a storm.

Mr. Hoyt heaved his man off and fetched him a good blow with his crutch, and another. I grabbed my man's coat in an effort to keep him down. I wasn't sure of my goal. Shrieks erupted from the skinny man, mixed with growls from my dog. People began to gather.

As suddenly, Mr. Hoyt and I were abandoned in the dust. I heard Bugle barking and growling, racing up the street. The skinny Baines man screamed, "Git 'im off me!"

A storekeeper helped Mr. Hoyt back onto his seat. A prospector helped me to my feet and handed me my hat. Bugle came back. The excitement over, people drifted away.

The prospector said, "Good hound ya got there," and went on his way.

Mr. Hoyt smoothed the pocket where he dropped Caleb's nugget.

I looked up the road. "I hope they won't come back."

"Well, we'll be ready for 'em, won't we?" Mr. Hoyt smirked, brandishing his crutch.

The day had gotten under way around our little fracas. Merchants opened their stores and set goods out on display. I saw one man selling potatoes out of the back of his wagon. Everywhere you looked, people were unloading wagons or loading mule trains. The sounds of hammering and sawing filled the air, as did the smell of fresh-sawn lumber. No one looked like they had time to give advice on how to hunt for gold. I made bold to try my idea on my partner.

"Mr. Hoyt," I began cautiously, "I was wondering, if you don't mind, I mean, if it would be all right…"

Mr. Hoyt leaned on his crutch and arched his eyebrows in mock worry. "'Sakes, lad, I'm dyin' of suspense." He started to chuckle but ended up coughing.

"I was thinking I could go out and have a look round. See how people are doing it. You know, looking for gold."

Mr. Hoyt studied me.

I tried a few more ideas. "I don't think we need to buy any equipment right now, until we can see what people are using." My real idea was to watch what the *successful people* were using, and buy *that* kind of equipment. "I wouldn't be digging or anything," I said. "I'd just be looking. Then I'd come back and tell you, and we could decide what to do."

Now Mr. Hoyt was rubbing his chin thoughtfully. "You've been giving this some considerable thought, haven't you?"

Maybe he thought I was trying to run the show. "Oh, no, sir. I was just thinking about how we could start."

"No digging?" He smiled.

"No, sir! No digging. Just looking." I didn't see how I could do anything more. I had no tools.

"I'll look after the mutt," Mr. Hoyt said. "No need to have him disturbing you."

"Oh! That's okay. I wouldn't want him to be a bother to you."

Bugle knew he was being discussed. He barked and licked his chops and went back to panting.

"But can I leave my pack with you?" I shrugged it off.

"Sure. I'll hold it for ransom." He smirked.

I felt odd about that, but I thought it best to humor him. "Okay." I grinned. "That's fair." I looked at Bugle. "You ready, boy?" I looked back at Mr. Hoyt. "Okay. I'll be back."

Mr. Hoyt watched my departure. I glanced back twice before I lost sight of him. My idea was to follow the miners as they set out for their diggings, and, of course, to keep my eyes peeled, as Gideon MacIver had so often said.

Grizzly Bar was a couple dozen buildings——if that——squeezed onto a flat space between the river bank and the canyon wall. Structures were crammed in any which way they could fit. The only open space was a meadow at the east end of town, cut in half by Simpson's Creek on its way to the river. If the town grew any bigger it would no doubt fill those two meadows. As I passed the last buildings, I saw the burly, scowling man from American House. To my surprise he was smiling. No, even more remarkable, he was laughing. He stood in front of a store with a shorter man, as if they were in conversation. Both cradled arms full of purchases. This other man smiled, too. As well as being shorter, he was clean and neatly dressed— definitely not a prospector.

I had never seen any person like him. He had a little wispy white beard and a shaved head with a long neat braid hanging down his back. He wore a loose suit of clothes composed of jacket and trousers— all shipshape and buttoned up. Nor did he wear boots in which to tuck his trousers. His shoes looked like slippers. The cloth looked much finer than the rough woolens and homespun that the miners wore. He looked like he belonged in a fine parlor, not out here in the dust and scruff. I came back to how clean he looked. I hadn't been that clean since we left St. Louis.

I went on my way, thinking that anyone who could make the burly, scowling man laugh must be a special person, indeed.

I joined the miners heading up Simpson's Creek, away from the American River. Many carried loads of provisions on their backs. One fellow showed off his new boots. Another read aloud from a letter he had received; his friends gathered close around to hear. Most of the miners ignored me, talking and joking among themselves. But a few took notice.

"Hey, Sonny. You lose hold of your momma's apron strings?"

"You lookin' for the schoolhouse, boy?" A pause. "They ain't built it yet!" The man laughed at his own joke.

"Comin' out to sing us a song?" That fellow must have been at American House.

A kid out here was rare as hen's teeth. I would have to get used to this silliness. Besides, Will, back home, could hurl gibes better than those any day, so I didn't pay them any mind. Except one.

"Hey, kid! I'll give you fifty dollars for your pooch, there."

I was stunned. Fifty dollars could get us started, sure! "No, thanks. He's not for sale." Someone else called out, "I'll give you seventy dollars for him."

"No. That's all right. Thanks just the same. He's not for sale."

Bugle looked at me.

"Don't you worry, boy," I smiled at him. "You're worth a lot more than any pot of gold."

I'm glad Mr. Hoyt didn't hear that. Partner or not, the last thing I wanted to do was put Bugle's fate in his hands.

The path roughly followed Simpson's Creek but was set back from it. The creek and its shores looked like a giant had taken a great stick and stirred up the ground. Piles of rocks and gravel heaped beside holes of all sizes. It was hard to tell where the original course of the stream had been. Some holes were filled with water as the creek found a new way down its ruined course. Bits of lumber and wrecked equipment were scattered around. Not many miners were working here, so I guessed there was no more gold left in this part of the creek.

One of the groups of prospectors still walking upstream with me was discussing selling their claim. I remembered Caleb Johnson, the first person we had met coming into Grizzly Bar, had almost offered to sell us his claim. I reckoned that the spot where a miner dug for gold was called his claim. As we got farther upstream, people dropped out of the general march to go to their claim, or to join partners already at work. A few headed away from the creek, up the steep sides of the canyon. I thought everybody stuck pretty close to water to look for gold.

"What's up there?" I asked a fellow who had come up and was walking beside me.

"Up where?"

"Why are those fellows heading away from the stream?" I asked. "Don't they need water?"

The man looked where I was pointing. Then he said, "They've more'n likely got dry diggings up on the flat."

"What are dry diggings?"

The miner smirked. "What's it sound like?" He swung away, toward the creek.

"Thanks," I called after him.

"For what?" he called back.

"For telling me that."

He snorted in surprise. "Well, I never."

I began to see construction that aided in the mining. Miners had built simple dams of trees and rocks to guide the water in the creek to where they wanted it to go. Many men were working with long trough-like devices that I later learned were called long toms.

Farther up the creek, I saw smaller groups with simpler contraptions. I watched one man pour a bucket or a spade full of dirt and gravel into a tray at the top of the device, while another man poured water over the gravel in the tray. A third man, worked a handle that moved the machine in a rocking motion. I looked more closely and saw the device was supported on two curved pieces of wood, just like a baby's rocker. But the miner's movements were much more vigorous than a mother's would ever be. The man doing the rocking bent down to forage in the bottom tray at the other end of the device. He found something of interest and held it up to his partners. It glinted briefly in the morning sun.

Gold? It has to be! His partners exclaimed their pleasure.

Most of the prospectors I saw used the simplest tool of all, though, the pan. Bugle took an interest in one of these men, and trotted over to introduce himself. I followed, hoping for a closer look at how things were done. The man knelt on one knee at the water's edge, tilting and twisting the pan, dipping in more water, with the sure movements of long practice. How long did it take to learn that? His clothes were faded and patched, his boots dusty and cracked. As I drew closer, I realized it was none other than Caleb Johnson.

"Well. Lookee you," chuckled Caleb, turning to Bugle. "Where'd you come from?" He set the pan down and scratched Bugle's ears. Both man and beast grinned in pleasure.

"He's from Vermont," said I, stepping up to them.

Mr. Johnson pushed back his battered hat and squinted up at me. "Say...ain't you the kid from yesterday? You lookin' for another nugget?"

"No, sir, I'm not." I smiled. "Thanks just the same."

Caleb nodded to Bugle. "I 'spect that makes you from Vermont, too."

"It does, sir." I held out my hand. "Bartholomew Pegg. I go by Pegg."

The prospector reached out and shook. "Caleb Johnson, as usual. Rhode Island."

Dad always said if you lay your kindling well, chances are you'll get a good fire. I'd watched him get his way with my mom many a time by such means. So I tried it then. "I'm just lookin' around. Seein' how things are set up. Don't mean to trouble you."

"No trouble. No trouble at all," he replied, still smiling and scratching Bugle.

My dog shivered with delight.

So far, so good. "Can I watch for a few minutes, see what you're doing? If you don't mind?"

Caleb Johnson turned fatherly in the blink of an eye. "Watchin' can't hurt, but the only real learnin' is in doin', Son."

I nodded. "I know, sir. I hope to be doing real soon."

He picked up his pan. "Well, this here's the best way to start."

The pan resembled some Mom had back home—easily held in two hands, made of metal, with sloping sides and a flat bottom. A pick and shovel seemed to be the only other tools needed. It was also easy to see that a miner could work on his own, washing the dirt he shoveled into the pan.

Caleb washed a new shovel full of dirt, going from sand and gravel down to fine black sand, but he got no color for his efforts. I watched him work one more shovelful, then thanked him and bid him good day. I called Bugle away from his exploring and returned to the trail.

Occasionally, smaller streams fed into Simpson's Creek. Most I could just hop across; many were little more than a trickle. The land got steeper as I followed the stream higher. Simpson's Creek itself became narrower and more disorderly, tumbling between rocks and boulders, zigzagging like a rabbit trying to outrun a fox. There was not much of a trail that far up, so I just kept to the stream as best I could. I saw one or two more miners, but we exchanged no words, and I kept moving.

At midday, with the sun right overhead, it was very warm for October. Bugle panted, but he had covered a lot more ground than me, with all his roaming. I found a shady spot to rest and sat down in the crunchy leaves. I took stock of my surroundings. Most of the trees appeared to be oaks. I was in a place where the miners had not yet come in search of firewood.

There was a type of pine I had never seen before. Its form was not the tapered spire I thought of as a pine or fir. The tree before me sported great, twisting limbs that went in every direction, willy-nilly, so that the shape of each tree was its own. The needles were longer than I had ever seen on an evergreen, the bark rough and grey. I assumed it was a pine by the smell and stickiness of the sap that oozed from cracks in the bark. That tree produced a great number of cones, round and fulsome, but only half the size of the sugar pine cones we had seen in the mountains.

Undergrowth crowded into the sunny patches. Two odd types were too big to be called bushes, yet too small to be called trees. One had a remarkable dark red skin, smoother even than a beech, while the other produced a large fruit. Those two I later learned were called manzanita and buckeye. I remembered MacIver telling me about Madrones higher up. They were more like real trees. Manzanitas were more like a real twisty bush.

I heard the cry of a blue jay and the sharp knock of the woodpecker searching for its dinner. That put me in mind of my own hunger.

I had no plan when setting out—just followed my nose. I certainly had made no provision for how long I would be away. I glanced around. Not much in the way of undergrowth. I may well have been surrounded with edible plants, but I knew none of them.

Suddenly, Bugle's head snapped around and he took off!

I turned just in time to see a deer—a beautiful eight-point buck—bound off into the trees above me. He wasn't a whitetail, like we had in Vermont; his ears and white rump patch were bigger. I called to Bugle, but he wouldn't give up. I settled myself to let him have his fun. He was a 'coon dog if he was anything, not a deer dog, but he didn't abide by such stipulations.

I thought about what I had seen so far. It seemed that gold mining was done in stages. The more you found, the more effort you put into finding even more gold with the aid of clever contraptions. And, clearly, with just a pan and a shovel, you could move quickly and often, and explore many spots without a lot of toil.

But once you had chosen a spot to prospect, how did you keep it? How did you let other people know it was yours? It had to be something more than just being cross with people and chasing them off. Such simple questions made me realize how much I had to learn if I was going to make a success of this business.

Bugle finally came back, panting harder than ever.

"Outran you, did he?" I grinned at him. The buck lost him in the brush and tangle, more likely.

Bugle flopped down and I gave him a rub.

Before we headed back, I climbed down to the stream for a drink. The water had formed a small, shallow pool before plunging on its way. I thought I saw a gleam in the sand at the bottom. I stuck my hand in and brought up a handful of sand and mud; no gleam. My action only served to cloud the water, which meant waiting for it to clear before I could have my drink. Bugle drank beside me. As I rose to leave, a second gleam, no more than a wink of light, teased me from the bottom of the pool. I chuckled to myself. *Wait 'til I get my pan and shovel. Then we'll see who teases who.*

Retracing my steps downstream, I had another look at what I had already seen. Bugle was tuckered out, or maybe bored, and stuck close. The shadows were already starting to grow long. Men worked energetically, as if every minute of daylight was precious. I came to a place that had collected more than its share of dross from past efforts. I spied an abandoned miner's cradle, sitting in the gravel on the opposite bank of the creek, and picked my way across. The water came only halfway up my boots, but I could feel the cold through the leather.

I approached the little cradle cautiously, expecting a challenge of ownership at any moment. Bugle trotted out onto dry ground, shook himself, and sat to wait me out. Parts of the machine were broken or missing. The top tray was gone, but I soon spotted it lying upside down in deeper water. The bottom tray and the sides were mostly undamaged.

If it was truly abandoned, why hadn't it been snatched up for firewood? Had the wrecking of it just happened? I looked around. Everyone completely ignored me.

I bent over the remains of the little machine and saw how the man this morning had found his little chunk of gold in the other cradle. The lower tray had little sticks nailed across the bottom, spaced like a ladder! The way the cradle worked was instantly clear. Mud and sand got washed down from the upper tray into the lower tray, and then moved along by the water. The little sticks worked like miniature dams, holding back the finer sand. They were too small to hold back pebbles, which tumbled out the end of the tray.

The gold probably got trapped behind those little sticks, too.

Even discarded, the little crosswise sticks were doing their job. I pushed my fingertip slowly through the sand behind one of the sticks. To my great surprise, I pushed out a piece of gold about half the size of a grain of rice. I could hardly believe my eyes! I made to shout, but then thought better of it. Did this belong to me? Or to the man who owned this cradle? Even if he abandoned the machine, did he still own whatever came from it?

I held the bit of gold tightly in my other hand while I pushed my finger along the back of another of the little sticks. Nothing. I tried a third. Two more bits of gold, tiny flakes that barely clung to my fingertip. *Where can I keep these two and not lose them?* By the time I had tried all the sticks, I had collected six pieces of gold. The last was the biggest, almost the size of a grain of rice. I felt like I had stumbled upon a bonanza. I found gold my first day! I couldn't wait to show Mr. Hoyt.

I put my haul in the little pouch that held my compass and called to Bugle, who was off exploring again. "Come on, Bugle! We've got to find Mr. Hoyt." We hurried back to town, running and leaping. We got more than a few puzzled looks, but I paid them no heed. As Will liked to say, *We're off to the races.*

CHAPTER 25

Music told me I was getting close to Grizzly Bar. I brimmed with all I wanted to tell Mr. Hoyt. *We can start making plans!*

It suddenly struck me we hadn't set a time or place to meet at the end of the day. I didn't think he would stay all day in one place, and, sure enough, he wasn't where I'd left him. If Mr. Hoyt went somewhere else, did he take my pack? That made me realize what a problem my pack must have been for him all day. I would have to store it someplace tomorrow, so he wouldn't have to be burdened.

I found my pack in front of a saloon called The Palace. I knelt down and opened it. Bugle stepped close, wagging his tail.

"Yeah, boy. I'll bet you're good and hungry, aren't you?"

Bugle whined. I got out the bacon and unwrapped it and cut off a big chunk. "There you go. I'll be right back." I found some water and filled my hat and brought it to him. He lapped up the water as eagerly as he had downed the bacon.

"I'm sorry it's only bacon, Bugle, boy." I petted him some more. "Soon, it'll be better. I promise."

After tying him to the pack I stood up again. I had little doubt that Mr. Hoyt was in The Palace. In my heart I said *sorry* to my mom and my dad, then went inside.

I likened it to walking into a storm of noise. The room, packed with miners, plus a few gaily dressed ladies, reeked of tobacco smoke and the smell of unkempt people. I stepped into the crowd the way I would step into a churning river. Almost every table hosted a game of chance. I found Mr. Hoyt at one such table, his back to me. If I needed convincing, his stiff, splinted leg, and the crutch lying at his feet, did the job. I decided to delay announcing myself, lest I should break his concentration.

I knew nothing of these games except that it was called gambling. Our preacher back home thundered against gambling almost as much as he did sloth and other dissipations. Five men were seated with Mr. Hoyt. Four were unmistakably miners. They had mud-spattered boots, simple woolen shirts, and patched baggy trousers. A couple of them, remembering their manners, had removed their hats. All sported whiskers in various stages of riot.

But the fifth man was clearly of another sort all together. Not a speck of dirt clung to this man. His clothes were expensive, tailored in the latest fashion. He wore a tall, shiny black hat, sticking up smokestack straight. His hands were long, pale, and clean. He was clean-shaven except for his moustaches, which were waxed to the shapes of twin swords. He displayed a casual air, as if lounging with friends. The other players, of whom Mr. Hoyt was one, were hunched forward, scowling over their cards and at each other.

The city slicker laid his cards on the table. The others studied this display for only a moment. One of the miners threw down his cards with a curse. The others surrendered their cards in turn, muttering expressions of disgust or frustration. A couple of them left the table. The city slicker, apparently the winner, calmly scooped up all the sacks of gold and colored chips to his place at the table. I thought it might be a good time to let Mr. Hoyt know I was back.

I cleared my throat. Mr. Hoyt did not turn. I guess my voice was lost in the general rumble. I tried again. A miner sitting to Mr. Hoyt's left turned to me. He understood my intent and cocked his head in Mr. Hoyt's direction. I nodded and the miner thumped Mr. Hoyt on his arm. Mr. Hoyt shifted with some effort, not pleased at being disturbed. But as soon as he saw me he broke into his lopsided grin.

"Ahh, Pegg, boy," he cried. "There you be. I was just saying to Bert, here," he swatted the miner in return, "maybe the coyotes had got you."

The miner who had noticed me nodded, smiling.

"No, sir. I didn't see any coyotes." I sounded like the dutiful student, not somebody who had just found gold in the gold rush.

"Did you see any gold, then?" Mr. Hoyt smirked. Then he laughed.

That seemed odd, but I smiled. This was my moment. "Yessir, I did." I pulled out my compass pouch.

"Did you, now?" Mr. Hoyt leaned toward me, suddenly intent. "I thought we agreed no digging."

"I didn't dig, sir. I found it in a cradle." I tipped the pouch onto the table, and the compass tumbled out.

"Now, that's the oddest nugget I've seen yet," drawled Mr. Hoyt as he looked around to his fellow players, who laughed with him.

"No, sir! Wait!" I leaned over the table and shook the bag gently.

Mr. Hoyt apologized to the city slicker. "The boy's confused. Give us a minute here."

The rice-sized nugget tumbled out. "There!" I exclaimed in triumph.

But before Mr. Hoyt turned to look, the little nugget rolled across the table and over the edge. I dove under to retrieve it, pushing among pairs of boots and chair legs.

I heard Mr. Hoyt's stern voice above me. "Are you fooling with me, boy?"

"No, sir, I'm not!" I shouted, still scrabbling in the sawdust and clods of dirt, pushing his crutch aside in my search. But the nugget was lost.

"Well, then, come out from there. You're making fools of us both."

Reluctantly, I climbed back to my feet and retrieved the compass, deciding not to risk losing my other specimens. I put the pouch away.

Mr. Hoyt addressed me in a parent voice. "Now, can't you see I'm trying to do my part here? I'm on a winning streak. Go find yourself some supper, and we'll have our little chat later."

He turned away. The miner named Bert shrugged his eyebrows at me, and turned away, too.

I waited a couple of minutes, hoping Mr. Hoyt would turn around again. *How can he be winning when the city slicker just took possession of everything on the table*? Two new players took the vacant seats. The city slicker began passing out cards to everybody. I walked back through the jostling crowd, trying to figure out why Mr. Hoyt wouldn't be interested in planning our next move. *What can be more important than getting started as quickly as possible so we can go home?*

I was outside before I remembered I had not asked Mr. Hoyt for money. Did every restaurant have a book to sign? I doubted the few tiny bits of gold in my pouch would buy me much to eat. I untied Bugle and slung my pack over my shoulder. "C'mon, boy. Let's go find some supper." He barked and wagged his tail like he was ready to do whatever I wanted to do. That cheered me up a little.

CHAPTER 26

Grizzly Bar sported almost as many places to eat as it did saloons. I trudged up and down the street, looking over my choices. Some were fancy, some not so. I passed American House, but had no wish to be stood up on a table again.

I came to a large tent with just three sides and a roof, open to the street. Instead of long tables and benches, I counted nine round tables seating six or seven customers each. As with the American House, every sort of humanity filled the tables. But here there was no pushing or grabbing. Most of the customers were eating out of bowls, not plates. Some were using short slender sticks, rather than forks and knives. A sign perched on top announced this was Chen's Garden. Underneath those words were a set of designs unlike anything I had ever seen. They reminded me of oddly shaped spiders. Next to the sign hung a long yellow flag.

Just then a man appeared through a parting at the back of the tent. He carried two steaming bowls. He was the same person I had seen that morning, laughing with the American House man! He set down the bowls before two of his customers and paused to survey his dining room. He noticed me, perhaps because I was standing still amid the general bustle of the street. He beckoned to me, smiling.

I looked around to make sure he didn't mean somebody else. It would be bad manners to just walk away now. It couldn't hurt to see what he wanted.

"Good eat. You like," he said as I approached. His customers were tucking in with a will. The food must be good and my stomach was growling. Hopefully, he had a book to sign.

The man waited while I tied Bugle to my pack, then he led me to a table with a vacant seat, an upturned barrel. Of the miners already eating, several were using those little sticks. What they were eating was a complete mystery. It looked like steaming yellow string.

The man who had invited me in, the host, for he acted very much like one, pointed to a neatly lettered board that hung on the side wall, high up. "What you like?" he asked.

I recognized only one word, rice, but I scowled at the menu like I was studying the choices carefully.

Before I could speak, a table partner next to me said with an accent, "Try the chow mien. It's excellent." He pointed with his eating sticks to his bowl of yellow strings.

I turned back to the host. "I'll have the chow mien, please."

"Chop, chop!" replied the host, and he hurried off.

"Excellent choice," said the man who had made the suggestion.

"What did I choose?" I said, completely forgetting to say thank you first.

"A delicious concoction of pork, bean sprouts, cabbage, onions, and noodles," he replied.

Pork and cabbage I knew. Bean sprouts named themselves. "What are noodles?" I asked.

He reached into his bowl with the slender eating sticks and lifted up a collection of the pale-yellow strings, only now they looked like very long, skinny worms. "My word. Have you never tasted one of the great culinary inventions?"

I didn't know "culinary" from a hole in the ground. "No, sir, I haven't." They looked slippery and slithery.

"These are made from wheat. Some are made from rice," he said. "Noodles come in all shapes and sizes. Think of them as very long bits of boiled bread." He brightened at his thought. "That's it. You could say they're boiled bread."

This man reminded me of Linnaeus Peabody. "Thank you, sir. I'm sure I will like them."

"You're very welcome, sir." He smiled and resumed his meal.

Let Mr. Hoyt have his noisy old Palace! I was going to enjoy my supper.

And how you gonna pay for it? snickered Will in my head. Maybe I could work off my debt.

The host brought me a cup. It was very small and had no handle. I decided to wait and see how my table partner picked up his. He paused in his eating and poured tea into my cup from a round, white teapot.

Once again, I forgot my manners and watched him eat. He used the two sticks as easily as I would use a fork. When he reached for his teacup, I said, "May I ask, what part of the world are you from?"

"You certainly may. Chiddingstone, Kent, England," he said. "My ancestors came from Scotland, but that was too long ago to tell." He took a sip of his tea. He held the cup along the rim. "And you, sir? Where do you call home?"

"Vermont. We have a farm outside Richford, Vermont. It's on the border with Canada."

The man lifted his eyebrows. "My. You've come a long way, then."

"Not as far as you," I replied, bold as brass. I knew England was across the Atlantic Ocean, but not much more than that. *Mom would certainly not be happy at such cheek on my part.*

The Englishman laughed. He didn't seem to take offense. He leaned a little in my direction, "Well, I'd say neither of us has come as far as Chen Yi, the owner of this fine establishment." He nodded to the man I had been thinking of as the host.

"Where's he from?" I asked.

"Oh!" he chided. "Come now. Surely it's obvious." He waited, but when I had no answer, he grinned. "China! Old Cathay, or as they would have it, the Celestial Kingdom."

I looked more carefully at Chen Yi. I remembered Mr. Pruitt's references to China. *So that is what people from China look like.*

"Yes," the Englishman proclaimed. "California is a magnet to the world." He indicated a man in a dusty, black slouch hat, sitting at our table. "Eduardo here hails from Argentina. The big fellow with the tattoos—he goes by Big Tiki—is from Molokai, in the Sandwich Islands. Gaspar Raspier, in the red shirt, is from France, Dijon, to be exact."

The Englishman held out his hand. "Ewing Galloway. At your service."

I shook his hand like a grown-up. "Bartholomew Pegg. You can call me Pegg."

"A pleasure, sir." He picked up his teacup. "To new beginnings."

Uncle Rafe always made toasts to this or that. I picked up my cup by the edges. "To a new farm, a better farm."

Chen Yi set before me a steaming bowl of chow mien and a set of eating sticks.

Mr. Galloway said to Chen Yi, "Perhaps Master Pegg would prefer a fork."

"Ah, so!" exclaimed Chen Yi. He went away and quickly returned with a fork wrapped in a napkin.

I forgot to say grace.

I learned to like noodles very quickly, but I had a heck of a time learning how to get them from the bowl to my mouth. Mr. Galloway showed me how to wind them around my fork. That helped a lot.

"If you don't mind my asking," Mr. Galloway said cautiously, in a quiet voice, "How close are you to achieving your goal?"

"Oh!" I almost laughed. "We just got here. We haven't even really started looking yet."

"Well, I'm glad to hear you are with family," said Mr. Galloway. "You seem a bit on the young side to be out here all on your own."

"I'm with Mr. Hoyt," I said. "He's a neighbor. My dad died of fever at South Pass." Suddenly, with no warning at all, tears began to run down my face. I was aghast and confused at such a display in front of a stranger, but I couldn't stop.

"Oh, my," Mr. Galloway said, "poor lad." He put down his cup and rested his hand on my shoulder. "I think I've met a very brave young man."

I wiped at my face with the napkin, but the tears flowed unbidden. Something had let loose inside, like river ice giving way in the thaw. *I'm not a little kid anymore. I shouldn't be crying like this. I shouldn't be crying at all.*

Chen Yi appeared from nowhere, very much concerned. Mr. Galloway and the Chinaman spoke quietly, their heads together. Chen Yi left us.

When I had quieted myself a bit, Mr. Galloway said, "I am sorry for your loss. But you have already done your father proud by completing such a difficult journey."

I will not encourage pity. Just to make sure, I said, "I'm okay. Don't worry about me."

Mr. Galloway patted my shoulder a couple of times and took his hand away. He took a drink of his tea.

"Don't worry about me," I said again. "Mr. Hoyt and I will make a good team."

"Where is Mr. Hoyt now?" asked Mr. Galloway. "He's missing out on some excellent victuals."

"He's at The Palace, collecting useful information," I said.

"I see." Mr. Galloway's tone was suddenly less friendly. He took another drink of his tea.

"He's good at it," I said. "He's been doing it all along."

"Oh, there's plenty of talk at The Palace," Mr. Galloway replied, his voice still wary. "Of that there is no doubt. But I'm not sure how much of it I would call trustworthy, much less useful."

I wanted to establish my worth in this situation. "I've been looking around myself, though, collecting my own information."

"That's more like it!" exclaimed Mr. Galloway, back to being full of cheer. He pointed at my bowl with his eating sticks. "Eat up, before it gets cold." And he dived back into his own noodles.

I didn't want the conversation to be over. It felt good to talk to someone who seemed to respect what I had to say. Perhaps if I offered him something we could start talking again. But I quickly realized the only thing I had learned for sure was that dry diggings were up out of the canyons and, well, dry. Everything else I had observed only raised a bushel of questions that needed answering.

Just to be polite, I managed a couple of forkfuls of noodles. Then I turned to him. "I learned about dry diggings."

"Capital!" he exclaimed with a grin. "What did you learn, then?"

I didn't know yet that I was supposed to be careful about what I said or what I found. And begrudging somebody just for being from somewhere else, which Mr. Hoyt appeared all too ready to do, was not what I had been taught. That idea seemed like an ill-fitting coat that made no sense to wear if you didn't have to. So I told Mr. Galloway what I knew about dry diggings and he listened so attentively that I was inspired to tell him about what else I'd seen that day. He asked lots of questions, which prompted me to remember better.

"You mentioned claims earlier," Mr. Galloway said after I had shown him the tiny nugget I had found. "What do you know about claims?"

"It's the name for a spot where you are looking for gold?"

"Good," replied Mr. Galloway. "Anything else?"

"Is there more?" In my head, my mom frowned at me, but I wasn't quite sure why.

Mr. Galloway got serious. "How do you suppose that spot is defined, marked, so that nobody else will use it?"

Mr. Galloway was asking me exactly what I wanted to know about! "I don't know, sir."

"Did you see any sticks in the ground today," he asked, "or stacks of rocks, near where the men were working?"

"I saw more rocks than you could count!" I smiled. "And lots of lumber scraps lying around."

"No," he said. "Stakes driven in the ground, as if you were marking out land for a farm, or a building. Or rocks stacked up like a post."

I thought back over my day's ramble. Suddenly I could see them! Sticks pounded into the ground! They had seemed so random, I had thought nothing of them.

Mr. Galloway could see that I understood him, so he went on. "Those stakes mark the limits of one man's claim, or the company's, if he has partners. It's usually ten to twenty feet square per man if the area is rich, larger if the area is poor."

"And where there isn't lumber handy, they use stacks of rocks."

"Exactly. Those are called cairns." He fished out the last of his noodles.

"What if you want your claim to be in the river?"

"Ah! Claims on the bank of a river are understood to extend out into the river itself, halfway across in some places, all the way across in others."

I felt like I was scooping up nuggets of valuable information! I could feel my dad smiling at me.

"But have a care." Mr. Galloway wagged his finger at me. "Different places have different rules. If you go up on the north fork, or up on the Yuba or Feather Rivers, they'll all be different. So when you go to a new place, you must ask about them."

"Yessir," I said, as seriously as a grown-up. I could hardly sit still. *I'm really in the gold rush!*

"Now. As long as you leave something of yours in plain sight—your tools, cooking gear, some of your kit, people will leave your claim alone." He let that sink in. "But!" He held up his finger like a flagpole. "You have to work your claim at least once a week, or you lose your right to it."

"Once a week?" I blurted out. "How are you supposed to find anything if you only look once a week?"

Mr. Galloway smiled. "Now, hold your horses. You've seen Simpson's Creek. Every place is like that. Most people are busting their butts." He paused a moment to let me reflect. "But what if you walk to Sacramento to mail a letter, or, better yet, receive one? That's two days each way! What if your claim is three days' walk from the nearest town, and you need flour, or a new shovel? And you get to town only to find out they've run out of shovels! So you wait a day, or two, or three for more shovels to arrive. There's a week, right there!"

I gulped. "And what if you get sick? You stumble into town to treat yourself to a real bed and some hot soup, and in your delirium you lose track of the time... Yessir. A week sounds pretty reasonable after all."

"Exactly," Mr. Galloway replied.

"But there's one really important thing I need to know."

He grinned. "Apart from all the other important things you need to know?"

"I understand you stake your claim once you've found a good spot. But how do you *find* a good spot?"

"You're a smart lad," said Mr. Galloway, pouring us more tea. "Some would say I've already said too much, but I'll tell you one more thing about placer gold."

There are different kinds of gold? "What's placer gold?" I asked.

"Loose gold," Mr. Galloway replied. "The kind we're finding washed down in these rivers. Placer means surface, or gravel. Some say it's all coming down from one huge deposit, a mother lode, somewhere way up in the mountains."

"So why doesn't everybody just head for that spot?"

Mr. Galloway chuckled as if he knew better. "Some do. Nobody's found it yet, that I've heard." He took a drink of tea, then refilled our cups again. "But let me ask you this. Would you chase after a rumor, if you saw perfectly good nuggets lying at your feet?"

He waited for an answer cheerfully enough, and I obliged him with a shake of my head.

He leaned a little toward me and spoke in a quiet voice. "But here's what you need to know. Gold is heavier, size for size, than most everything around it; sand and gravel and dirt. And that's as true of the tiniest flake as it is of a nugget the size of your fist."

I closed my hand into a fist.

Mr. Galloway kept talking. "That means gold, as the water pushes it along, is always looking for the lowest place to sink to, anywhere it can. The water will keep moving it as long as it can, but when that gold finds the lowest spot and settles in, nothing much can budge it. The water will leave it there, carrying everything else on downstream."

Mr. Galloway let me digest that. Then he said, "So you look at the water flowing, and the rocks it's flowing around, and think: if you were a little flake rolling along, where would you come to a stop so that you wouldn't want to move on, so you *couldn't* move on?"

I tried to imagine rolling and tumbling along under water. Mr. Galloway tipped the pot up, pouring the last of the tea. It seemed he was finished. But I had a dozen more questions.

He held up his cup. "To knowledge," he said.

I clicked my cup against his, like Uncle Rafe had taught me to do. "To knowledge," I said.

CHAPTER 27

I heard Bugle bark. It was his "somebody's coming" bark. I looked toward the front of the restaurant. In a minute, Mr. Hoyt hobbled into view. He looked down at Bugle and then into the tent. Several miners, waiting for a table, grumbled in protest when he moved into the tent, but he ignored them.

He weaved his way through the other tables to join us. He struggled more than usual with his crutch.

"How did you find me?" I asked.

"Saw the dog," Mr. Hoyt seemed in a dark mood.

I could smell liquor on him. *How much has he had?* I braced myself for an outburst.

"This is Mr. Hoyt," I said to Mr. Galloway.

Mr. Galloway had already stood up. "Ewing Galloway," he said, sticking out his hand. "Pleasure to meet you, Mr. Hoyt."

Mr. Hoyt shook hands with Mr. Galloway briefly, but didn't say anything.

Mr. Galloway looked concerned. "My word, sir. You do seem to have suffered some misfortune."

"Nothin' I can't handle," Mr. Hoyt grumped.

"Pegg spoke of you, but he didn't mention this." Mr. Galloway moved a chair so Mr. Hoyt could sit.

He lifted his teacup in the air and signaled to Chen Yi.

Mr. Hoyt scowled. "Has the boy been speaking out of turn?"

"Not at all." Mr. Galloway shook his head and smiled. "Indeed, he has shown himself to be a keen listener."

Mr. Hoyt merely grunted as he settled himself in the chair and laid his crutch on the floor.

Chen Yi came to our table with a teacup, put it down beside Mr. Hoyt, and waited a moment. He leaned forward just a bit. "What you like?"

Mr. Hoyt waved his hand, dismissing Chen Yi without even looking at him. Chen Yi went away. That seemed rude to me.

"Some tea, perhaps, Mr. Hoyt?" said Mr. Galloway.

Mr. Hoyt held up his hand, no, without speaking. Nor did he look at the Englishman.

"A most unfortunate mishap, indeed," Mr. Galloway continued. "When did it happen? I hope after you left the mountains."

"Awhile back," Mr. Hoyt allowed. "It slowed us up some. But we're here."

"Mr. MacIver set his leg," I blurted out.

Mr. Galloway smiled in relief. "It's fortunate that you had a medical man in your party."

I was happy to talk about Mr. MacIver. "He isn't a doctor. He was our guide, our scout. He's been all over. He can do anything."

"Well, from the looks of it, I would be inclined to agree," smiled Mr. Galloway.

"Mr. MacIver..." I started.

Mr. Hoyt broke in, looking at Mr. Galloway. "You mind excusing us? The boy and I have business to discuss."

Mr. Galloway looked cross for a blink and then composed himself. "Why, of course. How thoughtless of me." He rose to his feet. "I shall detain you not a moment longer."

It seemed right to stand, too. Dad did that with Mr. Pruitt.

Mr. Galloway put on his hat and touched the brim. "Pegg. It's been a pleasure. I wish you the best of luck." He put out his hand and I shook it.

Mr. Galloway gave a nod to Mr. Hoyt, who kept his seat. "May you enjoy a speedy recovery, sir." He touched his finger to his hat again. "Gentlemen." He went off to find Chen Yi.

Mr. Hoyt stared at the table until Mr. Galloway had left the tent entirely.

Chen Yi came to the table again. "What you like?"

Mr. Hoyt ignored him, glowering at the table. Other customers were standing outside the tent, waiting.

"Thank you, sir," I said. I reached into my shirt for my compass pouch. "We're done."

Chen Yi said, "Gentleman Galloway pay you supper."

I looked toward the entrance of the tent. What a remarkable fellow Mr. Galloway was!

Mr. Hoyt grumbled something under his breath. I scooted around to pick up his crutch. I waved to Chen Yi as we left Chen's Garden. He gave me a quick nod in return.

Even with Mr. Hoyt going slowly, I had to catch up with him after untying Bugle and picking up my pack. People filled the muddy street; shouting, laughing, arguing. Glowing lanterns held off the coming night. Eating places and saloons soaked up the throng. The chill air was rich with the smell of roast meat and manure, and the jaunty clatter of pianos.

"Did you have supper?" I asked, falling in with him. "The food is very good there."

Mr. Hoyt's thoughts lay elsewhere. "Leave the information gatherin' to me from now on," he grumbled, "you have to be careful of strangers."

I knew it was not my place to be frustrated with adults, but Mr. Hoyt wasn't making sense. "But we just got here. Everybody's a stranger." I expected a scolding, but my time with Mr. Galloway left me feeling bold.

Mr. Hoyt kept scowling ahead. "You can't go talking to just anybody. You never know what they have up their sleeve."

We threaded our way through the bustling throng, heading toward the west end of town. *Where are we going?* A miner shouted at me, "How much for the dog, kid?" I ignored him, and took a better hold of Bugle's lead. Mr. Hoyt swung his head left and right like an angry bear. I cast quick glances around, too. Nobody seemed the least interested in us.

I felt I ought to defend Mr. Galloway. "All we talked about was the gold mining I saw today. Mr. Galloway even talked about how to set up a claim."

"Then he's a fool. Just like the rest of 'em!"

Why would Mr. Hoyt say that? He knew nothing about what Mr. Galloway said. *Maybe he has even better information.* "What did you find out?"

"What are you talking about?" he growled. "Find out about what?"

"About gold mining. At the saloon."

"Hogwash! Nothin' but wild stories," Mr. Hoyt barked. "Spent perfectly good money on food and drink, and got nothin' but nonsense in return!"

"Was none of it useful?" I said.

Mr. Hoyt swept his free arm out in frustration, and then had to steady himself. "One of 'em said he'd found a nugget that weighed ten and a half ounces—one nugget!" Mr. Hoyt snorted like he didn't believe it. "Another said he filled his hat with nuggets in a day! One fool told me he had taken out eighteen ounces in his first four days on his claim."

I grinned in triumph. "I took out a few ounces in a few minutes!"

Mr. Hoyt stopped and turned to me. "I won't be made fun of, Pegg-boy. It's been a hard day."

"But it's true, sir! I did! Don't you remember? I showed you at The Palace. Well, I tried to show you."

Mr. Hoyt regarded me sternly. "We'll set aside for the moment that you weren't supposed to do any digging on your own." He looked around. Nobody was paying us any mind. "Did you show it to anybody else?"

"I didn't do any digging! I found it."

Mr. Hoyt glared at me and gritted his teeth. "Did you show that Galloway fellow?"

If drink did this to Mr. Hoyt, I had to hope he wouldn't do it often. My mom would call him a mean drunk.

He held out his hand. "Better let me safeguard what you've got there. No telling who might have overheard you talking to that foreigner."

I got out my pouch. This time I took out my compass first. I shook what remained of the nuggets into Mr. Hoyt's hand. The last two tiny flakes refused to come out. He closed his fist and stuffed it into his pocket without looking at the nuggets. They were so small I doubt he ever got them out again.

"It's only right. Your Pa wanted me to look after you." He hitched his crutch and set off again.

I caught up with him. "But now we know how to set up a claim! We can start!"

Mr. Hoyt said, "Word is the north fork of the American River has the richest diggings." He kept stabbing his crutch out in front and hauling himself forward.

Perhaps I could learn more from Caleb Johnson and Mr. Galloway, I thought. "I could try around here for a while. There must be some spots that haven't been taken yet. Then when your leg is mended, we could go to the north fork." I had no idea what Mr. Hoyt was thinking, so I kept going with my idea. "I could start with a pan and a shovel. That's all we need."

Suddenly, Mr. Hoyt stopped.

I stopped, too. *He likes my idea.*

Bugle trotted to the limit of his rope and then came back.

Suddenly, Mr. Hoyt turned aside and hobbled toward the door of a building. The sign over the door proclaimed it another hotel, *The Parisienne*. A second line offered: *Real Beds Available*. This hotel had windows. And the windows had lace curtains. In fact, it was one of the few buildings in town constructed entirely of wood—and sawn lumber, at that.

He opened the door and then turned to me. "At least in here I won't be rolling off the bed, now, will I?" He gave me a smirk, like I was in on a joke. "Meet me back here in the morning. We'll talk about what to do then." And without waiting, he went in and closed the door.

"Yessir," I said to the door. My partner clearly meant for me to find my own sleeping arrangements. I should not have expected better, having by now witnessed enough of his self-centered behavior. But it was still a disappointment. *Is this how partners treat each other?* Once again, I had forgotten to ask him for money.

I found Bugle looking up at me with his *What now?* look. "Let's hope we can find that barrel again."

We found the barrel, but somebody was already asleep in it.

"Any ideas, Bugle-woogle? Surely there's another barrel somewhere in this town, or maybe a crate big enough?"

Bugle worked his eyebrows at me and licked his chops.

"But before anything else, we've got to get you some supper."

I had no money. Mr. Hoyt would surely object to spending money to feed my dog. How could I get Bugle something to eat?

Three people had been friendly to me today, despite what Mr. Hoyt might say. I had no hope of locating Caleb Johnson or Mr. Galloway, who had disappeared into the crowd. The other was the restaurant man, Chen Yi. But I didn't expect him to give away his food. What could I trade for supper? My compass? Uncle Rafe's Bowie knife?

It was late when I got back to Chen Yi's restaurant. He appeared to have no customers at the moment. Another Chinese man was eating by himself at a back table. That man wore a big, grimy apron and a bandana around his head. *Maybe he's the cook.*

I could see right away that Chen Yi was in trouble, and what his trouble was. He was getting ready to swat an intruder with his broom. But the intruder was a skunk. The skunk didn't know what was coming. It was busy looking for scraps under the tables. We had skunks back home, but from the look of things, Chen Yi didn't know about them. I was still well back, out in the street. Skunks don't have very good eyesight. I took a tighter hold of Bugle's rope and raised my free arm to wave at Chen Yi. He saw me, thank goodness, and stopped. I waved my hand in two separate motions: One to say, *No!* and one to say, *Stay back!* Happily, Chen Yi did both. I nodded and he nodded.

Bugle shivered to give chase. I knelt down beside him slowly, holding tight his rope, and curled my arm around him. "Yeah, you see him, don't you?"

Shifting impatiently, Bugle never took his eyes off the critter. He knew about skunks. He'd had a run-in with one when he was young. Mom made Dad keep him out in the barn until the smell wore off. Since then he'd warn them off but knew to stay clear of their tail end.

I said real quiet, "Tell that ol' skunk he isn't welcome. Can you scare him off?"

Bugle barked twice. The skunk looked up. Bugle barked again. The skunk's tail went up in the air. I put my hand up carefully again to tell Chen Yi to hold still. The other man had stopped eating, but stayed where he was. Even in the shadows under the table, the white markings on the tail were easy to see.

We're not out of the woods yet. I waited. I patted Bugle softly. "Again, boy." He barked again. The skunk stopped and looked in our direction. I guess the critter didn't want any trouble, because it turned and trotted away from the tent, off into the dark. I waited another minute.

"Good boy." I gave Bugle a hug, scratching his ears. "Perfect. Good boy." Then we went over to Chen Yi, who was standing at the front of his restaurant with his broom, smiling.

"Friend of Mr. Galloway," Chen Yi said.

"Pegg." I held out my hand and Chen Yi shook it, but you could tell he wasn't used to the custom. I looked down at Bugle. "And this is Bugle. He just saved you a heap of trouble." I acted out about skunks and how they sprayed when cornered or attacked, mostly holding my nose and screwing up my face, and saying "bad smell" a lot. "And the bad smell stays a long time."

Chen Yi got a very worried look on his face. "Bad for business." He peered in the direction of the departed skunk. "Bad smell bad for business." And then he turned back, smiling. "Thank you, Mr. Pegg."

Then Bugle took matters into his own hands, well, paws. He sniffed around where the skunk had been searching, at least as far as the rope would let him.

Chen Yi looked down at Bugle and grinned. "He make bad smell?"

I laughed. "No, Sir. No bad smell. He's just hungry."

"Ah, so!" exclaimed Chen Yi. He went into his kitchen. It was separated from the tables by a canvas curtain cut down the middle. He was gone a couple of minutes and returned with a small plate heaped with chunks of meat and bones, no doubt the odds and ends that would be boiled down into soup. Chen Yi put the plate down in front of Bugle. He straightened up and said to me, "Chen's Garden happy not have bad smell. Customers happy. Chen Yi happy."

Bugle was not bashful. He was wolfing down his supper.

Chen Yi pulled out a chair. "Sit, please." He turned and spoke to the other Chinese man, who had remained still as a post during the entire commotion.

I sat down, suddenly fatigued. It was past my bedtime.

The man I assumed was the cook made a quick response and disappeared into the kitchen. A minute later he came out bearing a tray with a teapot and two cups. Chen Yi took it from him and set it on the table. Then he sat.

"Thank you, Sir," I said. "For Bugle's supper. Thank you very much. We sure do appreciate it."

Chen Yi took on a solemn expression, looking out into the street. "I appreciate. You do Chen Yi good deed, very good deed." Then he looked at me, worried. "That how you say? Do good deed?"

Back home we said, "good turn," as in you'd do someone a good turn, but deed seemed close enough. I smiled. "Yessir. That'll do fine." Then I remembered my mom's lessons. Even though Chen Yi hadn't exactly said thank you, he meant that. So I said, "You're very welcome."

Chen Yi stood. Lifting the lid, he peered into the teapot. With a nod I took to mean he deemed it ready, he turned up the tea cups, poured the steaming brew into them, then settled to drink with me while Bugle ate.

In our simple way we told each other where we were from, even though neither of us had any idea, for a certainty, where the other fellow's home was. I told Chen Yi I had a sister, a brother, and a mother waiting on me. He told me he had a whole village full of brothers and sisters and nieces and nephews, as well as aunts, uncles, and cousins. He looked old enough. But mostly we sat quietly and drank the tea. It was a good feeling.

Eventually, Bugle fell to gnawing on a ham bone. Otherwise the plate was clean. The tea pot was empty, too. It must have been long past Chen Yi's closing time. I reached down for the bone to take it with us.

Chen Yi stood. "Time sleep. You have hotel?"

I fell back on my old defense. "Don't worry about me. I'll be okay." I gained the front of the tent and turned back. Chen Yi had not moved, watching. The cook gathered up the tea pot and cups onto the tray. "Good night," I said, and held up the bone. "And thank you."

I walked up and down the street, sidestepping miners staggering in their excess, and turning down more offers for Bugle. Looking in the shadows between noisy buildings for an empty barrel or crate, I found a big barrel, what we called a hogshead, standing up, but when I went to tip it over, water—or some liquid—sloshed inside. Perhaps collected rain. In the darkness, it was hard to tell how much, but the sound said several inches, and tipping the barrel would only wet more of the inside. A second barrel, indeed, lay on its side, but it must have been recently emptied: it reeked of vinegar. At the end of the street, I came upon the livery stable. It had a corral with horses and mules and donkeys, all standing quietly in the moonlight. Behind that I found a large pile of hay. I turned to Bugle. "What do you think, boy? The Haymound Hotel?"

I hid my pack on the far side of the mound, scooping out a cavity at the bottom. Then I made a bigger hole, at about knee level, and lined it with my bed roll. After I climbed in, I turned to beckon Bugle, but he wanted no part of my scratchy cave.

"Suit yourself."

I shifted some of the hay to make a kind of door to conceal my presence, but also to keep the warmth in. Not long after I had settled myself, I heard Bugle growl. I poked my head out to see who was coming.

A Chinese man was standing there. He was the man I had seen eating by himself, the one I took to be Chen Yi's cook, who had brought out the tea. He had a wide face and a strong chin. The big apron hung past his knees. His shaved head gleamed in the cold light. He was small, but he was solidly built. I could tell he knew hard work. He looked around quickly and then beckoned that he wanted me to come with him.

I wasn't sure what to do. Mr. Hoyt had told me not to consort so easily with strangers. Bugle quieted as I climbed out of the hay pile. If it had been Chen Yi, I would not have hesitated, but Chen Yi must have sent him. The man beckoned again, this time pointing in the direction of the restaurant and acting out sleeping. I got my pack, redid my bedroll, and Bugle and I followed the cook back to the restaurant.

Chen Yi was nowhere to be seen. The man went past the tables and into the kitchen, holding aside the canvas curtain for me. The kitchen was half the size of the dining room. A big stove sat to the right, and a big work table took up most of the middle. It was warm and smelled of cooking. Boxes and sacks were stuffed into corners; tins and bottles crowded on the shelves. Piles of firewood and dishes and implements for cooking were stacked in orderly piles everywhere. The cook pointed to a collection of sacks of rice and flour close by the stove. These had been arranged into a kind of bench. Empty sacks had been piled on top. One sack was higher than the rest at one end. It was clearly meant to be a pillow.

I looked at the cook, if, indeed, he was the cook, and nodded.

"Thank you," I said.

I didn't know if he could understand me, but he nodded back. Then he turned and disappeared through a farther canvas curtain that must have marked off their living quarters. I got out my bedroll and climbed onto the bed.

I awoke to the sound of chopping. I sat up, remembering where I was. The cook was busy at the big table, cutting up ingredients for the day's cooking. At the other end of the table, Chen Yi was rolling out a very large circle of dough, just like my mom would for a pie. But his dough was more yellow in color, and he was rolling it out a lot bigger and much thinner. Pots were already bubbling on the big stove. I got up and packed my bedroll.

"You sleep good?" Chen Yi called out.

"Yessir, I did. Thank you."

He pointed to a teapot with his rolling pin. The teapot sat with a cup at the corner of the table nearest to me. "Breakfast," he said, and went back to his rolling.

I stepped close to the table and saw a saucer with what looked like two large dumplings. I poured myself some tea and bit into one of the dumplings. The dough was very white and moist, and there was a generous helping of dark brown paste hidden inside. I had never tasted anything quite like it.

"Bean cake," Chen Yi said, without looking up from his work.

While I was getting used to the taste, I discovered they were very filling. After two dumplings and two cups of tea I was ready for anything.

"May I have some water for my dog?"

Chen Yi pointed to a large barrel.

I filled my hat and had Bugle drink. I worried about how to pay for my bed and breakfast. I hated to lose it, but I put my Bowie knife in its sheath on the table.

"For my bed and breakfast. Thank you." The first thing I would do when I had some gold was buy a replacement.

Chen Yi regarded the knife with a serious face. "No good. No good."

"No. It's a good knife. Good steel. Very sharp. Good to cut anything," I began to draw it out of its sheath.

"No," he said. He had a troubled look on his face.

I stopped. I did not want to upset him.

He said, "You want pay, you insult Chen Yi."

"No, sir. I slept well." I pointed to the rice sack bed. "And you made my breakfast." I rubbed my stomach. "It's only fair I pay."

"You save Chen's Garden from bad smell animal," he said. "That no small potatoes."

I could tell he was getting more upset. I didn't want to wreck the good feeling we had. I shrugged and smiled. "Okay."

He got his smile back. "That right way? No small potatoes?"

I smiled, too, relieved we were back on good terms. "Yessir. That's right."

With his free hand he moved the Bowie knife back to me. "Good." Then his smile disappeared. "You busy, we busy. May ancestors smile on you." He put aside his rolling pin and began lifting the dough gently off the table. It was clear I was supposed to be on my way.

"Thank you, sir." I shouldered my pack and gestured to Bugle. I went off to fetch Mr. Hoyt. *Today we start!*

CHAPTER 28

Trudging up the main street of Grizzly Bar, I could see my breath puff out in the chilly morning air. I wondered what kind of winters this California place would have. October in Vermont was much colder. Adam would be chopping extra wood to stack on the front porch. Our corn crop would be cut and shocked. My mom would be putting potatoes and turnips and cabbages into the root cellar north of the house. In the smoke house hams and bacon would be curing. That had been one of my jobs this time of year, salting the meat, making sure the fire was producing the right amount of smoke and heat. Mom and Amy would soon be heading up the hill to pick apples.

When I reached The Parisienne, the sun was just rising above the horizon. I tied Bugle to my pack and went inside. Much to my surprise, the hotel clerk was a lady. The very few ladies I'd seen in Grizzly Bar had all been dressed fancy. This one wore a plain grey dress. She was a big woman—looked like she could fell trees with her bare hands.

I told her I was looking for a Mr. Hoyt.

She looked in her guest book and then raised her gaze, stone-faced, and jutted her chin as if to point to the hall behind me. "Room 12. End of the hall." I set off down a gloomy passage that burrowed deeper into the building. Her voice startled me. "And do us all a favor. See if you can teach him some manners."

"Uh, yes, ma'am."

I knocked softly on the door. I waited. I knocked again.

"Mr. Hoyt?" I waited some more. Then I knocked a little more firmly, and spoke up. "Mr. Hoyt?"

I heard footsteps in time to see the hotel clerk looming over me. She pounded on the door with her fist. The door shivered. "Check out time! Rise and shine!" she roared.

A muffled groan came from within the room.

She banged on the door a couple more times and went away.

I could hear shuffling and grumbling and bumping, and plenty of strong language, too. *This has to be the wrong door.* I had lived with Mr. Hoyt for six months or more, and I had never known him to be this foulmouthed.

Finally, the door jerked open and stopped short. But I caught the last of his speech, "Flea-bitten rat trap!" Mr. Hoyt lurched on his crutch. "Pegg-boy?"

"Good morning, sir." I backed up to let him come out of the room.

He reeked of liquor. He hobbled through the door. "Oohhhh, lad," he moaned in a trembling voice. "You don't know half the troubles I've had."

"What happened?"

"These pirates demand a king's ransom for the rat holes they are pleased to call rooms."

I let Mr. Hoyt go ahead down the narrow hallway to the front. "But it was a real bed, wasn't it? That's what the sign said."

"It felt more like a pile of rocks," he grumbled.

"I'm sorry. Did you get any sleep at all?"

We came into the lobby, where I saw a very large man blocking the front door, scowling at us. Mr. Hoyt took no such notice and continued his tirade. "And I'm expected to pay good, hard-earned money for such misery!"

"Five dollars, to be exact," said the lady from her desk.

Mr. Hoyt stumped up to confront the clerk. "I was told last night it would be four dollars."

"That was before we had to provide bedding," she said.

"Those flea-infested rags were filthy!" barked Mr. Hoyt.

I saw the big man by the door drop his arms to his sides.

"You could have slept on the floor for two dollars fifty."

"Maybe we should just pay the five, sir," I said. "We have a lot to do today."

Finally Mr. Hoyt saw the man by the door. He dug into his pocket and brought out the three nuggets he could find. He put them on the table.

"That's all I have," he said.

"It'll do," said the hotel lady.

But Mr. Hoyt wasn't done. "There's at least two ounces there. And I heard that gold is paying sixteen dollars an ounce. I figure I've got some change coming."

She moved the smallest nugget back to him with the tip of her finger. "Thank you, Gents. Come again soon."

The big man guarding the door had vanished.

"Outright banditry," growled Mr. Hoyt as we stepped through the door of The Parisienne.

"Love you, too, Lambkins," called the hotel lady.

Outside on the front steps, Mr. Hoyt reeled and threw his free arm over his eyes. "Ow," he wailed.

"Are you all right, sir?" I reached to steady him. I was learning to recognize the after effects of too much drink, though I had no idea what to do for it.

Bugle stood up and wagged his tail. I put my finger to my lips and shook my head. He seemed to understand. He sat back down again.

"So bright!" Mr. Hoyt winced.

"Let's sit down for a minute. Okay?" I tugged very gently on his arm and helped him to sit.

He held his head in his hands. I had to admit that Dad had been wrong about Mr. Hoyt. It turned out our partner had a weakness for the bottle. I was poorly equipped to know what this meant for our partnership.

I crouched beside him. "Should we get some breakfast? You'll feel better after some breakfast."

"And how do you propose we pay for it?" he groused without looking up.

"We have one nugget left. Would that be enough?"

Mr. Hoyt rubbed his face as if he wanted to rearrange it.

I tried again. "We can use some of our Vermont money, can't we?"

"Says you. How do you think I paid for yesterday?" Mr. Hoyt grumbled.

"How much do we have left?" I was getting a knot in my stomach.

Mr. Hoyt wasn't listening. "I was just lucky that a gentleman loaned me some money so I could carry on my business."

I thought, *What business?* But I kept my mouth shut.

Mr. Hoyt sank into silence again, resting his head in his hands. I tried to figure out our situation without his help. No matter how I came at it, I got the same answer: we had no money. Not for breakfast, not for a pan and shovel. Not for anything. I didn't know how much money we'd had left from Vermont when Dad died, but surely there'd been enough to get us started in California. According to Mr. Hoyt, it was all gone.

I stood up. "Can you wait here? And watch Bugle?" Then I thought better of leaving Bugle with him. He would probably sell him if he had the chance. Instead I asked, "Can you look after my pack? I'll be back in a little while."

I figured that wasn't too burdensome a request. There wasn't much to look after. The food had all been consumed except for some bacon I'd kept for my dog. My extra clothes had gone to the aid of Mr. Hoyt.

"I'll see if I can find a few nuggets to tide us over."

He nodded without raising his head from his hands. I slapped my leg at Bugle and took off up the street, back toward the diggings. Bugle raced ahead, but then came back, looking up at me as if to ask where we were going. I had a wild hope that the broken cradle had trapped some more nuggets during the night. And a desperate fear it had been taken up for firewood. I ran through the miners ambling on their way to their claims.

I found it right where it was yesterday. New sand had gathered in the bottom tray during the night. It almost covered the little cross bars. I pushed my finger carefully behind the sticks. Bugle scampered around, sniffing and marking stumps.

Some miners glanced at me as they walked passed. I hoped this old cradle didn't belong to anyone. I saw tiny glints in the sand, much too small for me to pick up. But there were no nuggets. I tried all the sticks. Finally I stood up. I had to come up with another plan. *When I do figure one out, do I have to go back and tell Mr. Hoyt?* Yes, I did. I had been brought up that way. Besides, we were partners.

The street in town was crowded and bustling with activity, I could not see Mr. Hoyt on the steps of The Parisienne. My pack sat right where I had left it propped against the wall. Bugle barked a couple of times as we approached it. I knelt down and scratched his ears.

"Where's Mr. Hoyt, Bugle-boy?" I ran my hand over the top of his head. "Where do you think he could've got off to?" I stood and looked up and down the street. I didn't want to use up the whole day looking for him.

I hoisted my pack and looked down at Bugle. "Come on, boy. Let's find a spot where we can figure out what to do."

My footsteps led me to the only friendly place I knew. Chen Yi was wiping down his tables. I had an idea. I approached him.

"Excuse me, sir."

Chen Yi left off wiping. "Ah! Boy with magic dog."

I grinned. "Yessir. Pegg. I'd like to ask a favor of you."

I had never known any Chinese people, but I could see him go on his guard. I went ahead anyway. "I'd like to ask you to look after my dog while I look for gold. He'll be no trouble."

"He keep skunks away?"

"Yessir. I'm sure he would."

"Then he welcome." Chen Yi smiled.

I set my pack off to the side and tied Bugle to it. I thanked Chen Yi and set off with an easy mind, at least with regard to my dog. The abandoned cradle had been a bust. I knew of only one other place where I had seen at least a hint of gold. I made my way to the little pool I had discovered yesterday.

I dug around in the sandy bottom until it was too muddied to see anything. Now I was really worried. Without tools, it would be hard to do any serious prospecting. I didn't even have a claim.

I started back down. Along the way, I poked around some of the smaller streams feeding into Simpson's Creek. There were no pools or resting places for sand to settle and gather.

By the time I gave up, the sun told me it was mid-afternoon. I had found no gold. I was hungry and full of stickers. *How much longer will it take Mr. Hoyt's leg to heal if he has to sleep outside in barrels? Signing ledgers and good will would only last so long. How am I going to feed Bugle?*

I still hadn't come up with any good ideas when I got back to the part of the creek crowded with prospectors. There was always a lot of noise, people talking and shouting; sawing and hammering, always the throaty gurgle of the water. Sometimes there were arguments. That day I came upon an argument.

Four miners were shouting at each other, throwing their hands into the air. They were across the creek and grouped around a brand-new cradle. Even at a distance, I could tell they were not speaking English. As I got closer, I could make out that it was French, the language Linnaeus had spoken with Mr. Fourier. Two of the miners held shovels, one held a bucket. The man with the bucket had the most to say, and directed his anger mostly at the biggest man of their company. I guessed that man was the cradle operator. The big man and the two shovel men seemed to be responding to the bucket man's fulmination.

The bucket man was clearly a greenhorn, as I had learned we newcomers were called. His clothes were city clothes, and while travel-worn, were relatively clean. Perhaps he had come by ship. The other three had the rough, patched clothes and muddy boots of seasoned miners.

A few prospectors in adjoining claims paused in their work, but most ignored the irate voices.

Suddenly, the man holding the bucket threw it to the ground and stormed off.

The Frenchmen continued to yell at each other, even though it was clear the former bucket man was calling it quits. In my rambles I had seen other cradles in use and I was pretty sure the man who was leaving had carried water from the stream to the cradle. The deserter shouted abuse at any of the other miners who dared to smile as he splashed across the creek.

The French prospectors watched their companion disappear down the trail toward town. The biggest man, still speaking angrily, bent to pick up the discarded bucket. He held it out to what I called the middle man, as he was shorter than the big man and taller than the third man. Then he held it out to the third man, the smallest of the trio. Both scowled and shook their heads vigorously, refusing to take over the job.

If they'll let me help them, I can see better how a cradle works.

"I can do that!" I called out as I crossed the stream towards them.

The three whipped around to discover who was shouting at them. By then, I was close enough to hold out my hand for the bucket. "I can do that," I said again.

Blinking in bewilderment, the big man handed me the bucket.

I filled the bucket in the stream and returned to stand by the cradle, ready to pour.

The Frenchmen gazed at me as if I'd just dropped out of the sky. The biggest fellow jabbered at the other two, who scampered off to shovel up some dirt. The big man sat back down next to the cradle and took hold of the handle attached to the side. He said something to me in a deep, mild voice. I couldn't understand a word, but I nodded and prayed what he had said wasn't important to the job.

Soon, the middle man, a lanky fellow who seemed all arms and legs, came up with a bucket full of dirt and dumped it in the top tray. The first time, I poured the water too fast. The big man didn't get mad. He just held up his free hand and patted the air, telling me to slow down. After a couple more buckets I got the hang of it, and the big man smiled. So we worked the rest of the day in harmony. The three chatted and laughed in a quiet, satisfied way, as if the rancor had never occurred.

I watched the cradle operator closely, to see how he rocked the cradle to get the dirt to spread out in the top tray and how it washed through the holes as I poured the water on it. The shovelers and the water boy, that was me, got a little rest whenever the big man dumped the rocks and larger gravel out of the top tray to make room for fresh dirt. This revealed that the top tray was not fixed to the rest of the machine, and that it had an iron bottom where the holes were cut.

A few times we would stop and the big man would scoop out the sand trapped behind the little sticks in the bottom tray. This he spooned into a gold pan. Then we would gather round to watch him wash away the last of the sand, in hopes of seeing some color. Color—that was one of the words I'd heard miners use for gold. The more he worked the pan, the more gray sand washed away. It left a very, very fine *black* sand. At last, as more black sand was washed away, we could see the glint of gold. With careful tipping and gentle washing motions, the big man was able to make the gold gather in one spot and the very last of the black sand in another.

Sometimes there wasn't any color, and when there was, it would be tiny flakes and grains. But it was unmistakable! When even the smallest fragment of that golden light winked in the pan, my breath caught in my throat. I couldn't believe I was at the very heart of the vast enterprise. I was peering at what I'd tramped thousands of miles to see. The desire to see yet more color in the next pan blossomed in my breast like a fire catching in dry grass. I couldn't stop grinning. The Frenchmen laughed at me.

When we stopped working, the sun had long since slid down behind the western ridge of the canyon. We had almost three teaspoons of gold to show for our labors. The big Frenchman carefully poured the dust out onto a cloth spread over a board and divided it into equal parts with a small folding knife. I was puzzled. There were only three of them, but he divided the gold into four equal portions. Maybe they still owed some to the man who had quit. The middle man sifted his portion into a small green bottle with his enormous, long fingered hands. He had carved a wooden stopper. The other shoveler, the shortest man, put his part in a worn leather pouch. I remarked that he had taken the trouble to stay clean-shaven while his two companions had let their whiskers flourish. The big man put his in an old tobacco tin. Then they all looked at me.

I looked back at them. *Could it be?* The big man pointed at the last portion with the blade of his little knife and then pointed the blade at me, making little stabbing motions that could only mean it was for me. I almost shook my head, but my friend Will screeched in my mind, *DON'T YOU DARE!*

I pointed at my chest and raised my eyebrows in question. My heart beat like a mad drum. I had butted in on their crew. They didn't owe me a thing. The big Frenchman nodded. I may not have dropped from the sky, but in that moment, I could have bounced that high. There was only one problem—I didn't have a container. That's how much of a greenhorn I was. The big man said something to me I didn't understand. Of course, he could see that right away, so he said the same thing again.

"I'm sorry," I said.

The man who had the bottle spoke to the big man and handed him a piece of paper he had taken from his pocket. *If he writes it in*

French, that won't do me any good either. Instead, the big man replied in a friendly way to his partner who had provided the paper, and they both laughed. The big man folded the paper so as to make a little packet and put my portion of the gold dust into it. He folded it up carefully and handed it to me.

"*Votre salaire.*" He held up the bucket and pointed at the packet.

I didn't understand those words either, but I thought I understood what it probably meant. "Wages," I said. "Thank you."

"Ah!" smiled the big Frenchman. "Thank you. *Merci beaucoup!*" He pointed at me and said, "Thank you." Then he pointed at himself. "*Merci beaucoup.*"

I grinned. "Yes."

He pointed at me. "Yes." Then at himself, smiling. "*Oui.*"

I grinned even more. "*Oui.*"

There were smiles all around. I put the packet in my compass pouch.

We worked out that I would come back the next morning and continue to be the water carrier. We did this mostly with gestures, like me using the sleeping gesture, and then picking up the bucket, or the Frenchman pointing at me and then at the ground where I was standing. We shook hands, and I headed for town to tell Mr. Hoyt of our good fortune.

At last, we were really in the gold rush! Dad would be proud we had some real gold dust to show for the first day's effort. I didn't think it mattered that the gold was in the form of wages. We'd come out here to get gold, surely wages would count. And they were honest wages: I had done my part, just like the shovelers. I was sure if I could continue to help the Frenchmen for a few days, we would have enough gold to buy a pan and shovel. Hopefully this early success would improve Mr. Hoyt's spirits, too, so he'd drink less and be ready to work when his leg healed.

Then our own search could begin in earnest.

CHAPTER 29

When I got back to Chen Yi's, Bugle was right where I'd left him. Except he had two bowls set next to him. One had water, the other had probably had food, but that was in Bugle's belly. The restaurant was alive with the contented hubbub of people sitting at their supper. Chen Yi was busy serving up steaming dishes, so I just waved at him. He nodded back. I knelt down and scratched Bugle good all over. "How you doin', boy? Huh? How you doin'?" While I scrubbed and scratched, I checked him for ticks. His tail thumped the ground. "You been good?"

Bugle licked my face and hands. I sat down and gathered him into my lap and gave him a good hug. I thought of my sister Amy for a minute— how we used to wrestle and horse around— and a sadness settled on me. *Can't start doing that.*

"You won't believe what I saw today," I said to Bugle. "Another deer. A doe this time. And some funny little plump birds, scurrying along in a line. And best of all, each one had a little black tassel on the top of its head that bobbed and jiggled as they ran."

Bugle looked up at me and licked his chops, then went back to panting contentedly.

"And I found a rattlesnake skin. Looked like he'd just shed it. I stretched it out. Best I could tell, it was at least four feet. You can bet he's bigger now. Let's make sure we don't run into him." I scrubbed Bugle's ears. "But best of all, we have some gold! Our first day in the gold rush, and we got lucky!"

I dug out my compass pouch and jiggled it above Bugle's head. He was not impressed.

"You dog good luck. Miners like," Chen Yi said.

I looked up. He wore a cap today, the same deep blue color as his coat and trousers. His cap was like none that I knew. It had no brim, and it was soft and round and sat low to his head. "You want supper? Today special: pork with black bean sauce."

I lifted Bugle out of my lap and got to my feet. "Thank you, Sir, but I want to find Mr. Hoyt and tell him of our good luck. Then we'll come back for some supper, if that's all right."

"Very popular dish. You hurry." Chen Yi smiled as he went off to tend to his customers.

I untied Bugle. "C'mon. Let's go find Mr. Hoyt and tell him we're in the gold rush!"

The street was busy, as usual. But the night sounds were different from day sounds. Day sounds were wagons and horses and people calling out, the thump and scrape of sacks and crates, hammering and sawing. Night sounds were music and laughter, loud talk, whooping and shouting.

I searched in vain for my partner. I didn't worry too much when he wasn't in the first couple of places. With his love of gab, he could be anywhere. After the saloons, I checked every eating place, sleeping place, every alley. *Where can he be? What could have happened to him?*

I thought of going down to the river to see if he had drowned, but I scolded myself. *That's silly.* The river would have carried him off.

There was nowhere else to look for Mr. Hoyt. "He can't have just vanished," I said to Bugle as we headed back to Chen Yi's restaurant. "He can barely get around with his crutch."

I'll just have to let him find me.

As unpredictable as he could be, and as much as I might disagree with his behavior now and then, he was my adult, somebody who knew me, even if it was just a little bit. If I couldn't have my dad, it had to be Mr. Hoyt. And Dad had said I should look out for Mr. Hoyt, too.

My stomach rumbled, reminding me I was hungry. *Wouldn't it be swell to run into Mr. Galloway at Chen Yi's?* I could show him my gold, and he could tell me more about mining.

The tables at Chen's Garden were all full, so after I tied up Bugle near his bowls, Chen Yi took me into the kitchen. The cook was dancing around his stove like a mad magician, stirring here, flipping there, splashing sauce in a pan. The side of the big table nearest the stove was lined with bowls and bottles of the ingredients they had prepared this morning. He reached back, hardly looking, for a handful of this or that, and threw it into a bowl-shaped frying pan. He had three, no, four of those pans going at once.

The cook lifted one of the pans off the fire and slid the contents smoothly into a serving dish Chen Yi held, not losing a drop. Chen Yi said something him and the cook nodded, then tossed the strangely rounded pan back on the stove to start another order. Chen Yi took the full dish out to the dining room.

I watched the cook, amazed at his agility. He could do all that and still know exactly when the stove needed another piece of wood to keep the heat just right. Before I knew it, he plunked a steaming bowl in front of me.

"Pork. Black bean sauce." He grunted, turning back to his stove.

I was too hungry to wrestle with the eating sticks. I'd heard the miners calling them chopsticks. Instead, I grabbed a fork and dived in. It was delicious.

I was determined to pay for my supper this time. After all, I had gold in my pouch, didn't I? I was a real prospector now. I was sure it would be enough. But, again, Chen Yi scowled when I brought out my pouch.

"I have enough. I had luck today. I have enough," I insisted.

"No matter. My debt bigger than one, two bowls supper," he said solemnly. "Think how many days bad smell keep customers away from Chen's Garden. That all tables, many times, three times day. Breakfast, dinner, supper. For how many days?" His eyebrows shot high on his forehead. "Think how many customers Chen Yi lose with bad smell." He looked down his nose, waiting for an answer.

I didn't have one.

"Food for you, Bugle dog, small price." He leaned forward and squinted through a tiny gap between his pinched thumb and forefinger. "Tiny price." Chen Yi settled back and closed his eyes. "No more speech on this."

I knew I had been put in my place.

Chen Yi took another dish out to a customer and I took my bowl over to the big tin tub that was their dishwashing place. I noticed that the water barrel was almost empty. I looked into the other water barrel. It *was* empty. It was late, but they would have a few more customers yet. I took up the bucket and headed out to the town's water supply. Chen Yi watched me weave through the tables with a suspicious scowl.

The last customers were leaving as I finished refilling both barrels. The cook was smiling, but he tended his stove. Chen Yi was cross as a wet hen.

I smiled at him. "You said no more speech on this, so I'm not saying anything."

"Doing good as saying," Chen Yi grumbled.

In the end, I helped with the dishes and filling up the bottles of sauces, then stacked more wood near the stove, all getting ready for the next day. Chen Yi tried to keep up his scowl, but I could tell by his quiet speech with the cook, he wasn't really cross. I felt better. I knew the cook was happy for the help. At last, Chen Yi pointed at the sacks of flour and rice and said in a stern voice, "Sleep here. Miners start early."

The flour sacks were only a bit softer than the ground, but I was just grateful for someplace to lay my head. It seemed like I had been asleep only a few minutes when I heard Bugle's warning bark.

A second later, Chen Yi was shaking my shoulder. "Town on fire! Town on fire! Go!"

The cook was loading a wheelbarrow with kitchen gear and bottles of sauce.

I had no sooner hopped off the rice sack bed, when he took three of them and threw them in the wheelbarrow. My mind went to Mr. Hoyt. He had to still be in town. I knelt in front of Bugle. "You have to wait here, boy."

I stood up and called to Chen Yi. "Will you look after my dog?"

He nodded without turning to me. Then I did what I shouldn't have done. I ran into the burning town.

To the west, a wall of fire leapt above the black silhouettes of buildings, the orange flames writhing like mad demons. Above the blaze columns of smoke boiled into the night sky. The fire must have started near the livery stable.

A man tried to stop me. "Don't go in there, Son. You won't come out!"

I pulled away from his grasp and kept heading toward the flames. *Partners look out for each other. I promised Dad!* If I lost Mr. Hoyt, I would fail in that promise, just like I failed in my promise to bring Dad home.

Furniture was being tossed out of second story windows. Other people carried their belongings out of buildings and piled it in the middle of the street: bedding from the hotels; bottles and furniture from the saloons; merchants their goods. In desperation, they pleaded with people to help. Some wanted to be paid, most just wanted to get away. A few carts and wagons were being loaded, but the teams hitched to them were plunging and rearing in the traces, their eyes rolling with fear.

The air was hot, thick, full of smoke and big chunks of flaming debris raining down. I swatted at drifting, stinging embers that landed on me. I darted into buildings, pushing against people who were scrambling to get out, searching each face. I had to hope he might have been in some back room during my earlier search.

Out into the street again, fighting through wild-eyed people hurrying east to the other end of town. Ahead of me, the leaping, hungry flames marched up the street like an invading army. My eyes and throat burned. The roar was deafening. A wind from the west pushed the fire along. Many of the buildings in town were only canvas tents. The fire gobbled these up as if they were paper. Many other buildings were partly canvas, and the canvas only helped the dry lumber to catch fire more quickly.

The air became a living thing, thick with searing, suffocating smoke and swirling cinders.

Somewhere, a bell rang frantically. People fleeing the flames filled the street like a surging river. Clouds of sparks drifted, landing on animals and on wagons, setting what people had salvaged ablaze. But those same people just kept bringing more out while they could. Then they had to give up their building to the advancing flames. Soon I would have to get back to Bugle.

I passed a man loading small sacks, each little bigger than a loaf of bread, onto a wagon. He dropped one, and it burst open when it hit the ground, spilling a treasure of gold nuggets into the dirt. He made no attempt to retrieve it. No one else gave it a second glance.

Suddenly a tremendous explosion erased every other sensation. The whole building that had been Radley's General Merchandise disappeared in a flash of blinding light. Burning lumber shot out and up in every direction as if fired from cannons. A piece of lumber hit me flat across the chest and knocked me off my feet. People ran for cover. Tools, boots, and clothing, much of it aflame, tumbled out of the sky to start new fires.

I went into The Parisienne, searched all the rooms. I found a man still asleep in room twelve, but it wasn't Mr. Hoyt. The man only groaned when I yelled at him about the fire, so I dragged him off the bed. He crumpled to a heap on the floor. I punched him and shook him until he roused himself.

I yelled at him like the hotel lady had yelled at Mr. Hoyt. "Fire! Get out! Now! Git!" and I shook him and prodded him some more until he crawled out of the room on his hands and knees. Smoke seeped in, orange light played on the walls. Finally, he looked around, stumbled to his feet, and ran. *Maybe Mr. Hoyt's in the dormitory upstairs.* I came back out into the lobby in time to see the side wall of The Parisienne sag inward. A building next door had collapsed against it. Flames licked in through gaps in the wall. The ceiling was smoking and starting to sag, too. That meant the dormitory on the second floor was already lost to the fire. The falling ceiling chased me out the door.

As I searched, smoke and flames replaced people pouring from the buildings. My eyes and nose were running. I desperately needed a drink of water. I tripped over a bucket and saw a line of them leading between two buildings toward the river. Somebody'd tried a bucket brigade but gave it up.

A building across the street was glowing from the inside like a furnace, top to bottom. A second later it burst into flame and melted before my eyes. The surge of heat washed over me, a suffocating blanket.

I found Mr. Hoyt's crutch lying in the street. The nearest buildings were already burning. I prayed he wasn't trapped in any of them, beyond my help. How was he managing without his crutch? Had smoke and heat overwhelmed him? My worries were cut short by the appearance of the lady clerk from The Parisienne. She was fleeing the inferno, but she herself was on fire. Where had she come from? I ran to her and thrust Mr. Hoyt's crutch between her ankles, sending her sprawling. I shrugged off my jacket and smothered the flames on her back. Her hair was all but singed off. She struggled to escape.

"Be still!" I yelled, patting furiously.

When she was out of immediate danger, I rolled off her, and she turned wild, staring eyes on me. Without a word, she scrabbled up her guest ledger and stumbled toward the unburnt part of town, shedding wisps of smoke and scraps of charred clothing.

She was one of the last. *Where had she been? Why did she wait so long? If I missed her, could I have missed Mr. Hoyt, too?* I looked in all directions. Burning wagons, abandoned merchandise, fallen, flaming timbers, burning canvas swirling like mad ghosts in torment. No Mr. Hoyt. I picked up his crutch, looking around to see what buildings I could still search. Cinders and flaming debris fell like rain. Sparks burned holes in my clothes and singed my hair. I couldn't remember where I had lost my hat.

All around me— nothing but flames!

I ran searching for Mr. Hoyt in the crowds. If he'd been trapped in one of those buildings, there was no saving him now. If I had missed him somehow in the crowds, I had to hope he was being helped to safety wherever everybody was going, most likely that big meadow east of town. Right now, I had to look after my own hide, and get Bugle out of harm's way. Turning in the face of a wall of fire, I sprinted back to Chen's Garden. The flames followed relentlessly.

As I got close to the restaurant, I met the cook coming back with the wheelbarrow empty. Where were they stashing their kit? I laid Mr. Hoyt's crutch on my pack.

Bugle was barking and whining and restless. I knew he was worried. I knelt down. "It's okay, Bugle-boy. We'll just clear a few things out and then we'll get away from this fire. Okay?" Bugle whined and shivered, even though I was petting him.

I found Chen Yi stacking dishes and cups on a blanket spread on the big kitchen table. I looked around for what I could do.

Chen Yi shouted, "Gao Chung help me. You help nephew! Please! Yang Ho store!" He pointed toward the east end of town.

"Keep an eye on Bugle, please! I'll come back for him!" I shouted and took off.

As far as I'd seen, Chen Yi, his cook Gao Chung, and the man I'd seen at Yang Ho's store made up the entire population of Celestials in Grizzly Bar.

I sprinted out into the street calling to Bugle, "Stay!" He couldn't do much else.

I still searched for Mr. Hoyt as I ran. I came into the store to see Yang Ho piling boots into a wheelbarrow. I figured we wouldn't be able to say much to each other, so I went straight to piling boots into the wheelbarrow, as well.

"Thank you, but who are you?" Yang Ho said in perfect English.

I was flabbergasted. This was a piece of luck. "Pegg. Chen Yi sent me."

"Ah!" He smiled. "The boy with the magic dog!" He loaded red flannel shirts. "Trousers! There!" He pointed.

I loaded trousers. How did he know English?

"Thank you! Your assistance is much appreciated," he said.

And not just a few basic words, like Chen Yi. Real English!

The wheelbarrow was quickly piled high and Yang Ho said, "Can you take the barrow? Sun Shu will show you where to go."

A second person had come in from the back room, loaded down with blankets. I couldn't see his face.

So there was another Celestial in town. Yang Ho spoke quickly to the blanket bearer in their language, and then turned to me. "When you get there, wet down these blankets and drape them over the merchandise."

I had only a glimpse of this Sun Shu as he rushed out the door with the load of blankets. About all I could tell was he was young, not many years older than me. The only odd thing was, Sun Shu didn't have a shaved head or braid like Chen Yi and Yang Ho. *Maybe that means he's a kid.*

I followed him quickly with the wheelbarrow of boots. The smell of burnt wood was everywhere, gunpowder, too. The night sky was full of sparks and smoke drifting our way. The fire had by then destroyed half the town. There was another explosion. More burning fragments started more fires. Some people had stopped running and were watching the inferno as if spellbound.

I had to keep stopping to pick up boots and shirts that fell off the wheelbarrow, but we were soon across the road and in the big, scruffy meadow that separated the town from Simpson's Creek, where it joined the South Fork. There was more meadow on the other bank of the creek. Some people had gathered there, hoping the creek would keep them safe from the flames. On that farther patch of ground Yang Ho and his assistant had already assembled a goodly heap of merchandise. They must have reacted quickly to have moved so much already. Sun Shu ran ahead and began soaking the blankets in the river.

I splashed across the creek with the wheelbarrow, almost losing it twice. I dumped out the load at the edge of the heap and went to him with the wheelbarrow. We held the blankets one by one under the water until they were soaked through and then heaved them into the barrow. Sun Shu was slight of build but did not shy from standing knee-deep in the icy water and getting thoroughly soaked while wetting the blankets.

We raced back to the heap of merchandise with the wet blankets and spread them. Then we rushed back to the store with the wheelbarrow for more to save.

The roaring flames were like a monster chewing through town. A fountain of sparks shot into the night sky as another building collapsed. The hills behind the town were lit with a dull red light.

We discovered that Yang Ho had piled more blankets and clothes out in front of the store, as well as bundles of canvas, kegs of nails, saws, hammers, rope. A second wheelbarrow was already loaded with more tools and kettles and frying pans, and wooden boxes with Chinese lettering on them.

"Spices," Yang Ho said without my asking.

Sun Shu brought more coils of rope out of the store. I started loading my wheelbarrow with picks and axes and shovels and gold pans, items I had hoped to be purchasing soon.

When my wheelbarrow was loaded again, Yang Ho handed Sun Shu a rifle and a box of ammunition, all the while speaking to him quietly. Then he turned to me.

"I've told her to stay out and guard the merchandise. Regrettably, she's only recently learned to shoot a gun."

Sun Shu is a girl! And a Chinese girl at that. California was full of surprises. She put the rifle and ammunition in with the spice boxes and headed back toward the meadow. She was clearly struggling with the load but she charged on. I piled on another bundle of shovels and took off after her.

We got back to the mound of merchandise in time to see someone carrying off a pair of boots.

I yelled at him to stop, but he ran off into the dark. A second person with similar ideas was crouched close to the boots, watching our approach.

I took the rifle from Sun Shu and checked to see if it was loaded.

"Hey, you," I yelled at the would-be thief. "This ain't your stuff. Git!" *That's how Dad would say it.* "Git!"

I pointed the rifle into the sky and fired a round. The sound was almost lost in the roar of the fire and the yelling. The man seemed reluctant to give up the easy pickings. I shot a second time into the ground about four feet to the side of him.

"Whoa! Be careful with that rifle, Sonny. You might hurt somebody!" He stood up, but still didn't leave.

I spoke a lot braver than I felt. "You lay a finger on any of this stuff, you'll know what hurt feels like, Mister!"

He scuttled away. I handed the rifle to Sun Shu. "If anybody tries to take anything, do that. Can you do that?" I didn't know if she understood me or not.

She clutched the rifle to her. Firelight played across her face. She was scared, but she nodded her head. I unloaded the wheelbarrows so she wouldn't see me shaking.

When I got back to Yang Ho's store, the buildings across the street were already on fire. I found him patting out sparks that were landing on everything he had gathered out front. The roof of his store was smoking. Maybe two buildings stood between us and the approaching flames. That meant that Chen's Garden was already gone. Had they got away? *Bugle!*

"I have to go find my dog!"

Yang Ho was frantically loading the wheelbarrow. "Did you leave him with Uncle Chen?"

"Yes!" I shouted over the roar.

"Then I'm sure he's safe," shouted Yang Ho. "Please stay. This is the last trip."

Relieved, I started throwing shirts into the barrow. I could have kicked myself for not bringing the other one back. We piled my barrow high, Yang Ho loaded himself down with coils of rope, and we headed back to the meadow.

Before long, the whole town was one big, long fire. Where Yang Ho's store had been was a raging, towering monster of flame. Unbelievably, a few people were still coming out of the maelstrom, clutching some precious object, their hair singed, their watery eyes staring. Everybody else was standing in the meadow beyond the creek, watching the destruction.

I took my leave of Yang Ho and Sun Shu and went in search of Chen Yi and Bugle. I wanted to run, but made myself slow down. It was still the dark of night, with the only light coming from the fire. People were scattered in disordered clumps. Many were in shadow, and the shadows were inky black. If I had any hope of finding Chen Yi or Bugle, I would have to go carefully. I prayed that Chen Yi had Bugle with him, and that I might even stumble across Mr. Hoyt.

Miners came in from their camps on Simpson's Creek to see the show. Everyone faced west, like a congregation, watching quietly, knowing they were powerless. I saw the big lady from The Parisienne hugging her ledger to her bosom. The scowling man from American House slowly folded up his apron. Some people stood in the river, trusting the water to keep them safe. Across the river, along the south bank, more miners stood watching, the ruddy firelight barely reaching them.

I crisscrossed back and forth through the people until I was sure I had looked in every corner of the crowd. I kept hoping for a bark that I knew. I called out, "Bugle!" until I was hoarse.

No Chen Yi, no Bugle, and no Mr. Hoyt. Could they be on the other side of the fire, to the west? Up on the side of the canyon? Then I remembered. My pack had burnt up with Chen's Garden, and along with it, Mr. Hoyt's crutch. Everything that remained to me was on my person.

If I lost both Bugle and Mr. Hoyt, I didn't know what I would do. I was alone in a big, dangerous, unpredictable world.

CHAPTER 30

I stopped searching and, like everybody else, watched Grizzly Bar burn to the ground. Beyond the town there was very little to burn. Almost every tree nearby had been cut down. The wide, tramped road, the scrubby meadow, and Simpson's creek presented further discouragements.

If I had truly lost Bugle and Mr. Hoyt to the fire, there was nothing I wanted to do more than go home. This was a hard, heartless place. There was danger around every corner. It no longer felt like an adventure. It felt more like a relentless string of calamities. *Maybe that's how Uncle Rafe felt after he near froze in that blizzard.*

But to head back home, I'd have to buy an outfit. And to do that would take gold. *Perhaps with daybreak, I'll find them,* I told myself.

There was nothing more to do but wait for the fire to burn itself out. I stood with Yang Ho by their merchandise. Sun Shu was on top of the mound with the rifle, turning now and then to keep watch on all sides. That seemed to be enough to keep people from mischief.

Yang Ho said, "I must thank you again. We could not have saved half as much of our stock without your assistance."

"Glad to be of help." I said it the way my dad did. For myself, I added, "I'm sure glad you can speak English."

Yang Ho laughed. "Ha! Yes." After a minute he said, "My father has been trading with the Yankees for thirty years. He insisted I learn English so I could conduct business when the time came."

I figured it might be okay to be curious. "How long have you been here?"

"I came to California in '47, heading for Monterey to establish a trading house. Chen Yi came in early '49, to bring my bride." He cast a quick glance up at Sun Shu.

That slip of a girl is his wife! It was a brave man who brought his wife to this rough-and-tumble place.

Yang Ho took no notice of my surprise. "Chen Yi decided to stay. He said he wanted a piece of the Gold Mountain. When this madness is over, we may go to San Francisco, or Monterey, and build our trading station. One thing I've learned here—anything is possible."

I was pleased that Yang Ho was speaking to me like I was a friend, an equal. I realized the Frenchmen had, too.

As dawn crept into the sky, the inferno seemed less menacing. Then the heavens took pity on us and sent rain to douse the flames that persisted. Miners went back to their cabins. Townspeople stayed put, despite the wet. There was no shelter left anyway.

When there was enough light to see good, I told Yang Ho, "I'm going to look for Bugle. I should have better luck with daylight." Yang Ho didn't have to know about Mr. Hoyt.

Yang Ho pulled out a pouch. "Please let me pay you for your invaluable help."

I was sorely tempted, but I put up my hand to stop him. "Everybody has to start over. You need that. Thanks just the same. I was glad to help. Chen Yi has been very good to me."

Yang Ho put the pouch away. "Well, then. You have credit at the store for anything you need."

"Thank you, sir. That's generous of you. I'll remember that."

"I wish you good fortune," said Yang Ho. "Thank you again."

I glanced up at Sun Shu to find her looking down at us. I gave her a wave and set off. *A girl! His wife!*

. . .

The fire was mostly out. After a night of roaring flames, the morning seemed strangely quiet. People were beginning to drift back to the smoking ruins. I stationed myself where the meadow narrowed into the street that ran through the town. I could watch everybody coming through.

While I searched the haggard faces, a sudden dread seized me. I would have to write to Mr. Pruitt. I remembered how I hadn't been able to write to my mom of Dad's death. Mr. Hoyt had to come to my rescue and write it for me. Now the awful task of informing Mr. Pruitt of his stepson's demise was mine alone.

On the other hand, Mr. Hoyt could be safe. There were dozens of cabins and shacks on the hills behind the town. There were even more along Simpson's Creek. He might be taking his ease in any one of them right now, enjoying a breakfast of griddle cakes and bacon.

Maybe it would be better to let him find me. After all, I was the only kid for miles around. But I couldn't bring myself to abandon my post while people were still straggling in.

Then Bugle found me! I heard his bark a second before he barreled into me, dragging his lead rope. I fell to my knees and hugged him for all I was worth. "There you are! There you are! Oh, boy, oh, boy. I was so worried!" I rubbed and scratched and inspected him for injuries. "I thought you were burnt up! You still got all your parts?" I was smiling to beat the band, scrubbing his cheeks. He almost wagged his tail clean off. "What did you do with Chen Yi and Gao Chung?"

I looked around. Gao Chung was running toward us, weaving between people. When he got to me he bent over, huffing and puffing.

"I'm glad you're safe," I said, hoping he would understand. "Where is Chen Yi?"

The cook pointed into town. He saw my look of horror and said, "Buy lumber. New store!"

I sagged in relief. I was pretty sure that meant Chen Yi was safe. That left only Mr. Hoyt unaccounted for. And Chen Yi was already planning a new restaurant. *But where is he buying lumber?*

"Go," Gao Chung said.

I didn't know if he meant me or himself. But he clarified quickly by sprinting off up the street, dodging between people and smoking debris.

"Let's go see!" I said to Bugle. I took up his lead rope and raced after Gao Chung. "Who knows? We may bump into Mr. Hoyt yet."

The smell of burnt wood filled the air. I had seen a burned-down barn once, the morning after it happened, and it was an awful mess. Blackened timbers were sticking up at all angles, lying on top of each other. It was very hard to tell that it had been a barn before.

This was a thousand times worse. A whole town was just stark, blackened skeletons of wood and heaps of grey ash. In some places you could see little caves of orange-hot coals glowing. Smoke still hung in the air. A lot of buildings, or parts of buildings, had collapsed into the street, so you had to pick your way carefully.

The few brick walls, built with confidence to withstand fire, were melted in sad, rounded humps. The fury of flames had twisted anything metal like a winter's leaf. A whole town full of goods— clothes, tools, food—had been reduced to ash. How would they replace all that had been lost? Would people just move to some other town? Go back home? Not so, these argonauts! Merchants and landlords were already directing workmen in clearing away the debris. Others were sorting out what could be salvaged.

Right in the middle of the street, a man stood on an upturned wash tub, letting everybody know that the fire was an expression of "Divine wrath!" Off to the side, a gentleman in fancy clothes sat at a rescued table, dealing out cards to miners eager to wager their gold. A few steps farther along, a man was serving drinks off a charred plank spread between two barrels.

I caught scraps of talk as I passed. Some people said the fire was an act of revenge, another said it had started in a greenhorn's camp next to the livery stable. A storekeeper said an organized gang had set the fire so they could loot during all the confusion. A little farther on, I heard a group of merchants, sorting through their charred goods in the street, coming up with ideas on how to prevent the same calamity from happening again.

"Outlaw canvas as a building material," said one.

"Have barrels of water on every premise," said another.

"Fine anyone who refuses to assist volunteer firemen!" proclaimed a third.

The first merchant pointed out that Grizzly Bar didn't have any volunteer firemen. I left them talking about forming a fire committee.

There was no question people were staying put. All you had to do was listen to the talk to know they were going to rebuild, bigger and better!

I came upon that burst sack of gold. Only the shredded sack remained, trampled flat in the road. It had not been completely ignored after all.

I got to the west end of town without finding a trace of Mr. Hoyt. What I *did* find, just beyond the livery stable, where the road came up away from the river, was a lively market going on. The road was choked with the mule trains and tall freight wagons of traders. They were surrounded by crowds of people, all trying to buy whatever the merchants had even before it was unloaded. People were shouting, waving sacks of gold. The really impatient ones climbed up on the wheels to see what was in the wagons.

Gao Chung had already found Chen Yi when I caught up with him. Chen Yi was bidding with another man for a wagon load of lumber. The trader stood facing them with his arms crossed over his chest, waiting to see who would offer the highest price.

I waited for them to take a breath, then I said, "Thank you, Chen Yi, for taking care of Bugle."

Chen Yi turned to me. He was more fired up than I'd ever seen him. "Run! Tell Yang Ho save nails for new Chen's Garden!" He turned back to bidding for the lumber.

I ran back to the meadow, with Bugle right beside me. Yang Ho was open for business, too, right where his merchandise was piled. Yang Ho and Sun Shu were running back and forth, looking like they were trying to serve everybody at once. I guess it should be no surprise. Most people had lost everything in the fire—everything except what they had on their backs. The only other thing they had was an eagerness to get going again.

When I worked my way to the front of the crowd, I got Yang Ho's attention.

"Chen Yi says to save him nails," I shouted above the other shouting. Then I worried that Chen Yi had not said how many nails. "Enough for a new restaurant!"

Yang Ho shouted back. "I will! I see you found your dog!"

"He found me!"

Someone else grabbed Yang Ho's attention and I let myself be pushed back by people who had more urgent business than me.

I had a decision to make. I could keep looking for Mr. Hoyt, or I could look after my own and Bugle's situation. I had about a teaspoon of gold to my name. I was sure that wouldn't buy me much. I couldn't look to Chen Yi for food and lodging anymore. He had his own concerns. The first step was to earn enough money to survive, so I could look for gold. I would see if the Frenchmen still wanted a water carrier. If not, I might get a job helping to rebuild the town. But who would hire a kid when they had hundreds of grown men to hire instead?

If worse came to worse, I could look among the debris for discarded equipment and get started looking for gold on my own. But that was too uncertain.

It was the beginning of November. The nights were cold. Not as cold as a Vermont November, but plenty cold enough. The days were getting chilly, too, and it was probably going to get colder, maybe a lot colder, in the coming months. *Does it snow here? How much? How can you dig for gold under four feet of snow or in a frozen river?*

I was tired of being hungry. I was tired of not knowing where I was going to sleep at night. And winter had followed us down out of the mountains.

Such thoughts produced one hard fact. If I didn't look after myself, I wouldn't be able to meet my obligations to my family or the partnership. *Try the Frenchmen first.* They'd wanted me to come back. The prospectors' first and only job was to find gold. They didn't have anything to rebuild.

Sure enough, by the time I got to the diggings, most all of the prospectors were hard at work, fire or no fire. I spotted the Frenchmen across the river. The shortest man, yesterday a shoveler, was now the water carrier. It was easy to see that he was slowing things down. I was still coming down off the trail across the beach when I yelled. Lots of people looked up, but only the Frenchmen answered my wave. I picked up Bugle and splashed across the stream.

I walked up to the Frenchmen, and set Bugle down. We were all smiling at each other. The shortest man dropped the bucket and fell to his knees to hug Bugle, babbling to him in French with the same affection that I babbled to him in English. The big man smiled down at these shenanigans and said something to the man in French. It could very well be that the Frenchman had a dog like Bugle back home. My dog, for his part, wagged his tail hard enough to knock himself over. I stuck out my hand to shake.

"My name is Pegg," I said. I pointed to my chest. "Pegg."

The big man grinned and shook my hand. *"Je suis Ormond,"* he said, pointing to himself. *"Ormond Bonnet."*

"Bertrand," said the lanky, middle man solemnly, holding out his hand. *"Bertrand Giraud."* He had kind eyes under his dark brows. His threadbare sleeve ended well above his wrist. My hand disappeared in his.

The shortest man stood up on bandy legs with a ready smile. *"Phillipe Arouet."* He shook my hand vigorously, covering our hands with his free hand. He gave me the bucket like he couldn't get rid of it fast enough.

"Bon," smiled the big Frenchman, Ormond. *"On commence."*

Mr. Pruitt back home sometimes said "…commence" at the beginning of a meeting. I wondered if it was the same thing. Anyway, I was pretty sure the Frenchman meant: Let's get going!

I took Bugle over to one of the few trees left near the stream. "Stay. And don't bother anybody," I pointed my finger at him and to the ground at his feet. He sat on his haunches and started panting. Then I went to fill the bucket.

The Frenchmen and I worked well together; I was pleased about that. It wasn't the most exciting labor in the world, except that your next shovelful of dirt could make you rich. But the rhythm of my task left me a minute now and then to look around.

Their claim was quite large, since there were three of them. Stakes marked it out all the way back from the stream to where the ground started to rise steeply. There were a lot of rocks and gravel that hinted where the stream used to flow. I saw several large boulders half buried in the ground. The bottoms of those boulders could be where the old stream bed had been a long time ago. But then I had to go get another bucket of water and concentrate on my pouring.

We washed forty buckets of dirt, or more, that afternoon, but we got no color. We would gather eagerly around the big man, Ormond, as he carefully washed the sand that he had taken from behind the little sticks in the lower part of the cradle. I later learned those little sticks were called riffles. I watched even closer as Ormond worked with the gold pan. He was very gentle in his movements, dipping more water into the pan, tipping the pan at a slightly steeper angle, just so. But there was no gold, no matter how careful he was. They stared into the pan with glum faces.

The shadows were getting long when the Frenchmen stopped work for a smoke. They gathered by the cradle and pulled out identical little white, clay pipes. I could tell by the tone of their talk they were discouraged.

I had messed around in creeks at home enough to know that flowing water always digs a kind of hole, or makes a depression, on the downstream side of a rock in the stream, especially a big rock. I put that idea together with Mr. Galloway's that gold always seeks the lowest spots, and thought that digging on the downstream side of some of those big rocks on the Frenchmen's claim might be worth a try.

I took up Bertrand's shovel and headed for a boulder where I thought the old stream would have been. On the downstream side of the boulder, I struck the shovel into the gravel close to it. Bugle came over to supervise. At first the Frenchmen didn't pay any attention to me, but when I kept at it, Ormond called out to come over and rest. At least, that's probably what he said.

I waved him off and kept digging. Bugle stood up, thinking he might get petted. I didn't comply, so he wandered over to try his luck with the Frenchmen. Phillipe gathered him up with a smile and scrubbed his ears, just like I did.

The gravels were loose, so I made good progress. I soon saw the boulder tapering inward. I was getting close to the bottom. *Will there be anything big enough to see without having to wash a lot of dirt?*

The Frenchmen probably wanted to call it a day. Ormond came over to watch me. *"Qu'est-ce que tu fais?"* It sounded like a question. He was not cross, just curious.

"I have an idea," I said, tapping my temple and pointing at the hole.

He watched me work a minute more and then went back to his comrades. They talked among themselves, probably about my foolishness. But I kept digging.

Three more shovelfuls and I saw what I had hoped for, a lump of yellow among the pebbles, tucked close under the boulder. It was about half as big as my thumb.

I brushed it off and held it up. "Hey!"

The Frenchmen turned to look. I held the nugget high, turning it so it might catch the sun. With a great show of indifference, they ambled over to my spot. Ormond looked around to see if any of the other miners were watching. He held out his palm. "*S'il vous plaît?*"

Phillipe and Bertrand crowded close.

I dropped the nugget in Ormond's hand. It was far, far bigger than anything we had found the day before. They were smiling. I was happy. Phillipe got down on his knees and peered into the cavity. He leaned in, reaching, almost fell in, and came up with another nugget. He spit on it and cleaned it on his sleeve. The gleam was mesmerizing. Ormond looked at me with a big smile. Then he turned to his mates and chattered some instructions. Bertrand picked up his shovel and went back to digging with Phillipe.

Ormond and I washed the dirt Phillipe and Bertrand dug up, just to be sure. But a lot of the material was large gravel and quickly washed. Phillipe and Bertrand soon had a hole about four feet across, down to the bottom of the boulder, which was about three and a half or four feet down. Ground water started to seep in. Phillipe stopped digging and bent down. Bertrand got down on his hands and knees and peered into the hole. They were muttering between themselves. Ormond and I looked at each other. Bertrand rose and turned to us, giving a tiny, sharp jerk of his head. Ormond and I sauntered over to them. Phillipe held up a nugget. It was partly crusted with mud and sand, but it was a nugget, for sure. It was about as big as two joints of my little finger.

Bugle sensed the excitement and trotted around, trying to get a look. Phillipe pointed to the bottom of the hole. *"Regardez,"* he said quietly.

I looked where he pointed. They had dug past the bottom of the boulder, into the depression that the water would have made. There, among the gravels and sand, were glints of gold. Phillipe crouched again and scraped away some of the damp sand to reveal more nuggets with his hand. He handed another nugget up to us. This one was almost as big as a walnut. Ormond, Bertrand, and I looked at it and then smiled big smiles at each other. I was just about to let out a whoop, but Ormond's eyes went wide and he held his finger up to his lips. "Ssshhhhh!" We heard Bertrand grunt and he held out his long, cupped hand. It held a nugget twice as big as the last one. Phillipe was standing in the hole with three more nuggets in his hand. We huddled close together at the edge of the hole and inspected them.

We filled a handkerchief with nuggets, and Ormond said in a low voice, "Eau," he looked at me and pointed to my discarded water bucket. *"Lavage, l'eau."* His voice was tense with excitement.

I took the bucket to the stream and filled it. We gathered around the cradle and I set the bucket down next to it. Ormond carefully laid the handkerchief in the top tray and we all crouched around and set to washing off the nuggets one by one. The Frenchmen were happily muttering among themselves. Ormond patted me on the shoulder. *"Merci, Pegg. Merci beaucoup."*

Phillipe and Bertrand both said *"Oui, oui,"* all the while scrubbing the nuggets.

Then I heard somebody shout, "Pegg!"

Bugle started barking. I knew who it was even before I turned around. Mr. Hoyt stood on the opposite shore of the creek with a new crutch. He had a big smile and he waved with his free arm.

My jaw dropped. I was so relieved he was alive that I forgot he had let me agonize over his fate for so long. He might have been an aggravation, but I would rather have him alive and aggravating than a remorseful memory.

But soon the realization Mr. Hoyt had somehow cheated death roused my ire. I wanted to rush over and find out what had happened to him. At the same time, I wanted to stay and wash the gold.

Mr. Hoyt decided for me. He shouted, "Don't let me bother your work." He paused a minute. "Got to make hay while the sun shines."

I wanted to ask him a dozen questions, but right now he was embarrassing me.

Mr. Hoyt shouted again. "I'll see you at American House."

I wondered why he would say that. American House, like every other building in Grizzly Bar, was a heap of cold ashes. I waved to him and nodded my head. I didn't shout back. I didn't wait to watch him head back to town. Maybe that was bad manners, I don't know. I went back to washing the nuggets. I guess I was scowling, because Ormond and the others exchanged glances, but left me in peace.

When the nuggets were all cleaned, Ormond divided them equally among us. He hefted each portion in his hand as if weighing it, making adjustments with the smaller nuggets. When he had four pretty equal little piles, he looked at each of us and asked, *"D'accord?"*

Phillipe and Bertrand nodded; long and thin Bertrand slowly, Frisky Phillipe fairly bouncing.

From that I figured, we were agreeing on Ormond's division. I nodded my head, too. For me, it was an unexpected bonanza.

We each got out our containers: Bertrand his bottle, Phillipe his pouch, and Ormond his tobacco tin. I got out my compass pouch. We each tucked away our treasure. When I dropped my pouch back down my shirt, it gave a good tug. I was very happy to feel that weight.

Ormond spoke to Bertrand and Phillipe and they went to fill the hole back up. Ormond went to the other side of the boulder and looked around to see if anybody was watching. Then he set three short sticks upright in the gravel, close under the boulder, so we would know which boulder to return to.

We went through the gestures of coming back tomorrow, smiling all the while. Then we all shook hands. Phillipe crouched down and gushed French and affection all over Bugle and the dog loved it. Phillipe looked up at me and said something in his language, and I just grinned and shrugged. But for good measure, I said, "No, he's not for sale." Just in case.

With lots of waving, Bugle and I splashed back across the creek to go find Mr. Hoyt. I was still in a lather about him just reappearing like that, like he'd only been out for a stroll, after me doing all that worrying that he was burnt to a crisp. But I was equally excited to show him our take. Now we could buy supper and stay at a hotel without worrying. In a couple of days we might even have enough to replace our packs and buy mining equipment. Then I stopped.

I had fists full of gold, but there were no places left to sleep, or eat. No stores to buy clothes and equipment. Grizzly Bar was nothing but a smoldering heap.

CHAPTER 31

Somewhere to the west of our canyon the sun was still up, but Simpson's Creek was already cloaked in shadow. I hurried past the meadow, jabbering to Bugle. "Wait'll Mr. Hoyt sees what I've got for him. This is the genuine article! We're on our way!" Bugle barked, drawing my attention to the near miracle spread before me.

The whole street, end to end, had been cleared of debris. It swarmed with people and activity. Lanterns and torches lit the scene like a country fair. Many businesses were already up and running. They might have only a barrel as a counter, or a stump to sit on, but business was in full swing! People had scrubbed their faces and hands, but soot still marked their ears and necks. Having no other clothes to change into, they conducted their business in the singed and soot-smeared garb that proclaimed their recent ordeal. The rare person with clean clothes had probably been up in the hills while the fire raged.

I could smell cooking along with the stink of burnt wood. People were tucking into their supper right next to people who were shoveling up ashes. A barber trimmed a miner's beard next to men pulling apart burnt timbers. Another crew of men wrestled with the twisted ruin of an iron stove. Other people were sifting carefully, patiently through the heaps of ash. *Why?*

I stepped closer to a man who had his hands plunged in the soft, powdery ash. "Can I ask what you're looking for?"

The man gave me a quick glance before returning to his work. "You must be new." He brought his hand up, trailing fine powder, clutching his prize. "This."

"A nail?" I blurted. "But you can get nails by the keg at the hardware store."

He snorted and looked around the area where he was standing. "This used to be the hardware store." Then he pointed. "There's your keg of nails." Several strange lumps of metal, in the shape of kegs, stood among the wreckage. I took a closer look. The fire had melted the nails in kegs to form the shape of the keg holding them!

"Thank you. Good luck." I left the man to his search. My dad would smile approval at such enterprise.

Many spots that had only tents before were already scraped clean and reoccupied. Nobody had a roof over their heads. What materials were available were being used to mark off space, or to build seating and shelves.

Among the jabbering and laughing, I heard someone playing "Old Dan Tucker" on a piano. Somehow, a piano had survived the fire!

I did what it seemed I spent half my time doing—looking for Mr. Hoyt. I couldn't wait to see his eyes pop out when I showed him the nuggets. I had a good hunch they were worth more than my dad made from our farm in six months!

I came to the spot that had been Chen's Garden. Gao Chung was cooking over an open fire. Now the tables were barrels standing on end with boards nailed on top. Chen Yi's customers were sitting on anything that could pass for a seat. He didn't see me, and I didn't interrupt him. The place was packed, and people were waiting.

I despaired of finding the rendezvous Mr. Hoyt wanted, American House, which was no more. Then, at a spot where I guessed the American House used to be, I spied the big, scowling man in his apron carrying around a huge chunk of roasted, dripping meat, carving off thick slices onto people's plates. One of his minions followed behind with a pitcher and a big brush to slather dark sauce on the meat for those who wanted it. People were sitting at long makeshift tables, just like the old place, with the same shouting and jostling.

Behind them I could see a whole beef roasting. I shuddered that Boreas and Yellowstone, too, had likely met the same fate. At another fire a man was ladling out beans from a great kettle with a shovel. I walked up and down among the diners, thankfully ignored, but I did not spy Mr. Hoyt. Bugle darted after scraps under the tables. Reluctantly, I moved on. The aroma of roasted meat made my stomach rumble.

I finally found Mr. Hoyt with a group of men who were standing still while activity surged around them. Mr. Hoyt was in the middle of the gathering, as if he were the center of attention. But he was listening, not talking. That was odd, right there. A tall, thin man dressed in fancy clothes was doing the talking. Like everybody else, you could tell these men had been through the fire. As I got closer, I could see that the fancy man was talking specifically to Mr. Hoyt. At one point, with a stern face, he held up his finger, like my mom did when she was scolding me.

Mr. Hoyt being scolded? That was hard to believe. As soon as I walked up to the group, the fancy man spotted me. His face changed instantly. No one else in the group acknowledged me.

"Excuse me," I said.

"Good day to you, young man!" he announced with a big smile. "Is there something we can do for you?"

The other men turned to look at me. Mr. Hoyt didn't.

"I'd like to speak to Mr. Hoyt," I said.

"What a coincidence!" The man reared back and grinned. "We were doing that very thing!"

The other men in the group rumbled with rough laughter.

The fancy man swept his arm into the air. "Speak away, young man. We're all friends here."

"It's kind of personal, sir." I felt in my bones these were not friends.

The fancy man made a surprised face and then recovered his composure. "Of course, of course. I understand perfectly."

Then he did an odd thing. He licked his fingers. He reminded me of a lizard.

Mr. Hoyt shifted his crutch and said, "If you gentlemen will excuse me. I'll be right back." His new crutch was just a tall, stout stick he hung onto.

"Oh! That won't be necessary," said the fancy man, still smiling. "I think we understand each other, don't we, Hoyt?"

"We do, Sweeney. We do," grumbled Mr. Hoyt reluctantly.

"Excellent," proclaimed the fancy man, grinning, as if he were laying on a blessing.

Mr. Hoyt clapped his free hand on my shoulder and hurried us away into the crowd. He got us well away into the busy street before he stopped. He lowered himself heavily to sit on a handy crate and laid his crutch aside. He was a little winded. He looked over his shoulder to make sure we hadn't been followed.

"I should lecture you on manners." He paused to catch his breath.

"I shouldn't have interrupted. I'm sorry."

He gave a faltering laugh. "Not at all, lad. In this case, your interruption was timely, indeed."

At least I could be glad of that. "Are those men important?"

Mr. Hoyt blinked at me a couple of times. "Indeed they are, Pegg-boy. They are the men who will shape the destiny of this country. They see the possibilities. Like myself, they champion ambitious plans, and they have the courage to pursue them." He looked around again for eavesdroppers, and then resumed, leaning closer. "They won't settle for splashing around in a stream with a pan and a shovel. No, sir. These men will move mountains, mark my word. And if we're smart, we'll move right along with them."

I was impressed again with Mr. Hoyt's ability to see a bigger picture, like his plans for a bigger steamboat. It stood to reason that the gold rush would attract such bold men. Still… "What was Mr. Sweeney cross about?"

"Oh, now, Pegg-boy!" he chuckled deep in his throat. "You're out of your depth here. It's dangerous to jump to hasty conclusions."

"Yessir, but he sure *looked* cross."

"Mr. Sweeney was just making a point in our discussion. A point I agreed with completely, I might add." He checked again to make sure we weren't being followed.

I got the feeling he didn't want to talk about Mr. Sweeney anymore. "Yessir. Well, I have good news. Our worries are over."

"Don't prattle, boy. It's been a long day." Mr. Hoyt didn't look at me. He lifted his hat and ran his hand through his hair.

I was tensed to reveal my treasure. I tried to keep my voice calm, but I couldn't control my smile. "I might have enough to pay for both our suppers and a hotel and…"

"You have money?" Mr. Hoyt eyed me like a hawk ready to dive.

"You could say that." Smiling, I poured out most of the nuggets into my hand. "Look!"

The little square of paper from yesterday got stuck inside the pouch. The compass tumbled out again, and I put it back. I had the brief satisfaction of seeing Mr. Hoyt's eyes go wide. He grabbed my hand and dumped the nuggets into his own cupped palm.

I couldn't restrain myself. "How much do you think they're worth?"

He dipped his head to inspect them carefully. "How did you get these?" He tested one with his teeth.

I was taken aback. *Does he think I stole them?* "I earned them," I said defensively. "In the diggings, where you saw me."

"Are there more?" Mr. Hoyt said, all his good humor gone.

I remembered Ormond saying "Sshhh." I clamped a lid on my excitement. "We don't know yet. We just found it this afternoon."

"We? It?" he barked, losing patience. He pushed nuggets around with his finger.

I was more cautious. "The Frenchmen. Where we found these nuggets."

Mr. Hoyt snapped his head up and gave me a smirk. "Come now, Pegg, boy. This is no time for games. Partners don't hold out on each other."

"I'm not! Like I said, we just found the spot this afternoon. But it looks like," I caught myself. "Well, like there might be a little more." I hoped I hadn't betrayed the Frenchmen too much.

Mr. Hoyt appeared not to notice my stumble. He went back to inspecting the nuggets. "Those others you're working with, did they get equal shares?"

"Yessir. Ormond was very careful. I got my fair share."

Mr. Hoyt was still staring at the gleaming, golden pebbles. "As it should be, as it should be." He sounded like he was thinking of something else.

"Let's divide them up," I said, preparing to shake out the couple of nuggets still in the pouch.

Mr. Hoyt closed his fist over the nuggets in a flash. "Whoa! Not so fast! Not so fast, laddie!"

My hands stopped and I guess I must have looked confused.

Mr. Hoyt checked the street and then carried on in a quieter tone. "It's not just you and me, Lad. We have people back home to think about. Winter's coming on. Our families will need extra lamp oil, food. Perhaps your momma could use a new winter coat."

I kicked myself for being so thoughtless. A few of these nuggets would make their winter a little more comfortable.

Mr. Hoyt went on. "And we can't forget our neighbors' stake in this. A little show of appreciation for them would be in order, don't you think?"

"Yessir." It was getting complicated. "I'll send my share to my family."

"There's a good lad," said Mr. Hoyt, patting my shoulder while he checked the street again. He turned back with his lopsided smile. "Now, don't fret yourself. I'll work it all out. We'll set up accounts for everybody at the express office. Compared to running those showboats, this'll be as easy as pie."

That was good to hear. Thank the Lord, the express office had been saved from the fire.

Mr. Hoyt cocked his head with an even bigger smile. "And for good measure, I'll send your portion home for you."

"Thank you, sir. I'd appreciate it." I didn't stop to think what I would live on. I was just happy an adult seemed to have matters well in hand. I knew nothing about handling money. *This is why Dad said stick with Mr. Hoyt.*

"Write a note," he added, "and I'll see that it goes along with the bank draft. I'll be doing the same for Mr. Pruitt."

I wondered where I could get some paper and a pen.

Mr. Hoyt said, "Of course, we'll have to look after ourselves."

I felt like we were finally being partners. I smiled. "Yessir. That would be good."

Mr. Hoyt grinned wider. "Or we won't be any good to anybody, will we?"

"No, sir." We were grinning at each other.

"We'll use my share to meet our needs." Mr. Hoyt gave me a wink. "And maybe a little of Mr. Pruitt's, if need be. I don't think he'd begrudge us an emergency or two, do you?"

I didn't know Mr. Pruitt well enough to say one way or the other. If anybody knew him well it would be Mr. Hoyt. And if we struck it rich, nobody would much mind anything!

"And if we're careful," Mr. Hoyt raised his eyebrows high, "there might be a little left over for a celebration when the time comes. What do you say?"

"Yessir. That sounds good."

He slipped the nuggets into his coat pocket.

"There's a good lad. We're good partners, you and I. Each doing our part." Mr. Hoyt was smiling wider than ever.

I dropped my pouch back into my shirt. "Let's go get some supper."

"Indeed, lad. Indeed." He fished out one of the smallest nuggets and handed it to me. "You go on ahead. I'll swing by the express office, set up these accounts, and catch up with you." He reached for his crutch and labored to his feet.

"But where will we—" I started as he turned his back.

"Don't you worry, lad. I'll find you. I'll find you. Just like I did today." And he hobbled into the crowd.

Why do I have the feeling that there is more to what Mr. Hoyt says than just his words? It would be worse than impolite to follow him to see if he did what he said he'd to do. I couldn't admit I didn't trust my partner. Everything would fall apart. But I did feel a little like a puppet, with Mr. Hoyt jigging the strings, lest the puppet look in the wrong direction. *But puppets don't find gold, do they?*

I shrugged off my doubts and went looking for dinner.

Chen Yi's was still busy, so I took my place in line. Bugle went around making friends with people. I watched Gao Chung cook. Even though he had almost nothing like his original kitchen set up, he was still jumping around like a mad magician. His bottles of sauce stood in a row to his left, like obedient attendants waiting to be called. A big kettle of rice was steaming to his right. Somehow he kept from burning himself over the open flames. Then I noticed he had used up most of his chopped wood. Without even thinking, I left my place in line and went around the eating area to his kitchen. He'd collected a big pile of tree branches and scrap lumber, but none of it was ready for the fire. I picked up his ax and set to work. I had no sooner chopped up a few pieces than he grabbed them and slid them into the fire. I guessed that was the right idea. I set to with a will.

Fortunately, I could chop faster than the fire could burn, so before too long I had a good pile of wood ready for Gao Chung. While I was chopping, I remembered that I had forgotten to scold Mr. Hoyt for being impossible to find while the town was burning down. I hadn't gotten to tell him how worried I was. Of course, it wasn't my place to be scolding adults. But it was all part of not being able to talk to him. Not like my dad, or my mom. They had a sense for when I needed to talk about something, and, if they could, they would stop and listen.

Mr. Hoyt was slippery as an eel. I didn't know where he had been during the fire. I didn't know where he was now. Heck, I hadn't known where he was for most of the trip, until Dad got sick. Then he was always around. Now he was back to his old tricks, disappearing and reappearing as it pleased him. Unpredictable is what he was, whether in his moods or his actions. I felt like I was on my own, except then he'd come swooping in, and I'd be jumping to his tune. Maybe, when his leg mended, and we were prospecting properly, so to speak, maybe then things would settle down.

That was the good thing about chopping wood. It gave you a chance to think things through. I was just splitting the last piece of charred timber when I felt a tug at my sleeve.

Chen Yi handed me a steaming bowl of chicken and noodles and onions. Like many of his dishes, it was as much soup as it was stew. Pointing to where Bugle was licking out a bowl, he went away without a word. I laid into that supper the way I'd laid into the wood. The evening air chilled the sweat I'd worked up. My shirt was drenched. But the good hot food warmed me right up again.

When I was done, I dug out one of the small nuggets still caught in my compass pouch. I tried to hand it to Chen Yi, but he wouldn't take it.

"You already pay supper. You chop wood," said Chen Yi.

"I only chopped a little," I said back.

"You want pay supper, you take this supper Yang Ho and wife." He handed me a bundle made of heavy cloth. "Careful. Easy spill." The suppers inside were probably very much like mine.

I took the bowls and mimicked his speech. "You make hard bargain." I smiled.

"You smart aleck boy," Chen Yi said, and jerked his head to send me on my way.

The bowls must have been very hot because the cloth itself was warm. I hugged them to me like a warming brick in the wintry night.

I called to Bugle. "Come on, boy."

I don't know how they did it. In the space of an afternoon, Yang Ho and Sun Shu had cleared the place where their store had been, made a simple rope fence to mark off their space, moved what was left of the merchandise back from the meadow, and set up a small tent in the back corner, just inside the rope fence.

Yang Ho had cobbled together some simple benches to keep their merchandise off the ground. They had it all organized: Boots and shoes in front as you walked in, clothing over to the left, mining equipment along the back, fancy goods next to the fence on the right. When I arrived, Yang Ho was helping a miner choose a pair of trousers. Sun Shu was nowhere to be seen. Bugle announced our approach. A moment later, Sun Shu emerged from the tent and hurried to me.

She smiled as she took the bundle from my hands. "Thank you. Uncle Chen is very thoughtful."

Yang Ho must be teaching her English. Sun Shu bent down and petted Bugle, who thumped his tail in delight. A few moments later, Yang Ho joined us. He arranged three of the spice boxes in front of the tent for us to sit. Sun Shu set the bundle carefully on the ground between them.

She untied the cloth and looked down in dismay. "There are only two bowls." She looked from me to Yang Ho.

"Oh! I ate already," I blurted out. "At Chen's Garden."

"Please excuse us then," said Yang Ho.

"Of course. Enjoy your supper." I got up to go.

They both looked at me in alarm. "No, no!" Yang Ho said. "We didn't mean for you to leave. Please stay." I sat back down. Yang Ho and Sun Shu muttered to each other in hushed voices, in Chinese. Then Yang Ho turned to me. "I must apologize," he said. "As you can see, my knowledge of the language is incomplete." He gave a quick glance to Sun Shu, who gave him a tiny nod. "I certainly meant no offense," he said.

I smiled at him. "Your English is better than mine."

"Oh! No," Yang Ho protested with a smile, shaking his head.

Finally, I said, "Please. Eat. It will get cold." It's what my mom always said.

Sun Shu took the lid off one of the bowls and handed it and a set of chop sticks to her husband. Yang Ho dove right in. Sun Shu sat still as a post. *Why isn't she eating?* After a minute, Yang Ho said something quietly to her in Chinese. She picked up her bowl and began to eat. *Had she been waiting for him to finish? Had she been waiting for his permission to eat?* If anything, at our house, Dad waited for Mom to sit down before he began passing food around. Things must be different in China.

Sun Shu seemed as delicate as a sparrow. She wasn't any taller than me, and her movements were smooth, like flowing water. My mom was small compared to many of the ladies in our neighborhood, but I'd bet she was almost a head taller than Sun Shu. I could tell Sun Shu was light boned, but still she'd wrestled more than one wheelbarrow load to the meadow last night. And she'd guarded the mound of merchandise by herself.

When Yang Ho was done, Sun Shu took his bowl and chopsticks. She said something in Chinese to him. He grunted.

"Sun Shu was agreeing with me," he said.

"About what?" I asked. In my head, my mom frowned at my forwardness.

"Well, it's a matter of some delicacy," Yang Ho said slowly.

"I'm sorry. I didn't mean to be nosy."

"It is not necessary," he said. "I've been fretting over how to bring it up."

Why do I get the feeling I'm involved in this?

"Well, my dad always said, 'Just speak it out plain'."

Yang Ho didn't. He fretted. "It's just that it's quite an imposition, so I do not raise the matter lightly."

He's the adult. He'll probably figure it out.

At last, he said, "Perhaps if I started at the beginning, so to speak, it would make more sense."

I nodded and waited. He took his time choosing his words.

"There are many opportunities for us here, I mean for Chen Yi and myself and people from our country. But there are also many challenges for us, as well."

To me, his opportunity had just burned down. It seemed a good place to nod.

"Now we have had this fire," he went on, "and everyone is in a great hurry to rebuild. But only so many miners are willing to stop prospecting to help build."

My first thought was to offer to help him and Chen Yi rebuild, but then I remembered of the good luck I was having with the Frenchmen.

Yang Ho said, "There are groups of my people in San Francisco, called tongs. Ours is the Hop Sing Tong. They will help us rebuild. Tomorrow I will ride to San Francisco to tell them of the fire and ask for their help. I will also buy supplies for rebuilding both my store and Chen Yi's restaurant."

I felt an urge to ask him to look for Linnaeus Peabody and check for mail from Vermont, but I held my tongue.

"I hope to be gone no more than a week or ten days." Yang Ho threw a quick glance to his wife.

I knew how far you could reasonably ride in a day, but I had no idea how far away San Francisco was, or the sort of country that lay between Grizzly Bar and there.

Yang Ho went on. "Uncle Chen and I have discussed the matter. He has offered to look after Sun Shu while I am gone, but such an arrangement would probably mean losing our store. I do not wish that to happen."

I knew almost nothing of the workings of towns and merchants. "Why? Why would you lose the store, I mean?"

"If we don't maintain a presence, others will consider it abandoned and take it over."

"Just like with the prospectors."

"Exactly," replied Yang Ho. He cast another glance at his wife before going on. "To come to the point. I would be most grateful to you if you would look after Sun Shu while I'm away."

I blinked at him. *Did I hear him right?* I found them both looking at me.

"I know full well it is a very great deal to ask," Yang Ho said. "I would ask Gao Chung, but Chen Yi needs him to cook. And I thought, since you do not yet have a claim to worry about...."

Boy! Am I in a fix.

We held each other's gaze over the fire. Sun Shu took the bowls and chop sticks away to wash.

Yang Ho was treating me like an adult. But agreeing to his request would mean giving up my spot with the Frenchmen, my first real success in the diggings. I didn't think Mr. Hoyt would be too happy about that. I was the only one in our partnership making any money, so far. If his leg was ever going to heal, he needed good food and good rest. But I could not help being flattered by the trust Yang Ho was putting in me. I was reminded half a dozen times a day I was a kid. Mr. Hoyt certainly never let me forget it. Taking responsibility for another person was a far cry from collecting eggs and chopping wood.

And what exactly did looking out for Sun Shu mean? Keeping her company all day? Making sure she had food? Guarding her from trouble?

When Sun Shu returned, she and her husband spoke quietly together for a few minutes.

Then Yang Ho turned back to me. "Excuse us. May I explain?"

Dad always said, when in doubt, listen. So I just nodded.

Yang Ho placed both hands on his knees and gave me a serious look. "Uncle Chen is certain that, as long as the roads allow, three times as many traders will be coming our way once word of our fire spreads. While I am away, he has offered to buy a quantity of goods for the store at the same time he is buying supplies for the restaurant." He gestured toward his wife. "These goods he will bring to Sun Shu." He gestured to the ground at his feet. "Here, for her to sell."

Where do I fit in? Should I give up my first real luck in the diggings to watch Sun Shu sell stuff to miners?

Yang Ho relaxed with a smile, spreading his hands wide. "If she has the good fortune to sell all that Uncle Chen brings on a given day, she has only to wait until the following morning to have more. Thus, everyone will know we are still in business."

I smiled back. "Let's hope she has good fortune." *And what do we do the rest of the time?*

He blinked. He hadn't expected well-wishing. "Yes, thank you. That is generous."

"And…" I started.

He waited politely.

"Well, what do I do?"

Once again, he consulted his wife, who provided only an encouraging nod.

Yang Ho gave me a sheepish smile. "You can help as you see fit. Many of the containers and bundles are burdensome. And, while it is necessary to watch the store at night, she should not be here alone."

That made sense, but if I didn't go back, the Frenchmen would certainly find a replacement for me, especially if word got out about their good luck. Will's voice snickered inside my head. *Ask him if Chen Yi will provide a fist full of gold each day to keep Pissy Hoyt happy.*

Sun Shu rose to her feet and went into their tent.

I glanced after her. "What about after the store closes?" Which was a silly thing to say. There were no walls or doors. The store was a patch of dirt marked off by a rope you could step over. He'd want me to stay here but not in that little tent with his wife.

"I will ask Uncle Chen to buy you a tent at his first opportunity. And he has generously offered credit for your meals while I am away."

Sun Shu came out of the tent with a small box, a tea pot and three cups, and knelt at the fire to make tea.

Yang Ho became serious again. "I realize this request would prevent you from prospecting, which could reward you handsomely. But if you'll accept my word, I will compensate you generously for each day I am away, once the store is up and running again."

So it won't be a complete loss. "And it would only be for a week or two, at most?"

I could tell he was relieved. He tried to stay serious. "It shouldn't take any longer. I hear supplies of every kind are pouring into San Francisco as fast as people are."

I stopped short in my thoughts. "I am not my own man in this. I will have to clear it with my partners." The Frenchmen were not, strictly speaking, my partners. But how quickly mutual regard had colored my opinion.

Yang Ho looked contrite. "I am sorry. But I must say I would not want to delay my departure more than a day or two."

I nodded, "I know where the Frenchmen will be. I'll have to chase down Mr. Hoyt." I scolded myself for not learning more about his perambulations. "Hopefully I can have an answer by tomorrow afternoon."

Yang Ho leaned forward hopefully. "If I can help persuade him—"

I threw up my hand. "No, no." It was rude, but I was caught off guard. "That won't be necessary" *It would be a disaster.* "I'll see to it."

I glanced quickly at Sun Shu. She dropped her gaze to her lap, where she held her teacup as if it were a fragile blossom.

"Thank you," Yang Ho said. "I am grateful to you."

We stood and shook hands. His firm grip told me he was well acquainted with the custom.

CHAPTER 32

The next morning, first thing, I found the Frenchmen where I knew I would, at work on their claim.

Beyond our names, we had acquainted ourselves with very few of each other's words: *yes, wages, good day, today,* and *tomorrow*. I used the bucket: setting it down and picking it up, and a lot of pointing—at myself, at them. I pantomimed the sun crossing the sky. Phillipe and Bertrand followed my movements avidly, grinning and tossing out what were probably guesses. Ormond stood reserved, stroking his mustache thoughtfully.

After I'd put across the idea of half a day by pointing from the zenith overhead to the western horizon, Ormond nodded and gave a satisfied rumble, "Oui. Un demi-journee. Je comprends." He looked at his compatriots and they nodded. He turned back to me. "D'accord."

I left the Frenchmen and hustled back to town. I had no hope my next negotiation would be nearly so genial. Mr. Hoyt had no truck with foreigners, and he would be dead set against anything that he perceived to jeopardize his inflow of gold. While I approached the Frenchmen with a willing heart, I was about to enter the same exercise with my official partner grudgingly.

I stepped up to a storekeeper setting out a display of picks and shovels. "Good Morning, sir. "Have you seen Mr. Hoyt? A tall man with dark hair—"

The merchant snorted, "Seen a dozen like that already." And he turned his back.

After getting similar answers from three more people, I decided to try a different way. "Excuse me. I'm looking for a man with a splinted leg and a crutch."

The man wrinkled his brow and looked off. "Last I saw him he was headed for Momma Loose's. But that was an hour ago, easy."

It was my turn to wrinkle my brow. "Momma who?"

He regarded me with pity and pointed off to the side of the town's wreckage. "See them tents yonder?"

I looked where he pointed. A row of tents sat beyond the crater that used to be Radley's hardware store. A large tent and six smaller ones, set in a row, as orderly as an army camp.

The prospector said, "If your partner's still there, Momma Loose'll know."

She was probably in charge of the tents. "Would she be in the big tent?"

He was already on his way. He halted and half-turned. "I reckon."

"Thank you, sir. I appreciate your help."

The large tent had no door on which to knock. The jolly voices of several people came from within. I thumped on the canvas flap. The hubbub died. A woman's voice called out, with no small helping of mockery, "Come in?"

I lifted the flap and stepped inside. The only furniture was a variety of seating and an assortment of trunks; all singed and smoke-stained. A small woman with a dusky complexion and a mass of bright yellow curls piled on her head occupied the only padded chair. She poured drinks from a stoneware jug for the four miners who seemed to be her visitors.

She gave me only a brief glance. "Take a seat, young man. It'll be a while."

"Thank you, Ma'am, but I can't stay. I'm looking for my partner, Mr. Hoyt. I was told he might be here."

"He might." Her smile had no humor in it. "But you all look the same after a while." She handed around the drinks.

What does that mean? "He broke his leg. He's getting around on a crutch."

"And he came *here*?" blurted one of the visitors, but another elbowed him to silence.

Momma Loose stubbed out her cheroot on the sole of her boot. "Isabel took pity on him. Tent on the end."

"Thank you, Ma'am." I touched my hat.

Rough laughter trailed me out of the big tent. Mr. Hoyt did not like to be discomfited in any way. I had a good hunch he would not look kindly on my interrupting his visit with the lady, Isabel.

I stepped softly up to the last tent in line. Within, the lady Isabel was humming a beautiful, wistful tune. Once again, I wished for a door to knock on. How to speak loudly enough for him to hear me but not so loudly as to embarrass him. "Mr. Hoyt?"

The sweet humming ceased. Then a man's voice spoke. Though muffled by the canvas, the throaty grumble was unmistakably Mr. Hoyt. Trilling laughter from the compassionate Isabel quickly followed. More moments passed. Isabel's voice cooed and giggled.

At last Mr. Hoyt appeared, awkwardly, with something between a crawl and a crouch, as a feminine arm held the flap open. He hauled himself upright and got his crutch under his arm. He had left his boots inside. He buttoned a last button at his throat. "Well, Pegg, boy. This is unexpected." His tone conveyed that it was also unwelcome. "Who told you I was here?"

"A prospector over the way." I gestured back to the bustling street.

Mr. Hoyt threw a scowl in the direction of my point. The look he gave me was merely grumpy. "What is so all-fired important that it couldn't wait?"

"Well, sir. It's just that Yang Ho wants to get started for San Francisco and—"

Mr. Hoyt's frown darkened. "What's that to do with me?" He threw a quick glance back at the tent.

Will hissed in my head, *Move it.* I stammered, "He wants me to help Sun Shu look after their store—"

Mr. Hoyt broke in again. "Did you tell him you have more important obligations? Namely looking for gold for us."

The lilting, tuneful humming began again. Mr. Hoyt's impatience increased noticeably.

I hurried. "He knows that, sir. He promised to pay me for the time I help Sun Shu, and—"

"And you believe him?" barked my partner.

The tent flaps parted just enough to reveal a round face with merry eyes and smiling, red lips.

Mr. Hoyt caught my stare and twisted. "I'll be right there," he said to the lady, but she did not retreat.

He turned back to me. "They're not to be trusted, Pegg, Son. How many times must I tell you?"

I sensed my time was running out. "It's only for a short while. Two weeks at the most, he says." Then I remembered. "And I'll still be able to help the Frenchmen."

Mr. Hoyt wagged his head. "I don't like it. They're taking advantage of you."

Isabel emerged further from the tent. She wore stockings with outlandishly bold stripes— and not much else. She stepped close behind Mr. Hoyt, perhaps for modesty's sake. He bent involuntarily; perhaps she was tugging at his suspenders. She started humming again.

Mr. Hoyt shifted to keep his footing. "As long as you keep bringing in the gold dust."

I grasped what I took to be his consent. "Yessir. To be sure."

He gave me a scowl. "Fail to do that, Pegg, Son, and we are ruined. Do you understand? Ruined."

Isabel stepped back toward the tent, taking Mr. Hoyt with her.

"Two weeks, no more. Thank you, sir."

The lady took his crutch and steadied him while Mr. Hoyt retreated into the tent. She gave me a wink as she herself followed him. That was a part of life of which I had only the foggiest notions. I hastened on my way, not least because I wanted to get back to Yang Ho.

When I got back to his store, I spotted a roan mare standing outside the tent, saddled. Yang Ho and Sun Shu stepped out of the tent. I gave them my good news and asked him to wait while I wrote a quick note to my mother, letting her know I had been having modest success in the diggings. I gave Yang Ho the letter. "Would you mind mailing this in San Francisco?"

He tucked it in his saddlebag. "It would be my pleasure."

After a quiet goodbye with Sun Shu, he was on his way. Gao Chung had already come and gone, leaving three wheelbarrow loads of blankets, clothing, boots, hats, belts, and tools—hammers, saws, chisels. On his third trip he'd brought bean cakes for our breakfast.

I helped Sun Shu set out the merchandise and as soon as we did, people started coming to buy. In her loose clothing, with her hair bound up, many miners completely missed the fact that Sun Shu was a female, even with her soft, respectful voice and graceful manner. Those who did realize they were in the presence of a lady transformed in a flash, burnishing their best manners, becoming as meek as lambs. It vexed me that some miners dismissed her as merely a foreigner not worthy of the barest civility.

She seemed unperturbed by this churlish behavior, portraying the same mild manner to all and sundry.

I found myself handling the tools. I had to ask her the prices for the saws and hammers. I knew prices out here were outrageous, to use Mr. Hoyt's word. Still, with the town in a fever of rebuilding and resupplying, everything was gone by noon.

Sun Shu took the money box and scales into the tent and reemerged a few minutes later with only the money box. "Would you like to have some dinner?"

I suddenly realized I was hungry enough to eat a horse. "Yes, ma'am. Very much." I untied Bugle and we headed to Chen Yi's restaurant.

Sun Shu walked a pace or two behind me. "Thank you for your help, Pegg. May I call you Pegg?"

I stopped and turned to her. "You're welcome. But I didn't do much."

"You were there. That counted for more than you know."

I scratched my ear. "Well, okay. If you say so."

We resumed.

I stopped again. "Why are you walking back there?"

"It is my place. It is the woman's place."

"It's odd to talk to you back there. Is that the way they do things in China?"

She didn't answer my question but simply said, "I will try."

We started again, and she hovered at my elbow, only a little bit behind. "Please forgive my directness, but I understand you are working with some Frenchmen?"

How does she know that? "Yes, ma'am."

"Perhaps, after dinner, we may pay them a visit."

It didn't sound like a request. "I thought you were going to stay with Chen Yi in the afternoons?" I smelled something afoot. I gave her what Will called my keen eye.

She didn't shy. "We have sold everything we had today. It was a good day. Everyone knows we are still in business. Now it is time to tend to other business."

I rocked back on my heels, owl-eyed. This was the most I'd heard her say—in English, anyway. More to the point, even though she used her same mild voice, she made it very clear the matter wasn't up for debate.

When we got to the restaurant, she gave the money box to Chen Yi for safekeeping. Gao Chung would return it in the morning. While we ate, Sun Shu told Chen Yi what items had sold the best, and what might be worth laying on a few extra for tomorrow, if he could get them. She had to do this in bits and pieces because Chen Yi, as usual, was scurrying between his crowded dining area and Gao Chung's leaping fire.

Afterward, with Bugle straining eagerly at his rope, we set off for Simpson's Creek and the Frenchmen's claim. The sun rode high but gave little warmth.

I fretted that this wasn't quite what Yang Ho had in mind. He probably wanted his wife to stick obediently by the home hearth, attracting no attention, avoiding any possible unpleasantness. Perhaps he was so confident in his expectations that he felt no need to give me instructions if she decided to do otherwise. The miners we passed gave no sign they saw anything amiss in our procession. We were just two soot-stained prospectors trudging up the road with their dog. Bugle, if anything, was the unusual part.

We came to the spot on the trail opposite the Frenchmen's claim. I called and waved as I had done before. Ormond, Bertrand, and Phillipe all turned and broke into big grins, waving. Agile Phillipe snatched up one of their buckets, held it high, and shook it. My job was still open. I turned to Sun Shu and pointed at the Frenchmen. "That's them."

Will snickered in my brain. *Do you think she could have worked that out on her own?* I felt like a dunce.

I stopped at the edge of the stream. I had boots I didn't mind getting wet, but Sun Shu had only her slippers. Even as I opened my mouth to speak, she slipped them off and stepped into the stream. The water was never going to get higher than her shins. She picked her way across like she did it every day. I closed my mouth and hustled to catch up.

Sun Shu was already ashore and putting on her slippers by the time I stumbled out with Bugle. The Frenchmen eyed their new visitor intently. Perhaps they were sharp-eyed enough to see in her slender, graceful hands and feet, the poise in her movements, that they were in the presence of a lady.

"Sun Shu, this is Ormond, Bertrand and Phillipe," I said, pointing to each of the Frenchmen in turn. Burly Ormond gave a short nod. Tall, gangly Bertrand solemnly bent at the middle, sweeping his hat off his balding pate. Little Phillipe fairly shivered with delight, bobbing his head up and down.

Then, grinning at my foolish friends, I swung my hand back toward Sun Shu. "Ormond, Bertrand, Phillipe, this is Sun Shu."

"C'est un plaisir, Mademoiselle," said Ormond, as if he was under a spell.

"Oui," she answered smooth as silk. "C'est un plaisir pour moi, aussi, Monsieur. Mais, s'il vous plaît, appelle-moi Madame. Je suis marié."

I stared at Sun Shu, saucer-eyed. *Where did you ever learn French? Does Yang Ho know French, too?*

They chattered on for some minutes like neighbors met over a fence, with occasional glances in my direction. I took the bucket from Phillipe. We slapped each other on the back, grinning like fools. Then there was much nodding and smiling from the Frenchmen, as if something had been decided.

Sun Shu turned to me. "Monsieur Ormond says they will be glad to have you back. I suggested tomorrow morning would be a good time to start this plan."

"But what about the store?"

She held up her hand, which stopped me as sure as interrupting me, but polite and proper. She gave me a pleading look. "Mr. Pegg. They need you as much as I do. So we have agreed, you will help me set up the store each morning and then come out to help Monsieur Ormond and his confreres. When I have sold all of the merchandise, I will come out to join you, so that I may be under your protection, as my husband intended. Then we will return to have supper in the evening with Chen Yi. It will be a good day for all of us, don't you agree?"

Only a toadstool would disagree, and I didn't want to be a toadstool. That night I slept outside Sun Shu's tent with the Colt under my pillow. Bugle and I helped keep each other warm. Before I fell asleep, I thought hard how I'd promised to look after her, and I made my own plan that would work with hers.

In the morning I woke up to find that sometime during the night, Sun Shu had come out and put an extra blanket over us. Gao Chung brought three loads of merchandise Chen Yi had bought for her at the makeshift market on the edge of town. On his last trip he brought bean cakes for our breakfast. Sun Shu and I set out trousers, shovels, and rope, among much else, while we munched on our bean cakes. It was chilly enough to see our breath.

Before I headed off to the diggings, I loaded my dad's Colt and gave it to her. She frowned and tried to give it back to me.

I shook my head. "If you insist on me leaving you here all morning and walking out to the claim by yourself, that stays with you—and Bugle, too. Then I won't worry that I'm not watching out for you the way I promised."

I'd figured that put it back on her to help me keep my word, and it worked. It took a moment, but she gave a sharp little nod to agree.

I handed her the satchel with powder, caps, and balls. "Do you know how to reload it?"

"Yes."

I took her word for it. I didn't want to think of her in a ruckus nasty enough that required her to reload. None the less, if she could hold a whole town at bay with a rifle, individual customers would mind their manners with the pistol in evidence.

By the time I got to the Frenchmen's claim, they were already hard at work. Bertrand and Philllipe brought a bucketful of dirt over to the cradle, where the four of us picked out the biggest nuggets. Many were as big as a robin's egg. A few were even bigger. Then they dumped the remaining dirt into the top tray for Ormond and me to wash and went back to dig out another bucketful. There was no jumping and shouting, but we were smiling a lot, quietly giddy with excitement. They'd mutter back and forth some in French, then chuckle. And it seemed with each bucket the nuggets got bigger. We could hardly believe our good fortune. But even in the dirt Ormond and I were washing, there was plenty of color in the black sand, specimens the size of pumpkin seeds, or peas, or rice, in addition to the finer flakes. This gold we put in a separate coffee can.

We enlarged the hole, thinking there might be more gold caught farther downstream from the boulder, but just after midday, our bonanza came to an end. We had perhaps five pounds of the bigger nuggets, and another pound of smaller nuggets and dust. At sixteen dollars an ounce, we had a tidy sum. Each of us could take home something over four hundred dollars!

We were considering our next step when Bugle splashed through the creek and near wagged himself to pieces to see me. It took a moment for Sun Shu to hove into view.

Imagine this dainty girl in a shiny blue coat and trousers, with her hair tucked up under her cap, striding up the trail like she owned it, a sack slung over her shoulder. The Colt, which probably weighed half as much as she did, was thrust through a bright red sash around her waist. She looked like a pirate.

She paused a moment to locate us among the many miners scattered along the creek. When she saw me, she doffed her slippers and splashed through the water.

"I have brought lunch, Mr. Pegg!" She swung the cloth off her shoulder, knelt down, and untied the bundle.

To my surprise, it looked very much like she had brought lunch not only for me but for the three Frenchmen, as well. "That's very generous of you, Sun Shu. Thank you."

The cloth held a collection of little round boxes, with tight-fitting lids, fashioned from a light-colored wood.

Sun Shu unstacked the boxes. "It is Uncle Chen who is generous. I am merely the bearer."

In my mind, my mom prodded me for my manners. "How can we thank him?"

She opened the lids. Wisps of flavorful steam drifted up. Inside were dumplings of different shapes and sizes. She lowered her gaze modestly. "You are all clever fellows. I am confident you will think of a way."

She handed out chopsticks, and we tucked in while she went over to greet Bugle. To everyone's surprise, each dumpling had a different filling. We showered Sun Shu with thanks in French and English. She covered her smile with her hand.

That evening I would take several gold nuggets to Chen Yi from four grateful prospectors.

When the last dumpling had disappeared, Sun Shu came back to gather up the little boxes and chop sticks, retied them in the cloth, and went over to sit under the tree with Bugle. I was sure this wasn't part of Yang Ho's plan. I kept looking over to see if she had gone back to the store. She stayed the rest of the afternoon, quiet as a statue, petting Bugle or letting him rest his head in her lap.

The Frenchmen decided to try their luck at some of the other large boulders scattered around their claim. As I watched them walk around, I had an idea. I waved to Sun Shu. Bugle noticed me before she did and barked. Sun Shu looked up. I beckoned her to come over.

"Tell Ormond—" I stopped and thought of my mom scowling at me. "Excuse me. Would you please tell Ormond I think we could try to track the old stream bed by seeing which of the other boulders forms a sort of line with this one." I patted the one we had just been digging by. "Those boulders might have a better chance of having gold under them."

"Yes, Mr. Pegg. I will be happy to do that," she said. Her face was very serious. *"Monsieur Ormond,"* she said in a firm, French voice. *"S'il vous plaît."*

The Frenchmen turned to face her, and she rattled off a whole bunch of French. I was just goggle-eyed. Ormond asked her a question, and she rattled off a whole bunch more French, sweeping her arm around the claim, pointing up and down the creek, and at the boulders. When she was done, she looked at me expectantly. She'd said about three times as much French as I'd said in English.

"Uh, thank you," I said. "I appreciate that."

"I am happy to help." She went back to sit under the tree.

So that's how we picked the next boulder.

Bertrand and Phillipe dug, while Ormond and I washed the dirt. Our luck held, not quite as bountifully as with the other boulder, but enough to keep everybody in a jolly mood.

Sun Shu sat with Bugle the rest of the afternoon.

Ormond called a halt to digging as the sun slipped toward the western rim of the canyon. We had maybe three hours of usable light left. I brought buckets of water from the creek, and we squatted around the cradle and washed the grit and mud off the big nuggets. Then Bertrand began washing the dirt from the coffee can. Ormond gave me lessons in using the gold pan to wash some of the same dirt. His instruction consisted of careful demonstrations and grunts of caution or approval. I got pretty good at separating the gold from the black sand.

When we had everything divided up into four portions, I had a lot more gold than my little compass pouch could hold, even more than my pockets could hold. The Frenchmen had the same problem. Mr. Hoyt was going to dance a jig, broken leg or not! Heck! I felt like dancing a jig!

Bertrand's bottle was filled up with just his portion of the gold from the coffee can. How would he carry his nuggets? Phillipe and

Ormond had quickly filled their containers as well, with most of their nuggets left over. I scurried around looking for discarded bottles and tins. But many other people had had the same idea long before me.

Sun Shu came over and said, "Please excuse me. I have an idea. Can you wait?"

I said, "Sure."

She turned and said something to the Frenchmen.

Ormond replied, clearly charmed. The other two nodded together.

"They will wait, too," Sun Shu said to me. "I will be back as quickly as I can."

By the time she got back, other miners were leaving their work and going to their camps, or heading into town. The smell of coffee and bacon drifted to us. Sun Shu unrolled a suit of long john underwear and asked me for my knife. She cut a leg from the garment above the knee, tied a knot at one end, and handed it to Ormond. He understood immediately and began filling the leg of cloth with his nuggets. Bertrand got the other leg, and Phillipe and I got an arm each. When he had put all his nuggets in his leg sack, Ormond tied the other end in a knot and slung it around his neck like a collar, smiling a big smile. The rest of us followed his example.

Sun Shu accepted our thanks with good grace but said, again very modestly, "My husband would be very unhappy with me if he knew I was giving away merchandise."

We understood and each gave her a small nugget from our portions.

The three Frenchmen shared a roughly-built shack a few yards up the slope behind their claim, and they invited us to stay for supper. But when I looked at Sun Shu, she gave a tight little shake of her head, so we declined and walked back to town in the deepening shadows. Bugle was very happy to be moving again, scampering ahead and coming back.

"I am sure they would have been honored to have your company for supper."

"That may be so, Mr. Pegg. But perhaps I have no wish to willfully disobey my husband's wishes more than I already am."

When we got back to Yang Ho's store, the last light was fading from the sky, but all the lamps and torches from surrounding businesses spilled plenty of light on the store's patch of ground.

Mr. Hoyt was waiting for us, sitting on one of the spice boxes in front of the tent.

"There you be, Pegg, boy! You had me worried," he called out as we approached.

"Mr. Hoyt," I said. "How did you know I'd be coming here?"

Mr. Hoyt made a smirk and tapped the side of his nose. "I know, lad. Never fear, I know. You can't hide from Fred Hoyt."

"I wasn't hiding, sir."

"I know, Pegg-boy. I know. I'm just pullin' your leg. No harm in that, is there?"

"Mr. Hoyt, this is Sun Shu. This is her store." I turned to Sun Shu. "Sun Shu, this is Mr. Hoyt. My partner."

Mr. Hoyt didn't stand up for Sun Shu the way I'd seen him do time and again out of respect for my mom. He just gave Sun Shu a short nod and said, "Ma'am."

"It's a pleasure to meet you, Mr. Hoyt," Sun Shu said seriously.

Mr. Hoyt looked around at the store—the rope fence, some benches, and the little tent.

"Looks like a good breeze could blow it all away." He grinned at me.

He said no more to Sun Shu. I thought that odd. Mr. Hoyt usually gave the impression he wanted to be everybody's friend. I felt bad for her. She didn't deserve that.

Sun Shu said, "If you will excuse me, Mr. Pegg, I will say good night." She went to draw the pistol from her sash, but I made a small gesture to stop her. She gave me a short nod of thanks and went into the tent. Mr. Hoyt stopped looking off into the distance and turned to me. He beckoned me closer and spoke in a hushed voice. "I have to say, Pegg, boy, I am concerned. Why would you want to be keeping company with foreigners when there's so many good, solid, American folk around?"

"I don't understand, sir." Actually, I had a pretty good idea what he was driving at, but it didn't make me feel good, so I wasn't about to just roll over.

Mr. Hoyt looked around to see if anybody was listening. "Well, I'm only looking out for your best interests." He got a worried look. "It's bad enough you working your fingers to the bone for those Eskydees"—he meant the Frenchmen—"for a pittance. But now this?" He cocked his head back toward Sun Shu's tent.

I drew back a little and lifted my chin. "This is what I talked to you about. Don't you remember? Yang Ho will only be gone a few days."

"So you said, so you said. The wench's husband." He shook his head.

I knew wench wasn't a particularly nice word. I wanted to protest his slur, but I wanted him to leave even more, so I held my tongue.

"And I don't suppose this Yan Hoo gave a moment's thought to the fitness of dumping such a responsibility on your young shoulders, did he?"

"Yang Ho," I corrected him. "He asked me, and I said I would."

"Whatever he's paying you, it isn't enough," Mr. Hoyt said.

I didn't want to argue with Mr. Hoyt anymore. I wanted to talk about good things. "We had good luck at the Frenchmen's claim today." I took the arm sack from around my neck and handed it to Mr. Hoyt. "Very good luck."

"What's this?" He pulled back, suspicious.

"What we took out today," I said, proud that I was learning the miners' language.

Mr. Hoyt hefted the bag, getting the feel of its weight. "A bag full of rocks?"

"It's gold." I took the bag back, untied it, and handed Mr. Hoyt a nugget. It wasn't the biggest one, either. His face lit up. He leered at me and then at the nugget. He tested it with his teeth. He gestured at the bag. "And the rest is rocks. Just to make a fool of me." He made his wry smile. "You'll have to get up pretty early in the morning to pull one over on—"

"It's not rocks, sir! It's all gold!"

He gave me a look as if he had been startled awake.

I upended the sack. Nuggets spilled into his lap and fell to the ground.

"Great Caesar's ghost!" he cried, looking down, leaping to his feet. The rest of the nuggets tumbled out. "You've done it, lad! You've done it! We're rich!" He teetered alarmingly without his crutch. I caught his elbow to steady him and helped him sit down. "Oh! My lad! Bless you! Bless you. You've saved our bacon." He stared around at his feet. The lumps of gold gleamed, reflecting torchlight. "More! You've set us on the road to glory!"

"Mr. Pruitt should be pleased," I said. "My family will be."

Mr. Hoyt chuckled with delight. "What a good lad! What a good lad."

I collected up the nuggets from the ground and piled them in his cupped hands. What he couldn't hold I put back in the arm bag.

He was staring, shaking his head, grinning. "No more groveling. No more begging."

Mr. Hoyt squinted at me. "And just to be clear. The Frogs got likewise portions?"

Frogs? I started putting all the nuggets back in the bag. Something about the way he asked seemed wrong.

"The Frenchies," he said, impatiently. He cast a quick glance back at Sun Shu's tent. "Has she seen this?"

Mr. Hoyt's attitude toward Sun Shu definitely rubbed me the wrong way. *He's got no reason to be suspicious of her.*

"She provided the bag," I said as I retied it. I didn't care that my voice might show him what little I thought of his question.

He reached for it. "Then I'd best get this into safe hands." He hauled himself to his feet with his crutch. "We'll get some supper, and…"

Mom would have had my hide, but I interrupted him. "You go ahead, sir. I have to stay here," I said. "I'll be fine."

Mr. Hoyt scowled at me. "But what about your supper?" Then he smiled and held up the bag. "We're not beggars anymore. We can order the best the House has to offer."

"I have to look out for Sun Shu. I promised."

"She won't know the difference," he said with a scornful whine.

"I would." I felt like my dad was standing right behind me. He'd want me to keep my promise.

Mr. Hoyt made a worried face. "You would put her welfare before your own?"

"I just think it's best I stick close by here. You go ahead. You know what needs to be done. My family should be mighty happy with my portion. I appreciate you taking care of it." That knot showed up in my stomach again.

Mr. Hoyt tucked the bag under his free arm. "I don't feel good, leaving you like this. I fear for your safety." He glanced up the street while he spoke, like he was impatient to be away.

I figured he felt he needed to say that as a matter of form. I didn't want to hear any more of it. "Don't worry about me. I'll be okay," I said. "Find a good bed to rest your leg."

"At least get your gun back," he said. Then he hobbled out to the street and turned in the direction of the express office.

After Mr. Hoyt was out of sight, I sat down on the box and tried to figure out why I wasn't happy, the way I should have been. We had plenty of gold. We could only hope there would be more. He certainly wasn't being very nice to Sun Shu. Was that it? He had no reason that I could see for being so rude to her.

I looked around the ground. A large nugget rested by the back corner of the box where Mr. Hoyt had been sitting. It must have been behind his heel when I was picking up the rest. I went to put it away and realized I had forgotten to give Mr. Hoyt the gold that was in my compass pouch. It was already stuffed full, so I put the nugget in my fire-making pouch, with the flint and steel.

I heard the canvas of the tent rustle and Sun Shu stood beside me. "Are you hungry, honorable Pegg?"

"Boy! Am I ever!"

Bugle perked up his ears and got up off his haunches.

She smiled behind her hand. "Let's see if Uncle Chen will make us some supper."

So we went off to Chen Yi's restaurant. Bugle romped around us. I smiled at him. "Maybe we can get you a nice hambone, boy. What do you say?"

We had no more than turned into the street when Sun Shu pulled the pistol out of her sash and handed it to me. "When we are together, you carry the gun. It is only proper."

I stuffed the pistol through my belt, secretly sorry I didn't have a red sash. I wanted to be a pirate, too.

CHAPTER 33

The trusty old Colt came to mark our days. At the start I'd hand her the gun, and at the end of the day she'd hand it back. In between, I worried that Sun Shu and I were not exactly carrying out Yang Ho's wishes to the letter. There might be harsh words when he got back.

The second day after Yang Ho left, Gao Chung brought a tent with his load, and he generously put it up while Sun Shu and I set out the day's merchandise. No shovels that day, but along with clothing, a half dozen kegs of nails and a score of hats. What Gao Chung brought depended on what Chen Yi could get. Many merchants were bidding for the same stuff. After setting out the inventory and sharing a bean cake breakfast, I gave Sun Shu the Colt and headed off to wash dirt with the Frenchmen.

Sometimes Sun Shu brought lunch when she came to the river. If she didn't show up around midday, I figured she was taking longer to sell the day's allotment. If she took too long, I would worry she might be in trouble. But she always appeared at some point, to my great relief, and sat quietly under the tree with Bugle.

I encouraged the Frenchmen to keep prospecting the old stream bed. Our luck held, for the most part, though nothing like that first boulder. We were taking out a hundred thirty to a hundred eighty dollars a day, which gave us each about thirty to forty. That may not sound like much, but my share alone was a month's wages, or better, back home. But you could see, the take was getting less, little by little.

I couldn't talk to the Frenchmen, except in the simplest way. I wondered if they were disappointed, but even on days when we didn't wash out that much, everybody seemed in a good mood. And, of course, each morning, Phillipe gushed all over Bugle. When Sun Shu showed up, she and Ormond would have a chat in French. It was funny to see Ormond, this big bull of a man, being so modest and respectful, and to see Sun Shu, who barely came up to his chest, speaking to him in quiet, confident tones.

At the end of each day, Sun Shu and I would find Mr. Hoyt sitting on the spice box, waiting for us. His manner was stiff, only "Ma'am," for Sun Shu. That's all. Sun Shu, for her part, replied simply, "Mr. Hoyt," and went straight into her tent and stayed there until he was gone. The feeling was so tense it soured the day, whatever our luck had been.

I gave Mr. Hoyt the day's take, and asked him how much the gold from the day before was worth. It was one thing to guess out at the diggings. The express office might measure it out differently.

"Fifty dollars," he'd say, or, "I don't rightly recall."

But his answers were so quick, so offhand, I got the impression such details were unimportant to him. He'd no sooner have the gold in hand than he'd have some reason to hustle off—the express office would be closing soon, a friend was waiting, he had important business. I thought I might follow him one evening, to see that he went to deposit the gold, but I didn't like the idea of being sneaky, and if he caught me, he'd never let me hear the end of it. But I promised myself I'd go to the express office soon and find out how much he'd sent back home to my family.

Truth be told, I was relieved he left so quickly each evening. I did not feel good about the way he treated Sun Shu.

Thus a week passed. Yang Ho's time away in San Francisco was half done. I imagined him buying wagonloads of lumber, a big stove for Gao Chung, hiring crews of eager carpenters. Two weeks at most, he said. In a few days I could start looking out for his return.

Grizzly Bar was rebuilding at a furious pace. The road leading up from the river was crammed with traders' wagons bringing lumber and bricks and nails and furniture, and every other thing you need to rebuild a town. The commotion of hammering and sawing and shouting was even greater than on a regular business day. Scores of miners, mostly those who weren't having the best luck, left their diggings to earn steady and generous wages as carpenters, masons, laborers, and blacksmiths. For many, these were the very jobs they had left back home, so the work went smoothly and quickly.

The smell of fresh-sawn lumber filled the air. Sawdust and wood shavings covered the ground. An itinerant sign painter was kept busy day and night, making new signs for all the businesses.

In the middle of Yang Ho's second week away, Ormond called a halt to work a little early. Phillipe and Bertrand dumped their shovels of dirt back where they had dug them. I had my bucket of water ready to pour. I looked to Phillipe and Bertrand and got the sense they knew what was afoot. While Ormond walked over to Sun Shu, I set the bucket down. *All will be revealed soon, no doubt.* Bugle got up and approached the big Frenchman for a scratch. Ormond bent and obliged.

After speaking together for a few minutes, Sun Shu and Ormond returned to the three of us.

Sun Shu fixed me with a solemn gaze. "Your friends have asked me to speak to you on their behalf."

I threw a quick smile to the three and got cautious smiles and nods in return.

Sun Shu went on. "They say with the claim yielding less gold each day, they have talked about going to work in town. They would like to ask you to keep working the claim, so they could keep it. Would you be willing to do that?"

I looked from her to their anxious faces. I thought about it a minute. It made sense, since it was doubtful anyone would hire a fourteen-year-old for building work when they had experienced grown men to choose from.

"Sure I would."

Sun Shu spoke to Ormond for couple of minutes more and they all nodded to her. Then she said to me, "I proposed they let you keep whatever gold you find. They have agreed to this."

"Thank you, Sun Shu." That they agreed told me they thought as I did, that the claim might play out sooner than later. I stepped up to the Frenchmen, and we shook hands all around.

Sun Shu retrieved the thick cloth she had brought lunch in. We said our goodbyes for the day, and she, Bugle and I headed back to town.

I turned to her. "Thank you again for helping talk with the Frenchmen."

"You are very welcome, Mr. Pegg." She furrowed her brow for an eye blink. "But I am afraid my mother will not be happy that I am making deals, especially for a man who is not my husband."

I smiled. "I've been doing some things my mother wouldn't be happy with, either. Maybe we can blame it on California!"

She laughed. It was the first time I had ever heard her laugh. I thought to myself, *What a good day.*

The Frenchmen got work right away, Ormond as a foreman, Bertrand as a carpenter, and Phillipe as a bricklayer. Sun Shu still came out to the claim each afternoon and kept Bugle company. Each day that went by I had less and less gold to give Mr. Hoyt.

The second week slipped away and Yang Ho had yet to return. I scolded myself that it was too early to start worrying about him. I had to worry about the claim. Some days would yield more than others. The only thing I could do was start each day with hope. But only a blind man would deny that the take was growing less, slowly but surely. I was determined to wash every last thimbleful of dirt on their claim. It was my livelihood, after all.

No matter what my luck had been, at the end of each day, without fail, Mr. Hoyt would be waiting to collect whatever I had for deposit. He always sat on the same box, his crutch laying on the ground beside him like a faithful pet. After curt greetings, Sun Shu repaired to her tent.

Then two claims downstream, Orville Tunner struck a bonanza that lasted all of an afternoon. Everybody around him started digging harder. But I still didn't see much color that day. When we got back to the store, I handed Mr. Hoyt a teaspoon of gold dust in a tobacco tin. I didn't feel like sitting or being companionable. If he stayed true to form, he would be off soon enough.

He stared in dismay at the meager take. "Lad, lad! What's happening? Are those Frogs demanding more than their fair share?"

I stepped over to pick out some kindling from the meager heap of firewood Sun Shu and I had gathered. "No, sir. They all took jobs in town. I'm the only one working the claim, so they're not taking anything, but working alone it takes longer." I was sure he wasn't interested in details.

Mr. Hoyt poked at the small nuggets, as if prodding them could make them grow, or multiply.

"The claim may be playing out, running dry." I knelt and began laying the kindling.

He leaned forward and nudged my boot with his own. I looked up, and he said with a leer, "Or maybe you're spending more time chatting with your little doxie, eh?" He winked. "Could that be it?"

My friend Will liked to use that word when talking about girls, but it was rude. To use it in reference to Sun Shu was an insult.

I know I blushed beet red. "No, sir! It's not that. The claim is probably running out."

He reared back like an indignant uncle. "And you're not sneaking candy and treats behind my back, are you?"

Now it was my turn to scowl. "No, sir. I'm not." I stepped away for more firewood.

Mr. Hoyt settled and rubbed his chin thoughtfully. "Well, well. This is something of a problem."

"Maybe we can use some of our gold to buy another claim."

"Easier said than done, lad, easier said than done," Mr. Hoyt was still distracted. Finally, he worked up a smile. "There's a good lad. Maybe you'll do better tomorrow."

"I'm doing my best, sir. But you've heard the stories, same as me. A claim can be a bonanza one day and bust the next. I just don't think we should expect too much more out of this one." I didn't want to lay any more fuel before I got the fire going. I moved one of the spice boxes that didn't need moving.

"My associates will not be happy to hear that." Mr. Hoyt sat up straight and puffed out his chest.

I stopped fussing with the box. "Your associates?" *Does it mean they're new partners?*

"The gentlemen I am in negotiations with." He slipped the tobacco tin into his coat pocket.

"Is that Mr. Sweeney?"

"Among others," Mr. Hoyt said airily, waving his hand. "But I must say no more, for your own sake."

Partners aren't supposed to hold out on each other. "Has anybody suggested any better places?"

He bent to pick up his crutch and labored to his feet. His voice had pity for me. "Pegg, lad. These are financial men, managing the wealth of the land." He put on a smirk. "Not scrabbling sandhogs."

He left me with a bushel of questions. What was he telling these associates? Why was he so eager to stay in their good graces? And what did less and less gold have to do with that? A cold fist squeezed my heart. *Is he buying their friendship with the gold I'm giving him?*

. . .

The very next evening, when Sun Shu and I got back to her store, Mr. Hoyt greeted us in a new suit of clothes. When he saw us approaching, he stood up to give us a better look at his yellow and black checkerboard trousers, a black silk vest, and a fawn-colored coat! He had finished it off with a yellow silk cravat, all puffed out at his throat, like a prairie cock, and a black silk top hat, every bit as fancy as Mr. Sweeney. He also sported a freshly carved crutch. How could he afford such fancy duds if he sent most of the gold back East?

He held the jacket open. "Direct from New York City." He tossed a new felt hat at me as I walked up. It was black, with a wide, flat brim. He grinned. "There you go, lad. A little something to pick up your spirits."

It was a fine looking hat, but it was a little too big and sat on my ears.

"And there's more coming with the hat," Mr. Hoyt grinned. "Radley didn't have anything to fit you, so I put in a special order. He knows a seamstress in Sacramento. New coat, britches, the works!"

I was so startled, I forgot my manners. "I don't need any fancy clothes!"

His mouth dropped open and his eyes went wide with hurt.

Now what have I said?

"Your generosity, Lad, not to mention your hard work, have been weighing heavy on my mind."

I took a step back. "My generosity?"

He wasn't exactly listening. He plowed on like he had a speech to deliver. "It's the least I could do to replace the duds you sacrificed to bind me up." He patted his splinted leg "in the mountains. For that I am in your debt, and won't soon forget it."

I blinked at him. The man was full of surprises. I felt like an ingrate. How could I turn away such a gesture? "Thank you, sir. That's real nice."

Mr. Hoyt flipped his coat tail up with his free hand and lowered himself back onto the spice crate. Then he laid down his crutch. "'Course, I don't expect to see you muckin' around in the river with 'em. Save 'em for when we're flush." He ended with a conniving wink.

"Of course. Yessir." I took off the new hat and set it carefully on one of the empty crates.

He tugged at his silk vest, then smoothed it over his belly. "To gain respect," he pronounced, "you have to look respectable." He checked to see if I was listening. "You'll realize the importance of that someday."

He gentled his features and spoke amiably. "So. Did fortune smile on us this fine day?"

I handed him the day's take, not even a teaspoon of dust, and a few tiny nuggets in a little medicine bottle stoppered with a stick. It probably wouldn't buy him a handkerchief. He lost no time putting the bottle in his pocket.

Despite his unexpected generosity, my mom's hardheadedness asserted itself. *How much flour and bacon or tools could we have bought with the gold that went for the fancy duds, his and mine?* The concern forced its way past my manners.

"How much did it all cost?"

Mr. Hoyt gaped at me like I'd slapped him. Anger snapped in his eyes and was gone.

I took a deep breath and spoke on, "How much did all these new clothes cost? How much of the gold did you use?"

He swept his hand through the air in frustration. "Too much, of course! You know that! But we are at the mercy of these vultures! We have no recourse!"

I held his gaze. I waited for him to say how much he had spent.

He broke into a ragged laugh. "Oh! Oh! I see your thinking." He pushed back his shiny top hat and leaned forward with a pleading look. "Do you think I would forget your mother or Mr. Pruitt? Do you think I would neglect my duty?"

I forgot about being an ingrate. There was only one way he could have paid for those clothes. "Is there *any* money left?" I dreaded the answer.

He blustered for a minute, as if confounded. Then he laughed. "All right. I confess. I had a little luck at the faro table last night. My modest investment of our resources yielded handsome returns, indeed." He patted the lump in his pocket. "Besides, there's more where that came from. There's bound to be!" He leaned forward and whispered, "As long as you don't let those Frenchies, or anybody else, take advantage of you." He flicked his head in the direction of Sun Shu's tent.

Watching him, I startled myself with a terrible thought. *It's not them I have to worry about, it's you.*

He took up his crutch and got to his feet. "My money's on you, lad. Don't let me down."

He hobbled off, calling over his shoulder. "If you need help while the Frogs are in town, put the girl to work. She's just sitting on her keister out there, anyway—-not that she's good for much else."

I watched him lose himself in the boisterous street. *How does he know Sun Shu comes to the river?*

Will snickered in my head. *He may be buying favor from his betters, but he's no doubt paying for favors from the worms beneath him.*

Sun Shu came out of the tent.

"I'm sorry if you heard that," I said, when she came to stand beside me. "He had no right to say that. He doesn't know anything about how hard you work. I don't understand. He wasn't like this on the way here."

"Mr. Pegg, do not worry about me. I understand the kind of man Mr. Hoyt is. I understand, so his words cannot harm me."

I turned to look at her. She might be as dainty as a hummingbird, but she had the steady gaze of an owl, the heart of an eagle.

"Would you like to get some supper?" she asked.

We made our way along the street to Chen Yi's restaurant. The air grew chillier as darkness fell. The smokey tang of roasting meat mixed with the whiff of new-sawn lumber and manure. Buildings were in every state of reconstruction. Saloons and gambling halls spread amber light onto the muddy thoroughfare, inviting revelers eager to spend their gold. One or two stores were still open.

Bugle wanted to explore everything. With so few other canines in evidence, he thought he had the world to himself and marked almost everything that wasn't moving. I had to keep calling him back. As always, miners offered good money for him. I stopped answering and just waved my hand, no. Finally, I put him on his lead rope. Sun Shu offered to take it. Bugle trotted right beside her. I frowned at my dog. "He behaves better for you than he does for me."

She smiled, looking down at him. "You love Bugle very much, Mr. Pegg. Did you bring him from home?"

"Yes, I do. And, yes, he walked all the way with me." I leaned down to scrub the top of Bugle's head. "Didn't you, boy? Every step. Every desert, every mountain."

Sun Shu said, "It is good to have such a faithful companion. And, if I may ask. Where is your home?" She spoke so modestly, it sounded like she expected me to not tell her.

"Vermont. It's way in the East." A drunk careened toward us. We parted to let him pass. "It's about as far away from here as you can get, and still be in the United States, that is." But then I remembered what Mr. Pruitt said. "But maybe it's not as far as you've come."

She hid her smile behind her hand. "I think you may be right."

We came to Chen Yi's restaurant. He had managed to buy some tables and chairs, but others were just barrels and planks. He had rigged up a sheet hung on poles to separate the kitchen from the dining area, but Gao Chung was still cooking over an open fire. The tables were full and people waiting. Sun Shu, Bugle and I took our place at the back of the line.

Bugle strained at the rope. She held it firm. I glanced at her sideways. Even her ears were delicate. She seemed very calm. *What can I say that won't be stupid?* For all the time we'd been spending together, we hadn't really told much about ourselves.

"Can I ask where your home is? In China, I mean." The line inched forward when a table came free.

She spoke without turning. "I grew up near a small village in Guangxi Province, in the mountains. It is very beautiful there. My village was far away in the forest, but perhaps not as far away as your Vermont." Then she asked, "Did you live in a town or in the country?"

"We have a farm. Not a big one. My mom and my brother, Adam, and my sister, Amy, are looking after it while we're out here prospecting."

She turned to me. "But Mr. Hoyt is not your father?"

I flinched. "No, he's not."

"Is your father looking for gold at another place?"

I braced myself to not cry. "My father died of fever at South Pass. That's in the mountains, before we got here."

Sun Shu looked stricken. "I am very sorry, Honorable Pegg. I am truly very sorry."

The way she said it made it very hard not to cry. "Thank you, ma'am. I appreciate that very much."

We got to the front of the line. Three miners left a table close to the kitchen curtain, paid their bill, and brushed past us on their way out. Chen Yi caught our attention and pointed us to that table. Two miners remained. Whatever tongue they were speaking was unknown to us, so we made do with nods of greeting. They wore decorated shirts and trousers baggier than I had ever seen. They jabbered away and paid us no mind. They seemed thoroughly practiced in the use of chop sticks, which is more than I could say for myself. No sooner had I settled Bugle, than Chen Yi brought a tea pot and two cups.

"Evening. Chen Yi," I said.

"Good night. Welcome," he replied.

I didn't have the heart to correct him. He didn't have the time for an English lesson, either. Customers were calling for more tea, or to pay their bill. He and Sun Shu exchanged a rapid smattering of their language and he hurried away.

Sun Shu checked the tea. "I hope you don't mind. I told him to fix what Gao Chung can do quickly, so we are not a burden."

I gave her a big grin. "I've never been disappointed yet."

She hid her own smile. "Thank you, Mr. Pegg."

We watched the bustling scene. Chen Yi looked almost run off his feet.

Sun Shu spoke again. "And now your family is waiting for you."

"Yes, ma'am."

"Your ancestors have smiled on you. Soon you will be able to buy a new farm, perhaps a bigger farm?"

How did she know about that?

She got a worried look. "I am sorry, Mr. Pegg. I have spoken improperly. Yang Ho has said I must put a lid on my curiosity. Please forgive me." She knitted her brow and reached to check the tea again.

I didn't want her to feel bad. "No, no. It's okay. Please, don't feel bad. Yes. We are going to buy a dairy farm. My dad always wanted a big dairy farm. Holsteins. They give the most milk."

She checked the tea a third time, then she poured. "Permit me to ask, Mr. Pegg. Does your mother know that your father has gone to meet his ancestors?"

"Yes, she does. Mr. Hoyt wrote her a letter right after."

Chen Yi brought a platter heaped with slices of pork and vegetables in a dark gravy. He rushed away and returned with two plates, chopsticks and a serving spoon.

"Gao Chung Special. Nowhere else." He called as he rushed away the second time.

Sun Shu took up a plate and spooned on a generous portion. "So now you are the patriarch."

"Ma'am?"

"You are the head of the house, the family," She put the plate in front of me and nodded to the chopsticks. "Please begin."

I remembered her waiting so patiently for Yang Ho to tell her to start eating. I wondered if I was supposed to do that now she was calling me a patriarch. She served herself a portion. To my relief, she didn't wait. We tucked in in earnest, same as always.

After a few minutes Sun Shu had more to say about patriarchs. "The patriarch is the leader. The family looks to him for his wisdom, for which path to take. His word is law. After the Emperor, of course."

"Oh," I said. It sounded like a big job. This talk called to mind a story my dad told about how Uncle Rafe, being the oldest son, was entitled to inherit grandfather's farm, but turned it down to go trapping in the mountains. "What about my brother Adam? He's older than me."

"Well, then he is the patriarch."

"But he'll be married soon, if he isn't already. He wants to start an ice business."

She looked perplexed. "I'm not sure, but whatever the rules, I would say your family is counting on you."

CHAPTER 34

The line of people waiting for a table wasn't getting any shorter. The two miners in the colorful shirts left and three other prospectors sat down at our table. They were a lively, noisy bunch. They spoke English but that wasn't necessarily to our benefit, for their exchange consisted almost entirely of hurling droll insults at each other, peppered liberally with vulgarities, or challenging each other's masculinity.

Sun Shu and I looked at each other. She whispered, "This is difficult. May we continue later?"

I just nodded, and we bent to our supper. I slipped Bugle several slices of meat.

Sun Shu cast a glance my way. "Bugle will be very well-fed tonight. I've already given him two slices."

I looked down. My dog was lying on his side, licking his chops contentedly.

Walking back to the store, the mood of celebration had intensified. Now that it was full dark the lights seemed brighter, the shadows deeper. Piano music and laughter billowed out from the saloons. We had to avoid more than one drunk. Ahead of us, one man, reeling, passed out and dropped like a felled tree, face first into the street. I flipped him over on his back so he wouldn't suffocate in the mud.

Sun Shu looked down at his mud caked face. "He is fortunate you happened by.

We moved on, and a moment later Sun Shu said, "You have walked across America." Her back was ramrod straight. "You can do anything you need to do."

I wanted very much to believe what she said.

Her profile was edged with golden light. She walked so poised. Did Guinevere, in the tales of King Arthur, walk that way?

I smiled back and nodded. "May I ask you a question?"

Her eyes widened in surprise. "Ah! Your curiosity has no lid, either?" and her graceful fingers flew up to cover her grin.

I had to laugh. Bugle barked. "Yes. No lid," I said, still laughing.

Eight or more miners tumbled out of a saloon at our right, bashing, kicking, shouting oaths. We didn't move aside quick enough. A wild swing, intended for someone's jaw, knocked Sun Shu's cap off her head. Her hair came loose from its pins and flowed loose past her cheek. We both lunged to retrieve the cap. I snatched it up and we scurried to the far side of the street. She calmly re-pinned her hair.

"Are you all right?" I held her cap gingerly in both hands like an offering.

"Yes. Thank you." She took the cap and settled it firmly.

We went on our way. The sounds of the fight were soon lost in the general hubbub.

Sun Shu said, "I'm sorry, Mr. Pegg. What question may I answer for you?"

What is she apologizing for? "Oh! Yeah, right. My question." I'd forgotten it in the ruckus, and watching her pin up her hair. "My question." I fumbled with my hat. "How did you learn to speak French? Does Yang Ho know French, too?"

"I learned French long before I met Yang Ho. He is teaching me English, Yankee English."

"Would you tell me that story?" I felt like I was asking to open a new box of treasures.

We came to the little rope fence that marked out their store and went in past the benches. Tomorrow morning they would display new merchandise. There was no guessing what it might be. I went to our stack of firewood to gather fuel for a fire.

Sun Shu stood near the spice boxes. "Forgive me, Mr. Pegg, but may I ask that we save that story for another time. We need our rest. Gao Chung will be here before the sun." She tilted her head and tucked in her chin. "Do you mind?"

I straightened up, kindling in hand.

"No… Sure. Another time," I stammered. "That's fine."

Have I been too nosy? I dropped the kindling back on the pile.

She lifted the flap of her tent. "Goodnight, Mr. Pegg. Thank you. Rest well." She went into her tent.

"Goodnight, Sun Shu." *What is all this thanking for?*

I didn't go into my tent right away. I sat on one of the boxes and stared at the grey ashes from last night's fire. Bugle curled up at my feet. I thought about my mom and Adam and Amy. It really *was* up to me. If we were going to have anything better, I had to find enough gold to get us a new farm. I took out the little piece of paper that my dad had given me. It had just one notation written on it: Fifteen thousand dollars. That seemed like an impossible fortune to me.

I remembered from the discussions my folks had that fifteen thousand would get us a couple hundred acres, a herd, a barn, and a house. But, according to my dad, we, now I, would have to bring home twice that much to pay back what was owed. Would I be lucky, like some of the people in the stories, and find one stupendous bonanza? Or, would I live out my days wandering the hills, scratching out a bit here, a bit there? How long would it take to accumulate thirty thousand dollars? *How much have I sent back so far?*

. . .

By the middle of the third week, Sun Shu's husband was still not back from San Francisco. She had even been working the cradle as Ormond had, without my asking. The Frenchmen's claim was about played out. I had tried everywhere. I washed piles of the dirt we had already washed. I had even gone back to our first bonanza boulder and dug some more there. I could easily contain the day's take in the little bottle, which Mr. Hoyt had returned to me.

Trudging back to town with Sun Shu at the close of day, I brooded on my discontent. I felt like I was playing the part of the dutiful peasant and Mr. Hoyt the gloating tax collector. After all, I was doing all the work. He was still using the crutch, though he seemed to lean on it less. His part, depositing the gold, took only a few moments. What did he do with all the rest of his time? Of course, it would be rude in the extreme to challenge him directly. Best to come at it sideways, see if I could draw him out.

I stood before him, two teaspoons of gold in the little bottle in my back pocket. "Did you have a good day?"

Mr. Hoyt guessed my intent right off. "Well, I can't do much with this leg." He patted his trussed limb affectionately.

"Yessir. I know you can't be digging just yet." If he got my nudge, he didn't show it. I waited for him to offer something more. My silence must have vexed him. He shifted on his seat, wincing like his leg hurt him.

"I look after our interests, lad. That's my main concern." He chuckled deep in his belly. "I have to be extra careful since our means are so limited."

So I should be bringing you more gold. I returned his gaze, but said nothing.

He glanced away, smiling, his laughter silent now, only jigging his shoulders. "Even with this blasted crutch, I must be on my toes." He looked back up at me, expecting praise for his wit.

It was clear he didn't want to tell me anything more about how he spent his time. I held the bottle out to him.

Mr. Hoyt took it and inspected it with worry wrinkling his brow. He shook it. "You're sure you've tried every last square inch of the place?" he said. "Maybe there's some deeper yet. Have you tried that?" It almost sounded like he was pleading.

I was out of ideas. "Maybe your associates could offer some advice."

He stared at me a moment and burst out in a harsh laugh.

I jumped. Bugle shifted nervously.

Then Mr. Hoyt collected himself. "I know you're joking." He dropped the bottle in his pocket. "It's just that you've got us in a tight spot here."

I stared at him. *Us?* Whatever tight spot he was in, he had got there by his own efforts.

He got to his feet. "What I meant to say is, the gentlemen I've been dealing with will be disappointed. They have certain expectations. Their patience is growing thin."

"Yessir." This was adult talk meant to discourage questions.

He tried to sound fatherly. "See if you can do a little better tomorrow, for all our sakes." And he hobbled off.

I knew that was supposed to be encouragement, but it sure didn't feel like it.

It wasn't just the work load that rankled. It was our talk. I told him everything and he told me nothing. He expected me to spread all my cards on the table while he held his close to his chest. I didn't think partnerships should be like that. His words were slippery eels. I didn't have, and wondered if I would ever gain the wit to counter his clever hogwash. If only I could strike it rich, and we could go home, and I could be rid of him. *No wonder Mr. Pruitt wanted to ship him off.*

Sun Shu came out of the tent, and we went to supper.

I was still in a lather the next morning, not in a talkative mood. Sun Shu gave me questioning looks while we set out the day's merchandise. She had her own worries, she needn't take on mine. The benches were soon loaded with long johns, trousers, wool shirts, coats and boots, winter garb for the coming cold. This batch should sell well.

When it came time to head for the diggings, I took my bean cake with me. By now Bugle didn't budge. He knew his place was with her for the morning.

Sun Shu said, "Good luck today."

I managed a halfhearted wave. "I'll see you later." I hoped she knew I wasn't mad at her.

At the Frenchmen's claim, I dug dirt like a mad man, willing the gold to be there—foolish desperation. Sales must have been lively, because Sun Shu appeared at the creek before midday. She brought lunch wrapped in the heavy cloth, and took Bugle over to their usual spot by the tree. I worked a while more, then she beckoned me to come eat.

Steamed dumplings with pork and cabbage inside. I tried to be civilized and asked her how things went at the store, but our talk fell like leaves scattered on a river of silence.

As we finished, she said, "I think you have a lot to think about. Shall I leave you?"

"Oh, no! Don't!" I blurted. "I'm sorry for being such poor company."

"Ah, no," Sun Shu smiled. "You are the best company." Then she concentrated on the knot she was tying.

That caught me by surprise. That kind of honesty was new to me, and I didn't know quite how to accept it. "Likewise!" I grinned, hoping to hide my confusion.

She offered to work the cradle in the afternoon, while I brought dirt and water. Somehow that made things better. We worked later than usual, well after most around us had quit for the day.

We headed back to town with perhaps a tablespoon of dust, and three nuggets, one the size of a grain of rice, the other two, half that. The surrounding hills were black silhouettes against a sky filled with red-orange clouds lit from underneath. These shed a soft, rose-tinted light on the canyon floor. Campfires glowed in rough camps behind the claims, coffee and bacon aromas rode the fitful breeze. Across the creek, someone broke into song. Most of the miners who were going into town had already left the diggings. We had the wide, well-trod path pretty much to ourselves.

We walked a ways in silence. Then Sun Shu said, "May I offer something, Mr. Pegg?"

"Yes. Sure. Of course."

She spoke like she was talking about her favorite thing. "In my country, a very long time ago, there lived a sage who collected wise sayings—proverbs that were even older."

I remembered somebody Linnaeus had told me about. "Is a sage like a philosopher—like Aristotle?"

"Yes." She smiled. "Aristotle is deep in your history, as Lao Tzu is deep in our history. That is the name of the gentleman I am speaking of, Lao Tzu. He was very odd, but very wise." Sun Shu paused. "One of these ancient sayings Lao Tzu collected was, 'Roiled as a torrent'."

A man overtook us. He touched his finger to his hat. "Evenin'," he said in a gravelly voice, and kept on his way.

"Evenin'," I said back.

Sun Shu could see that I was bewildered by her exotic words. She spoke softly like we were sharing a secret in a crowded room. "Roiled is like being all mixed up, or upset. You're in great confusion, and you don't know what to do. A torrent is a wild, dangerous body of water, like a river in flood."

"I will own to being mixed up, and I know what a river in flood is like." I glanced at her. "Roiled as a torrent. Never heard 'roiled' before."

"Yes," she said. "There is a further part to the saying, which completes it." She waited to see if I was ready. "Lao Tzu asks a question. If you are 'roiled as a torrent,' how will you figure things out, how will you make a good decision?"

Bugle pulled on his lead. Out of the gloom on our right a sleek, beautiful doe bounded over a stump, arced high over the pathway, splashed once in the creek, and bolted up into the gloom on the far bank. She had been little more than an arm's length in front of us.

When we caught our breaths, and settled Bugle, we continued on. Now the clouds were a deep, somber red, going to purple. I wanted to hear more about making a good decision. "What were you saying about good decisions?"

She took right up again. "Lao Tzu's answer was, you must have patience. You must let whatever is troubling you settle, let the water become calm and clear before you can see the best way, make the best choice."

I instantly thought of a bucket of muddy water settling out until the water was clear. Talking with Sun Shu reminded me of talking with Linnaeus. And that felt good.

CHAPTER 35

As that third week wore on, cooler days were warning us that winter would be here soon enough, and with it, no doubt, rain and snow. Enough wet would make the roads an impassible mire. They couldn't leave the store open to the skies through the whole winter.

Yang Ho hadn't returned with building supplies. *What can be keeping him?* Was he having a hard time finding materials or hiring men? Had he run into some kind of trouble, himself?

I beat down my misgivings with the pick and shovel at the Frenchmen's claim, flailing like one possessed. I didn't care that other miners close by made a joke of it.

Orville Tunner called out, "Slow down, Pegg. You'll find yourself in China."

Another miner, upstream, said, "Ease up, kid. Yer makin' us all look like layabouts."

But these jests were said with good humor, so I let them roll off.

I took out a few pinches of dust each day, rarely more. In some places I had dug down to bedrock. River water seeped into the deepest pits I dug.

In the afternoons, Sun Shu worked the cradle. I sensed she needed the distraction, too. She grew more and more quiet. I tried to lift her spirits. "He'll be here tomorrow, sure," I'd say, or, "He's probably past Sutter's trading post already."

She'd smile without joy. "Thank you, Mr. Pegg."

I felt bad for her. She was up before dawn and worked hard all day, but she never said a peep about being tired or discouraged. I knew how much my mom and dad counted on each other. When one was down, the other lifted them up with a good word. Sure, they were man and wife, but they were also best friends. You could hear it in the way they talked to each other. Sun Shu must be really missing Yang Ho.

Two more days went by. On the second evening I presented Mr. Hoyt with a thimble's worth of gold. He regarded the take with dismay, shaking the little bottle. "Lad, lad. We have to do better than this. We'll never get home at this rate."

Of course, he meant *I* had to do better. I was too weary and too worried about Yang Ho to muster a response. I could not make the earth hold more treasure than it did. Mr. Hoyt dropped the bottle in his pocket and rose to take his leave. *No exhortations, no encouragement?* Maybe he was too burdened with his own worries about his associates.

Sun Shu came out of her tent. Mr. Hoyt gave her one hard glance, saying nothing, and hobbled away.

As Sun Shu and I made our way to supper at Chen Yi's, the street was filling with carousing nightlife, jostling and shouting. She and I had to walk closer together to hear each other. She walked almost beside me now.

I felt I had to apologize for my rude partner. "I'm sorry about Mr. Hoyt."

Sun Shu looked at me then looked away. She didn't reply for a few steps.

Is she choosing how to lambast Mr. Hoyt?

At last she replied in a quiet voice. "Permit me to say, Mr. Pegg, I am glad he is not your father."

I looked over at her. "I wish you could have met my dad. I wish you could meet my family." Just saying that hollowed my insides out. When would I see them again?

After a minute more, she said, "We take so much for granted when we are children. Our mother puts food on the table and we eat, without worrying. We squabble with our siblings and our father makes us see both sides. We learn unwritten rules to live by and assume the rest of the world lives by the same rules."

During supper I told her of the many different kinds of people I'd seen on the emigrant trail. City boys who didn't know the first thing about guns blasting away willy-nilly, grown men breaking down when their wagons did, a woman who lost her husband and most of her children to cholera but kept on, and then here in California, generous miners and cranky miners.

After we got back from Chen Yi's I set about laying a fire. While I was lighting it, Sun Shu brought more wood. She sat on one of the spice boxes and watched me. When the fire took hold I sat back on another. Bugle came over for a scratch.

Sun Shu said, "The other day you asked how I know the French language."

I sat up straight with a big grin. "Yes!"

Of course, I didn't want to hear just about that. I wanted to hear her whole story. I had a good hunch it would be a story full of things I'd never heard of—strange doings. Things even Will's wild imagination wouldn't think of.

Sun Shu put her hands out to warm them. It was like watching a flower open. "I am not as good a storyteller as Uncle Chen, but I will try."

"You speak in the nicest way I've ever heard," I replied.

She looked down at her lap, smiling. "Ah, Mr. Pegg. You make the heart glow with your words."

I gazed at her, dumbstruck. That was almost as good as one of my mother's hugs.

She cradled one hand in the other as gently as if she were laying a babe in a crib, and began. "You remember I said I grew up in the mountains."

I didn't want to break the spell. I just nodded. The din of the rowdy throng in the street seemed to fade as I leaned in to listen.

She went on. "My father was a dealer in teak and other woods. When I was five years, a French missionary came to our village. With the help of the people, he built a school and a church. I pleaded with my father until he let me go to the school. He had only himself to blame. He had taught me to read and was teaching me calligraphy, to write."

She could read at five? She did better than me.

"My curiosity had no lid, even then. My mother was shocked. A girl going to school was unheard of. It was this missionary who taught me the French language."

I nodded again. Even back home, schooling for girls was a sometime thing.

Sun Shu bowed her head. "His name was Father Sebastian Cuvier." She paused a moment, perhaps recalling him. Then she looked up and smiled, "He, too, could not keep a lid on his curiosity. He was a wonderful teacher." She waved her hand in an arc at the night sky. "He also taught me the names of the stars." Then she made a motion like she was smoothing something on a table. "And maps. He made beautiful maps. He had been in China many years. Of course, he could speak *our* language perfectly."

I was making pictures in my head as fast as she revealed them. "I'll bet you were his best student." My own schooling was pretty patchy. My mom had tried to make up for that. "How many years did you have him as a teacher?"

Her smile faded and she gazed at the fire. "When I was ten years, a warlord, Zhou Chow, descended on our district. He lay waste our crops, destroyed our village and a dozen more. Many of our men died defending our homes. Among them my father and Father Cuvier."

That jolted me. "You lost your father, too? I'm sorry." My throat filled up with rocks. I realized I hadn't thought of my dad in a couple of days and that felt like I had betrayed him.

Sun Shu stared into the flames. "Yes. It seemed like the world had ended. It emptied of all meaning." She sat quiet for a minute. "Those of us still alive hid in the forest, waiting for the monster Zhou to go away. It was weeks before we could return to rebuild our homes.

"A year later a famine came. My mother starved herself, rather than see her children go hungry. In the end, I lost her and my siblings. People were eating grass and the leaves from the trees. I would never tell you the things I ate to stay alive."

I stared at her, nudged by unease. These were not happy memories for her, not by a long shot. I chided myself for being so eager to hear the story.

But then her voice brightened. "Uncle Chen, yes, this Uncle Chen, found me alone in our house. He was one of the merchants who came for the teak wood. He took me home and raised me as his daughter, even though he already had three. He had a large house. I had my own room for the first time. He let me read books from his library and took me to see his warehouses. That was my first glimpse of the wider world." She paused again, making a quick gesture down and across her chest with two fingers, almost like a cross. "I have so much to be thankful for."

I got up to get more wood for the fire. As I came back, she said, "There's not much more to tell. I do not wish to bore you."

Feeding chickens and building fences made for a boring story. We had only gotten to her eleventh year. Yet here she sat: a married woman. Surely there was more to tell. Questions crowded into my head like hogs trying to get to the trough. But only one managed to get out. "What happened next?"

Sun Shu smiled and tilted her head, glancing away. "My new stepsisters were nice, but I knew they thought me a coarse, country bumpkin. They had had their feet bound, starting when they were very young, to improve their marriage prospects. But Uncle Chen said it was too late for me. I knew I had to live with my big, ugly feet, and hope for the best." She shifted her feet, tucking one behind the other. "I was sad, but not for long. Uncle Chen gave me an entire set of *Encyclopedia Britannica*."

To me, her feet seemed as dainty as the rest of her. "What does that binding do?" I thought I saw her shudder.

"It changes the feet in such a way that makes it almost impossible to walk," she replied, "which I am sure makes husbands happy. It's a long, painful process, but a girl with such feet can expect to make a very good marriage."

"But then you wouldn't have been able to be part of the gold rush," I chirped.

She laughed. Her slender fingers came up to cover her lips, but then slipped away again. "I must continue my story, or we will be up all night."

I tucked in my chin. "I'm sorry. I promise, no more interruptions."

She folded her hands once more, dropping her gaze. "When I was thirteen, Uncle Chen's brother, a merchant from the coast, began to bring his son with him when he came to do business. My stepsisters were very excited and, while I made the tea, they argued over which of them should serve it. How he came to know of my existence remains a mystery to me. He knew I had big feet, but it made no difference to him. We exchanged messages. If we had been discovered it would have been awful for both of us. But he was very clever. Then the messages became poems."

The next interruption was not my doing. "Hey, there," raised above the general din.

We glanced over. A clean-shaven, portly man in a long coat and tall boots stood at the rope. His stance made it clear he'd merely paused in his stroll up the street. He wore an eager expression. "How much you want for this plot?"

I looked at Sun Shu. She made the slightest shake of her head. I turned back to the man. "Sorry," I called, "Not for sale." And gave him a friendly wave.

The man was not deterred. "Name your price."

"Sorry. Can't help you." I gave him another wave and turned away.

He wanted the last word. "Let me know if you change your mind. Name's Wilson."

I turned to see if he would offer any more particulars, but the reveling throng had already swallowed him up. When I turned back to Sun Shu she said, "His is by no means the first offer. I will be glad when we have a building again."

I leaned forward, adding another scrap of lumber to the fire. "So there you were, writing secret messages…"

She sat back and settled, a smile playing at her lips. "Oh, dear. Are you sure you want to hear more?"

"We're just getting to the best part." I instantly regretted my choice of words.

She began again, seeming to look inward. "At first I was afraid of him because he had traveled so much, but he did not boast of it. He was not put off by my education. And he answered my questions tirelessly. How could I resist that? We were married when I was fourteen. He was twenty." She looked up shyly and switched which hand was on top in her lap. "I'm sure you've guessed that young man was Yang Ho. By then, he was already helping his father as a trader."

I waited a bit.

She glanced up, but then dropped her gaze just as quickly. "Of course, I went to live in his father's house. His mother was very demanding." She paused again. "I believe Yang Ho has told you the rest—Uncle Chen bringing me to join him in Monterey."

"Yes. He did."

Sun Shu sat up straight, as if collecting herself. "He is a good husband. Permit me to say, Honorable Pegg, I hope you find a good wife—when the time comes."

I sat back and blinked. *Didn't see that coming.* I had more immediate problems. *A wife?* That prospect seemed as distant as China itself.

Fishing through my compass pouch, I dug out the compass and held it out in my palm. "This has been to China."

She regarded it for a moment. "Perhaps you may visit there someday, after you have made a success of your dairy farm."

That would be an adventure to tell Uncle Rafe about.

We watched the fire burn down. I told Sun Shu about my sister, Amy, and about life on a small, rock-strewn Vermont farm. The street lost some of its clamor. You could hear the music better: a piano up the street, a violin farther off. When only glowing coals remained, Sun Shu rose to her feet and bid me good night.

"Yes, ma'am. You have a good night, too. And thank you for telling me your story."

After Sun Shu went to bed, I wrote a letter to my mom, telling her bits of Sun Shu's amazing story, and wondering if they would ever be able to meet.

I rolled up in the blankets that night imagining what I would be willing to eat just to stay alive. Will and I had challenged each other once to eat a worm, when we were little kids. I fell asleep wondering what Sun Shu's village looked like. Did it have a main street, like Richford? Did they have a blacksmith and a livery stable? Was Saturday their market day, when everybody came to town to do business and shop, for a haircut and the latest gossip?

Bugle woke me up in the dead of night. A single bark.

"Shhh. You'll wake Sun Shu." Bugle was looking toward the front of the tent. I thought, *Another fire?* Then I heard my name. I fought my way out of my blankets. A man's voice outside my tent. Hissing. Urgent. "Pegg!"

I scooped up the Colt and stumbled out, hugging the blankets around me.

Mr. Hoyt leaned precariously on his crutch, tense, like a cornered animal. "Pegg, we must go. Now. Not a moment to lose."

I was still befuddled with sleep. "Go? Go where? What's wrong?"

Mr. Hoyt, his eyes wide and darting, hissed, "San Francisco. Anywhere! It's too dangerous for us to stay here."

The saloon across the street was still going strong at this late hour. It provided just enough light for me to see something in my partner's face I'd never seen there before, and never expected to see—fear, soul-rattling fear.

I'd seen Mr. Hoyt grumpy, rude, high-handed, thoughtless, yes, but never afraid. He was not a man easily intimidated, even if his arrogance was often misplaced. Maybe he had finally brought real calamity down on his head. And mine, too, according to him.

What danger can there be? Go away? What about looking out for Sun Shu? What about the Frenchmen's claim? "What happened? What's wrong? I can't go. I have to wait for Yang Ho to come back."

Hoyt stretched out his hand in pleading. "But don't you see, lad. If we value our lives, we must get away." He glanced nervously toward the center of town.

Just then Sun Shu came out of her tent. She held up a lantern and clutched a robe around her. Her long hair fell loose to her waist. "What is the matter, Mr. Pegg?" she said. "Is there danger?"

"Sorry to disturb you, ma'am." Mr. Hoyt touched his finger to his hat brim. "But there is the gravest of dangers."

Sun Shu took a step back, staring at Mr. Hoyt. I stared, too. Why did Mr. Hoyt suddenly feel the need to be civil to Sun Shu? Was the threat against him so dire that it erased his high-handed disdain?

He glanced over his shoulder again. Turning to Sun Shu, his voice became desperate. "We must run for our very lives. Make him see sense, Missy. If only for his sake."

She held the lantern higher. "If your life is in danger, Mr. Pegg, you must go."

I could see the dread in her eyes, but also concern. "But I promised Yang Ho I'd look out for you 'til he got back."

Bugle sensed my turmoil, dancing around my feet, whining.

Mr. Hoyt snarled, "What is a promise against your life, boy?"

I knew he meant a promise to a foreigner wasn't worth keeping, especially a Celestial, a Chinese person. A cold anger seized me. I had to say something he would understand. "No. I can't go with you."

That stopped him cold. He straightened out of his fugitive crouch. "Are you daft? You have no choice."

Nothing to lose now. "Tell me the truth."

He glanced toward the center of town again. "There's no time now. I'll explain when we're away."

Sun Shu held the lantern steady, but she stared toward town.

I didn't move. "Who's after us? Why are they after us?"

Mr. Hoyt got a better grip on his crutch. "Men who would cut out our livers without a second thought." He put on a derisive sneer. "Is there more you need to know?"

Bugle pressed against my leg. I reached down to touch him. *It's okay.* I tried to keep the tremor out of my voice. "If my neck is in the noose, I want to know why."

He made a fist with his free hand. "Blast it, Boy——"

I braced for his anger. "Does this have to do with money?"

He grimaced like I had aired a dirty secret, gnashing his teeth. "If you must know, I fell prey to treacherous men. They sailed under false colors." He threw out his hand as if to say, How was I to know? then let it fall to his side. "They made generous promises, then went back on their word." He paused to see if that was enough.

I waited.

He shook his head and slapped his good leg in frustration. "I explained that my means were limited, but they had no sympathy. The more I reasoned with them, the angrier they got."

"Why'd you have to drag me into it?"

The lantern light wavered. I glanced over to Sun Shu. She lowered her arm with an apologetic look.

Mr. Hoyt caught my glance. "Is that it?" he exploded. "Is that why you're hanging back?" He made another fist and leaned toward me, sneering. "If you're worried about losing your doxie..." He flicked his own glance at Sun Shu. "...I'll buy you another one." He leaned back, smug that he had struck true.

I held his eyes. My fingers itched to use the gun. "I think it's time for you to go."

Mr. Hoyt broke into a triumphant grin. "That's my boy! Grab your gear and let's make tracks. They'll——"

"Not us. You." I held my face still. I was quaking inside. "You got yourself into this. You can get yourself out of it."

Mr. Hoyt, his weight shifted to flee, stared at me in disbelief.

I finished. "It has nothing to do with me."

He turned back to face me, his heavy brows arched in concern. *What ruse will he try now?*

His voice faltered with emotion. "I cannot abandon you. I made a solemn promise to your father to look after you. He wanted you to stay with me."

So I'm supposed to honor your promise and forsake my own?

Hoyt's fear seemed to have robbed him of his cleverness.

"Dad was wrong. He didn't have a chance to learn what kind of man you are."

My partner reared back in righteous indignation. "Now you're talking balderdash." He shifted his weight to set off again. "If you won't listen to reason, I am forced to leave you to your fate." He gave a dismissive wave of his hand. "I'm better off without you getting in my way." He hobbled off toward the rope that marked the edge of the store, away from town. Only uncertainty lay beyond.

When the night had swallowed him up, I stepped over to Sun Shu and took the lantern from her.

She still watched where Hoyt had gone. "What will we do if they come here, looking for him?"

Could I lie to them? Could I willingly send them after him? I peered into the night's black. "We stood here talking for fifteen minutes and nobody showed up. One thing I've learned is that Mr. Hoyt is capable of considerable balderdash, himself."

Sun Shu finally took her gaze away from the darkness and regarded her store, the rowdy town. "This is such a savage place. Are you not concerned?"

"Yes."

She went into her tent and came out soon after dressed in her dark blue jacket and trousers.

I fetched wood from our pile and got the fire going again. I checked the Colt. A full cylinder. I had to hope it wouldn't come to that. "I'll keep watch. Let me walk you over to Uncle Chen's. Stay with him until this blows over."

She sat down on one of the crates. "Yang Ho would want me to protect the store. I will stay." She touched the loose sleeve of her jacket. "Yang Ho took the rifle with him, but I have my 'chaperone.'"

I had never heard the word. "Chaperone?"

Rather than explain the word, Sun Shu drew from her sleeve a long, truly wicked-looking knife. The blade ricocheted firelight. "This is my chaperone."

Uncle Rafe's Bowie knife was a great slab of metal; Sun Shu's knife was sleek as a viper. She tucked it back into her sleeve. "Perhaps it is enough to say a chaperone is someone who protects."

We watched the fire. Bugle came over for a scratch and then curled up by my boot. Whenever a burst of shouting or gunfire came from the town, all three of us looked that way as one.

I remembered Sun Shu's talk about, 'roiled as a torrent.' That was me that night. Where would Mr. Hoyt go? Would he find a way to get back home? I had an odd feeling of desolation at the thought of him getting home before me. Maybe Dad was right. I needed an adult to do the things I couldn't do.

But I had adults! Chen Yi and Sun Shu. The Frenchmen. People I could call friends and could trust. Even Mr. Galloway if I chanced upon him.

My uncle Rafe flashed to mind. He could come out and help me find gold! He'd probably be really good at it. He knew how to read the land. He didn't mind living rough. He could travel fast and light. He'd be an ideal partner.

He also had a growing family and a booming business. My spirits sank.

Besides, even if he did agree to come, I'd only be putting him in harm's way. For I could not completely dismiss the possibility that Mr. Hoyt had, indeed, made mortal enemies. If I stayed here, no matter who my partner was, I would live in fear every day. And not knowing who they were, or when they might strike, would be worse than trying to evade an enemy who was in active pursuit. I couldn't hide and hope to find gold at the same time.

Then go home. Once again my hopes leapt to Uncle Rafe. Maybe he could come and get me. But if he helped me get back home, how could I return with nothing to show for all these travails? Without my father? Without the one thing Mother asked me to bring back? To say nothing of a dream turned to ashes. No!

•   •   •

Two hours and more passed and the angry men had yet to appear.

Sun Shu put more wood on the fire. She watched off toward town. She stood ramrod straight, but still looked like she could lift away on the breeze.

"This is not your trouble, Sun Shu. Please. Go to Chen Yi's."

"You are thoughtful, honorable Pegg, but my place is here." She came back to sit on the crate.

A silent owl swooped overhead. I felt the air more than saw the shape. I flinched after it was gone. The gibbous moon hung fat-bellied in the sky.

Some timid part of my mind insisted it was I who was better off without Mr. Hoyt, rather than his view of it. I thought through the times he had acted carelessly, or thoughtlessly, selfishly. In fact, I had taken care of him as much as he had looked after me. I'd cooked his meals, readied the tent every night. On top of everything else, once we got to California, I'd kept him supplied with gold, regardless of what he did with it.

The fire popped sharply and Sun Shu shook herself awake. "Honorable Pegg. Would you tell me some stories of your wagon trip? Then, if we aren't interrupted, I could tell you about sailing across the great ocean."

I knew her worry had subsided some, but neither of us would sleep tonight. "I will, if you'll tell me why you say 'honorable Pegg.'"

She smiled and nodded.

I told her the story of the Buffalo Chip Gang getting lost and fending off the wolves through the night. "The next morning, my dad said the best thing he could have said to me. 'You kept your head, you didn't panic. And you kept everyone else from losing heart.'"

Sun Shu smiled at the glowing coals. "I think I would like your father."

Bugle looked up at me for a scratch. I obliged him. "Mr. Hoyt has scorned me plenty of times for a helpless whelp. Dad saw better qualities in me. Now we'll get to see which one of them was right."

COMING SOON

EXCERPT FROM
PEGG'S PROGRESS: BOOK 2
in the *Gold Rush Odyssey* Trilogy

The jury put their heads together right where they sat. A jug was passed.

I couldn't help but worry about how much that jug might influence my fate. I would not belittle my Maker by "praying" for this situation, I just hoped the jury would find in my favor. Mr. Mahoney's claim was my first real entry into the gold rush on my own steam. I had no idea how much he had taken out before he gave it up. It was no bonanza, or he wouldn't have walked away from it so easily. But there were stories aplenty of people taking over "played out" claims, only to find new wealth.

The crowd dissolved as men remembered their own thirst.

A quarter of an hour passed. The plaintiff, yours truly, fretted. The defendant, Mr. Louis Absolom Shrivington, spent most of the time looking annoyed or superior. A miner brought Judge Bovee a fresh bottle of beer, which he polished off in short order. The judge stared at the jury to his right, as if willing them to finish their work. At last, the tallest man on the jury stood and nodded mutely to the judge.

"Gentlemen," exclaimed the wizened magistrate, taking a fresh grasp of his beer bottle gavel.

This roused the dozing bailiff, who obediently bawled, "Order in the court!" to nobody in particular. The onlookers, reduced by half, quickly reconvened.

Ira, the judge, glared at Ned, his bailiff, who retreated.

Ira addressed the tall man. "Mr. Hawthorne. Has the jury come by a verdict, so we can all get back to our business?"

Mr. Hawthorne cut an impressive figure. He squared his shoulders and raised his chin. "We have not, your Honor." His proud bearing wilted a little. " 'Pon my word, Ira, we are at an impasse."

Ira made a fist and shook it in frustration. "Goldangit, Pete. Your job ain't to get stuck at impasses. Your job is to get over 'em." He pounded the bench once.

"It's neck and neck, 'far as we can see, yer Honor. Without Mahoney—"

The judge swept his hand to shut the man up. "That's good corn liquor gone to waste if you boys can't settle on a verdict."

Hawthorne braved the judge's ire. "We looked at it six ways from Sunday, but these two fellas have 'xactly the same story, not countin' the amendments by Simpson, there."

The judge turned his stormy brow in our direction, muttering, "King Solomon had it easy." Then he swiveled back to the jury. "I got a good mind to hang the bunch of ya." Turning back to us, he muttered on. "No court of mine is gonna end in a pussyfootin', prevaricatin' hung jury." He cast his gaze around, vexed. "Here's what we're gonna do. We're gonna have us a race." He ignored the confusion that announcement provoked. "From here to Mahoney's claim. Whichever of you two rapscallions gets there first, gets the claim." He slammed his bottle on the bench to ratify his ruling.

Bailiff Archer stepped forward. "Court is now---"

Judge Ira thumped the hapless bailiff on his arm. "Shut yer trap, Ned. We ain't done yet." The codger hobbled out from behind his bench and came over to the two of us. He squinted at us for a moment as if we were livestock. He bent with some effort and, in the space between the toes of his boots and ours, drew a line in the mud with the neck of the bottle. "From here."

Someone called out, "You got 'em pointin' the wrong way, Bovee." The judge looked around and had us move to stand on his side of the line, facing south toward the river canyon.

Louis asked, "What are to be the rules?"

Judge Bovee blinked at Louis Absolom Shrivington as if the green-suited man had just dropped out of the sky. "Rules?" he cried. "What rules? It's a race." He lunged closer to Louis. "No kickin', bitin', or eye-gougin'! How's zat?"

During that exchange I sized up my opponent. He was half a head taller than me, which gave him a few more inches in the leg. Properly employed, those few inches could, by the end of the race, add up to a sizable lead. But only if he was a runner. Long legs weren't the whole answer. Hunched on a bookkeeper's stool day in and day out doesn't make you a racer. But he was lean and sinewy; he could easily be fleet of foot. Whatever his capabilities, I had to win this race.

I gave my two friends a worried look. Richard said. "Don't worry, Mate, we'll be your seconds."

R. C. scowled at Richard. "Maybe you can. I ain't run a hunert yards since I was his age, much less four mile."

I handed R.C. my Colt, my knife and the pouch around my neck.

R. C. eyed Louis and spoke in a low voice, echoing my concern. "We got no idea if that varmint is fleet as a deer or if he'll give out after fifty yards." Then he held his finger against my shirt. "Pace yourself. Save some wind for the end." He stuffed my Colt through his belt. "You'll need every break you can find." He gave me a wry smile. "Since you're so partial to the swimmin' line, you might keep that in mind."

The judge interrupted our huddle. "Ready?" He turned to a gaggle of miners idling close by. They were showing the effects of the jug. "Hawthorne, Belshaw, Connoly. You pace 'em. Make sure there ain't no hanky panky goin' on."

Hawthorne replied, "Sure thing, Ira."

"No Hinkle pinks," blabbered Belshaw and sagged in a heap, laughing. Connoly reached down carefully and helped him stand again.

Judge Bovee held the bottle gingerly by the neck out in front of him. "Ready?" After a heartbeat, he let it drop. We were off!

I sprinted up the street. Behind me, the sturdy bailiff yelled, "The court is now adjourned," amid shouts of encouragement for us.

Even as we reached the top of the rise at Rich Flat, the big miners, Hawthorne and Connoly, were already huffing and puffing. Shrivington and I were neck and neck. He was a good runner. Richard used his long legs to advantage. To my surprise, Belshaw, a small, wiry man, was right on our heels. We turned westward onto the wagon road and charged on. A few riders on horseback overtook us and sped on, calling, "We'll see you there!"

Louis said he just came from Coloma. How well does he know the country along the north fork? He knew enough to find Mahoney's claim, but maybe he was directed. For people who don't know the country, they'll probably keep westward on the stage road. But then they'd have to "know," or guess, when they are opposite Rattlesnake Bar off to their left, to cut south to reach the river. The fact that Louis had even agreed to the race meant he had a pretty good idea where Rattlesnake Bar was.

Louis, Richard, Belshaw and I formed a small knot pounding down the road, while Hawthorne and Connoly— Connoly was a giant—were already lagging behind.

After another half mile or so, I glanced at Richard and tossed my head to the left. He nodded. I picked a clear spot with not too steep a drop and veered off the road. Richard stayed right with me. Louis skittered to a halt. Belshaw all but plowed into him.

"Hey!" shouted my opponent. "What are you doing?"

"Tryin' to win this race!" I called back.

"That's not the way."

I didn't answer. I concentrated on picking out the next twenty feet.

Behind me, voices shouted, getting fainter as I plunged and lept down the slope. They were arguing what to do. Hawthorne and Connoly caught up and joined the debate.

I wasn't running perpendicular to the road, but angling south and west, picturing a diagonal line from the road to the river. I knew I was well short of Rattlesnake Bar. Once I reached the river, running west, I could look for a place to cross, so as to be on the south shore for the last leg of the race.

I glanced up at the road. Louis was still there, a little ahead of me, pounding hard, with Belshaw some distance behind him. The other two referees were nowhere to be seen. Louis and Belshaw were still arguing as they ran, but I couldn't make it out. Their voices were soon lost in the crunch of leaves and snap of twigs Richard and I were making.

Smaller water courses crossed my path, cutting their way down to the river. Many were choked with brambles and blackberries. Fortunately, the first one I came to that I couldn't jump had a bridge. A tree, one of those Digger Pines had fallen across it. So, while the first half was a straight trunk, the upper portion, lying on the far half of the gully, was a great jumble of limbs. That slowed me down some. I wasn't used to traversing these trees. Back home, Will and I would gambol over such a crossing without a second thought.

Gaining the other side, I heard a shrill oath higher up on the slope. My adversary, in his dandy suit of clothes, had finally left the road. He trailed me by several hundred yards, above and behind. No doubt he had given up the road reluctantly.

I glanced back. He had lost his hat. He was going cautiously, clearly not familiar with negotiating steep, unkempt terrain. Belshaw, yet farther back, being drunk, made most of his progress by rolling and tumbling. I was rattled. Louis A. Shrivington was showing remarkable grit—and gaining quickly.

That glance cost me. I tripped and went down, sprawling. Scrambled up, flailing, and plunged on.

I couldn't worry whether Mahoney had promised his claim to two people or ten. His claim was my first real chance to make a success of this whole mad enterprise. I could feel my dad looking down on me, a steady smile in his eyes. I imagined my mom and Amy hoping and praying. I had to win this race.

A faint, sibilant thunder came to me. The river. The canyon welcomed me like a wide trough. Richard stumbled and fell. "Keep going," he panted, rubbing his knee. "I'll catch up."

R. C.'s suggestion had found fertile ground in my mind. The river wasn't an obstacle; it was a means.

The lower I got, the easier it got. So many of the trees had been cut, harvested for cooking fires. A stitch stabbed in my side. Nothing to do but wince and look forward for your next twenty feet. Stumps to dodge. Slipping on dry leaves. My throat burning dry, my lungs about to burst. Is he gaining on me? He can't be. He's a city slicker; he needs orderly sidewalks, neat pavements…

I didn't go right down to the river. I stayed up on the slope maybe fifty yards, until I could recognize features of the land that told me I was close to Rattlesnake Bar.

Suddenly I spotted a familiar outcrop on the south bank: a disordered tumble of gray stone jutting into the channel. I was a mile short of the bar. Downstream of the stones, the eddy had formed a pool. It was time to use the river.

I clambered my way down to the rock strewn north shore. Out of my clothes in a flash. Long johns, everything. Louis had no doubt reached the more open ground by now. He would be making better time.

I splashed into the cold water and swam like a madman, the current adding to my progress. Just above the warble of the water, I heard a frustrated howl far back upstream: "No fair!" That had to be Louis.

He must have found my clothes, and was loathe to follow my example— or couldn't. Where was Richard? Louis, if he couldn't swim, would have to look for a crossing place. There were several, if you knew where to find them.

I stroked for the south shore, keeping an eye out for the old oak tree that marked Mahoney's claim. The river ran strong, but was a modest echo of its force the week before. I concentrated on getting across, to be ready to leap ashore once I spotted the tree.

Louis's shout sounded again, closer, maybe a couple of hundred yards away. "Treacherous scoundrel! Blasphemous rogue! No fair!"

I stroked harder; the tree would be coming soon—There! The stout old monarch with its heavy, winding arms, set back from the shore.

A crowd of prospectors surrounded Mahoney's claim, awaiting the outcome. A few perched up in the limbs of the oak. I recalled the riders overtaking us early in the race. All watched the bright green of Louis's suit on the north shore. He was making the most noise.

Then the miners spotted me and set up a shout. Four more strokes and I felt the bottom. I took a heartbeat to look across to the north shore to see Louis running along the water's edge. His fist whipped the air; his shouts heaped terrible abuse upon my character. He must have more wind in him than we gave him credit for. This was the finish of four miles of "flat out."

Even that brief pause in my effort carried me farther than I had planned and I clambered out and ran back upstream to the claim. The miners parted and let me walk to the center of Mahoney's claim. I stood beside the umbrella, waiting for my rival, dripping and shivering like the last leaf of autumn. Somebody threw a blanket over my shoulders. I was treated to claps on the back, cheers, and praise.

"Din't know you was part fish!"

"The Mississippi's just waitin' for ya!"

"Hell! Go for the Atlantic!"

Through the gaps in the crowd I spied Louis picking his way across, a dozen claims downstream, even so, in up to his knees. I looked upstream for Richard, hoping his fall was not serious. But there he was, some ways up, loping steadily along the north bank, his long legs eating the distance, my clothes tucked under his arm.

I hoped our referees would appear soon.

Amongst the well-wishers stood Osher Phelps, who had the claim on the other, upstream, side of Mr. Mahoney's. We had exchanged greetings but not a lot more. He was a mild-mannered, good-hearted sort from Missouri. Osher wore a big smile.

"Could we build a fire?" I chattered, pulling the blanket tighter and pointing to the ground at my feet.

He nodded with a sharp shake. "For the champeen swimmer? You bet."

In minutes a goodly fire burned warm and welcome. I huddled as close as I could without burning the blanket. Some of the miners drifted away; others came up, curious about the commotion.

Louis stepped through and confronted me. "There was nothing about swimming. I call it a foul." His fancy green suit had suffered from the snags and twigs that caught at it. Clinging leaves attested to one or more spills along the way. His trousers from the knees down were plastered to his bandy shanks.

Our referees arrived, winded and disheveled.

Louis Absolom Shrivington lost no time in making his case. "He cheated. He should have stayed on the road." Louis puffed out his chest and glared down his nose at them. "I insist you disqualify him and declare me the winner."

ABOUT THE AUTHOR

Frank Nissen grew up in the heart of the gold country, roaming the hills and canyons through which the American river flows. Though this is his debut novel, he's been a lifelong storyteller. Frank started writing and illustrating comics in middle school. He went on to work in animation for over forty years doing visual and story development for projects such as *Mulan*, *Dinosaur*, *Treasure Planet* and *Tarzan*. After retiring from Disney Studios, he returned to the landscape that inspired this novel and is focusing on his writing career. He currently serves as president of Gold Country Writers. He is also a member of the Placer County Historical Society, which is a rich source of the kind of arcane knowledge he loves weaving into his stories.

NOTE FROM THE AUTHOR

Word-of-mouth is the best kind of recommendation. If you enjoyed *Fortune's Call*, please contribute a review online—at any site of your choice. Even if it's only a sentence or two, I would appreciate it very much.

Thank you and, good reading!

Thanks!
Frank Nissen

We hope you enjoyed reading this title from:

BLACK ROSE
writing™

www.blackrosewriting.com

Subscribe to our mailing list – *The Rosevine* – and receive **FREE** books, daily deals, and stay current with news about upcoming releases and our hottest authors.
Scan the QR code below to sign up.

Already a subscriber? Please accept a sincere thank you for being a fan of Black Rose Writing authors.

View other Black Rose Writing titles at www.blackrosewriting.com/books and use promo code **PRINT** to receive a **20% discount** when purchasing.

CPSIA information can be obtained
at www.ICGtesting.com
Printed in the USA
LVHW040113060822
725039LV00003B/5